A HOLY GHOST
IN MEXICO CITY

JoaNN —
It's been a pleasure getting
to Know you over The years.
ThaNks for your support,

Len MacQuarrie

For Marilyn

A HOLY GHOST IN MEXICO CITY

W. Lea Macquarrie

CHB Media, Publisher

ISBN 978-1-9460-8860-4
LIBRARY OF CONGRESS CONTROL NUMBER: 2016962416

CHB MEDIA, PUBLISHER

(386) 690-9295
chbmedia@gmail.com
www.chbmediaonline.com

First Edition
Printed in the USA

"Behind events are evolutionary forces which transcend our ordinary needs and which use individuals for purposes far transcending that of keeping those individuals alive, safe and happy."
— George Bernard Shaw (writing on Joan of Arc)

"Whosoever does not give up all that he has cannot be my disciple." — Luke 14-33

Confessions of a Peeping Tom

1960

My sole defense for what I am about to tell you is that I was too young to be so much in love. Linda Grigsby was a high school cheerleader and teen dream. I was an outcast dunce and poet geek. No one could understand what she was doing with me, me least of all. Everyone wanted to date her but no one could because she was mine. She was my inspiration, a vision, a beautiful wet teen dream. A tantalizing suggestiveness animated her radiant blue eyes; a shyly seductive smile lingered on her provocative red lips. When she looked at you she seemed to intuitively understand and accept everything about you. Oh, she knew you wanted her all right, and you did. Everyone did. Who wouldn't, a girl like her?

She developed a woman's body earlier than other girls her age, with lovely voluptuous breasts and a perfectly shaped behind. She wore short skirts, tight sweaters, and strolled the halls at school with a voluptuous swing of the hips that turned our heads so fast she caused whiplash. Guys were walking into walls, crashing and tripping into lockers, banging heads, and colliding with each other from watching her so intently. Half the male gym class was wearing neck braces. I was proud of her. She validated me and gave me value. I gave up everything for her—my funky beatnik personal style for her preferred collegiate attire, my love of jazz for her Johnny Mathis records, my literary novels for her vapid television shows, friends she didn't like, attitudes she found disagreeable. Whatever it took to lie between her sweet wet thighs and lose myself inside the paradise between her legs I would do. Once I was there, I didn't care. I forgot everything else, and nothing else mattered. I even took on her Pentecostal religion, no matter how falsely, pretending to be a Christian and attending Church with her family. Oh, how I walked the walk and talked the talk. God bless you, Mrs. Grigsby. Glory halleluiah praise God. Praise the Lord. Oh, it was low, I admit it, but I'd do it all again and so would you.

But it wasn't all just sex and serious heartfelt talks, either. Linda loved to goof around and play, to wrestle and tickle. We were often silly and laughed until our sides ached. We were going to be married, have children. We thought we would be together forever. She wanted one boy, two girls, a family dog and brick house with a fireplace somewhere in the countryside where she could keep horses. I was going to be a writer; in the country I could work undisturbed.

But we were too young to handle an emotion as volatile as love. We didn't know what we were doing or how to behave. The more I wanted her, the more I became fearful of losing her. Her fierce streak of independence threatened me. I mistakenly interpreted normal, innocent outings such as nights "out with the girls" as defiance. I made demands I had no right to. I recognized this but couldn't seem to change it. I didn't know how. I felt trapped, manipulated and resentful. I hated myself for this.

Not that she acted any more maturely than I did. She became possessive and critical, subjecting me to excruciating interrogations that went on for hours: Do you love me? Why didn't you telephone me? Where were you? Why didn't you come over? Who was the girl I saw you with? Why were you looking at my friend Sheila that way? You were staring at her breasts. You were too. Don't deny it. I saw you.

Both of us were pathologically jealous and suspicious. I knew I was supposed to be trusting rather than suspicious, rational instead of reactionary, supportive rather than argumentative, but my self-defeating behavior was the exact opposite of what I wanted it to be and knew it should be. I was a spectator locked in my own mind without influence or power over it. Linda said it was the same for her. We were like lab mice trapped in a maze of complexity neither of us understood. We played our roles in this high school melodrama as we thought we were supposed to, but with no real idea of a mature relationship. During our increasingly frequent fights one or both of us usually ended up crying. Afterwards we apologized, begged forgiveness and made impossible promises, kissing and petting and then having beautiful makeup sex. Then the cycle would start all over again.

Senior classmen waiting for her to dump me rubbed their hands together in greedy expectancy. They were the campus celebrities, their status ostentatiously displayed on the sleeves of their letter sweaters. I was jealous and contemptuous of them. So what if they were football heroes who would go on to college on athletic scholarships? I was a poet, wasn't I? Didn't that count for anything? Poetry was as valid as athletics, wasn't it? But I was envious and resentful of them.

Linda and I went on to find new subjects to argue about. I began attacking her taste in literature and television. She read Ayn Rand, Grace Metalious, and hospital romances with love affairs between doctors and nurses, books with titles like *Magnificent Obsession, Forbidden Medicine* and *His Healing Hands*. She read them openly, without apology, shame, or explanation. I told her these novels were shit, that she should put false book jackets over them like people did over books of pornography, because they exposed her as a literary dilettante and shallow dimwit bimbo of subhuman intelligence. She argued that the books I read—dark, angry, despairing accusatory novels like *Death on the Installment Plan* by Louis Ferdinand Celine or *Nausea* by Jean Paul Sartre, were exhausting, bitter and no less contrived and false, but at least her novels were entertaining and unpretentious and fun to read. Sure, I said, fun if you are a teen age bimbo cheerleader with the brain activity of a peanut. And what about her television shows? Garbage, excrement, vomit, contrived intellectually bankrupt scripts utterly lacking in imagination with predictable plots acted out by wannabe thespians with pretty faces and mediocre talent.

"What about you and your pretentious Ingmar Bergman films, Raymond? The *Seventh Seal*? People being burned at the stake? Some entertainment, Raymond. You really know how to romance a girl, take a girl to a movie about the Plague, of all things. God, Raymond, how could anybody actually *enjoy* something like that?"

* * *

According to Linda, most girls we knew were "saving themselves for marriage." Not, Linda though. She was much more adventurous and less cautious about sex than I. I remember a night under a blanket in the darkness of a covered wagon during a church youth group hayride when Linda, pretending to be asleep with her head in my lap, unzipped my fly and took me in her mouth. I was so frightened of being discovered I initially tried to discourage her but she was persistent. She once gave me hand job on a Ferris wheel at an amusement park. I had to walk around the amusement park all afternoon with a large visible wet spot on my pants. Acts of covert public sex were a game with her. It turned her on to initiate sex play in public places, surreptitiously, without getting caught.

But we *did* get caught, and under the worst possible circumstances.

It happened on a Saturday afternoon, inside her father's chapel, which we were supposed to be cleaning in preparation for Sunday services. When her father walked in I was on my knees and she was standing over me, one hand clutching her panties in her fist, the other holding the hem of her dress over my head, which was buried between her legs. I will never forget the expression of betrayal in her father's eyes when I emerged from under her dress, my wet face glistening with vaginal fluid. It was, of course, a hurtful act of betrayal against her father and an unforgivable violation of his trust in me. Linda and I were forbidden to see each other again, though we did, whenever possible, in secret.

But it was difficult under these new, clandestine circumstances. We saw each other less, and it was the beginning of the end. We graduated from high school and she started dating. I became obsessed with jealous fantasies of her with other men. I did a lot of accusing, name calling, shouting, pleading, begging, and crying. She in turn became defensive, angry, and ultimately, I realize now, bored. It didn't take long before I had lost her. She answered my telephone calls, but our conversations were brief. Later she didn't so much as answer, and I was told by whoever did that she was out.

I lost track of her for a while. I watched my peers go off to college, some settling down into jobs with promising opportunities, sensibly working toward stable, productive futures. Many traded their hot rods for sensible nice late model family cars and their jeans and tee shirts for shirts and ties. Some married and began having children and making payments on homes. I applied for work in every bookstore in Seattle, in record stores and downtown Seattle pawn shops specializing in rare books and used musical instruments, but no one would hire me. I went out to Boeing Aircraft and Bethlehem Steel in Seattle and the Weyerhaeuser Lumber Mill in Everett, less exciting than working in a bookstore but better paid. No luck. No one wanted me. My self-esteem plummeted. I became depressed and sat on the couch in my underwear until the late afternoons, nostalgically watching Linda's favorite television melodramas as if we were still together. I was no longer critical of these scripts, but tried to understand what Linda saw in them. I unfavorably compared myself to the handsome young leading males, who were not much older than me, but so much more sophisticated.

These young television personas I had never before wanted to be and now envied wore unwrinkled tailored suits and had perfect hair always in place even when driving their sporty convertibles, while I seemed always in rumpled disarray no matter how I dressed or tried to groom myself. How did they do it? What was their secret? They were men not much older than me who knew how to select French wine, order five-star restaurant items like snails and pâté, and how to prepare and serve cocktails I had never even tasted, much less mixed. They wined and dined glamorous women in elegant restaurants, taxied them in foreign two-seat convertibles to modern, bachelor luxury suites where they mixed martinis to the sound of Dave Brubeck playing on the Hi Fi. How could it be these men had become so sophisticated and urbane at such a young age? I didn't even know how to tie a necktie. It was no wonder Linda didn't want me.

I don't know why I watched these television shows. In the past I had been hostile and verbally critical when watching them with Linda, who swooned over the handsome actors and, to my embarrassment, wept at their failed melodramatic love affairs. Now I watched these shows for hours on end. I was hardly even reading, much less writing. Of course, these debonair young men on television were only actors, and not very good ones at that, and the women they seduced probably didn't even exist in real life, but I didn't know this, and besides, I saw, on the streets of Seattle, men close to my own age who looked every bit the part, young lawyers, bankers, doctors, speculators and financial advisors, all upwardly mobile and living the life I had previously rejected as beneath me and which now, in an ironic turn of events, rejected me.

Around this time she came by my parents' house a couple of times. I was miserable and disgusting but managed to elicit enough sympathy to be given pity sex, which I accepted gratefully and shamelessly, in her car. But when she next dropped by unexpectedly, for the last time as it turned out, I knew I would not be getting any sex. Not even pity would inspire her, or for that matter anyone else, to have sex with me. I was so depressed I didn't care. Unwashed, wearing torn pajama bottoms and a chocolate-stained white tee shirt, my teeth not brushed and breath probably bad, I mumbled some lame excuse about not feeling well. She said she had only come to say goodbye, because she was going away to college in Texas.

She didn't give me her address, explaining she hadn't yet received a dorm assignment. Later, during the months I persistently wrote in care of the University in Texas, her letters came back marked "addressee unknown". I called her parents but they wouldn't help. They said it was over between Linda and me and sounded happy about it. Meanwhile, I had earned the reputation of town loser. Linda was the only thing I ever had going for me. She alone had given me credibility and status. People had figured that since Linda and I were a team and would probably be married, there had to be more to me than met the eye. But no more. After all, I had lost Linda. Now I was nothing, a pathetic beatnik bum who wrote bad poetry, an embarrassment to myself, family and community.

I accepted my fate and perused the TV Guide, planning my weekly viewing schedule in advance. I was no longer looking for work. What was the use? If I was an employer, would I hire me? No fucking way, José.

One night I found myself screaming at the television. It surprised me and frightened my mother, who stood aside wringing her hands while saying over and over, "What is it, Raymond, what's wrong?"

Everything was wrong. What people had been saying about me wasn't fair and wasn't true. And television was the biggest lie of all. Young doctors in love? Handsome attorneys who saved beautiful women in distress? Comparing myself to these make-believe television fakes had been the wrong way to assess my worth. I didn't want to be a doctor, lawyer, or an actor for that matter, whether on screen or in life. I wanted to be writer. I *was* a writer. I had always known this. Why had I had forgotten it, given it up? And for what? The flickering shadow images on a 24-inch television screen? I had been trying to emulate unreality. Well, I was through with all this striving to be what I was not. I was as good as anyone. I had value, a future; I was an artist, a writer. I was going to prove it.

I went to work in earnest, writing and smoking, pacing and sulking in my room. I locked the door and wrote without revision or reading what I had done, page after page, reams of it, expressing everything I felt, all that was important to me. I knew I couldn't stop to revise because what I was writing was too vitally important; the momentum had to continue because I was on my way to greatness. This novel, this confession, exorcism, or whatever it was destined to become, would redeem me. I would show them all, Linda, the upperclassmen who had mocked me, my neighbors, parents, everyone who had thought I would never amount to anything or accomplish anything of value. I would write my way to validation, fame, and greatness.

But a hundred and seventy pages later, during a ruthless night of objective reading, I saw clearly that what I had written was not the insightful important document I had thought, but mere narcissistic teen whining. I wasn't ready yet to be a writer; I hadn't lived sufficiently, hadn't suffered or paid my dues for my art. I was like the men on television. I was just acting. And I was only writing to forget about Linda. I wasn't over her. Far from it. I still loved her. I both wanted her back and loathed myself for it. I didn't know what to do with my life. If I couldn't have Linda, I didn't know what I wanted.

Months later, she came home for a vacation from college. We sat in her Impala convertible by the twittering silver nightlights of a ferry landing in Edmonds, the quiet suburban township north of Seattle where I lived with my parents. We kissed and confessed we still loved each other. She talked about her life in Texas, how she was on her way to a career in business management. I had no career, no job, no car, and no money. All I had were scribbles on paper and they were worthless. They could not get me what I wanted and needed in life. They could not get me Her.

I determined right then and there to relinquish ambition to be a writer or anything even slightly extraordinary, to grow up, settle down, and be grateful to be what they call a "regular guy." Find a good, working-man's job or get into college, maybe toward a teaching degree. I promised this to her. I opened the car door and got out and knelt on the damp hard pavement and promised on bended knee. She said she was sorry, she would always love me and never forget me, but it would never work; we couldn't go back; it was too late. She said it wasn't anyone's fault; we had both been too young.

That was when she told me the truth. She hadn't even been to college. She had been with relatives in Texas, having an abortion. I hadn't even known she had been pregnant. We had killed our baby. We held each other and cried. I wanted another chance. I wanted her back. I wanted our baby back.

* * *

She went back to Texas and I didn't know what to do with my life. I was broken. I moped around forlornly in my underwear until late afternoons. I was clinically depressed but at least had given up television to begin reading again. That was something. It was a start. Any change was good.

I began getting up early and taking long walks. I hiked from my parents' house on Blueberry Hill, down the steep dirt path through the woods, jumped the creek and came out of the woods into Edmonds, slinking down Main Street past its mom and pop grocery store, its one and only movie theatre, hardware stores, barber shop, diner and waterfront bait and tackle shop. I watched majestic white ferries glide like floating castles on the crystal-blue ice-cold surface of Puget Sound to our single pier and dock. I thrilled to the sound of their fog horns. The beach was strewn with strange stinking organic sea life such as jelly fish, whip-like ropes of sea kelp, and strange unidentifiable sea creatures which might have dropped down from another planet in a haphazard combination of odd gelatinous life-forms making me think of a painting by Joan Miro.

I'd often seen magnificent Orca whales surface in Puget Sound, while some of the largest octopi on the planet were said to lie submerged in the Sound's depths. The deceptively calm waters are shockingly, breathtakingly cold, far too cold to comfortably swim, and are of surprising depth, rich with submerged organic life, and at times alarmingly odiferous, as are the beaches, strewn as they are with seaweed, kelp, and barnacle-encrusted driftwood.

A fence separated the beach from the railroad. I climbed it, walking the tracks. The seawall was bordered by giant rocks. I leapt from one to another, carelessly daring fate. It would have been easy to lose a footing and break a leg or worse. The view was beautiful here, and the solitude welcome. Walking the tracks, I had a view to the thickly forested San Juan Island fjords, which thrust upward out of the blue sea like emerald-green jewels and which, perhaps because they were so perfectly situated, possessed a gentle tranquility reminiscent of a Zen rock garden. The surrounding geography was rugged and mountainous, with the snowy Olympic Range across the sound to the north, and the Cascades to the east, while the imperious volcanic entity that is Mt. Rainer watched over the city skyline to the south, giving the distant buildings of downtown the impression of being in miniature.

Sometimes I walked between the parallel train tracks and once became caught between two trains traveling in opposite directions. When trains came around blind curves, I was forced to leap from the tracks to the rocks. I hiked these tracks hour after hour, sometimes north to Mukilteo and Everett, sometimes south to Ballard Bay and Seattle. Then, after a few months of this, I got a job.

It was pumping gas at a local gas station, a kid's job without promise, status, or glamour. It did nothing to elevate my standing in the community. I was still a bum, just an employed one. But at least with some money in my pocket I was spared the shame of having to always beg for cigarettes or, worse, scrounge butts out of ashtrays or off the ground, as I had done in the past. I took my money and put it in an empty coffee can and counted it every few weeks. I was living rent free and took all my meals at home, so it was surprising how it added up. I told my parents I was saving for college. Pleased and encouraged, they began matching my funds.

* * *

I was working at the gas station when I heard she had moved back home. I was so excited I could hardly finish my shift. It was all I could think about. I was so distracted I found myself pumping gas with a lit cigarette in my mouth. I was overfilling gas tanks, and we came up short at the end of my shift. I made up for the shortage at the register with money out of pocket and dashed across the street to the phone booth. My pants pockets were so heavy with dimes, nickels and quarters their weight threatened to pull me down. Coins were falling to the street and I didn't even bother to pick them up. My hands were shaking so badly I dropped a few more trying to feed the slot. My fingers trembled so hard I could hardly dial. The phone rang and rang, but nobody answered. I drove home, took a shower, and drove right out to her house. Nobody home.

I called all night, but no one answered. Early the next morning, still in my pajamas after a fitful night, I called immediately. The phone was answered by someone who sounded like Linda's mother, but who hung up when I asked for Linda. I quickly dressed, snatched my mother's car keys from the kitchen counter and immediately drove out to Linda's house. Her father answered the door but refused to admit me or even notify Linda I was there. He said I was not welcome, to go away and stay away.

But I had to see her again, had to talk to her. I began parking down the street, watching for her car and an opportunity to inconspicuously follow her. The first time I did this I followed her to the local grocery store. I filled a shopping cart with random articles I had no intention of purchasing and trailed her from a safe distance through the aisles, pretending to be coincidentally shopping and unaware of her presence. She stood at the Deli counter and didn't see me hiding in the cereal aisle, watching her. Her cart was loaded with coffee, toilet paper, bread, jars of peanut butter and jelly, frozen pizza and bottles of chocolate and white milk. I had forgotten how unpretentiously pretty she was. It surprised me. Linda's sexiness is not the first quality one observes and appreciates in her, but it eventually becomes apparent, and then one can't forget about it. Her appeal otherwise was not obvious, not at first glance. Her beauty was a secret that revealed itself incrementally over a period of time. One could not guard against it or prepare oneself for it. It was captivating. The longer one looked, the more smitten one became.

Linda's personality had always been what I would describe as warm and convivial. I had forgotten how she seemed to personify genuine interest in others without trying no matter with whom she was talking or what the subject and, watching her now, I was reminded. She was chatting with a slightly plump young mother with a beehive hairdo. The beehive woman was pregnant, with a baby in a stroller and a toddler hanging on to her housedress. Linda's tone with the other shopper was inquisitive and warm, even more than I remembered. No wonder everyone liked her.

I kept a safe distance, hiding among the boxes of Cheerios, Wheaties, Corn Flakes and other cereals, appreciatively watching and admiring her. It was hard to believe a woman such as this had once loved me. Her presence made think of a song my mother used to like: *This Nearly was Mine.*

As if having become unconsciously aware she was being watched, she unexpectedly and inexplicably turned around, and when saw me lingering in the aisle, there it was: her beautiful bright winning smile. I had missed it for so long now. Her eyes shone and face seemed to flush. It was clear she was glad to see me. Her voice rose slightly in excitement

"*Raymond*," she exclaimed. "Dear, dear Raymond."

What she wore was nothing special, not especially figure enhancing or provocative, just an unpretentious pair of faded blue jeans and a clinging lime-green cardigan sweater I remembered from long ago. Her sweater was open at the throat and she wore a necklace of tiny pearls against her long pale neck. She was wearing her hair shorter than I remembered, and while I preferred it long, the new style added a quality of seriousness that made her look adult and interesting. I loved the glasses, which added a new depth of intelligence to her beautiful blue eyes. Her face was a little fuller and she had gained a little weight since I had last seen her, but it looked good on her. I on the other hand was probably too thin, but unusually well dressed for once, in clean new jeans and a decent if wrinkled white shirt, and my recently cut hair was neatly combed. I saw her look me up and down in assessment.

"You look nice," she said.

She asked how I was and I said I was working, saving money in preparation to attend a community college. She said that was great; she was glad to hear it and it was nice to see me again. For a reason I do not entirely understand I irrationally blurted out I had a girlfriend.

"It's pretty serious," I said. "We may get married."

It was stupid and I don't know what I was thinking except probably I was hoping to catch her off guard and eliminate any concern she may have had that I was following her, which of course I was. And maybe, pathetically, I hoped to make her a little jealous. But it didn't work.

"I'm happy for you," she replied. "Who is she?"

"You don't know her. She's not from around here. Her name is Lucy."

Don't ask me where that came from. It was the first name that came to mind for some reason. Probably I had been watching too much *I Love Lucy* on television. Linda asked a few polite questions about "Lucy" while we were in the checkout line. I didn't answer them very well and could see she became dubious. When we got outside of the supermarket I walked her to her car in the parking lot and helped her load the groceries into the trunk.

"What about your groceries," she asked? "You left your cart in the store."

"I'll go back. I have a few items to get yet. Listen, can we go out sometime?"

"Raymond, no," she said, getting into her car. "That would just be trouble. I'm sorry. Besides, you have a girlfriend. A fiancé. Lucy. It was so nice to see you, though. Good luck to you, Raymond. Take care."

I blew her a kiss goodbye and, hoping to avoid suspicion,

headed back inside the grocery store. When I returned to the parking lot, her car was gone. After that I began following her whenever I thought I could without being discovered. This went on for several weeks.

* * *

One afternoon I trailed her car to the Edmonds City Park. It was a moderately warm day for Seattle, during a dry spell. The sun was up for a change, and people were taking advantage of the good weather. A tennis game of doubles was in process, and some college kids were throwing a football. A teen-aged girl wearing bright yellow sneakers with red satin basketball shorts ran across the lawn trying to lift a dragon-shaped kite. I wandered the park until I found Linda sitting on a park bench facing a small duck pond. I hid behind some trees and watched her read a book on her lap. Sometimes a gust of wind blew the pages and she had to find her place again. I watched her probably around ten minutes or so and then pretended to be lost in thought and unaware of her presence while hiking the path that led around the pond and past her bench. I wanted it to seem our encounter was entirely unintentional and accidental. She glanced up from her book and then resumed reading as I walked on by.

"Raymond," she called after me.

I turned around in feigned surprise.

"Linda. Why, hello. What a pleasant surprise. What are you doing here?"

"I was going to ask you the same question," she replied suspiciously. "Are you following me, Raymond?"

"What? Me? Why, no. Of course not."

She snapped her book closed and glared at me.

"I don't believe you," she said. She got up and began walking off, then stopped and said, "Stay away from me, Raymond. I mean it."

I had never heard her talk to me in quite that tone before. It was like she hated me.

* * *

The thing is, I had thought I was getting over her. Seeing her in the grocery store had brought on all the old feelings. I was in love with her all over again or more precisely had been all along, but not facing up to it. I began bombarding her with love poems. Sometimes I wrote her two or three a day. I didn't even read them over, just wrote them and put them in the mailbox. Not all the letters were poems or love letters, though. I sometimes wrote a conventional, newsy letter. I was still pumping gas at the Shell station at the time, so mentioned it if someone we both knew stopped in for gasoline or oil, which was often since there were only two gas stations in the town. In this way I kept her updated on any high school alumni gossip of possible interest to her, thereby dispensing evidence of our connectivity through a shared past.

But mostly the letters were declarations of eternal love and devotion. As time went on they became more provocative. Some of them may have been angry. I expressed my hurt and frustration of being shut out and ignored. I told her we were meant to be together. I told her I would never stop loving her as long as I lived, there was nothing she could do to change it; it wouldn't make a difference even if she got married and had children, I would never give up trying to win her back. These letters went unanswered until finally she sent a card telling me to stop writing them. After that my letters were returned with an official postal mark saying "refused." So instead I sent post cards.

* * *

One night Fred Henderson pulled into the Shell station in his souped-up Studebaker Hawk. He got out, spat on the pavement, and lighted a cigarette. I pumped a dollar's worth of gas, wiped the windshield clean, and checked the oil. He had the radio turned up to a popular teen rock and roll station. Henderson was one of those big loud pushy guys who was always spitting and never seemed to be without a longneck bottle of beer in his hand. He was a braggart with a story to tell, usually of beating someone in a fistfight, of a woman he had seduced, or a big cash pot he claimed to have won in one of the local card games his crowd always seemed to be having. He had never been friendly to me in high school, but in the way things change after graduation, he now acted like we were buddies bonded by a common experience. His overtures of friendship may have been genuine; after high school he had lost the audience for his stories of conquest and glory and no one seemed to care anyway. It was Henderson who told me Linda had a serious boyfriend, an older guy who dressed collegiate and drove a fancy foreign sports car. He seemed happy to tell me this. I think it was the only reason he came in to the station. He didn't need the gas; the tank was mostly full.

I couldn't get it out of my mind. I kept trying to picture Linda's boyfriend, imagining what he might look like, whether he was handsome, what model of car he drove, whether he came from a good family, if he was a nice guy or a loudmouth braggart and cheat, if he was a working professional or maybe a medical or law student or an athlete on a scholarship. I had to find out.

Thinking I might catch a glimpse of Linda and her boyfriend, I began hiding in the bushes across the street from the Grigsby house. Eventually I became bolder and moved in closer, hiding behind some trees next door, a behavior which escalated to the point where I began dressing in black, blackening my face and sneaking right up to the side of the Grigsby house to crouch in some bushes near her bedroom window. I saw her undress one night. It wasn't my intention and I knew it was weird and wrong, but once she started taking her clothes off I couldn't stop watching.

That's where I was when I saw him for the first time. I was hiding in some bushes near the side of the house with a view to her bedroom window. It was a clear quiet night with only a few scattered clouds and an almost full moon. I heard his car before seeing its headlights round the corner and come down her street faster in my opinion than it should have for a residential neighborhood. A row of hedges flanked the driveway. Hoping for a closer look, I crawled along them, my hands and knees on the damp grass. The car was an Austin Healy, a British sports car. Its headlights shone on me briefly as they pulled into her driveway. I crouched low to the ground behind the bushes and was not seen. He got out of the driver's seat and went around to the passenger side to chivalrously open the passenger door for Linda. I could see him clearly under the porch lights. He wore neatly pressed white dress slacks, a white shirt, tie and jacket. He was handsome, very much like the leading men on the television shows we once watched. But this guy was real. There was no way I could compete with someone like that. He took her hand and helped her out of the car and they kissed in the moonlight. Their kiss went on for a while. I cried so loud I thought they would hear me and had to back away into the bushes.

* * *

There is more to this story but I am ashamed to tell it. I continued hiding in the bushes outside of Linda's window almost nightly. She always left her window open, and undressed for bed at the same hour. And I was always there. One night I was so absorbed in her undressing that I did not hear Linda's boyfriend sneaking up behind me. He stepped on a twig which snapped and caught my attention, and then I saw him, but too late.

"I know who you are," he said. "You're Linda's former boyfriend. You're a little old to be playing Peeping Tom, aren't you?"

Then Linda appeared in the light of the front porch. "Don't let him go," she said. "I'm calling the police."

I threw a few punches Linda's boyfriend blocked easily. He was older than me and had the benefit of reach, strength and confidence, and probably experience. He could have kicked my ass if he had wanted to, and I wouldn't have blamed him. He had every right to do so. He could have made a big show of it for Linda, but in retrospect was a pretty nice guy because he didn't take advantage or exploit his athleticism in a show of manliness.

I tried to run but he tackled me. I struggled to break free of his grasp but he was strong and held me until I had mostly exhausted myself.

Linda went indoors for her father who came out and called me a pervert, loser, psychopath, communist, Satanist, peeping Tom, sex fiend, and a number of other choice names, a litany that went on and on until the police came. Linda stayed in the house and didn't return until the police had me cuffed in back of the cruiser. I was arrested, booked and charged with sexual predation and trespassing. Both of these charges were later dropped, but a court restraining order of protection was awarded to Linda.

I went back to hiding in the bushes outside of her window. I saw her naked and even masturbated once but couldn't finish and broke down crying from shame. I loved her so much, and I was so wretched, so stricken. I stayed away for a week or so, but couldn't stop thinking about her open window, and her disrobing. Drunk and miserable, I wrote a love letter and poem and wrapped it around a large stone and threw it through her bedroom window, which I assumed to be open. She *always* left that window open. But not this time. The window shattered in airborne projectiles that became imbedded in her face.

Her father took unfairly grotesque photographs of everything. The newspaper printed a sensational shot of Linda in which she looked head-on into the camera, her bleeding face so contorted with betrayal, fear and rage that at first I did not recognize it. Police photographs of jagged pieces of exploded shards of glass on the floor and bed later appeared in court as evidence.

I got to see her again during my trial, where she testified against me. She wore a white blouse under a University of Washington letter sweater, and a pleated skirt. I couldn't see any scars at all, though I did note she was wearing more makeup than usual. But she was so pretty, so winning. Who could not believe the truthfulness of her account? Even I was convinced of her accusations against me. No wonder the judge ruled against my attorney's request for leniency under court supervised conditions.

I believed myself innocent of the charges against me but deserving of punishment because it had been a stupid thing to do. Either way, I felt horrible about it. The last thing I wanted to do was hurt Linda. Funny how a single moment can change your life. How a poem tossed toward a lover's window can result in the exact opposite of what was intended, and cause so much harm

The prosecution attorneys said I might have blinded her. They said her scars would not heal. They said I had done this deliberately, that I was an enraged, jealous, predatory boyfriend bent on revenge, intent on disfiguring his former girlfriend so no other man would look at her.

Later, found guilty of assault, voyeurism, and sexual predation and sentenced to the Snohomish County jail, I had plenty of time to think about it. I went over it again and again in my mind. Had I been the vengeful person the prosecution had described in the courtroom? Maybe there *had* been intention on my part, and

23

I was guilty of a crime against a woman I was supposed to love. Maybe I couldn't face the truth about myself or what I had done.

The men I met in jail were all guilty, but none were criminals. They were men who, like me, had made mistakes, but who were ashamed of what they had done. Most were surprised to find themselves in so much trouble. I was no better than them. You are no better than me. Any of us can make a mistake. Many of us will. No matter what road you take in life, trouble waits. We think we know ourselves but we don't.

Leaving Home

If you make mistakes like I did in life and are ashamed, I will forgive you. You don't even have to explain. I understand trouble, and shame. I came home from jail to a press release in the Edmonds newspaper. Since nothing criminal or even memorable ever happened in our small town, and because my earlier arrest and conviction had been all over the town newspaper and had been sensational, my release was considered newsworthy. Now I was the town disgrace, a notorious peeping tom, jailbird and reputed sexual predator. There was no one in Edmonds who did not know of me, or what I had done. People shunned me. I may as well have worn a leper's sack over my face and gone around shouting, "unclean, unclean." The leprosy metaphor was spiritually if not physically accurate. When I looked in the mirror a confused and ashamed Seattle boy stared back in uncomprehending bewilderment. I was this boy, but I did not know him. I knew only there was something wrong with me, that I was somehow emotionally and spiritually ill, fearful and stricken with self-loathing while on my way to becoming a man so much less than what I had once expected of myself.

So now, a month short of my 20th birthday, on this drizzly, gray September morning so typically melancholy, wet, chilly, and characteristic of Seattle during this time of year, I hoped to distance myself from my past and all who knew me. Dad was driving, clearly taking the longer route to the freeway to avoid the Grigsby house, where I had hoped to catch a last glimpse of Linda through the windows. I of course was not allowed within two miles of her or anyone in her family. A violation would return me immediately to the Snohomish County Jail.

The promise of dawn announced itself faintly on the glimmering horizon but had not yet fully arrived, as if the muted morning light had not yet decided and hesitated between night and day, light and darkness. Neighborhood street lights reflected glistening sleek rainwater on the road as we drove. Drenched glistening evergreen, towering spruce and Douglas fir swayed in the wind as if saying goodbye, their rain-bathed limbs waving from within the beams of our headlights

Of course we were early, Dad and I. My father had an almost pathological fixation on punctuality. It was a kind of behavioral code of honor with men of his generation, I guess. I didn't understand it. There was a lot I didn't understand about my father, an officer and purser with the Merchant Marine who had spent more of his adult life at sea than at home. Probably because he was away so much of the time, we had never much shared our thoughts or feelings, and were somewhat awkward in each other's company. He was basically a private man who mostly kept his thoughts to himself.

During my time in the Snohomish County Jail, Dad had been mostly at sea and had visited twice. He came probably because mother had set him up. She often complained, justly so, that with Dad at sea most of the time she had to take on the role of both mother and father. A common threat all through my childhood had been, "Just wait until your father gets home." It must have been disappointing to her when the time finally came and he called me into his study for an accounting, because his heart did not seem to be in it. When he got home from sea he just wanted some quiet time without a lot of problems. I did not blame him for that. He had earned it, keeping us comfortable and well provided for in our upper middle class suburban home of which, because of his absence at sea, he was seldom the beneficiary. My father was not a punitive man. He was one to sometimes offer advice, but not to scold or belittle. It was not his way. My father was a practical man who focused on the future.

"You have a criminal record now," he said during his visit. "It won't be easy finding a good job when you get out."

It was his greatest fear for me. That I would not settle into a career, become a solid wage earner, my life consequentially defined by poverty and financial struggle. I knew it to be the fear of many men who had grown up during the depression.

I wanted to reassure Dad but it was hard to do, considering I had proven myself inclined toward lapsed judgement and poor impulse control, and now had a criminal record, so I merely said, "I'll be all right, Dad. You don't have to worry about me."

"But I do worry about you. I don't know what's out here for you when you get out. You've pretty much sabotaged any hope you may have had of getting hired with Boeing. They won't want you now. I don't think I can even get you in at the Sailor's Union of the Pacific. You're basically limited to minimum wage dead end jobs with no future."

"Well, that's nothing new. I was already working one at the gas station."

"Yes, but then you still had options. Besides, is that all you want from your life?"

"I've already lost what I wanted."

"Well, I'm sorry, son, but face it, it's over between you and Linda. It's time you accepted it and moved on. The best you can do now, Raymond, is to complete your education. With a college degree, you would still have a chance for a future."

I had already considered this, briefly considering teaching, preferably English literature, but with my criminal record, that was probably out now. Dad turned the car radio to a popular generic music station. Mantovani and his one thousand and one regurgitated generic strings, a vacuous offense marketed as "easy listening," but which he, to my vexation, referred to classical music. To say that I found this music objectionable would be an understatement. I was offended by it to the degree that I had been known to announce to surprised grocery and department store clerks that I would no longer patronize their establishments because of their policy of playing Muzak, a declaration usually met with indifferent shrugs by uncomprehending clerks and incredulous head-scratching bewildered management officials.

Dad and I may have been in opposition about music, art, politics, religion, and many other subjects I cared deeply about, but make no mistake about it, I loved my father. We loved each other but were afraid of open acknowledgement, and especially of the words. I wanted to tell him I loved him but we didn't talk that way in our house. We didn't talk much at all. Who could guess his thoughts? Not I, and he wasn't likely to share them. Not with me anyway. Maybe not with anyone. He was a seafaring man, accustomed to solitude and the silent company of great empty ocean landscapes.

I turned off the radio and Dad did not object; he probably expected it. We did not speak then, and listened to the metallic patter of rain on the roof, the slosh of tires on wet pavement, and the wipers clicking back and forth across the windshield.

We crossed the Aurora Avenue Bridge with a view to the University District's vast campus and impressive new football stadium, then saw Lake Union and its industrial barges, shabby houseboats and fishing vessels. The Smith Tower and other landmark buildings of the city skyline became visible against the massive volcanic backdrop of snowcapped Mt. Rainer. We exited downtown to a convergence of funky narrow back streets and steep, rain-washed slippery hills, red brick tenements, railroad tracks, trolley cars and traffic.

I had come of age prowling these streets, rummaging through First and Second Avenue Seattle pawn shops and the hidden treasures of curiosity shops, or investigating the thousands of esoteric books on the dusty shelves of downtown used bookstores. I used to hang around Pioneer Square and talk to bums, listening to their tales of riding the rails during the Depression. I smoked filtered Camels and shared bottles of wine on the waterfront's docks reeking of marine life and salt.

If there is truth to reincarnation and the transmigration of souls, I want to come back as a Chinook king salmon. I'd merge with thousands of them in their exodus up the swift foaming rapids of the Columbia River, eluding opportunistic fishermen and hungry foraging black bears, slithering over slippery lichen-covered submerged rocks and the egg-swollen bodies of other salmon in a genetically coded preordained return to ancestral spawning grounds. There we would finally release our precious cargo of translucent pink eggs and die flopping on the rain-spattered river bank. What could be better than this, a genetically fated life cycle, preordained, without possibility of deviation or error, without blame or shame, just fate?

But I was leaving Seattle for Mexico City. Why? I didn't even know the language. I wanted it that way. I wanted to wipe the mirror clean of all that reflected who I was, all I could identify as "me"—friends, family, country, even language. I didn't yet know there was nowhere to run. You can't hide from who you are and what you have done. I knew only that if I was going to live, I wanted it to be as someone else. I wanted transformation. I wanted to become the person I always knew I was supposed to be. I wanted to become Holy.

* * *

Dad found a parking place at a curbside meter a block and a half from the bus station. He shut off the engine but kept his hands on the wheel, staring thoughtfully out the windshield. My father rarely spoke his mind directly without first thinking it over carefully and knowing exactly what he wanted to say. It was obvious this was one of those times, and it was awkward for him. I could almost hear him thinking.

He shook a Camel from a pack, lit it with his Zippo and said, "You know, Raymond, your mother blames herself for your trouble. She says she should have seen it coming. Of course now she's worried sick. She's convinced you're not ready to go off on your own."

"I know. She told me and told me and told me. What's your opinion on the matter, Dad?"

"About you leaving home, your mother, or why you got in trouble?"

"All of it."

"Well, you're no criminal, Raymond, that's for sure. You're basically a good boy who got in some trouble and ended up in jail because of a dumb youthful mistake. I honestly don't know what you could have been thinking at the time, Raymond, but I hope you have learned from it and smartened up. I think you're leaving

29

home because that is what young men do. Your mother will worry because that's what mothers do. She'd keep you at home until you were eligible for social security if she had her way, but I think it's important you cut the apron strings because you can't become a man at home. She just doesn't understand, Raymond. I know what it is to be a young man with a thirst for adventure and his whole life ahead of him. It's why I joined the Army during the war and why I shipped out with the Merchant Marine afterwards.

"It's good to put distance between you and Linda, too. I understand how you want to grow up and get on with your life and it's the right thing to do, but I want you to be careful down there in Mexico, Raymond. Be smart and stop doing stupid shit that gets you into trouble. You don't want to go to jail in Mexico, that's for sure. And don't just play around writing little poems in your journal, either. Focus on your studies at the University, learn the language and the culture, and come home safely with some college credits you can transfer and build on."

I shook his hand, promised to write once a week, and promised I would follow his advice. He opened the car door, went around to the trunk and removed my seaman's duffle bag. We stood awkwardly by the car as morning traffic hummed by.

"Well," he said.

I thought I might have seen his eyes mist a little. It was uncharacteristic, and it took me by surprise. I had the impression that he wanted to hug me, and I wanted him to, but I knew he wouldn't. We just shook hands.

It had been drizzling earlier but now the rain began coming down hard. I remember watching him duck his head when entering the Plymouth and taking the wheel. He stared at me from behind the rain streaked window, his countenance expressive of a solitary man quietly resigned to separation by great distances.

And then he drove away.

Goodbye

Road weary travelers and rain-drenched Seattle vagrants took shelter in the downtown bus terminal where some kind of disagreement was taking place at the ticket window. I waited behind a family of Asians who seemed to be upset about something, remained in line until the matter was settled, then purchased my ticket for Mexico City. The noise level made it necessary to shout when purchasing my ticket. I looked for places to sit but none were available. A crowed gathered near an igloo-shaped juke box flashing red and blue lights while blasting James Brown. A man so tall and thin he might have passed for a professional basketball player jitterbugged with his buxom woman. His confident, agile footwork was loose but precise. His woman followed his steps with graceful synchronicity. People around the juke box shouted them on encouragingly.

An obese Indian woman sprawled on a bench, her head resting on her bulging backpack for a pillow. God knows how she could sleep for all the noise. Asian teens with slicked back hair congregated territorially near a cigarette machine where they smoked and spat on the grimy floor. They wore elaborate greasy haircuts and red satin jackets with gang patch appliqués sewn on the back. Piles of luggage were stacked haphazardly everywhere. Announcements of departures and arrivals on the public address system were made continuously in English, Spanish, and an Asian language I didn't recognize. (Seattle has a large Chinese, Philippine, and Japanese population). I waited for a vacant stool at the restaurant counter and ordered a coffee I didn't want or intend to drink, paid with a ten-dollar bill and asked for change in quarters for the phone booth. I left the coffee on the counter but took the quarters, closing myself behind the glass doors of the phone booth, listening to the change ring down. The phone rang four times, then four more, and then I quit counting. I was prepared to let it ring until my bus arrived, if necessary. Maybe things would work out. The phone rang and rang. I waited nervously, hopeful that Linda would answer and not her father.

"Hello?"

"Is Linda there?"

"Yes, one minute please, I'll get her. No, wait. Who is this? Is this you, Raymond?"

Her father's voice was wary and vaguely accusatory.

"Yes, Pastor Grigsby. Hello."

He sighed audibly on the other end of the line.

"Raymond, you know you aren't supposed to call here. There remains a court protective order against you and Linda doesn't want to talk to you. Your persistence only upsets her and prolongs your grieving. Linda's too, for that matter."

"Linda is grieving? I didn't know that".

This seemed a hopeful indicator. Maybe she missed me.

"Let's just say she grieves for her life as it was before you entered it, Raymond. We all do. Anyway, you are not supposed to call her and Linda doesn't want to talk to you."

"You'd be surprised how many Christian people are in jail, Pastor Grigsby. When you think about it, all the early Christians were considered criminals. They were persecuted, imprisoned, and martyred."

"Well, you are definitely no martyr. You weren't in jail for your beliefs, Raymond. You were incarcerated for crimes against my daughter."

"I know what I did. And I'm repentant. But I'm just saying, a lot of good Christian men are in jail. I was one of them. I joined a prayer group, contemplated my past mistakes and trespasses, and asked forgiveness, which I received. Now I'm going to Mexico City on a mission of repentance and atonement."

"With what church group?"

"None. I'm going alone."

"Not a good idea, Raymond. I advise strongly against it."

Pastor Grigsby's admonition felt good. It was like when he used to like and trust me. I wanted him to again, but I had failed him more than he even knew. When working for him as a volunteer assistant youth pastor, although I organized basketball games, camping expeditions, rallies, teen prayer meetings and fund raisers for mission trips, I was a liar and a spy. All I could think about was sex. At Bible Camp, during our silent prayer vigils, heads bowed and eyes closed, I stole surreptitious peeks at girls' legs and breasts. When we prayed or sang Hymns while sitting cross-legged around the campfire, sometimes I looked up girl's skirts to see their panties. I'd ogle their young budding breasts, the outline of their nipples under their church T-shirts. I don't want to tell you how young some of these girls were. Too young for me to be indulging in fantasy while gawking at their underpants and budding young nipples, that's for sure. People trusted me and I took advantage. They thought I was a Christian, which I was supposed to be and wanted to be, but I was no better than a depraved old pervert. Sure, I was a teenage boy with raging hormones but that's no excuse. I was a faker, a joker, a spy in the house of God.

"You're supposed to be my pastor. You're supposed to forgive me."

"I do forgive you, Raymond. I've told you before, you're welcome in my church, but not during late service when Linda attends, not anywhere near my home, and not at all if you persist in stalking my daughter."

"But I never stalked her. That's a misconception. It's not like that. It never was. You had no reason to fear me. I meant you no harm. I loved you. I still love you. I'm no danger to you guys. I don't park in front of your house or spy in your windows or do anything weird and creepy like that. Not anymore, anyway."

"But you did, Raymond, exactly that, and more than once. Need I remind you of the incident when Linda and her college friend Gregory caught you hiding in the bushes? That was stalking, Raymond. And still later, after the restraining order was issued, you persisted."

"But you didn't have to call the police."

"You broke our windows, Raymond. *You hurt Linda.* How did you expect we would react?"

"I didn't mean to hurt her. I was only trying to get her attention."

"You threw a brick through our window, Raymond. She might have been blinded. If it had hit her in the head it could have killed her. It's possible she may have scars on her face for the rest of her life."

"It wasn't a brick; it was a large stone. But I know. It was stupid. It had a love poem wrapped around it. I thought I was being romantic, but I miscalculated. It was an accident. It wasn't meant to hurt her. I thought the window was open. I'm sorry, Pastor Grigsby."

"You deceive yourself, Raymond. You still haven't accepted your criminal intent. You deny stalking, which you were, and that was the least of it. The fact is you were convicted in a court of law for assault and sexual predation. And now, despite the risk of violating the terms of your probation, you persist. I don't know why I am even talking to you. I should be calling the police and reporting this call."

"Practice what you preach, Pastor Grigsby. Walk the walk, not just talk the talk. You need to forgive me and you need to take me into your family again."

"Again? What do you mean again? You were *never* a member of our family. You were Linda's boyfriend, not her husband, and not the one I would have chosen for her. I have a responsibility as a father. It's my daughter I'm watching out for now. She had an abortion because of you. How do you think that makes me feel, as a pastor and father? The one good thing that has come out of this is Linda no longer wants anything to do with you. I'm hanging up now, Raymond. Please don't call here again. If you do, I'll report it. Remember, you could go back to jail just for calling here."

Out the window a black and white squad car screeched to a stop and two uniformed police officers came into the terminal. The people around the jukebox scattered and vanished like cockroaches. An overhead light in the booth kept flickering. The inside reeked of ash and stale cigarette smoke. The floor was littered with cigarette butts and candy wrappers. The PA system announced the imminent departure of a bus for Chicago.

"*Raymond?* Is that *you?*"

It was Linda, probably on the upstairs extension in her bedroom. I loved the lilting soprano sweetness of her voice. She was everything to me, my one great love, my ultimate hope for a life worth living.

"Yes, Linda, it's me, Raymond Watson, who loves you more than his own life, more than any man ever will so long as you shall live. The man you promised to marry, cherish, honor and obey."

"I never promised any such thing and you're not supposed to call here. You know that. I'm hanging up."

"I'm leaving the country for Mexico City, Linda. I'm in the bus station right now."

"That sounds crazy even for you, Raymond."

She was right. Mexico was a fool's idea born of desperation I hoped to be talked out of. I always take things too far. I can't seem to find any middle ground. I become like a brush fire that needs to be put out.

"I'll stay if I have even the slightest chance of making you love me again."

"Well that's not going to happen, Raymond. I'm not sure I ever really did love you. And whatever misguided decision you make about what to do with your life, whether it's Mexico or an equally foolish alternative, I'm not responsible for it. Mexico, of all places. Where did you come up with that idea? Leave those poor people alone, Raymond. They have enough misfortune down there without you adding to it."

"Can't you forgive me a little?"

"I'm trying to, but every time I look in the mirror I see the scars on my face and hate you."

The juke box still played, but the police had dispersed the crowd and no one was dancing. I was too choked up to speak into the telephone. A pregnant woman squatting over a large suitcase on the dirty floor rummaged furiously through a heap of rumpled clothing. We were both crying.

"Playing the old crying card again, Raymond? It won't work anymore. Everything you say and do is just to manipulate. You're all fakery and trickery. And you're not a man. I don't know what you are, but you aren't a man. Stop it, Raymond. Stop crying like a little sissy girl. I can't believe that I was once in love with you."

"I can't stop crying because I can't stop loving you, Linda. It doesn't make me less a man."

It was hopeless. She would never take me back. I knew this, had known it for a long time, but couldn't let it go. I still can't. It's what sent me to jail. Love.

I couldn't stop crying; I was half falling to my knees in the phone booth. I had to steady myself to remain standing. I heard Linda hang up the phone and then a dial tone. I was about to leave the booth when the phone rang.

"Sir, you owe another two dollars and fifty-five cents."

I hung up and wandered outside to the loading docks. The smell of exhaust and diesel fuel hung in the air. It was still raining, but the wind was slight. The overhang kept the pavement and piles of stacked luggage dry. I slumped to the concrete and put my wet face in my hands and wept.

Crossing the Border

In the El Paso bus station a man without legs who claimed to be a veteran of the Korean War sold pamphlets in which he exposed a conspiracy of aliens from the planet Venus to take control of the Earth by manipulating human thought. Satan was said to lead their army, and was responsible for addiction and sexual perversion meant to enslave human kind. The bus station was hot and lurid, with dirty light cascading through filthy plate glass windows. A blast of hot air and a sharp whiff of diesel fumes entered from outside each time the doors opened.

With time to kill before changing busses, I wandered down the street and ordered a hamburger, fries and a milkshake at a Woolworth's lunch counter. A lean young cowboy about my own age took a stool next to me and ordered coffee. Sandy- haired, pale and obviously not Mexican, he nevertheless spoke fluent Spanish when ordering coffee from the pretty Mexican waitress. He wore jeans and imitation snakeskin cowboy boots and a western shirt with the sleeves rolled up. His hair was in need of a trim, and his teeth and fingers stained with nicotine. He had a skull tattoo on his arm. A snake was wrapped around the skull, the name Jesus tattooed on a flag below it. The fingers of his right hand were tattooed with letters spelling the word *Life*, and the left with the word *Death*. Smiling, he offered me a smoke, which I politely declined. His stubby teeth were slimy with a pale coating of mucus. He pointed at the seaman's duffle bag at my feet and said, "Coming or going?"

"Both," I said. "I just got here, but I'm crossing the border into Juarez."

"You better be careful," he advised. "Juarez is a badass town. Mucho frigging dangerous amigo, especially for people who don't know their way around. Same here in El Paso for that matter. You could get in a lot of trouble, robbed, beat up, killed even. I've seen it, man, more'n once, and it ain't a pretty sight."

He smiled briefly and crushed the cigarette he was smoking into the ashtray as if it was a living bug and he was destroying it. He reached over and took a French fry from my plate and said, "Shit, man, I've had to rescue unsuspecting gringos who were kidnapped by their *own freaking guide* and sold as sex slaves in Mexico. Not just women, either. Some were men, sold to all-male whorehouses servicing queers in Juarez and Tijuana. Lucky for you, you are in the right place at the right time. I'm probably the best guide around."

He removed the saucer from under his coffee cup and squirted some ketchup in it. He helped himself to another French fry and dipped it. His effeminate long fingernails were filthy.

"I know my way around Juarez real good," he said. "You'd be safe with me because everybody knows me and knows not to fuck with me. Last guy who tried ended up in the hospital. Oh, you'll be safe with me, amigo, I can promise you that."

He squirted more ketchup from the container but it was near empty and came out in spurts that splattered on the counter and on his hand and grimy fingers. He licked his ketchup-spattered hand and fingers with his tongue. It was the longest tongue I had ever seen, way too long for a human tongue. Maybe he was part aardvark.

"Waitress," he called. "More ketchup for these fries, por favor."

He wiped his hand and fingers with a wad of napkins and tossed the mess onto the counter. Again he glanced to the duffle bag at my feet, but quickly, furtively, as if I might not notice his abiding interest. Finally, he just came out and asked.

"So what's in the bag? You're traveling kind of light, aren't you?"

"Not much of anything, really. Some clothing, a few toiletries, an English-to-Spanish phrase book and my Bible."

I had nothing of value. No rings, no watch. Other than toothpaste, underwear and socks and this journal, my bag contained only one change of clothing. My only article of value was my motorcycle boots, which I had purchased new before leaving, which would serve me well. Meanwhile his pilfering of my lunch escalated. He took a pickle and a generous handful of French fries from my plate and laid them on his coffee saucer, which had become his own little plate.

"Listen here," he continued, "I can take you places and get you things not available to the usual tourist. I can bring you to live sex shows, get you the very best dope available, as many women as you want as young as you want. I can get you anything and everything, buddy. And guess what? You're in luck. Because I'm in a good mood and I like you, you don't even have to pay for my services. We'll just share in life's sweet abundance; you dig? Get us some tequila, some good smoke, maybe a little speed, *definitely* a motel room and some women, maybe even three or four so we can switch off. We'll party all night long. All *week* long. Let me tell you, amigo buddy, that's heaven."

His eyes kept flickering from me to the duffle bag at my feet. He pointed to my milkshake and said, "Are you going to finish that?"

I gave it to him and said I had a bus to catch, that I was not staying in Juarez but continuing on immediately to Mexico City.

"Too bad," he said. "We could have had us some kicks. You're gonna miss out."

"No offense," I replied, "but I don't drink or smoke or do drugs or anything like that."

"Well then, what do you do for kicks?"

"I'm not really interested in kicks. I'm trying to be a Christian."

His tone shifted abruptly as he pointed to a small golden cross around his neck and said, "I'm a Christian too, but I don't go around talking about it like I'm better than you. Being a Christian don't exempt you or save you from what's coming down. Shit, man, we're *all* sinners. What's the matter with you, you don't know that? I know it even if you don't. We're all tempted; we all want to indulge in secret fantasies and take pleasure in what is forbid-

39

den. And we all do. It's elemental, you dig? To be human is to be tempted. It's part of life. We all make mistakes and do stupid shit we regret, and we all need relief even if it's in shit that's bad for us. Read Ecclesiastics, my pious friend. Vanity, it's all vanity.

"And I'll tell you something else, my jive-ass holier-than-thou Christian hypocrite amigo buddy, give you a little history lesson here, free of fucking charge. This soil you're standing on? It may be called Texas, but *fuck* remember the Alamo and all that rah rah patriotic yahoo bullshit, because before the Alamo, it was Mexico. We fuckin' stole it. This is *still* fuckin' Mexico, dig? We're just enemy occupation troops. The point is, just about everyone you meet here is Mexican and devout Catholic and so what? Nobody measures up, in the end. Everybody sins, suffers, and dies alone."

"I know," I said. "We live in a fallen world. It's sad."

"Yeah, but that's it right there. You said it right there, man. We *live*, brother. Fallen world or not, we live. And that's what we damn well *should* do. Live it up. Laugh in Satan's face. Eat the fucking apple and spit it in his eye. Drink the liquor, screw the woman, and party in Hell. And you know what?—it turns out it ain't so bad down here. Shit, man, I can take you to bitches who could make you forget everything but how good you can feel. Show you some heaven on Earth, so to speak. Git us some of that God-given consolation. Some of that sweet juicy balm of Gilead."

"I don't think so," I said. "This is interesting but I have a bus to catch."

"There's always another bus. You queer or something?"

I couldn't tell if he was serious or mocking me. "No, nothing like that," I replied indifferently. "But look, I really have to be going."

"That's a shame, man. Well, if you change your mind, just ask around for Jive Jerry. Everybody knows me, and I'm easy to find."

I left him chattering with the waitress at the counter as he finished what remained of my hamburger and fries. I didn't tell him that I was a practicing celibate who had taken a vow of chastity. No one understood that, or could be expected to. It wasn't the sort of information you shared with just anyone. I'm reluctant to record it here.

The abstinence was deliberate. It was an act of contrition and a vow I intended to keep. I was not a good Christian but wanted to be. I was a sinner, but believed in the possibility of redemption.

* * *

From Juarez our bus set out along a promising modern four-lane highway toward Mexico City, but very soon began veering off onto dirt side roads, stopping in dusty little outlying villages along the way. I repositioned myself again and again in my seat in an impossible attempt to get comfortable, sometimes dozing, but waking at stops where the bus loaded and unloaded freight. Because I was the only Anglo on board, with minimal Spanish language acquisition, there was little chance of engaging in conversation with other passengers, so there was nothing to do but look out the window, read my Bible and write in this journal.

We entered a vast desert wasteland without vegetation other than cacti and an occasional solitary withered jacaranda tree. Sunset announced itself in a soft explosion of crimson. Strange tropical light glared off the sands and rocks. The Aztecs believed the sun's brilliance would diminish and become defeated by darkness unless continuously fed on the spiritual energy of sacrificial human blood. I tried to imagine the hearts, souls, and minds of a people founded on a theology of murder. Their cannibalistic God seemed insatiably cruel, horrific and utterly inconceivable to my Christian concept of a loving, forgiving deity. Their concept of time was sophisticated, but their cosmology less so. The sun will not flicker and die like a candle flame but burn incrementally until becoming a raging, fiery nova. I watched this Aztec sun set behind the dunes and the moon rise slowly over the desert. The night became as dark as indigo ink, the vast sky above brilliantly speckled with thousands of luminous jewel-like stars. The beam of our headlights reflecting off the road ahead provided the only ground light as we continued over moon-shadowed hills and dunes and across flat sandy wastelands.

The next morning an exploding blood orange sunrise appeared out the bus windows. We drove on, winding slowly into a high desert landscape. Hours of sharp, treacherous turns gave view to steep precarious embankments as the bus wound slowly up mountain roads without guardrails. Elderly female passengers dressed in shapeless black sack dresses made the sign of the cross and fingered their rosaries. The abandoned rusted skeletons of crashed automobiles were strewn in deadly ravines below. A sad procession of overburdened donkeys carried mountains of goods on their backs. Every few miles an overheated roadside automobile was attended to. Stranded passengers stood helplessly around malfunctioning cars or trucks while men changed tires or added water to steaming radiators.

Eventually the road became congested with slow moving pickup trucks and flatbeds overloaded with Mexican workers crowded in the beds. We passed through a bleak run-down city of water towers, railroad yards and slaughter houses before continuing on into harsh desert. Indian men and women of all ages, from children to grandparents, toiled in the unrelenting desert heat while carrying burdens piled so high on their backs that it seemed impossible their legs would not buckle. They did not as much as glance at us.

Chased by mangy packs of barking mongrel dogs, we passed through stranded outposts in still more desert towns consisting of solitary gas stations, tire repair shops, junkyards, auto-body shops, markets and cantinas. Each town we stopped in, no matter how small, had a prominent Catholic Church as its center.

Night found us in a vast desert where there were no ground lights and only a few lamps burning in the distant windows of randomly scattered adobe houses. Darkness loomed on the horizon, with only a few solitary reading lights inside the windows of the bus. I looked out the window and saw the garish illuminated reflection of my haunted oily face staring back at me accusingly.

My shame was right here, riding along with me, staring at me disapprovingly from my reflection in the window. Why was I was here, on this bus? What did I think I might accomplish? I was running to Mexico because I couldn't face the truth of who I was and what I had done to Linda, who I was supposed to have loved. In Mexico no one would know me, or my history of failure.

The bus rumbled and bumped along deteriorated roads to isolated dismal locations where passengers boarded or disembarked and freight was loaded and unloaded. Indian women and children sold bananas and oranges, avocados and mangos. Vendors sold cold beer and bottles of soda and water. Women boarded the bus selling goat meat tacos and tamales. I watched men devour enormous tacos made with meat soaked in hot sauce. Juices dripped down their arms and hands and fingers. I heard the sound of juicy mangos being chewed and sucked. I watched the moving Adam's apples of men as they gulped down rich creamy milk that frothed on their mustaches, which they happily licked.

I was hungry but had been warned to beware of street food in Mexico. Suppose the meat in these tacos was disguised in a smothering of lethally hot sauces? Suppose it was in fact Mexican dog meat? What then? I was terrified of sickness. I would rather be dead than sick.

I went to sleep hungry and woke to the artificial light of a bus terminal, the hiss of hydraulic bus doors and hollow thud of luggage thrown in the compartment below. It was night, and the lights on the loading dock spilled yellow liquid light on the pavement. How long had I slept? Not long enough. How much farther? Too far.

A plump Mexican woman boarded with a wooden plank held in place at waist level by hemp ropes strapped around her neck. Her hair was streaked gray, she wore a woven shawl over her shoulders and carried a large basket and several knives on the plank. Her brown face was wrinkled, her smile warm and friendly.

"Torta," she sang, "torta".

Sleepy passengers groped in their pockets, fumbled with wallets or rummaged through purses while waving for her attention.

"Aqui! Aqui! Torta por favor!"

She began slicing large baguette style rolls on a wooden sandwich board, slathered the roll with a thick helping of refried beans, added ham and tomato, chilies and sliced avocado. The finished product looked delicious and closely resembled a harmless American sandwich. I watched with an almost prurient absorption that bordered on pornography as she sliced avocados taken from her basket and lathered bean dip across the rolls, then added ham or sliced chicken. She worked quickly and efficiently, preparing her delicious sandwiches and accepting cash from eagerly awaiting passengers with a smile and quietly intoned gracias.

The sandwiches sold out quickly. The woman exited the bus and stood outside under the golden light of the terminal. She waved goodbye as the bus pulled out. I slid down in my seat, heartbroken with disappointment. If only I had purchased a torta. Now I could only watch as passengers activated the reading lights over their seats and bore down into serious, focused devouring. They chewed noisily, smacking their lips with what seemed deliberately cruel exaggeration. It was as if they were intentionally teasing me, chewing ever so slowly, relishing each bite, slurping and licking soft avocado from their fingers.

I heard their grunts of pleasure, the smacking of their lips. I watched them down to their last bites, to the patting of their mouths with their napkins and the gentle sweeping of bread crumbs off their laps. I heard their sighs of satisfaction as they turned out their lights and slumped back in their seats. *Ahhh.* I heard their soft belches of satisfaction, their gentle farts and snoring as the bus headlights streaked ahead into the starry darkness. I dozed fitfully, awakening with hunger pangs and the haunting, erotic memory of tortas. I couldn't get them out of mind. All the way to Mexico City, everywhere the bus stopped, I woke vigilantly, alert for more tortas, but none were forthcoming.

* * *

My thoughts during lonely nights, were of Linda. I remembered our last brief conversation, in the telephone booth in Seattle, when she had said terrible, hurtful things to me. I knew it was because I had hurt her and she wanted to hurt me back and feel her pain, but her words were daggers in my heart. I wanted her forgiveness so bad I would have let her burn me at the stake if it would help. Yes, I had hurt her, but why didn't she understand that everything I did was because I loved her?

She accused me of not being a man, of being manipulative, a "crybaby" when confronted with the truth about myself. Guilty as charged, then. I cry because I am ashamed and in love with a woman who wants nothing to do with me, who no longer respects me. Even thinking about it makes me want to cry.

What would you prefer, Linda? Would you respect me more if I was a "real" man, one that society seems to esteem, the kind you seem to most admire—one able to laugh off personal failures or violations of ethics with cocky sarcasm, bravado, or a false show of tough-guy indifference?

My problem is that societal expectations reflect me unfairly. I am held in comparison and expected to conform to a standard of masculine ambition, aggressiveness and covetousness that I don't care to emulate. I reject the striving for status and acquisition of wealth and power that my peers engage in, and do not share the materialistic values of what others define as success. I believe in reparation, atonement, holiness. Success is when you have given everything away. When all that remains is Love.

* * *

Barren sandy wasteland of dust and sagebrush. Strange, isolated whirlwinds. Dead tumbleweed rolling slowly along the thirsty shimmering desert. Thunder and a sudden, inexplicable explosion of rain battering the road, pounding the bus without forewarning. After the rain, the shimmering desert sands give the strange illusion of audibly hissing. A misty vapor rises slowly from grotesque cacti. Huge isolated boulders steam in the sand. A magnificent rainbow expands across the entire horizon.

We turn off the main highway onto a nameless dirt road. Red mud one-room shacks placed far apart pepper the landscape; there is no town, no telephone poles, nothing. In the distance is a random, isolated shack without a road leading to it. Small dark children play in the forsaken remains of expired autos. At another stop, buzzards swarm the carcass of a dead dog in the dusty unpaved street. Why have we come here? There is no explanation. No one gets on or off the bus.

More desert. Distorted shapes of huge cacti twisted into grotesque parodies of human form. Phantoms and ghosts of the desert moonlight. A city of grandiose Spanish style haciendas with red tile roofs and high stone walls topped with implanted sharp pieces of broken glass. Behind the walls, guard dogs roam the grounds. We pick up speed and are back on the four lane highway. On a two lane road, at the crest of a dune, two Mexican men astride magnificent horses watch us from their saddles as we pass. They wear sombreros and gun belts and have rifles across their laps. They do not wave and their expressions are stern. Who knows their intent? They might be highway bandits, or armed resistance fighters awaiting the revolution. One thinks of Zapata, Villa, Indian uprisings.

We drive through stranded outposts where idle unshaven men sit in rockers silently watching. Who can guess or imagine their thoughts? They are old beyond their years, perhaps burdened with memories, secrets, and too much dying. There is nothing they have not seen or experienced. We pass Pemex stations, cantinas, bus station loading platforms, white stucco churches with bell towers. Dogs lay panting in the dust with their tongues hanging out and rib cages showing. They are too forlorn and sun-weary to chase after us. Women everywhere suckle infants. Are there no women in this country who are not either pregnant or nursing?

* * *

I did not yet know that the border I had crossed had been more than geographical. Bernal Diaz de Castillo, a soldier with Cortez during the conquest of Mexico, wrote that upon the conquistadores first sighting of the ancient capital of the Aztec civilization known then as Tenochtitlan and today as Mexico City, "some of our soldiers asked whether what we saw was not a dream." Their minds could not assimilate or believe what they saw as they gazed at the mouth of a volcano into an island mega-city floating on the glittering turquoise waters of Lake Texcoco. Tenochtitlan was equal in size, architecture, and engineering to any city in Europe, larger and more populated than Paris, its inhabitants numbering between five and six million. It was a grandiose capital of elaborate monuments and palaces, complex pyramidal towers, exotic zoos and floating gardens. Cortez wrote of it that it was "the most beautiful city in the world." He subsequently destroyed it completely.

Approaching the city by road at night, as one drives over the high volcanic mountains that hem it in on three sides, the sight of the lights of Mexico City spread out across the valley is spectacular. The new city that replaces Tenochtitlan—Mexico City or Ciudad de Mexico, or just Mexico, as its citizens call it, is built on the ashes of the old. Lake Texcoco has been drained and the new city is built on the underlying soft clay. Its bedrock is soft and spongy, the city itself unstable, sinking at the rate of a foot a year. It is said that eventually the old part of the city will have disappeared, having sunk into the mud below it. Because of this lack of stability, there is frequent seismic activity, and it remains a strange, ancient land of volcanoes, earthquakes, preternatural phenomenon and supernatural apparitions recorded throughout history, ranging from the miraculous appearance of the Virgin of Guadalupe in the year 1531 to recent sightings of large formations of flying saucers witnessed by thousands of astonished spectators and investigated by UFO researchers from all over the world.

I first saw the city from the windows of the bus after a long winding drive over volcanic mountains. Upon my first sight of it, spread out for miles in the valley below, I gasped audibly. My journey into the heart of Mexico was about to take me from all that I thought I knew about the world and myself.

PART TWO

Jesus the Beggar

The first person I met in Mexico City was a nameless beggar we'll call Jesús Sanchez. He seemed to be dying right in front of me. Later he began appearing in my dreams. Once I thought he waved to me from a park bench, but he vanished when I reached it. Another time I watched him briefly in the mirror in my room, but it may have been his ghost I had seen. There are many such ghosts here in Mexico City. I may be one of them.

I had been on the bus to Mexico City for five hard mind-numbing days and blurred narcoleptic nights during which I had not changed my clothing, bathed or even brushed my teeth. I was dirty and grimy with sweat. My hair and skin were oily. My sticky underwear felt like it had been pasted onto my body. My mouth tasted like sour garbage. My stomach rumbled. I stood outside the city bus station, exhausted, astonished, exhilarated and unprepared for the exotic carnival that was life in Mexico City.

The crowded broad sidewalks writhed with activity, everyone bumping into each other in the melee. I felt myself pulled along, not entirely voluntarily, with the flow of pedestrian traffic to a large central paved square. The Metropolitan Cathedral of Mexico City encompassed the entire forward view. Its magnificent golden dome, smooth and peaked with a silver cross, glittered in the sunlight. The steps to its magnificent doors were festooned with brilliant yellow and red roses and white hyacinth. Vigilant winged gargoyles and gilded seraphim clung to its ledges and cornices.

Those who ascended its steps made the sign of the cross. Even without knowing anything of this city, its culture or its people, I knew that for them it was sacred ground. Women with braided hair wore embroidered peasant blouses and bandanas with woven belts around their long skirts. Many sold crafted Catholic trinkets such as small brightly painted figures of Jesus, hand hammered silver and tin crucifixes, crosses and rosaries spread out on blankets. Vendors sold exotic fruits, hand woven baskets and serapes, blankets and pottery, bird cages and bright talking birds. Shoeshine stands were on every corner. Young boys roved the streets hawking Chiclet gum, lottery tickets, newspapers, chirping birds, cigarettes by the pack or in singles. Everyone was selling something and any and everything was for sale.

Everyone seemed to be shouting. A continuous blare of automobile horns insistently blasted at frustrated drivers stalled in congested traffic. There was no emission control in Mexico City, and the mountains hemmed in the exhaust. The air was thick with soot; smoke and smog made my eyes burn and water.

Thousands of bicycles wove through traffic. People seemed to be talking at a high rate of speed. A permeating drone of sound was everywhere around us. I passed a street musician who serenaded with a guitar but couldn't find his voice because it was lost in the ocean of noise. Male and female voices young and old, crying babies, barking dogs and shouting roosters competed with radios from tenement widows and the unceasing blare of automobile horns on the street. Overhead, far above, was the distant rumble of a passenger plane that glittered silver in the sky. The music of the city was an inspired symphony composed by a madman. The streets and sidewalks and buildings and windows were pounded with it.

I wandered without plan or purpose, without destination. Drifting clouds of charcoal smoke rose from portable make-shift kitchens on sidewalk street corners. The aromatic tang of tacos, tamales, beans, and sizzling meat filled the air. Women knelt over curbside cook fires where they patted tortillas while their naked, smudged- faced children crawled around them.

The street was a slow undulating anaconda of traffic; fleets of bright taxis and automobiles that barely ran coughed clouds of black smoke. Busses, delivery trucks and automobiles maneuvered haphazardly without discernible order or pattern or were stalled in the melee. Crowded windowless trolleys that looked as if they had been built in the early 1900s transported shoulder-to-shoulder passengers along an antiquated rail system. Men rode on the roof, clung to fenders or clutched anything that offered a handhold. Dark little children darted between the trolley tracks selling lottery tickets. A procession of amputees who had lost their legs working these tracks rolled along on wooden platforms.

This is when I first saw him, the man I will name Jesus Sanchez, who would later haunt my dreams and startle me with appearances that may or may not have been apparitional. He was the first beggar I had ever witnessed. He staggered forward in my direction, lurching unsteadily as if wounded. One leg didn't seem to work as it should. It wobbled and periodically gave out as if in refusal to obey. His back rose in a pronounced hump, his footsteps so precarious it seemed certain he would trip and fall, but with each lurch and stumble he corrected himself at the last second.

A nun stepped off the bus and reached in her coin purse and gave him some money. He tried to embrace her but she skittered away without looking back. Two gnomish old women dressed in black made the sign of the cross but did not give him anything. Several merry, laughing young Spanish schoolgirls dressed in Catholic School blue blazers with gold buttons and crests passed by him without so much as giving him a glance. I saw a man push him out of the way. The momentum sent the beggar stumbling into the gutter. A shriek of angry horns rose in protest as vehicles swerved or braked to avoid him.

His eyes brightened, as if he recognized me. As he began making his way toward me, I had the impression he was so determined to make contact with me that had I been standing in shark infested waters and he on the edge of a high cliff, he would have marched right off the precipice, never taking his eyes off me.

It was impossible to ascertain his age. Everything about him looked old and broken. Even his eyes looked old. His face was a library containing epic volumes of misfortune and resignation. His face was so deeply lined it was like granite on which the entire history of human suffering had been etched. His clothing hung from him in ragged shreds that were like filthy unraveling bandages. His gray patchy long hair was coated with dirt and ash, and his beard appeared to have not been washed in months. He was barefoot, and one arm might have been deformed—he kept it hidden under his ragged serape.

His other arm reached out to me, hand open, palm up. He grasped my sleeve and spoke to me in Spanish. His breath was putrefying; it reeked of disease. I turned my face away. He raised his fist, not to my face, but to the heavens in some impossible, desperate petition. It was the first time I had ever seen the filth and degrading misery that was the life story of most of humanity.

I had been forewarned about these beggars on the streets of Mexico City: that they would be legion, and I would have to beware of trying to benefit them or attempt to mitigate their fate. I had been advised that these were the lives they were born into, their destiny and lot in life. There were hordes of them here and there was nothing anyone could do about it. If you gave to them, there would be no end to it. You would be left with nothing. I had been warned about all of it: the tacos made from the meat of mangy dogs, bandits who would hijack your vehicle, kidnap and hold you for ransom, the beautiful tempting prostitutes whose dark thighs held incurable venereal disease. One needed to be wary, one needed to be vigilant, one needed to be hyper-alert to every one of the multitude of terminal pitfalls and entrapments in the dangerous spiritual whirlpool that was Mexico City.

I, who had said that I wanted to give all that I had until only love remained, ignored his outstretched begging palm and intoned one of the few Spanish phrases I knew, *no entiende,* which means, translated, *I don't understand.* But how could one not understand this universal gesture of begging and need? His very being was an expression of it. He reached inside his serape to present what I initially thought was a black stone about the size of a misshapen tennis ball. He held it out for me to examine and pleaded again, *"Por favor, señor."*

There was no anger in his expression, no aggression in his gesture of begging. Then I saw that the stone was really a piece of bread, blackened with soot. *No Entiende?* There was no pretending to misunderstand *this* gesture of begging.

I experienced a flutter in my chest; my breathing quickened as if I could not fill my lungs with enough oxygen. Everything around me seemed to go still; there was only this moment and we were the only two people occupying it. I could hear people all around me but he was all I saw. I had to get away. I reached in my pocket for some money. I gave him a few coins. I didn't know what I was giving him. I had no understanding of Mexican currency, no idea what the coins were worth translated to dollars, no idea what he could buy with them. He took them from me, and then he embraced me. I felt his old, frail, pitifully thin body under the layers of dirty clothing, felt the stubble of his beard. His stench was pervasive and hideous. I worried that he might have a communicable disease.

I pulled away, abruptly aware once again of the crowded street, people passing by, indecipherable fragments of conversation, the sound of automobiles and radios and voices all around me. His eyes would not leave mine. They were wet and glistening. His gratitude was enormous and effusive and seemed far beyond what my meager gesture of giving deserved. I couldn't understand what he was saying but it appeared that he was thanking Jesus, his mother, the Virgin of Guadalupe, saints and whatever holy mysterious orchestration of God that had providentially guided him to his fortuitous encounter with this American boy. One might have thought that I had given my very life for him.

I was on the verge of crying. At that moment he was beautiful to me. I wanted to save him from his life but where would it end, caring for a soul such as this? Where would the act of giving end? You would have to give all and still it would not be enough. The man was probably dying. I stepped into the swiftly moving flood of pedestrians and disappeared from his sight.

Later, after becoming familiar with Mexican currency, I learned the coins I had given him were probably insufficient to buy more than a small loaf of bread. How account then for his effusive display of gratitude? Had his poverty been so great that his thankfulness had been for these pitifully few insignificant coins dropped in his palm, or was it instead for a simple act of human kindness on his behalf?

Or rather was I, as a sheltered privileged American, so separated from the poor fellaheen of the Earth that I simply did not understand how a few coins and a loaf of bread could mean the difference between life and death?

Welcome to Mexico City, which posed these questions, but did not answer them.

* * *

Two major intersecting boulevards deliver continuous traffic into the commercial heart of Mexico City. The Paseo de la Reforma, beginning at Chapultepec Park, is one, and is known for its historical castle and museum of natural history and expansive gardens. It merges with downtown Avenida de Insurgentes, a major wide boulevard of elegant upscale hotels, gourmet restaurants, boutiques, exclusive department stores and banking and business institutions. Eventually this busy interconnecting thoroughfare gives way to clean and reasonable but less elegant restaurants, middle income department stores, second class movie theatres and construction and demolition pertaining to city restoration projects. The street ultimately descends into the low income working class tenement barrios at the end of the line.

Dazed and culture shocked after hours of walking without purpose or destination, I found myself on this major hub of tourism and traffic. Almost everyone does, especially foreigners. Sanborn's, a gathering place for American tourists and expatriates is here, as is Brentano's, a bookstore stocking books printed in English, and also the American Express, where I opened an account, set up a mailing address and exchanged dollars for Pesos. Here I was given the name and address of the Hotel La Paz, said to be clean and priced appropriately to a student's budget.

Cabs maneuvered through thick traffic on the avenue and I found one easily, with an English speaking driver who said he had once resided with relatives in Chicago. He accepted the address of my hotel but declared it unsuitable, taking me instead to a half dozen of the many upscale, brightly lighted Las Vegas styled hotels along the commercial section of the Paseo de La Reforma, where he was probably trying to collect a commission from management. I refused to even so much as step foot upon the threshold of these garish monstrosities.

The driver continued along Insurgentes, stopping at hotels there as well, but eventually gave up, presumably accepting the fare in the back of his cab was not the prized rich American he had initially mistaken me for.

Situated on a quiet side street in a working class neighborhood, the Hotel La Paz was definitely on the funky end of its three-star rating. Without a neon sign or marquee over the La Paz entrance, only its name painted on the narrow glass front door identified the building as a hotel. The entire block consisted of tenement buildings. Across the littered windswept street, a Chinese laundry seemed oddly misplaced.

It was early evening. The front windows were dirty and the inadequately lighted lobby reeked of stale cigarette smoke. A leather couch and mismatched lounge chairs that had once been luxurious had seen better days. The tiles were stained with accumulated grime, the maroon carpets faded and worn so thin in some areas you could see the tile flooring beneath. Exhausted and irritable, I checked in with the English speaking desk clerk, who addressed me in English.

"Your luggage, sir?"

"I have only what I am carrying."

He frowned disapprovingly at my seaman's bag and lack of luggage otherwise and replied, "I see."

I signed the register; he took my passport, issued a room key and directed me to the lone elevator. I found my room on the uppermost floor, at the end hall left of the elevator. It was a disappointment, cramped and stuffy, with overhead lighting glaring off a dirty linoleum floor. A water stain blemished the ceiling over the single bed, which supported a spongy mattress. A tall wooden dresser contained six drawers, one missing a handle, while a writing desk set with a carafe of water provided the only other furniture. A solitary framed print depicting an armored conquistador on horseback hung on the wall behind the desk and single chair. The small lamp on the desk's surface was burned out. A rickety wooden clothes tree stood incongruously in the corner. The bathroom, separated by an opaque Plexiglas door, was claustrophobic but clean. I raised window blinds streaked with dust and grease and was rewarded with a view to an air vent and tiny sliver of hallway. So much for a view, or fresh air.

The room was so cramped and unadorned it might have served as a study in sensory deprivation, but it was all I needed and cheap. I could pay three months in advance. My plan was to record my experiences in this journal, stretch my money and remain in Mexico until whatever fate intended for me here was accomplished. My parents, by prearrangement, had been instructed to wire a hundred dollars a month to American Express, where I would pick up my mail. I'd made them promise to ignore requests for additional funds without exception regardless of what emergency I might present.

Now, whether from the bus ride or long walk through the city, I was ready to collapse. My limbs ached and I hadn't had a shower or bath in five days and six nights during which I had been cramped in a seat without stretching room. I was too tired to decide whether to take a shower or just fall into bed.

I heard a light tapping on the door. The desk clerk asked permission to enter, then opened it with his pass key, pausing at the threshold without entering. Again he frowned at my sea bag and lack of luggage. He stood just inside the door, aimlessly as far as I could see, while I wondered what he wanted and hoped he would go away soon.

He bowed slightly and said, "Greetings, Señor Watson. I hope I have not disturbed you. My name is Ricardo. I am at your service. Is everything agreeable?"

"Fine, thank you."

Although he presented himself with officious subservience, I found him haughty and disagreeable. I disliked him immediately. Slender and slightly effeminate, he wore his greased black hair combed straight back with a narrow pencil line moustache traced over his thin upper lip. His oily dark face climaxed with his pointed nose, his eyes were dark, shifty, and rather calculating. He was immaculately groomed, but because of his pointed nose, narrow face and thin little moustache, I would soon come to think of him as Ricardo the Rodent Desk Clerk.

"Perhaps," he suggested, "you would like some company?"

Why would I want his company? I didn't want anyone's company. I was exhausted. I had not been in prone position for five days and I wanted to go to bed.

"Thank you for asking, but maybe another time."

He tweaked his moustache and said, "I understand." The diamond ring on his finger glinted. "You are tired after your long journey." Ricardo spoke formal textbook English and actually used the word "journey."

He smiled coyly and left. Afterwards I felt foolish. I understood too late that he had not been suggesting his own company, but a woman's. Ricardo, in addition to being a desk clerk, was apparently a pimp.

I would have liked to soak in a hot bath but had to settle for a shower in the confining stall in which there was barely room to move and only intermittent hot water. Afterwards I unpacked my tote bag, which contained all that I had or would have during my exile here: underwear, socks, toothbrush, a denim shirt, and one other pair of jeans besides those I was wearing. I had not packed any additional footwear because I was wearing motorcycle boots, which I expected to last in all kinds of weather.

In addition to the Spanish phrase book and Bible, I had my notebooks and writing paper and pens. I liked to think of myself as a writer and I suppose, since I write daily, that's what I am—a writer. A writer without a message. A writer with no universal truth or connection to the human family.

A writer without a story.

* * *

A week later I can't remember where I am and can't see anything, not even the palm of my hand. I grope along the wall for the light switch, but where is it? Damn! I just stubbed my big toe against something, but what? I think maybe I jammed it against the chair leg. It hurts like hell. I'm cursing and hopping up and down on one foot. How can a tiny little toe cause so much freaking pain? OK, I have found the light switch and turned the toggle but now everything explodes in light and I see someone who should not be here sitting in the chair.

It's Jesus the Beggar again.

His image vanishes instantly and then I am alone under the light.

Again I had dreamed of him. He had clutched that same lump of bread but offered it to me. He tore a piece and handed it to me to eat in communion. I refused it. It was filthy with grime from his dirty hands and when I looked closely it was crawling with miniscule brown insects. I don't know what this dream means, but it frightens me. I *am* hungry though. I don't know what is safe to eat here in Mexico. I limit myself to fruit at the outdoor markets, oranges, pineapples, bananas, anything organically sealed within its own peel. I'm afraid of the most tropical fruits, which are unfamiliar and somehow look alien, and the vegetables look nasty.

I'm suspicious especially of the meat here. Grotesque naked animal carcasses hang upside-down from enormous iron hooks, but what are these mutilations? I don't know what this meat is they serve in these tortillas. Dog meat, iguana, monkey, boar, jaguar, donkey? Who knows? Men who resemble beasts tear into huge hunks of it right in the street where it is cooked over improvised fires. Grease runs down their chins. They wipe their mouths with their hands, their hands on their bodies. There is plenty of chicken, but I have seen too many in the process of decapitation, too many with blood on their feathers or naked and headless in obscene poses representative of human brutality, horror and murder. I've seen too many boiling pots of stews with chicken feet surfacing in the bubbles. I'm nauseous from the stench of raw and cooked flesh and overripe fruits and vegetables.

The dream of the beggar is already fading from my mind. But he will be back, I know. My gaze falls to the notebook of my neglected autobiography and journal, which seems to regard me in a manner vaguely accusatory. I think I am supposed to be writing of the beggar, telling his story, but I'm not qualified. What do I know of his life, his suffering?

Let me do the telling, he whispers.

* * *

My view from the lobby's dirt streaked windows is to a net-work of tenements with clattering fire-escape steps and landings with flowerboxes, potted plants, hanging laundry and birdcages. I recognize some of the women at upper floor windows as they lean over their painted flower boxes, chattering with one another as if sharing neighborhood gossip. Women sweep their stoops or wash them on their hands and knees. Men are less in evidence. By this time of day, they have left the neighborhood for work. Children are off to school. No one here knows me, or has ever spoken to me.

It is hard to imagine, just a few blocks away from this improb-ably sequestered side street is the interminable maze of intercon-nected neighborhoods which comprise the enormous, monstrous, dissonant honeycomb of copulating humanity that is Mexico City. The city is a teeming, seething, writhing megalopolis, a throbbing nebulous life form, swollen with hope, spilling itself in an ecstatic frenzied abandon. It is a hydra-headed incomprehensible entity, a pregnant Mayan serpent goddess giving birth to billions of auto-mobiles, trillions of screaming children, crowded open markets, taxi cabs, women, inconceivable armies of insistent vendors.

For weeks I walked its streets day to night. My socks became like rags. My feet became swollen and bloated, raw and blistered in my punishing steel-toed motorcycle boots. I wandered as if sleep-walking, trancelike, with no destination in mind, no understand-ing of where I was at any given time, no intent except to lose myself in the physical act of walking. I roamed until my legs were so weak I had trouble standing. I don't know why I did this. I questioned it myself. Maybe I was lonely. Maybe it was more than that. Maybe I was driven by the need for an event that confirmed I was not dead.

No one spoke to me. No one acknowledged me. My life was taking place in a city that I had no connection with. I was invisible, a peeping tom, an eavesdropping ghost as I prowled the streets or took second and third class busses, challenging myself to get lost and find my way back. It was a game I played with myself. The sky-scrapers of the Insurgentes and the Paseo de la Reforma were like the lighted necks of sea monsters.

Sometimes, utterly exhausted after my wanderings, it seemed so impossibly far back to the hotel that I was ready to join the armies of the homeless sleeping in vacant door wells, alleys and on park benches, not because I had no place to go, but because I was too tired to get there. Legs aching, feet throbbing, lungs hurting, mind shattered in a maze of embarrassing, shameful memories relieved only by the physical pain of my forced march, I staggered like a shipwreck survivor into the rude unforgiving glare of the of the hotel lobby. The brightly lighted hallway to my room seemed elongated, a surreal corridor miles distant from my room.

It sometimes took twenty minutes to get the boots off my swollen feet. Sometimes I was too tired to remove them and gave up. After cursory prayers more similar to recitation than communion, I'd descend into the oblivion of sleep. In the morning, every limb protesting, I'd rise to stagger into the shower to wash the blood off my feet and soak in whatever hot water might be available, dress and carefully force my raw blistered feet into my motorcycle boots. Then I'd start all over again. I walked without intent or destination, wherever my feet led me. Sometimes, either by accident or the exertion of an outside spiritual force, I ended up in barrios where homeless men sat on stoops or slept in the street. I hoped against reason that I might miraculously stumble on Jesus the Beggar. This time I would not fail, but give to him generously.

I cannot explain this beggar's persistence in my memory or his spontaneous and intrusive appearances. There is something extraordinary about it. I've dreamed of him a few times so strongly that it's spooky. I've wakened in the middle of the night, convinced he's in my room. I know it's crazy but I end up having to turn on the light. Believe me; if it happened to you the way it does to me, you would do the same.

* * *

Whenever it wasn't raining, I walked aimlessly, all day. No one spoke to me. No one so much as acknowledged me. I was in the city but not a part of it. I had no connection to life around me. I was invisible, a ghost lingering among the living. I took second and third class busses, challenging myself to get lost and find my way back. It was a game I played with myself. During times of heavy unrelenting rainfall, there was nothing to do but write in this book. Other than the Bible, it was the only book I had. I was famished for books, newspapers, and the English language. Sometimes I even tried talking with Ricardo, if only to hear English spoken in return, but he just seemed annoyed. I spent rainy days napping. There were times when I slept all day. I loved to sleep, to dream. In my dreams I had an identity and was real. Dreams were my refuge, my solace, my comfort.

Autumn leaves drifted languidly in the crisp afternoon breeze. Linda and I sat in the rocking chairs on her front porch. Her sister Jenny played fetch with her frolicking new puppy on the freshly mowed lawn. Me, my mother and father and little brother Mickey ate hot dogs at Mickey's little league baseball game in Edmonds Park. We sailed Puget Sound on a small boat. Whales surfaced magnificently and then disappeared in the aquamarine depths.

My loneliness has made of me a ghost. I hunger for conversation but I haven't learned the language. I walk these streets like an apparition, silently, without speaking. Only the sound of my motorcycle boots on the pavement give evidence of my substantiality. What is my mission? Why am I here?

I don't know. I pray, but no one answers. It's like I am talking to myself. I can no longer trust my perceptions. Sometimes when I prowl the city streets I see a young attractive woman, maybe at a restaurant table or standing on a corner waiting to cross the boulevard, and I freeze, stunned at what I see, unable to believe my eyes. I know it's impossible, but it's Linda! Linda! I seize her by shoulders and turn her around to face to me. But it is not Linda. Of course it is not Linda.

El Puño

On a slightly chilly late morning, the streets damp and crisp after a hard rain but good for walking, the air brisk, the wet pavement glistening with freshly fallen rainwater, I began. Dodging trolley cars, taxis and morning delivery trucks, I crossed the trolley tracks that divided the city economically and geographically and continued until the sun was high in the sky. I wore no watch but the lighting and temperature suggested I had been walking for hours. I found myself to be in an unfamiliar industrial area of manufacturing plants. Factories spewed columns of grey toxic smoke and gas into the already polluted sky. I wondered what was manufactured here, whether these buildings were meat packing plants or slaughterhouses of some kind. There seemed to be no end to them, some with broken windows and the grinding hum of machinery inside.

Men with picket signs congregated at some of the factory entrances. Women at busy lunch-truck taco stands sold lunches to workers on mid-day break. A lone pair of uniformed soldiers walked their beat with their rifles over their shoulders and no apparent interest in what was going on around them. They passed me but did not stop me to ask for identification or otherwise give me notice.

I had no idea where I was or how long I had been walking, but my legs felt like they would no longer support me. I boarded an old, beat-up, third class bus that shook so violently at the curb it might have had epilepsy. Gray haired women with shopping bags loaded with bread and vegetables took up most of the seats. I was squeezed between standing passengers who with each stop were pushed further toward the back of the bus by the momentum of new passengers boarding. Infants cried in their mother's laps or were nursed at their mother's breasts. Toddlers clung to our legs. Chickens squawked and pecked at our ankles. All the windows were down; the weather was humid, and there was no air conditioning.

Two enormous Mexican women with shopping bags kicked at a scrawny Chihuahua who kept trying to pilfer their grocery bags. The women often missed their target and kicked my ankles instead. The dog persisted, snapping at the women's legs and going for whatever was in those shopping bags. I had to keep shifting my position to keep from being bitten.

Those of us without seats swung from handheld straps while propelled forward with the momentum of the bus. Sometimes we collided with one another. Each time a passenger needed to disembark from the interior a wrestling match ensued. Passengers continued to board until squeezed together so tightly we couldn't move, much less collide. The breeze through the open windows offered no relief. The bus muffler must have been damaged. Coughing, our eyes watering, we were subjected to the thick black emission of toxic smoke from the vehicle's malfunctioning muffler.

I had no idea where we were, or how long I rode, but eventually there were few of us left, and fewer who boarded. The few passengers who remained read newspapers or quietly stared out the window. In the aisle opposite me a young woman nursed her infant. In the seat directly behind the driver, a man and woman were kissing. The man had his hands down her unbuttoned blouse and the driver's eyes in the rear view mirror seemed to be as much on them as the road ahead. Their petting caused me to think about Linda, who liked to have clandestine sex in public place. I found myself fantasizing about sex, but then remembered my vow of chastity, which I intended to honor and which was important to me.

Somewhere along the way I fell asleep. I meant only to doze but slept hard. When I woke it was night and I was the only one on the bus. Even the driver was gone. I stepped off the bus into a dark vacant lot where the driver, his head and face hidden under the lifted hood, held a flashlight while examining the motor. Another man, underneath the bus with his legs sticking out, was banging on something with a wrench.

Streetlights here were mostly burned out but a few couldn't make up their mind and flickered on and off. My shadow danced against the walls as I passed unlighted adobe buildings. The distant twittering lights of downtown Mexico City were only faintly visible, and were like a mirage. The man under the bus crawled out and wiped grease off his face and hands with a soiled rag. The driver returned to his place behind the wheel and turned the starter while the other man worked at the carburetor with a screwdriver. The engine failed to start and after a while the starter gave out and the driver gave up. He and the other man walked off into the darkness and then I was alone and could see them no more. I knew they would not return tonight and began toward the direction of the distant lights that hopefully were in central Mexico City.

I was in an unpopulated neighborhood of warehouses, junkyards, inoperative manufacturing plants and vacant lots. There were no storefronts, nothing functional open to the public, or in operation. I walked damaged streets flanked by boarded buildings without seeing another human being. I don't know how long.

A filthy man wearing multiple soiled layers of rumpled clothing was either homeless or sleeping one off in the street. I could not be certain he was not dead. Mosquitoes and ants had feasted on him and his face was raw from scratching. I knelt at his side and heard him breathing. He was alive, and stunk horribly of urine and grime. I couldn't be certain if the ground he lay on was a road or a vacant lot. The streets had been dirt for a half hour or more by now.

Because I thought I could faintly discern what might be tire tracks, it seemed possible the man was in danger of being run over. I took hold of his feet and began dragging him. He woke briefly, mumbled something in Spanish that sounded like a curse, and passed out again. One of his shoes came off in my hand. I got him to the side of the "road" and left him there. A shadow ran across the lot that might have been a large dog. The sound it made was vicious, and if it was a dog, I suspected it was feral and dangerous.

Frightened, I found a board with a large rusty nail thrust through it and carried it as a weapon. I had lost sight of the lighted skyscrapers of downtown Mexico City, which were no longer even faintly visible. I was really lost now. Clouds obscured the moon, making the darkness absolute. Other than the barking of dogs in the distance, there was utter silence. It began to rain, a mere drizzle, but one that dampened my clothing and amplified the chill that hung in the air. The moon came out from behind some clouds and I slogged through puddles in a labyrinth of dark unnamed dirt streets and steaming misty alleys.

From within the shadows, drifting slowly, snarling feral dogs appeared in the mist. A dozen or more mangy, foul smelling runt Chihuahuas with bared teeth and drooling mouths gathered, snipping and sometimes biting at one another in their agitation. They backed me up against a dripping wet building with nowhere to move but through them.

They charged without warning as a group. I kicked many away with my motorcycle boots. They went flying off like footballs into the darkness, but some clung to my ankles and pants legs. The others quickly regrouped.

I saw The Beast, a pit bull mix breed, it's smashed face a mass of scar tissue. Its teeth were dripping saliva, its mouth a gob of foam and spittle. I recognized it as capable of knocking me off my feet and tearing out my throat. I struck it with the board and nail midflight during its charge. It howled and backed off. Screaming, I continued, swinging wildly. I was on the move, walking backward, defending myself. The pack followed.

Snapping its immense drooling jaws, the pit bull lunged again. I kicked out with my steel toed motorcycle boots, but missed. It had my leg and was trying to take me down as I dragged it toward the flickering light of an open doorway. A dozen or more mutts followed. I heard my pants tearing and then felt their jaws and teeth on my ankles and legs. I was dragging them with me, through the open doorway, as many as half a dozen attached to me. I stumbled and lost balance, and then the pack pulled me down and was on me.

Men at shadowed tables watched silently while I was mauled on the dirt floor of a small, dimly lighted windowless cantina. The dogs were biting me all over in a mad frenzy. The Beast moved up my chest on its four legs. Its spittle was in my face as it tried to seize my throat. I had its head in my hands and was trying to strangle it. My hands were wet with its saliva. Its breath was hideous.

A man with the build of a Sumo wrestler carried a length of heavy pipe as he came slowly from behind the bar. He swung the pipe, scattering the smaller dogs, giving him passage to the pit bull on my chest. He brought the pipe down hard on the animal's head and it fell to the ground howling in pain. Several of the men around the tables burst out laughing. The bartender struck it again and it howled some more, hung its bloody head and slithered backward on its hind legs out the door. Patrons returned to their prior conversation as if nothing at all unusual had taken place.

I hobbled to an empty stool at the rickety plywood bar. Other than the candlelight in the interior, a perilous industrial tubular light over the bar provided the only illumination. The faces of men around the tables in the interior were shadowed. There were no windows here, only the open doorway. The floor was unevenly distributed dirt in some areas, worn stucco in others. Mostly it was loose dirt.

I put some cash down on the bar and the deadpan bartender poured tequila from a bottle into a shot glass. My hands shook so badly I could hardly drink it. The bartender's dark brown eyes, set close together in an unshaven pock-marked face, stared down at the money as if deliberating before picking it up. His swollen, venous nose looked recently broken. He opened a bottle of beer and placed it beside my empty shot glass. He left a few peso notes and some change on the bar and wandered off. My mouth tasted like garbage and fear. I drank gratefully, though I hated the taste of the tequila.

I couldn't stop my hands from shaking. The dog bites were beginning to throb. Welts were erupting where I had been bitten on the legs, arm, chest, neck and face. I raised my hands to drink but they were trembling so badly I was near to dropping the beer bottle.

I had no idea where I was. I was without access to a taxi or bus or even so much as a comprehension of the native language to ask for directions back to the city, but at least had shelter and was safe from the dogs, which may have still been out there somewhere. I glanced cautiously around the room. Because of flickering candle light on tables, men's faces were ghoulishly distorted and vague. I, on the other hand—and I was just now realizing this—was illuminated under the neon tube light over the bar.

Three men playing cards at a corner table in the adjoining room exchanged punches in a game I did not understand. At the showing of hands, the loser pushed back his chair and stood in preparation for a hard punch to the stomach. Sometimes the loser stumbled with the blow. If so, he was mocked with laughter and derision, but usually the man receiving the blow stood firm and was awarded a congratulatory shot of what I assumed was tequila from the bottle on the table. One of the three men at the table did not participate, but only watched. There were no women present. I was bleeding on the floor below the barstool. No one seemed to take notice or care.

Men occasionally staggered to the bar for drinks. One tried to strike up a conversation. He asked in a mix of Spanish and broken English whether I was a gringo from Los *Estados Unitos* and I said yes. He nodded and said something I didn't understand and went over to the table where the men were playing cards. He spoke to them and pointed in my direction.

Several stools down from me a man at the bar was either asleep or passed out, face down on the plywood countertop. He teetered precariously on the rickety stool as if he might fall, but righted himself at the last possible moment. The bartender poured another shot of tequila and opened another beer. He took some of the bills I had placed on the bar earlier. I was uncertain how much more money was in my wallet but didn't feel safe showing it. I only sipped the tequila, chasing it with the beer, while noticing my hands and fingernails, which were filthy with canine saliva, dried blood, grime and mud.

A cockroach the size of a child's open hand lumbered awkwardly along the surface of the wet bar. Wobbling erratically as if its legs might have been broken, its swollen crustacean body seemed too large and cumbersome for its spindly legs to support. It reached the sleeping man and crawled up his arm. The man woke, opened his eyes and blinked as if not sure if what he was seeing was real or alcoholic delirium. He swept it off and went back to sleep. The enormous roach continued along the bar toward my beer. The deadpan bartender watched it until it had reached my glass and then swept it off the bar. It was so big I heard it land. In the darkness I could no longer see it but sometimes thought I felt it crawling up my leg. After a while I forgot about it.

The three men who had been exchanging punches between hands of cards might have been banditos in a western movie. They were not. They were frightfully real. The candle-lighted table they occupied was in a dark corner. Their voices had become agitated, their presence troubling. From time to time I stole wary apprehensive glances at them. One of the men was bare chested and hairy, with arms like steel cables. He wore a thick shaggy moustache in the shape of inverted handlebars. A large sombrero shaded and partly concealed his face. Another man at the table was massive, with broad hairy shoulders and a large cruel ugly face that looked like it smiled only at the misfortune of others. A third man was cleaning his fingernails with a large hunting knife

The drooling unconscious man passed out six empty stools down from me awakened. He wobbled precariously along the empty barstools in my direction, placing his hands on the bar to steady himself along the way. Twice he stumbled and almost fell, but at the last moment corrected himself. He collapsed on the stool next to me and I smelled his alcohol saturated breath in my face. He was unshaven, his pants torn and ragged, his fly unzipped. His oversized dirty white shirt was missing several buttons, the remaining two or three buttoned in the wrong holes. It was hard to guess his age and I didn't want to look at him long enough to try.

He clutched my sleeve and started to say something, but then his face smashed the counter and he was out, face down on the bar, his shoulder against mine for balance. I moved a few stools away from him in revulsion. Without me to prop him up he almost fell, but again regained his tenuous balance and went back to sleep.

He later woke and resumed his attempt to occupy a stool next to me. This time he managed it, stumbling but not falling. He smiled intimately, as if we were in on a private, funny secret unknown to the others. He had very few teeth, and his breath was foul as he talked into my face. I kept monotonously repeating that I knew only English, hoping he would go away. Undaunted, he kept on, incomprehensively smiling the whole time while trying to put an arm around my shoulder like we were comrades-in-arms out drunkenly celebrating the victory of the revolution. Spittle flew from his mouth and sprayed my face. I tried to get away but he had a surprisingly strong grip on my arm. I didn't know what he was saying but he wouldn't stop talking. A sharp ammoniated odor of urine rose to my nostrils and I realized he was pissing himself. His pants were soaked, and a steaming pool of urine was forming on the ground under his stool. He didn't seem to notice and went on talking the entire time he was pissing himself. I pushed him away in revulsion and he fell off the stool and landed on the dirt floor, and did not move.

The bartender, sauntering out from behind the bar, wiped the wet barstool previously occupied by the incontinent drunk with the same rag he had been using to wash glasses. The steaming dirt floor reeked where the drunk had urinated, and the bartender turned the urine-soaked dirt over with a shovel. Muttering what sounded like soft curses, he pulled the drunken, incontinent man by the feet to the filthy, foul-smelling toilet in back. The toilet was a hole dug into the ground. The smell of feces was pervasive and nauseating. Patrons were presumably to use a shovel conveniently placed in a tall pyramidal mound of loose dirt to cover one's excrement in the hole but rarely did. The unconscious man was left face down in front of the stinking hole. As the night wore on, drunken unsteady men using it pissed on him. It was difficult not to.

A shirtless man wearing loose denim overalls over his bony reeking unwashed frame limped up to the bar and slumped on a stool beside me. I could smell his hairy pits as he sprawled across the bar on both elbows while holding a shot of tequila with both hands to his quivering lips. He drank the shot down, swiveled on the stool to face me and began coughing so forcefully with such relentless duration that I feared he might go into some kind of convulsion and die. No one seemed to notice or care. I clapped him on the back a few times, but that didn't seem to help, though he did manage to mutter *gracias* between coughs. I poured him a glass of water from a pitcher on the bar, but he began choking again, spewing water from his mouth and nostrils. I didn't know what to do to help him. Eventually, though, his coughing subsided. He smiled broadly and pointed for permission to a pack of cigarettes I had on the bar—in my opinion the last thing he needed—but I nodded consent and he fumbled with the pack and lighted one.

"*Muchas gracias, señor*. You Americano, no? Me speak Eengleesh leetle beet. I was een Texas. My name, Felix."

He removed his baseball cap and smoothed his greasy black hair, which was dirty, receding, and matted from the cap.

He turned his pockets inside out and shrugged as if in demonstration of his penury and said, "Me *pobre* Mexicano. You reech Americano. Buy Felix drink, si?"

It was the usual erroneous presumption; because I was American I was rich. But okay, probably compared to him I was. I put another bill on the bar and motioned to the bartender to pour us each a shot. Felix knocked his down immediately, then quickly drank mine and gestured for another. One of the banditos at the table in the darkened corner slammed his fist down hard on the table.

"*Chinga Los Estados Unitos*," he shouted. He kicked an empty chair into the room. The other men at his table laughed.

"*Si*," they agreed. "*Chinga Americanos. Chinga gringos.*"

They glared at me malevolently.

"Never mind heem," said Felix. "He ees *El Puño*. Do you know *puno*? It means theese." He pointed at his clenched fist.

"Do you mean fist?"

"Si, si, feest. It is said he once beat down a bull with his feest. He hates Americans, but don' warry. Nobody likes heem. He just got out of prison and is *muy* angry. He always trouble and we are sorry to see heem return from the prison."

I made the motion of turning a steering with my hands and said, "Felix, I need a taxi."

"No, señor, no taxi acqui."

I began dialing an imaginary telephone while holding a receiver to my ear.

"*Telephono?*"

"No, señor, no *telephoto*."

Something was pecking at my leg. I looked down saw a large red rooster. Felix swatted it away with his foot. It squawked in outrage and fluttered toward the low ceiling, its feathered wings flapping audibly. It settled on an empty table in the darkness.

Meanwhile, it seemed El Puño had lost a hand of cards. He stood positioned firmly in expectation of the winner's punch to his stomach, digging his boots into the dirt for a foothold, legs spread wide for balance. The punch never came. Instead the winner of the hand pushed him backwards and kicked his legs out from under him. El Puño tumbled backwards into a chair, which broke beneath his weight. His sombrero came off and he ended up sprawled in the dirt. The man who had pushed him danced on the sombrero victoriously while men at tables and on stools at the bar laughed loudly.

El Puño was not laughing. He retrieved his flattened sombrero, corrected the shape with his fist, put it carefully back on the table and shouted a command in Spanish I did not understand. Everyone instantly quieted. He strode to the bar and stood right next to me. In the enhanced lighting of the industrial hanging neon lighting I saw his face clearly for the first time. It was unspeakably ugly and frightening, with a huge misshaped nose that had probably been broken many times, and massive sagging jowls. His bald head was pitted with many small cuts and scars. The man was a goliath with an enormous stomach, the shoulders of a bull, thick muscled arms shaped like ham hocks and fists like anvils. His resemblance to the pit bull that had attacked me earlier was uncanny. He turned his scarred face in my direction and fixed me with an expression of contemptuous disregard that one does not directly engage and prays will be of brief duration, a mean, hateful stare that is like impalement. It terrified me.

He spat at my feet and returned to his table. I don't know why I watched him; it was foolish, but there was something about him that mesmerized me. He took a long drink from the bottle of tequila on the table. The man who had won the round gestured impatiently for him to pass it along.

No, said El Puño. "*Chinga tu madre.*"

The other man began arguing with him, grabbing for the bottle, which he clearly wanted but which El Puño denied. El Puño just stared at him. He drank from the bottle and put it down between them. He did pass the bottle to the third man at the table, but not the man who had pushed and humiliated him earlier. Each time El Puño set the bottle down on the table the man made a grab for it, but El Puño was faster. This went on until finally El Puño picked it up brought it down hard on the man's head. The sound was sickening. The man fell to the ground, where El Puño began kicking him. El Puño's adversary was limber, though, and rolled away quickly. He rose to a crouch, drew his hunting knife and slashed El Puño's face, which ejaculated a stream of bright red blood. El Puño swung a massive fist in retaliation but blood was all over his face and seemed to impair his vision. He wiped his face and swung again, missing. His face continued to spurt blood. His adversary swung with the knife a second time but El Puño grabbed the man's arm and broke it. You could hear the man's bones snap. The knife went clattering to the floor.

El Puño knocked the man down and commenced to beat him with the tequila bottle with such force that it broke. He jammed the jagged broken end of the bottle into the man's grimacing face and began twisting it around and around. The man screamed horribly. His eyeball hung loosely by a thin gelatinous strand. He was trying to push it back in with his thumb. El Puño rose and stood over him victoriously, one foot on the ground and the other on the man's chest as if he were a big game hunter and had just killed a lion. He held the bloody broken bottle aloft like a human head and shouted triumphantly into the air. The injured man crawled across the bloody floor and rolled into fetal position. He continued trying to insert his detached eye.

The place went quiet. Everyone seemed to be looking at me.

El Puño especially.

Felix, his hand clutching my sleeve, leaned in and whispered, "It is not safe for you here amigo. Leave quickly."

But how?

The men blocking the front door seemed to be doing so intentionally. Their cold expressions were fixed on me exclusively. I knew I would never get past them. I rose slowly from the stool and entered the back hallway toward the urinal. I hoped for a rear exit at the end of the hall but there was none.

Then I noticed a curtain, pushed it aside, and a door was behind it. I opened it, stepping into what at first appeared to be a windowless storage room. The door locked from the inside with a dubious flimsy eye hook. Cases of canned goods and other supplies were stacked in a corner on the concrete floor. The remaining space consisted of a working toilet, hot plate, sink and small table and cot. A framed portrait of Christ hung on the wall over the cot. A shotgun stood in a corner beneath it. Men were pounding on the door, which was threatening to give. Behind a tattered shower curtain, I found yet another door. I opened it to an alley in back, where it was raining hard.

Retreat

I ran until I dropped to my knees and vomited. Soaking wet and filthy with mud, I knelt in a large puddle beside trash cans piled high with garbage. My jeans were weighted with rainwater and my boots heavy and waterlogged. I shivered; my teeth began to chatter. The moon came out from behind drifting clouds. A garbage can lid rattled and a large black rat dropped to the ground. I could hear more scurrying in the darkness around me. The hard rain lightened to a continuous drizzle.

I groped along an alley between squat adobe buildings with boarded windows and came out in a vacant lot where junkyard tires were stacked. The hulking remains of dead autos and discarded appliances were piled high behind a locked chain-link fence. Snarling junkyard dogs leapt at the fence, which sprang back and forth during their vicious attempts to jump it. I reached the end of the block and entered another shadowed street, this one riddled with potholes filled with rainwater.

It was no longer raining at all now, the unobstructed moonlight giving improved visibility. Windswept tree limbs dancing in the moonlight made a phantasmal grid-work on the ground. In a littered clearing the vague shapes of human shadows moved in and out of the flickering light of campfires. I heard the crash of breaking glass; it sounded like someone throwing a bottle. I heard laughter but it was not joyous or pleasurable. It sounded mean and hardened. I was exhausted and near shaking with fear.

I kept moving, hoping blind luck would lead me to an area I recognized and from there to the hotel. It seemed unlikely. Emerging from the clearing, a car rumbled up the street, slowing when it neared me. Someone shouted out the window but I ducked into an alley much too narrow for them to follow. The alley intersected with another, slightly wider, where blankets were hung over the doors of lean-tos made from flimsy particle board. I could hear a baby crying from behind one of the blankets.

I came out of the alley into a street where cars were parked at curbs alongside inhabited buildings with curtains in the windows. The promise of light became faintly visible on the horizon; dawn was very near. I had the impression of seeing dawn incrementally, as if developing in a photographer's darkroom. Eventually a soft gray morning daylight arrived but gave no view to high-rise city buildings downtown that might guide me back to familiar surroundings.

The silence that had been so prominent began to be replaced with the singing of morning birds. I heard radios and televisions from behind tenement windows. An elderly man with a long white beard, denim coveralls and a straw hat was making his way toward me. He herded two small donkeys, both loaded high with burlap sacks filled with wood twigs and charcoal. His back was bent and stooped. He had a slight hump and carried a tall walking stick. He looked ancient

"*Buenos Dias*," he said in passing.

The likelihood that he spoke English was so slight that I didn't even bother to inquire.

I kept walking and the neighborhood changed again. In a wide dirt street wet with running rainwater and drifting sewage, a small young girl ran through the soggy mud with two skinny malnourished dogs.

"*Hola*," she said.

Her clothing hung far too large for her small frame. The wet hemline of her tattered skirt dragged through puddles. She smiled brightly and I saw that the wicker basket she carried contained several soft yellow baby chicks. Her young face was dark and beautiful. When she smiled her eyes and teeth shone.

She petted the chicks tenderly, carefully removing one from the basket. She held it in the palm of her hand, and I could see it quiver with each breath. She carefully placed it in my open palm, smiling as I stroked its tiny downy head with my index finger. It was such a delicate, fragile creature. I could feel its ribcage expand with each inhalation, its muted heartbeat and warm breath on my fingers, as if with each inhalation it was taking in the life force itself. Somehow it seemed to me that we were all connected by this same life force, the girl and I, the infant yellow chicks hovering in her basket, her two lingering, panting dogs, even the circling buzzards, stray dogs, feral cats and rats. But how fragile, how imperiled, and transient we were. We were so vulnerable, so temporary, we living creatures. We were but one breath away from disconnection and death. I couldn't help myself. I began crying. The girl wrapped her arms around my legs as if to comfort me.

"*Para tu*," the girl said sweetly. She was offering the chick to me, but I returned it to her. How could I protect such a delicate creature? How would I forgive myself if it withered under my care?

"*Donde es la ciudad*," I asked. Where is the city?

She pointed toward a sloping distant terrain where vultures circled. I staggered toward it, my protective motorcycle boots protecting my feet as I tromped over broken glass, rusty tin cans, discarded nails, bloody rags and other hazards. Piles of garbage smoldered everywhere. I was in some kind of a dumping ground. The air was thick with flies, their buzzing a continuous, pervasive drone. Dogs sniffed through the infested rubbish, but paid me no mind. Rats were abundant. I nearly stumbled and fell into the carcass of a dead, maggot- swarmed donkey.

On the far side of the dump, beyond a succession of garbage mounds, I heard the laughter of young children huddled inside a large cardboard box that might have once contained a refrigerator or stove. A naked, filthy little boy with a distended round stomach chased after a scrawny dog. He saw me and stopped, stared at me with haunted eyes. He peed indifferently, innocently, leaving long visible streaks down his dirty legs. His penis was impossibly teeny for the amount of urine produced. He seemed to urinate for an inordinately long time. His urine was the wrong color and smelled foul. Open infected sores drained from his dirty knees.

A woman wearing a soiled torn dress and a filthy tattered shawl silently opened a burlap rag serving as a door to one of the shacks and chased after a naked child. She looked far too young to be anyone's mother, but when she dropped the shawl I saw that she was pregnant. Another child came out from behind the ragged burlap curtain and followed her.

I staggered into a neighborhood of cinderblock tract homes that might have been part of a recent but failed low income housing project. Damaged rusted railroad tracks ran through the center of the neighborhood but there was no sign of any train and the tracks ended at a mound of dirt. I climbed the mound and gazed toward what I hoped would be the towers of the city center, but there were only more unrecognizable buildings. I marched toward them and found myself in their midst.

A tall man wearing overalls and a baseball cap stepped out onto his porch and lighted a pipe. He wore high rubber boots and carried a tin lunchbox. I hurried to overtake him but he got behind the wheel of a pickup truck and drove off. People were leaving their homes now, men for work, women dressed in maid's uniforms, students dressed in catholic school uniforms. The sun was out in full and my clothing had begun to dry. Torn, filthy with mud and streaked with blood, they reeked in the morning sun.

A man approached with a wagonload of yellow and green bananas pulled by a donkey. I stopped him and bought three with the change in my pocket. It was then I discovered my wallet was missing. Thankfully my passport was back in the hotel but I had only enough money for the bananas, which I ate while sitting on a stoop. My package of cigarettes was damp and ruined and my matches would not light. I kept walking.

I came into a neighborhood of modern buildings with locking front doors and panels of intercom buttons in the vestibules. Occasionally a building had an awning over the entrance and a doorman. Out of one of these came a man dressed in a three-piece suit and tie who carried a briefcase. I approached him hopefully.

"*Habla Ingles?*"

"*No, señor. Espanol solamente.*"

He walked off briskly, a newspaper under his free arm. There was traffic on the streets now, but no taxis. I saw a bus stop but there was no bus and who could say where they routed and my wallet and money were gone.

The neighborhoods were declining yet again. I was among peasants, Indians, homeless men and stray dogs. Men squinted in the morning daylight while going through trash cans for food. Hungry, I thought of joining them. I had been up all night with only bananas to eat and was so tired I considered making my bed in the street until run over by a car and taken to a hospital or picked up by the police. But there were no police here, no ambulances or taxis. And I was still lost. I had a headache. I had walked all night and all morning and was no closer to home than when I began.

A small whitewashed neighborhood chapel with a large cross and small bell tower glistened in the late morning sunlight. In a small grassy park nearby, voices rose from a swing set, benches and picnic tables. Many children were present. I heard them before seeing them, their young voices joyous with laughter and cheering. Adults sat on benches at wooden tables. Elderly men gathered around a domino game in progress. Some read the morning paper or ate tortillas spread with chilies or snacked on fruit and sweetbreads. The sight of food made my mouth water. My attempt to communicate with the men was met with puzzlement and shrugs. No one understood my broken, inadequate Spanish and no one spoke English. The women mistakenly thought I wanted only their food. They offered tamales and fruit, slices of watermelon and sugar cane. Their kindness moved me to tears and I began crying.

I cried hard, unable to control myself. Women gathered around me and put their hands on me and began praying. A plump matriarchal woman with braided long gray hair who made the sign of the cross on my forehead with her index finger prayed over me intently. She wiped my tears and said her name was Isabel.

"I'm Raymond," I said, sniffling.

"Si. Ramon."

She wore a bright woven shawl over her shoulders and sandals on her bare brown feet and seemed to be their appointed spokesperson. Her eyes were kind and beautiful. She huddled with other women in a conference in which everyone seemed to be talking at once. By now our numbers were swelling. Our group had grown to as many as a hundred. More were coming into the park to discuss my situation. It began to seem as if the entire neighborhood was present. Almost all were women. I was confident they were trying to decide how to help me but there seemed to be much disagreement over how to go about it. They debated in a huddle for what seemed a long while, but finally seemed to agree, nodding their heads and saying *si, si, bien, si.*

The woman who had called herself Isabel crossed the street and vanished into a tenement building. Later she returned in the company of a pretty adolescent Indian girl wearing the navy blue gold-buttoned blazer and matching blue pleated skirt of a Catholic School uniform. The girl was probably no more than twelve or thirteen years old but spoke with a poised, adult-like serious tone. Her dark brown hair was expertly braided with meticulous care.

"My name is Maria," she said in English. "I am a student learning English. I do not know it well so please speak very slowly."

"I'm lost," I replied. "I have been walking all night. "

"I understand, señor. Where do you live?"

"In the Hotel la Paz."

"I do not know this place."

"It's in la Colonia Guerrero."

"I am sorry. I do not know this Colonia. There are no taxis here. It will cost very much for one to come out from the city, if one will even come. If I call for one, you will wait and wait, perhaps forever."

"If I can find my way to Insurgentes or the Paseo de la Reforma, I could find my hotel from there. I have no money for a taxi. I don't even have bus fare. My wallet was stolen."

"Ah," she said. "I understand."

A matronly Indian woman gave me hot coffee. Another offered sweet breads and orange slices. An elderly man who seemed unable to stop smiling shared his pack of cigarettes. Another offered tequila, which I declined, though I accepted a bottle of beer. I seemed to have been taken in by these people. My mind was not working right. Maybe I would be adopted by them and they would be my family now. That would be fine with me. Just give me a bed, somewhere to sleep.

Maria returned in the company of a plump, dark-skinned

middle-aged woman dressed in a brown maid's uniform.

"This is my cousin, Marta," she explained. "She does not speak English but is a laundress in one of the hotels downtown. She will take you there by bus."

"But I have no money," I replied.

"Jesus Christ will pay your fare, señor."

She pointed to the chapel and indicated the money was coming from the Church.

Marta led me off by the hand as if I were a small child. Everyone applauded happily as we left. Smiling shyly, Marta remained silent all the way into the heart of the city, a long ride requiring transfers on several busses that took over and an hour and a half. By the time we reached the hotel where she worked I was back in recognizable surroundings.

We lingered, she in her starched brown maid's uniform, I out of place in my muddy clothing, in front of the elegant chrome-trimmed revolving glass doors of the upscale hotel on Insurgentes where she worked. I thanked her repeatedly. I watched her enter the luxurious gleaming mezzanine. She waved one last farewell at the bank of elevators. The elevator doors closed and she ascended.

When I finally returned to the La Paz, the lobby was empty of guests. I did not want Ricardo to see me in this condition. My misfortune would bring him far too much pleasure. I managed to enter the alcove where the vending machines were, which offered the stairs as an alternative to passing the front desk to the elevator.

I sat in a chair in my room and struggled to remove my wet boots, which were thickly coated with dried mud. It took a while to get them off. I threw them in the shower stall. My grimy clothing, damp with perspiration, clung to me as if pasted there. I threw my pants and shirt in the shower with the boots, turned on the hot water, got in and closed the shower door behind me.

I was probably the only person in the hotel using the hot water at this time of day, and there was plenty of it for a change. Working up a thick soapy lather and scrubbing with a washcloth that felt like sandpaper, I soaped my body, which was riddled with dog bites. I washed my clothing with the bar soap, scrubbing hard and wringing out excess water, and then repeated the process. Afterwards I hung my clothing to dry and went to bed naked. I slept deeply, but not peacefully. My dreams were of enemies. There was no safety. I was no longer an innocent spectator. Mexico was a land in which unseen principalities were at work. I was afraid and unprepared for the spiritual warfare in which I had been conscripted.

Prisoner of the Hotel La Paz

I believe I am under attack. Three days ago, facing a busy intersection when standing at a traffic light, someone tried to push me into oncoming traffic. Or did I only imagine their hands on my back? Perhaps someone was accidentally pushed into me. Or I merely stumbled. But I don't think so. I believe I am the subject of a focused spiritual attack by invisible forces that control this city and its inhabitants. Everyone I see looks like a murderer. Everyone who makes eye contact with me seems to regard me with malevolence. Every automobile appears designed to run me down. The city wants my soul. Its armies of foraging beggars, its legions of roaming predatory dogs, its opportunistic pursuant street vendors conspire against me. I shudder at the sound of the city's codified language and choke on its strange dangerous tainted food.

People stare at me with contemptible expressions of hatred and menace. They gather around sidewalk kiosks in sinister impromptu conferences, hovering and whispering like malicious old crones in their incomprehensible language. It's like I'm the butt of a malicious trick and everyone is in on it. Even the air seems lethal; smog and gas fumes hang over these streets like a poison. The continuous city grinding of gears is like a mechanical, mocking death rattle. It drills into my brain. I cover my ears, grit my teeth, and grimace helplessly.

My previous wandering and exploration of the city has ended with the abruptness of a car crash. I can't leave my room, much less the hotel. My knees get weak and legs feel like they are going to buckle. I end up breaking into a sweat, my breathing becomes shallow and I can feel my heart pounding in my chest like an iron piston. I'm serious. It's actually physically painful. I become light headed and dizzy and think I am going to faint. At most I manage to sometimes pace the halls of the hotel or circle the lobby for a little exercise, but as often as not the mere *intent* to leave here can launch me into a panic attack. A couple of times I had panic attacks before I even managed to get down the hall as far as the elevators. Well, the truth is I can't take the elevator much anymore—I keep thinking the cables will snap and plunge me to my death. I'm taking the stairs almost exclusively now. Believe me, I'm working with this, I know I have to overcome it, but the more I try and fail the more difficult the next attempt becomes.

Stop it, Raymond. Stop whining, you sissy. You can't be Holy without risk, danger, and suffering. It is what connects you to the human family. It is what rescues you from shallow mediocrity. It's why you came. You knew that. You accepted it. You don't know what is to suffer. Think of Christ and his agony on the Cross. *That's* suffering.

* * *

My life has gone to the toilet. This is not a metaphor. It's real, stinks horribly, and owns me. I'm sitting on it right now, shitting while writing this. Montezuma's revenge, they call it. Amoebic dysentery. It seems impossible that a tiny microscopic one cell organism can bring a grown man to his knees in helpless submission but I'm trapped here. I don't dare even leave my room to get help. I'm enslaved to this foul porcelain throne from which I dare not wander more than a few steps. I recently got as far as the elevator but felt an imminent gush of diarrhea and had to turn back and make a break for my room. If you had seen me you would have laughed at the sight of me, hopping like a sack race contestant with my pants around my ankles. Oh, I made it into the room in time, but not to the toilet. I had to wash out my shitty clothing in the shower stall. Another time I vomited into the bidet. I didn't even know what a bidet *was*. I had never seen one before. I thought I would be able to flush it like a toilet. It wouldn't flush. The maids had to clean it out and I think they hate me now.

* * *

I'm losing track of time. Ricardo the rodent desk clerk has provided, undoubtedly at marked-up cost, anti-diarrheal medicines, but I suspect they contain narcotics because I end up feeling disoriented and strange, and that is the last thing I need, when everything is already so unfamiliar and frightening. Recently I shit myself in the back seat of a taxi when returning from a horrifying trip to my American Express post office box to pick up my monthly check. It was my last, and singular excursion outside of the hotel. I don't even leave my room except when compelled by hunger. I limit myself to eating only candy bars and pre-wrapped crackers from the lobby vending machine. The machine is getting low and no one is restocking it. Only crackers remain in it, and they are stale and going fast. This little room in which I live is shrinking by the day, the walls closing in on me. There is no window to the outside, just a small view to the air vent and corner of the outside hallway. My Snohomish County jail cell gave as good a view as this.

Companionship is provided by a conquistador in a framed print on the wall. He wears body armor and a golden pointed helmet and sits regally on an armored gray warhorse. I find his presence offensive but he's all I've got. But I let him know I hate him and his shameful decimation of indigenous peoples by sword yielding, musket carrying, armored conquerors enslaving in the name of Christ while lusting for gold, rape, and slaughter. Enraged, I tear him from his place on the wall and throw him in the empty closet.

Now there is nothing. No picture, no photograph or memoir. There is only the mirror on the dresser with its haunted face. The walls of the room that has become my world seem to vibrate under the harsh glaring overhead light. The faded linoleum floor is scarred with cigarette burns and rippled with water stains from a leaking ceiling. The bed is narrow, the spongy mattress far too soft. The mirror is accusatory. I cannot remove it despite my attempts. The face in the mirror regards me with revulsion, as if it had caught me in some unspeakable perversion such as coprophagy.

I have lost all track of how long I have been confined here. There is no event, no separation from one day to the next. I pace the room. It's ten footsteps from wall to wall, including the bathroom. I walk in circles and have conversations with myself. Mostly I vomit and shit and sleep feverishly. I have taken the conquistador out of the closet again and put him back up on the wall. His eyes follow me as I pace the room; he never stops watching me. His expression is accusatory and disagreeable. He's mad at me for putting him in the closet. Once we argued so loud Ricardo called up to report a complaint. Oh, I'm not hearing voices; I know that I am making them up. I have complete control over this. It's a game I play with myself to pass the time. On the other hand, I should stop playing, because it's dangerous. Once when I was about to take down the conquistador and put him back in the closet again I heard him say, *"I wouldn't do that if I were you. I'm all you've got."*

I rise from the hotel room bed, the room spinning, and have to grasp the desk to keep from falling. Wobbling on weak, unreliable limbs, I down huge carafes of water from the sink, both for hydration and to ward off the hunger pangs, but the water churns around in my stomach like soggy rumpled clothing in a washing machine. I run to the toilet and explode horrid liquid feces from my bowels. I lay in the bed, sweating and immobilized, groaning, cramping, shivering, my wet clothes clinging to me. I open my Bible at random for comfort.

Ecclesiastes 9:10: *Anyone who is among the living has hope – even a live dog is better than a dead lion! For the living know that they will die but the dead know nothing; they have no further reward, and even the memory of them is forgotten. Their love, their hate and their jealousy have long since vanished; never again will they have a part in anything under the sun that happens.*

Where is the comfort in this passage? Before Mexico I did not fear death. I considered it a merciful deliverance to a promised landscape of light and tender shimmering beauty. Death was a coming home to Heaven and Christ. In Mexico, death is a mocking, dancing skeleton.

How horrible it is for us to live with the specter of Death, to have to leave everyone and everything, to die. To no longer hear the melodious story-telling of morning birds or feel the bracing wind on one's face, to never again gaze upon the sparkling sunlit ocean at the seashore or smell the wet freshly mowed dewy lawns of summer. We die and they throw dirt over us, and the worms and maggots crawl over our once beautiful faces that have become obscene mocking grimacing skeletal death masks. We stink and rot until only our teeth and bones remain. Later our names might sometimes come up in conversation, a few stories are perhaps told about us, and then we are forgotten and even the memories of us are no more. We are not even a memory. We were never here.

Who can even imagine it? Death is a divine jest, a cruel trick played by a jokester God. How can we be expected to endure under this eventuality? And yet how can we not? If we ignore our deaths we are denying the one central fact of our existence, the one certainty of our being. If we face it and acknowledge it honestly and fully, we are immobilized by its hopeless, stark inevitability. There is no exit from this impasse, no possible hope of not dying.

We are dying now, as I write this, all of us, you, me, everybody—some slowly, some sooner then they know, some will be dead in the morning without having ever suspected the end was near. Death is all around us. We don't want to see it. We don't want to face the inevitability of our own decay. We don't want to acknowledge the sick who stagger among us. We close our eyes and our minds to the central fact of our existence. We don't want to hear the lamenting, the wailing and crying, the weeping widows, orphans and bereaved lovers. We don't want to hear the eulogy, listen to the sermon, the spooky organ music or the true funeral music, which is the hissing of crematory flames or final harsh thud of a coffin dropping into the grave.

We all are marching to our deaths. Perhaps a man you saw today is dead now. Perhaps he passed you on the street or stood behind you in line or asked for spare change. Maybe you were the last person he saw, the last person who spoke to him. Maybe I am that man. Maybe as you read this, I am dead. You may be next. Look behind you. Death is right there. It's gaining on you. It's a rigged game, and you will lose. You are going to die. Think about it.

* * *

Dear Raymond –

In all the years that I have been going to sea, other than sending a postcard, this may be the first letter that I have ever written you. I apol-

ogize for that, but I'm not much for writing, and I'm told that I'm not much for talking either. But I miss you and Emily and Mickey. I always did but it was a comfort to know that when I got back to home port at Pier 51, you would be there. It's true, there's no place like home. You're young and have to do a lot of traveling yet to find that out, but you will. Anyway, here I am writing without much to say.

I am in Bombay, India. From here we go through the Suez Canal to Cairo Egypt, then to Istanbul, across the Atlantic to the Panama Canal and home. Should take about three months allotting for time loading and unloading cargo.

When you write, please tell me how your studies are going at the University. Tell me what classes you are taking, how you manage in Spanish.

Funny, I have been around the world more times than I have fingers and toes but I have never once been to Mexico. Never had much desire to either, I must admit. I'd rather be home.

Five more years, Ray, then I can retire to be with you and your mother and Mickey full time. Maybe, if I get bored, I'll take a part time job close to home.

Well, anyway, like I said, not much to say, I just want you to know that I am thinking of you, proud of you, and miss you.

Oh, one last thing. I'm sure of course you know not to drink the water. It will make you sick as a dog with the dysentery.

Love,
Dad.

* * *

Stupid, stupid, stupid! Why had I not remembered the water here caused dysentery? Well, I'm exclusively drinking sodas from the machine now. Smoking like a fiend too. It helps stifle hunger pangs. I'm still eating mostly what is available in the recently re-stocked lobby vending machines. Ricardo occasionally sells me fresh fruit, which I eat only if it has a peel that can be removed. Nothing that needs washing. I'm certain Ricardo makes a huge profit on this. My cash stash is dwindling. Meanwhile he delivers oranges, pineapple, cantaloupe. Once he brought me a coconut. What was I supposed to do with it? I had no hammer; he might as well have delivered a stone. I pounded it in frustration for half an hour with my steel-toed motorcycle boot, gave up and tossed it in the closet with the conquistador.

I've got charcoal sticks and a sketchbook for amusement, but what is there of interest to draw, in this bare room? I've tried a few self-portraits from the mirror, but the drawings inevitably turn out to be portraits of Jesus the Beggar. I think he's inside of me somewhere trying to get out. Maybe that's what the cramps were about. Maybe it wasn't the water after all.

A dead lizard decomposes in a corner by the heating duct. Its distorted pose is one of writhing agonizing slow death. How did it even arrive here, I wonder, from its natural tropical habitat, to die here on this dirty linoleum floor in this little room situated in the center of the largest city in the hemisphere?

The elevator doors open and the tenant, suspended between departure and arrival, exits at the uppermost floor, his soft-sole shoes silent on the carpeted hallway. As he strolls the lengthy hallway to his room he hums a little song from his childhood, but is not aware of it. He doesn't even consciously remember the song. He is also unaware that a lizard has crawled from his pants cuff to his shoe, and is now leaping silently for the carpet, escaping down the hall. He does not see the lizard slip under the door to my room.

Hello, lizard. I am very hungry.

Maybe I should eat you.

* * *

Dear Dad –

I never realized before that you were tired of going to sea and looking forward to your retirement. I always thought when you were home you were mostly anxious to get back on a ship.

Don't worry about getting bored when you retire, Dad. You are always gardening, working in the yard; you're good at it, and it seems to be something you really like.

To answer your question about my studies at the University, I'm in special classes for exchange students. The classes and assignments are partly in Spanish and partly in English. We set aside part of the day for speaking only in Spanish, but a few of my classes are in English only and attended by exchange students, many of whom speak English only as a second language. They come from all over the world. The course work is demanding, leaving me without as much time as I would like to see the sights, but I'm taking notes and recording my experiences in a journal, and I'm excited and happy to be here. I do miss home, though, especially Mom's cooking. The food here tastes good but makes me sick to my stomach. I'm told this will pass eventually, as I accommodate to the higher bacteria content of the food. I'm already on my way there, getting more native every day.

Well, it's exciting and educational to be in a foreign land. "Broadening" is the term they used to use if I am not mistaken, but you know all about that, having sailed around the world many times. I will never catch up with you and am not even going to try. Anyway, no real news here, I miss and love you,

Raymond

* * *

I'm on my bed staring up at a large water stain. The ceiling is sagging. It looks unsafe. Someday it may fall in on me. I've reported it but no one has repaired it. (*Let it come down, right, Paul Bowles?*) I've said it before. Mexico City is built on a volcanic lake and is sinking. The La Paz itself is a shambles. You have the sense when you enter that you can feel its deterioration under your feet. No one takes care of anything. Rooms are cleaned but there is no real maintenance here; the plaster is peeling, the radiators knock, the trash-strewn lobby reeks of cigarette smoke. The hot water is haphazard and sometimes rusty. I haven't washed my clothes or had a proper shower in weeks. I shower mostly for warmth when I'm cold, if indeed I'm lucky enough to get some of the intermittent hot water, which never seems to last long enough for a really good soak. The single bar of soap is scummy, with tiny dead bugs embedded in the surface like fossils. I can't remember when I last used it. I really don't care anymore. I piss and miss the toilet. I ignore the ashtray and throw burning cigarette butts on the floor. I often refuse the maids.

I rip pages from this journal, light them and watch them ignite. The pages become minuscule black particles of drifting ash. I've been taking lots of sleeping medication. Last night I dreamed Mom and Dad and I were sitting in the bleachers watching one of my little brother's little league baseball games in Edmonds Park.

Mom and Dad were kind of cuddling; she had her head on his shoulder. He had his arm around her. We were eating hot dogs in the stands. Mickey, my little brother, stood next in line behind the batter's cage. On deck, as they say, holding his favorite bat slumped over his shoulder. He looked up at us, his plump young face angelic, beautiful. He smiled shyly. I loved him more than my own life.

I dreamed that I was mowing the lawn on a bright sunny day, and when I stopped to wipe my face and looked out across the embankment that overlooked the quaint little township of Edmonds and shores of Puget Sound, a ferry was coming in, brilliantly white against the shimmering blue sea. When its horn sounded, I felt a thrill go through me.

I dreamed that my novel was published and my father came into my bedroom with a mail sack stuffed with fan letters he dumped on my bed. Many were from beautiful women who had enclosed their pictures. They wanted to meet me. Their letters contained airline tickets to exotic sites where they lived.

Several were from famous authors praising my work. My editor wanted me to move to New York. Set me up in a penthouse suite, all expenses paid while I began my next masterpiece. No, I replied, I like it here at home, in Edmonds north of Seattle.

I dreamed that Linda wanted me back. She was in love with me and wanted to have my baby. Her face was wet with tears. *How could I have left you, she cried. What was I thinking? We were perfect together.* She opened her robe and was naked. *Here, she said, this is yours, all yours and only yours, Raymond. Take me, Raymond; lay me down on your bed.*

No, I replied. You are too late. Now that I am a rich and famous author, many women love and want me. You had your chance, bitch.

I wake as if from hibernation, from death itself, confused, still tired, relieved to be alive but disappointed to be awake. My legs feel filled with cement. It is a colossal effort to lift them. I lie here, immobile. The room in which I lie stinks of body odor. *My* body odor. My clothing is so dirty it might have been handed down from Jesus the Beggar. Looking in the mirror, it's shocking how much weight I have lost. My rib cage is skeletal. My shoulder blades are like hatchets.

Sometimes I take the back stairs to the roof where the maids live in single-room concrete bunkers. Children play while their mothers wash and hang laundry from clotheslines. I watch and admire them. I am nothing to them. They don't see me, longing for a conversation, a hug, a smile, anything at all to confirm my existence.

I stare into the darkness. I hear the elevator rising in the shaft. The doors open and I hear approaching footsteps in the hall. My heart flutters in anticipation. Will the footsteps end at my door? Has someone come to me at last? A door opens down the hall and closes.

Silence.

* * *

Dear Raymond –

We are just so worried about you. Please write or call home as soon as you read this. After all, to go off as you have to a foreign land, ostensibly to attend the university there, but then to stop writing and just disappear, what are we to think? Mexico City is one of the largest cities in the world and we hear it can be quite dangerous. What if you were to get sick down there? Of course we worry! Why wouldn't we? I am so upset, angry and afraid, Raymond. If we have not heard from you by the end of the month, know that we will not wire another installment of your money until we do.

I have to be honest with you, Raymond, I never wanted you to go to Mexico because I don't think you are altogether well. Your father, who as you know has traveled the world, said it would make a man out of you and would be good for you, but I don't think you have the temperament for foreign travel. You have always been a moody, sensitive, nervous boy, too much of a loner. You know how I feel about that, we have talked about this. I remember how you began to turn away from us, spending all your time in your room reading and writing and asking us to leave you alone and to tell people who called for you that you were not at home. It frightened me, Ray. We didn't talk anymore like we used to. I didn't want you to go to Mexico and now you don't even write.

I must insist you send us your actual physical address. It will not do to continue to write you care of American Express. We want to know where you are staying, and how to reach you quickly if there is an emergency. If we do not hear from you very soon we will know that something has gone very wrong and will call the American consul in Mexico City. I am counting on you not to make that necessary, Ray.

But if you are in some kind of trouble down there, no matter what it is, please, don't be ashamed or afraid to ask for our help. That's what mothers are for, Raymond. All right, enough of a mother's worries. I know you will write and send me the address of where you are staying as I ask.

There is not much news here; your father is at sea after two months at home between ships. It was the longest period of uninterrupted time we had together all year. We did a lot of work in the yard. Your dad built a fence and worked very hard in the nursery. I did a lot of weeding and trimming, and you know how we both enjoy that. The weather held up for us pretty good but it's been rainy lately. We miss you.

Love,
Mother

* * *

Dear Mother,

I'm sorry I didn't write sooner but I have been busy getting settled, learning the language, and finding my way around the city. The reason I haven't sent you a physical address and instruct you to write care of American Express is because I am not yet settled and have been kind of hotel hopping. As soon as I have a permanent address, I will send it on, I promise.

My health is excellent and generally I am robust and energized by all the good food down here and from walking all over the city. I am very happy. The only problem I have encountered so far is that I do have some problems with my digestion. I suppose that is what they call the tourista and I am told it normally passes as one adapts to the higher bacteria content of the food. I have made so many friends down here so quickly, many of them fellow Americans, but also Europeans and Mexicans. I am hardly ever alone and there is always much to do. We usually play tennis during the day, sometimes drive to Cuernavaca where we lunch and then ride horses in the late afternoon. I have gained about ten pounds since arriving. The difficulty, with so much social activity, is finding time to write. But I promise I will now write you at least once a month. Meanwhile I miss you and love you very much and assure you that you have nothing to worry about concerning my health, mood, or any other aspect of my life down here.

Much love,

Ray

I look up from what I am writing at my desk to see my unshaven face in the mirror stare at me accusingly as if to say, *Liar.* But it's not that simple. It's complicated. What am I to say?

Dear Mother, how nice to hear from you. Pacing back and forth in this tiny hotel room, I have become reduced to the human equivalent of a trapped bug walking circles within an inverted water glass.

I wish for death.

Love, Raymond.

No, it's better to lie, better under the circumstances to be kind than honest. The truth is I'm probably not coming home, ever. I have so much anxiety I can't even get myself a few steps beyond the front doors of the hotel. Some mornings I can hardly even get out of bed. The room begins to spin a little and I teeter as awkwardly as a newborn antelope calf on new untested legs. And then, when I have risen, shaking, naked, gasping, I wonder why I even bothered. But isn't this what I wanted? A monastic, hermetic life, to practice self-denial, to suffer?

That's fucking crazy, Raymond.

No, talking to you is what is crazy.

* * *

I enter a house of chocolate cake and sit in a rocking chair on the back porch. My fishing pole rests over a railing of sharp Vermont cheddar, it's line dangling into a river of root beer with ice flows of vanilla ice cream in which maraschino cherries bob. Slow moving boats parade, their thinly sliced prosciutto sails furling in the wind. Barges pass with cargo of fresh salted tomatoes in virgin olive oil, crispy cold salads with vinaigrette dressing, corned beef hash, bacon and eggs, pancakes. Oh! I think I have a bite on my fishing line. I hope it's a hamburger!

I'm so hungry I can't think straight. Flying cheeseburgers

twirl in my dreams like seductive chorus girls. Their warm sexy buns are lips I long to kiss. I want their munchy little secrets. Dozens of darling little patties sizzle naked on a hot grill. Sexy hotdogs steam in warm covered kettles.

Oh, oh. Someone's at the door. Hot melted cheese sticks to my feet as I open the door to bright sunlight, traffic and the sound of whistling birds. A torta stands on the porch. It tips his bun hello. A torta sandwich with thick crusty slices of bread spread with refried beans and piled high with sliced cold ham, tomato and avocado.

Danger lurks in the hallway. I press the button on the panel at the elevator door but it opens far too eagerly, as if it has been waiting here specifically to entrap me. I stand in the hallway staring into its mouth, listening to it hum in the silence. It sounds hungry. I ease in, just a little at first, then further, but the walls seem somehow malevolent and I quickly back out again. The elevator remains as before, insidious, brightly lighted and cunning. I extend one foot into the interior, step out again. It's no good. I can't do it. It's too dangerous. I decide to take the stairs.

They're not much better. The stairwell is too narrow and the walls are closing in. I've barely got room to move in here. I'm going to be squeezed like a smelly old trash bag in a garbage compactor. Besides, I should be in the lobby by now. There are many more stairs than I remember. Someone keeps adding flights. I'd turn back but my legs are moving so fast I can't stop them or slow them down. My feet can't keep up. I'm tripping, falling, tumbling, down I go. My face impacts against the stairwell landing below and makes a sound like a barge smashing against pilings.

The empty lobby reeks of stale cigarette and cigar smoke. The clock over the check-in desk says it's just past midnight. The witching hour. Except for the erratic crackle and ping of an idiotically flickering light over the check-in desk, it's quiet. No one is behind the desk or on the shabby couch or wingback chairs facing the dark street. I step up to the window. My dirty reflection gazes back, hair grown down to my shoulders, looking more like Jesus the Beggar every day. The vending machine is empty. My forehead throbbing, I wipe it with my sleeve which comes back with flecks of blood.

I don't care anymore what happens to me. I'm too hungry to

care. I must have a torta. Nothing else matters. This is the first time I have left the safety of the hotel in weeks, maybe months. It's absolutely quiet out here; not even a dog barks. A certain dreamlike unreality inhabits this quietude. I could be sleeping and dreaming this except the night air is bracing and my nose is still throbbing from my accident on the stairs. I suck the night air into my lungs like nourishment. It sustains me.

It feels wonderful to be outside in the fresh air again, to feel the wind in my face and the unconfined freedom of movement, the stretch of legs and swing of arms while listening to the tap of my boots on pavement. It's exhilarating. Why have I not done this earlier? What was I so afraid of? I feel a part of the world around me again. I am not a ghost. I am real. Hunger has made me corporeal. I am a human being inside of a body, and this body that I am inside of is ravenous. I inhabit this hunger. It walks.

Two women are visible through the iron grating pulled down over the door and windows of a small bodega; I'm guessing them to be mother and daughter. The daughter is pretty, about my age, maybe a little older. She disappears from my view, exiting somewhere in back. A gray-haired Indian lady remains. She wears an apron around her plump midsection and seems to be busy with something behind a counter. I tap on the window for her attention and point to my open mouth to indicate I am hungry.

She shakes her index finger diagonally and says, "*Cerrada*".

Closed.

"*Torta! Comida! Mucho hungry por favor!*"

My Spanish remains shamefully limited; I have not put the inadequate vocabulary I have learned from my Spanish dictionary into practice. I have failed to conjugate verbs or correctly pronounce nouns. *Stupid!* Why have I not studied this beautiful language more earnestly? Why have I spent my time in this unfathomable country idly sleeping, daydreaming, or aimlessly walking? By now I might have been, if not fluent in Spanish, certainly at the very least able to make rudimentary needs known to others. Instead I am reduced to shaking and rattling the grating while idiotically shouting *torta, torta, torta* as if by sheer volume and repetition I might make myself understood.

The old woman begins sweeping the floor. I take some bills from my pants pocket and wave them. That seems to work. The universal language. She leans the broom against some shelves, approaches the door and unlocks it. The inside is vibrant gumball blue and banana yellow colors which, under the bright overhead lighting, lend a hallucinatory quality. It's beautiful in here. Everything is an adventure now. I see candy apple red, dark shimmering green. Everything is vibrating color. I'm alive, in the world. And hungry! I see stacks of newspapers, bags of flour, sugar and charcoal, cans of vegetables and sweet condensed milk and a cooler of beer and soda, but no sandwiches. No torta. This is obviously the Mexican equivalent of a convenience store.

The old woman, perched now on a tall stool behind the counter, watches me intently. Her rough brown hands are folded in her lap upon which lies a heart-shaped fan she occasionally uses to cool her lightly perspiring face. She is brown-skinned, with eyes of such depth one could swim in them. Her face is elongated, with high prominent cheekbones and a long sloping Mayan nose. Her gray hair is braided with red and blue ribbons, her smile a flash of gold and silver. She wears a black, beaded rosary around her neck. It's easy to imagine she had been a beautiful young woman once. She is *still* beautiful. The younger woman, who I only caught a glance of from outside the window, is in back somewhere, out of sight.

The shop is stocked with toiletries, antacids and pain relievers, bottles of soda and beer, bags of sugar, flour, and other sundries. Behind the counter are shelves of cigarettes and stacks of boxed matches and hanging strips of lottery tickets.

"*Por favor, Señora, torta?*"

"*No, señor. No torta.*"

I hear a radio playing in back. Someone is laughing but it sounds like it is coming from the radio. I feel myself breaking up like an airplane that is shaking apart from too much turbulence. This hunger owns me now. I am on the verge of tears.

"*Torta,*" I reply. "*Torta torta torta.*"

There is power in this incantation. It's as if by chanting torta I might conjure one. I can hear my strident voice verge on hysteria.

The woman's fiercely beautiful daughter emerges from behind

the beaded curtain. She's dressed in a tight white sweater and leopard skin pants with a silver belt and red high heels and looks like she might be going out to a dance club. Her long hair is fashioned stylishly, with silver hoop ear rings and dark red lipstick that matches her fingernails. She's drop-dead gorgeous but her eyes frighten me. I see violence in them. She fixes them on me like daggers.

The older woman is talking, but I don't understand a word of it. The daughter joins in. A brilliant large Toucan with rainbow-colored feathers joins the chatter. Now there are three entities talking in a language that I do not understand.

The daughter points to the door dismissively and says, "*No señor. No torta acqui.*"

I pound my fist on the counter. I hear myself shouting.

The old woman's silver bracelets rattle as her wrinkled brown hands gesture in an attempt to communicate something in her language, which I cannot understand. But these women understand *me;* they know what I want, why I am here. It's not fair. They must have tortas here. They are lying. They hate me because I am an American. I am aware that I am screaming, banging on the counter with my fists.

I see the fear in their eyes. They think I am mad, a crazy drunken Americano, possibly dangerous. Maybe they are right. I feel crazed, desperate, capable of anything. The younger woman picks up the telephone and makes a call, her gaze nervously shifting from me to the phone. Is she calling the police?

But no, it is not a police car that pulls up in front of the shop but a taxi. She gets in and rides off into the night, maybe to her dance club. I'm left alone with the smiling old woman behind the counter, a smile I now find to be subtly cunning and malevolent. I'm convinced she and her daughter have set a trap for me. The hag smiles, a flash of silver and gold in her mouth. She motions for me to sit on a wooden chair under a painting of a tortured Christ crucified on blue velvet.

I give up. There will be no torta for me tonight. The taxi returns with the young beautiful daughter. She enters the shop, her bracelets clattering as she hands me a package the size and shape of a large shoe wrapped in butcher block paper. I can feel its warmth through the wrapping. Something the size of a small kitten is alive inside and breathing. Am I imagining this? It is too strange to be real.

I begin cautiously unwrapping the package, just an outer edge of it initially. I do not trust these women.

Inside the package is a fresh perfect torta.

The women smile benevolently in unison say, "*Si. Torta, señor.*"

The kindness of this moves me to tears. I am crying again, but from happiness. I hand over a wad of money damp with my tears. I have no idea how much it is. She takes some, returns the rest. I thank them repeatedly, bowing, my hands held as if in prayer, *gracias, gracias, muchas gracias.*

It is six long blocks back to the hotel lobby. The elevator seems to buzz happily when the doors open. I step right in and push the buttons for my floor. My luck seems to have changed.

The unwrapped sandwich is beautiful and enormous, exactly as I hoped and everything I had wanted. The bread is crusty on the outside and doughy within, the ham thickly layered, the tomatoes fresh and ripe. The avocado and bean spread add a distinctive flavor that blends perfectly. I sit on the bed in my room gorging, breathing like an asthmatic. I eat shamelessly, urgently. I've eaten over half of it before I am willing to pause. I look up from the torta, *and there is Jesus the Beggar!*

All this takes place in the blink of an eye, but somehow time is elongated, slowed in a way that defies laws of physics and cannot be. The image is so pervasive and hyper-real that while my reason tells me this is impossible and must be taking place only in my mind, my sensory perceptions give indisputable evidence to the contrary. I see the beggar's sad beseeching eyes as he stares at my sandwich and I'm flooded with shame. He is ghastly thin, his hair shoulder length as in Renaissance paintings of Christ, and his clothing hangs off his emaciated frame like torn rags. He looks as if he is dying of starvation. Maybe he is already dead and doesn't know it. Maybe it is his ghost I see. I reach out to touch him but his image is disturbed and disassembles like ripples made in the reflection in a pond when you stick your hand in it. How to explain this? What is happening to me?

And then I understand.
And burst out laughing.
I was seeing *my reflection in the mirror*!
What a relief!

* * *

Dear Raymond,

Don't you think it is about time that you wrote us again? We have received your post cards but without a return address other than care of the American Express. We still don't even know where you are staying. I know you have always been rather absent-minded and lose track of time and forget about just about everything else when you are writing, but how much time does it take to sit down and write us a long informative letter telling us some of what you are doing down there and how you are feeling? After all, you consider yourself to be a writer, so how hard can it be? I want you to write me as soon as you finish reading this letter and put it in the mail! You say you write letters and then forget to mail them, but no more excuses! In this envelope you will find plenty of stamps.

Your father says if you are getting sick down there to avoid dairy products and most importantly stop drinking the water! He says eventually you will accommodate to the higher bacteria content of much of the food, but to stay away from the water, milk, and especially the cheese, which is not pasteurized and not from the milk of cows, but goats, sheep, donkeys and who knows what, maybe dogs or even worse. He is away again, in Japan as of this writing. Unlike his ungrateful selfish son, he loves me and writes me letters once a week.

I do have some news. Do you remember Carla Johansen? Well, guess what? She is in Mexico City! Her mother told me Carla was studying Spanish and Mexican culture at The University of Mexico. When I told her you were in Mexico City at the University learning Spanish and writing a novel, she was thrilled to hear it. She wants your address and phone number to give to Carla, who is excited about seeing you again.

I'm sure you must remember Carla, even though she graduated a couple of years ahead of you, she was so active and prominent, a member of the drama club and student council and everything. Didn't she edit the high school literary magazine for a while? Oh, I'm sure you remember her. Her mother used to be in my book club, remember? I think she was two years ahead of you, tall and pretty, and very active. You must have known her because she was so smart and popular. Such a smart, nice girl, and very pretty too! Isn't it nice to have someone you know down there the same time as you? And she can help you with Spanish!

Well, anyway, that's all for now. Don't forget to write and send us your address. I'll make sure Carla gets it, but be sure to let me know as soon as you meet with Carla how it goes.

Love,
Mother

PART THREE

Carla Johansen

Of course I remembered Carla. When my family first moved from the Wallingford house in Seattle to the Edmonds suburb, her family was already living in the same Hummingbird Hill neighborhood. I was just a pubescent kid at the time, shy and young for my age. I remember her as not afraid to play contact sports with the boys, a tomboy known to love horses. She wore grass-stained jeans torn at the knee from rolling around in the dirt playing tackle football. I didn't know her well, but it was a small town and I saw her around, and when I did, I watched her. We never became friends, but she fascinated me. We never spoke. This was during the summer. I would be going to a new school in the fall. We rode the same bus but never sat together. We shared no classes. She was older and ahead of me in school. When she went on to High School I didn't see her around much anymore, but I heard things. The story I got was that she was dating, and had changed.

By the time I caught up to her in high school her tomboy days were long gone. She had filled out and become voluptuous. We shared a few classes, because I was assigned to advanced courses. It was a great distraction when she rose from her desk and walked to the pencil sharpener in the front of the classroom. It was difficult not to stare at her breasts. We boys watched her intently in immobilized silence. We were stupefied by the sight of her. Not a pencil scratched until she sat back down. It was like we all stopped breathing.

She wasn't a tomboy anymore, and we weren't kids. Not in our pants anyway, and she was the subject of much locker room conversation. I didn't take part in these testosterone-fueled locker room conferences. I was as dirty minded as the next boy, but secretive and private. Besides, I was one of the smart kids. They would never include or invite me. I was too weird.

Carla didn't go out with any of these apes. She was a star pupil, fluent in Spanish, a member of the debate club, left guard on the girls' basketball team, drama club treasurer and senior editor of the school magazine and yearbook.

I remember Carla in her senior years as a naturally beautiful robust Scandinavian girl with a healthy eggshell complexion who wore her thick golden hair the color and density of wheat braided regally on the top of her head like a crown—an unfashionable style at the time, but one she pulled off easily.

She mostly dated college boys who were both academic and athletic, but remained genuinely friendly and gracious with the rest of us, no matter how little prestige we may have had. She couldn't help being sexy but was not exhibitionistic or a tease, and unlike so many of the girls who were part of her clique and out of our league, when she asked us questions or otherwise expressed interest in us, we felt that her inquiries were genuine. I knew her mostly from the poetry magazine, which she edited and for which she wrote some very bad poetry while lavishly praising mine. By then I was going steady with Linda. Carla graduated and went her own way, and I basically forgot about her.

Carla and I had never been friends, really. I liked her a little, but it had been a long time ago and even then I had been suspicious of her popularity. I didn't like any of her friends at the time. So she's here in Mexico City now, making problems for me, calling the hotel desk and asking if I'm in. How did she even know I was here, in the La Paz? I'm going to have to move, somewhere where she can't find me. I'll begin looking for another hotel tomorrow. But starting right now, I need to get this squared away with Ricardo.

He's abrupt and impatient when answering the phone, but cooperative when I tell him my problem.

"Don't send up any calls to my room Ricardo. Especially not from the woman you say has been calling here. I don't care how you do it, but get rid of her. Tell her I checked out without leaving a forwarding address. This is important to me, Ricardo. Please do right by me this time.

"Of course," he says. "We are both men. I understand and sympathize. The woman was bossy and rude on the phone. I will enjoy lying to her."

He hangs up and I breathe a sigh of relief.

Now to start looking for another hotel.

* * *

The telephone on the night table rings some twenty-five damn times before I begrudgingly accept that the only way to stop its infernal nagging is by answering it. Already angry, half hanging off the bed, groping, fumbling and dropping the receiver once or twice, I've wakened hard and against my will from a sleeping-pill hangover. I consider this intrusion deliberate harassment on Ricardo's part and intend to let him know it.

"I'm still sleeping, Ricardo. I thought I told you to hold my calls."

"Wake up, sleepyhead. It's me, Carla."

Someone has thrown the equivalent of a bucket of ice-cold water in my face. Damn! Ricardo strikes again! He's probably listening in right now, snickering under his breath, near to pissing his fancy pants from the effort of stifling his laughter. I imagine later he will entertain the entire staff with his account of how he betrayed me. They will reward him with applause and boisterous cheers. None of the staff here like me anymore, not even the maids. They love to belittle me. I'm their stupid Americano. They all give me dirty looks when I pass them in the hall or in the lobby. But now I have a more immediate problem to consider. Carla.

"Oh. Wow. What a surprise."

The Nembutal I took for sleep has left my mouth so dry I can barely speak. I haven't had a shower in a few days and my armpits itch. I can't stop scratching. I place the receiver on the bed, take a quick drink from a half-full bottle of flat soda left on the night-stand from the previous night.

"Didn't your mother tell you I was in the city and planning to look you up?"

The receiver slips from my hand, reducing me to groping on

my hands and knees on the dirty floor again. When it's secure under my chin again I light the first cigarette of the day.

"She may have," I reply. "It might have slipped my mind. I haven't heard from her in a while."

"So I hear. That's one of the reasons I'm calling. She's worried sick about you. She doesn't even know where you are staying. All she has is the address for the American Express."

"So how did you find me?"

"I found you through Jake Egan. You mentioned to him in your post card that you were staying in the Hotel La Paz."

Egan. Shit. I did send a few notes and post cards from the hotel. None were answered, either. Fair weather friends.

"Does my mother know I'm here? Did you tell her I was at the La Paz?"

"Not yet, sleepyhead. Why haven't you called me? Haven't you been receiving the messages I've been leaving at the desk?"

"I had no idea you were trying to contact me, Carla. I've received no messages at all from the desk."

"Well, I did call, and just about every day. So when do you want to get together."

She voices this as a command, rather than a question.

"Well, I don't know. Wow, Carla, let me think about that."

Why do I keep saying "wow"? I never use that expression and can hear how forced and deceitful I must sound. It's probably obvious I'm stalling. I can imagine how it must sound to her and I'm embarrassed.

"It's really good to hear from you, Carla. We definitely have to get together. No doubt about that."

"Okay, good then, fine, but when?"

"Well, unfortunately, I'm not in a position to say right now. But I hope soon. It's just that I'm so busy these days I don't even know myself what my schedule looks like for this month. Next month is mostly wide open though. Will you still be here? Why don't you leave me your number and when I get a break in my schedule I'll give you a call."

Does she believe this? Hard to say. She does give me her number though. I don't even write it down. In my head I'm already planning to check out of the hotel. Move to a new neighborhood where she can't find me. My rent is up anyway.

"What is it that has you so busy, Raymond?"

"You wouldn't believe my course schedule, how spread out it is. Worst of all is I've fallen behind a little in my studies and have to catch up. You know how it is—homework, homework, homework. It's definitely not like high school. And wow," (there's that word again), "all these *papers*. There is so much *research*. I don't know how they expect us to manage it all. Sometimes I think about getting a sleeping bag and just moving into the library, it would be a lot easier."

I laugh blithely into the receiver, into my rhythm now. This isn't so hard. I can do this. I've almost convinced myself of my lies.

"Bullshit, Ray. You're not even in school. I checked."

"*Well*," I reply, "I think you are wrong *there*." She's obviously bluffing. "You better check again, because I am definitely enrolled."

"I have a friend in the registrar's office, Raymond. They looked you up and have never heard of you. I'm here at the University now."

"Well, that explains it then. I'm not enrolled in the University. I'm enrolled in Mexico City College."

"Oh," replies Carla. "My mistake then. I apologize, Ray. What are you studying?"

"Well, you know. The usual. Mexican history, Spanish."

"Good for you, Ray. Hey, speak some Spanish to me. I would love to hear your accent."

"I don't speak it very well, Carla. I mean, I'm learning the vocabulary and everything, but my accent is rather embarrassing."

"Come on, Ray. Don't be shy. I won't judge you. Say something to me. I insist. You can't improve if you don't practice. If you're studying Spanish, there must be a few common phrases that you can speak correctly."

"Donde es mi casa en la vida con mericosa del especial?" I reply. I have no idea what I am saying. It's ridiculous. "Uh, I told you I was behind in my studies. I'm probably failing Spanish. It's humiliating for me."

"You mention you are taking courses in Mexican history. Who was the first president of Mexico after the execution of Emperor

Maximillian and the liberation from Spain?"

"That's easy." I reply confidently. I know this one. "It was Poncho Villa. Or was it Emiliano Zapata? I always get those two mixed up."

"Neither. It was Porfirio Diaz. Villa and Zapata were part of the revolution that freed Mexico from Diaz. Come on, Ray, we knew that in high school, or at least I did. You're not enrolled at Mexico City College or anywhere else."

"Okay, okay. You're right, Carla."

"Of course I'm right. I knew it all along. You're not that good a liar, Ray. "

"Well, I was enrolled and attending classes until recently, but then I got sick with the tourista and fell behind and couldn't catch up. I tried to, but it was hopeless and I finally had to drop out or I would have lost all of my tuition."

"I don't believe you."

"It's true. I was sick as a dog, Carla. You should have seen me."

"That part I believe. I got it too. Everyone does. Anyway, now that the truth is out and you have nothing to hide, when do you want to get together?"

"I don't know, Carla. I'm not feeling very well right now. I really don't want any visitors for a while but I *will* call you. I promise."

"When?"

"Soon."

"Ray, I really don't understand why you are putting me off like this. I thought we were friends. Don't you want to see me, Ray? Don't you like me? Your old friend from high school? Do you think I am insufficiently hip? I might not be the way you remember me. It's been a long time. You're not the only one who can change, you know."

"Of course I like you, Carla. And I always liked you fine just the way you were."

"You don't act like it."

"I know. I'm sorry, Carla, it's a long story and I don't think I can explain it right now but I'm really not feeling very well at all and that's the truth."

"Well, I'm disappointed, Raymond. I thought it would be nice if we got together. After all, we are both a long way from home and we did practically grow up together. You know, our parents still see each other."

Yes, I agree silently. And there is the problem exactly.

"You're right, Carla. I want to see you again and I'm going to get better soon. When I do I'm going to call you and we'll get together and talk. Honestly."

"Really?"

"Absolutely. I promise."

"All right then, Ray, but don't take too long. My mother has been pestering me to death asking questions about you. Your parents are worried that you might be sick or in trouble. Our mothers do talk, you know."

"I know. So what are you going to tell them?"

"Just that you are alive, Ray. That's all I know for certain."

"Are you going to tell them that I'm not in the University? Please don't tell them where I am staying."

"Ray, what do you think I am, the FBI or something? I won't tell them anything you don't want me to."

"Thank you, Carla."

"Thank me by calling when you feel better."

"I will. I promise."

* * *

It's good to be loved, but the people who love you seem to end up meddling in your affairs and putting you in positions where, if you want to be true to who you are, you must either be deceitful for their sake, or hurt then with honesty. I'm not proud that I lie to my mother and father, but how can I tell people the facts of my circumstances when the truth of the matter will only hurt them? Where is the honor in that? Which is better, to be honest but hurtful, or deceitful but kind? What I *want* is just to be left alone and not put in positions by others where I have to lie or compromise my principles. And it's true that that I am not feeling well. Not well at all, actually. Worse by the moment in fact.

It's all Carla's fault, of course. Thanks to her, my secret hiding place is no longer a secret. If Carla reports to her mother that I'm unwell or in trouble, her mother will tell my mother, and there is no telling what *my* mother might do. She'd get me back even if she had to pay thousands of dollars to some yahoo cowboy bounty hunter to knock me out and put me on an airplane. At the very least she'd cut off my funds. I can't let this happen. It would mean that my entire experience here was for nothing. I'm not finished yet, hardly even started in fact. I have come to Mexico for a purpose and will not leave until I know what it is and have accomplished it.

Of course it's not *entirely* Carla's fault. Ricardo is equally complicit. I don't know why the rodent hates me, but he does. I try to follow Christ's dictum to love my neighbors as myself, but it doesn't work when I have to deal with people like Ricardo. Of course I'm supposed to rise to the challenge and love him anyway and maybe that's why people like Ricardo are the way they are—to challenge the rest of us with opportunities to become more tolerant. I'm going to have to find another way. If I want to be a Christian, I'm going to have to find a way to do it without the fellowship part.

I find Ricardo tweaking his pencil- line moustache while reading a nudie magazine behind the desk. He's wearing a designer suit that must have cost more than what he can afford working at this hotel, and smokes expensive imported cigarettes. His white jacket is immaculate and worn with a silk Hawaiian shirt open at the throat, a thin gold chain necklace around his brown skinny neck. His slick black hair is combed perfectly straight back with pomade. His beady brown eyes are calculating and lifeless. His gold watch is ostentatious and probably genuine. So probably are the sparkling rings on three of his effeminate, manicured fingers. This man is no mere desk clerk. Who knows what he's into? He's intently flipping the pages of the nudie magazine, knows I'm standing in front of the desk but he doesn't even look at me.

"Hey!"

He takes his time about looking up, lays the magazine down slowly on the counter. It's open to a lurid, vibrantly colored photograph of an obscenely posed fat woman with enormous sagging brown breasts and wide open fat legs. Ricardo slides off his stool behind the counter and stands. He blows cigarette smoke in my face and says, "*Buenos Dias*, Raymond Watson."

"I'm checking out," I announce.

"When? Now?"

"Tomorrow morning."

"But why?"

"I asked you to hold my calls, Ricardo."

"Please try to understand, Señor Watson, this lady friend of yours, she is very persistent. She made many threats and demands, stating you were officially classified as a missing person with the United States Embassy here in Mexico, and that an international investigation was in process. She went on to say that if I did not cooperate she would notify the American consulate. She left me with little choice, this friend of yours. I apologize sincerely, Señor Watson, but we cannot get involved in an international incident."

Ricardo regards me with an expression of respect that I have never experienced from him before. It is as if he suddenly finds me less a subject of ridicule, the events in my life now of heretofore unsuspected interest. He leans over the nudie photograph and even though no one is present but the two of us, glances surreptitiously around the lobby.

"This woman? She is your wife?"

"No. "

"Perhaps then," he says hopefully, "she is a lover you have made pregnant during an affair?"

"No, nothing like that."

His disappointment is visible.

"Please, Ricardo. Give me an eight o'clock wake up call. I'll come down then and settle the bill and check out."

* * *

I wake to the maids tapping on the door and know that I've overslept. They never come to this room before one in the afternoon. Sometimes they don't come at all, since I rarely admit them anyway. Ricardo has probably set this up so he can bill me an extra day for missing the 11 a.m. hotel check-out time. I'll refuse to pay. What are they going to do, evict me? I'll lie here in bed another few hours and check out of the hotel later. They're still knocking on the damn door though. What's a Spanish word for *leave*?

"*Luego*," I shout. I think that means later. It's pathetic. I should know this by now. But they are unusually persistent this morning.

I get out of bed, pull my beltless cotton pants up over my skinny thighs, and lurch for a nonexistent handhold. *Woah, Raymond, hold on.* The room spins around and around. Shirtless and barefoot, holding my pants with up with both hands, carefully stepping over tangled dirty ash smudged sheets, empty soda cans, half eaten chocolate bars and dozens of cigarette butts, my right foot sinks into a warm and slippery muck that sends me skidding head first into the door. I drop to my knees, my pants fall down to my ankles, and I'm naked. The knocking on the door persists. Seething with anger, head throbbing and ears ringing from the collision, I pull up my pants and abruptly open the door.

It's not the maids.

Standing in the hallway with a large purse slung over her shoulder and a denim jacket folded over her arm, is Carla Johansen. She's wearing a black leather skirt that comes to her knees, black ankle boots and a plum red cardigan sweater with tiny black buttons up the front. The sweater is unbuttoned to the third button and gives a generous view to her appealing cleavage. I had forgotten how pretty she is.

As for my appearance, the expression on her face says it all. I know without looking in any mirror that I have probably the look of someone who had only just escaped from a lunatic asylum. I have not shampooed, showered or shaved in weeks; I am wearing only my beltless pants, which because of weight loss I now hold up with one hand. Weighing in at an average of around 135 in high school, I have always been thin, but then I was toned and in good physical condition, while I now resemble a concentration camp survivor, with arms and legs that look like sticks and a visible rib cage. As if that weren't bad enough, I haven't shaved in weeks, my hair has grown down to my shoulders, and I can smell my armpits. Embarrassed and ashamed, I witness her initial smile of anticipatory excitement change to fear and trepidation, and from there to revulsion.

She looks me up and down apprehensively, searching this dirty unshaven face and skinny unwashed body for a remnant of the person she once knew, and by the time her expression of confusion and surprise has begun to change into one of loathing and gradually accepting recognition I'm trying to slam the door in her face and lock it before she can enter or even speak. It doesn't work. She has her foot in the door, and without so much as a hello bullies past me, pinning me against the wall. Again the door hits me in the head and again my pants fall down. I hike them up quickly while her back is turned, and clench the belt loops in both fists.

She's standing in the center of the room now, frowning and looking around. The bed is a mess and takes up almost all of it. Dirty sheets hang from it to the dirty floor. Because the altitude and thin air of Mexico City have been giving me nosebleeds, the pillow on the bed is faintly bloodstained. The only chair for her to sit in is draped with a discarded pair of my fart- stained dirty underwear.

She frowns at the messy bed and reluctantly sits, fumbles in her green leather bag for a cigarette. I have long since stopped using the ashtray, which at the moment is probably lost in the tangle of sheets, since I normally just throw my cigarette butts on the floor.

She lights her cigarette and tosses the extinguished match with the comment, "How can you live like this?"

I'm surprised to see her smoking. This is apparently not the old Carla. She inhales and makes a face as if she smells something unpleasant.

"It's early," I explain. "The maids haven't been in yet."

I look down at my bare feet and see that they are brown from having stepped in a half-eaten chocolate bar, which explains what I slipped in when I rose to answer the door. I see Carla staring at them. They look like someone shit on them.

"It's not early, Raymond. It's almost three o'clock in the afternoon and it doesn't look like any maids have been here in months. But if they do come, maybe they could turn on the shower and encourage you to go in. I'm trying to find a gentle way to say this, Raymond. How should I put it? Oh, I know. How's this? You stink, Ray. You don't look so good either. Actually, you frightened me. I thought I had knocked on the wrong door. You're so skinny I didn't even recognize you. I see now why your parents wanted me to find you and report back. What's wrong with you? Are you sick? Are you on drugs or something? And what's with the hair? You used to be a good-looking guy, Ray. Now you look like a skinny Lenore Goldberg."

Lenore was the dirtiest, meanest, most unpopular girl in our school.

Carla's expressive blue eyes are the same as I remember, but have become the eyes of an intelligent adult woman, not the girl I had known in high school. I can't help noticing that she's gorgeous, even better looking than I remembered. She stretches her legs on the bed, her black leather skirt exposing the hem of her panties.

She seems either unaware of it or unconcerned and says, "What's the idea of not calling me or answering my calls?"

There is something different about her. She is more directly engaging somehow, commanding in initiating conversation, as opposed to being mostly receptive. Her assuredness is unnerving.

"I don't understand. We talked just last night."

"Yes, and you were being evasive. You had no intention of getting together with me."

"That's not true, Carla. I was going to call you today."

"That's not what the desk clerk said. He said you were checking out today."

Damn! Ricardo strikes again. I should have known better than to trust him.

"Your mother is worried about you."

"That's what mothers do."

"Well, it honestly looks like she has every reason to worry."

"I'm fine, really. If you knew my mother better, you'd understand."

"Nevertheless, you look like shit."

"Thanks. You, on the other hand, are as beautiful as I remember."

"I never thought you noticed."

"Are you kidding? Everybody noticed. Half the male graduating class was in love with you. What are you doing here? I figured you to be a rising young Republican by now, married to a lawyer or junior senator, house in the suburbs, two perfect kids, seat on the school board, all that."

"Not a particularly flattering supposition, Raymond. I suppose that would have been a logical conclusion based on how you knew me in high school, but I've changed and you're way off base. I was at the University of Washington for two years and went off in an entirely different direction with a lot of history and political science courses. My education politicized me. But what's with the banter, Raymond? I detect a note of hostility. If you must know, I've been converted by the inspirational examples of Fidel Castro and Che Guevara. People change, Ray. Well, maybe not you. You are still weird."

"Did my mother pay you to come down and spy on me?"

"She hired me to drug your coffee and put you on an airliner."

"It wouldn't surprise me."

"Well, for the right price I might have, but she didn't offer enough. Too bad, because it might have covered tuition. But I'm here as an exchange student taking advanced Spanish and Latin American studies on the campus of the University of Mexico where, according to your mother, is where you're supposed to be. By the way, you look like shit, Ray. Did I mention that?"

"Several times. If it's any consolation, I feel like shit. It's embarrassing to have you even see me like this."

"Well, it was a shock when you first opened the door. I didn't even recognize you." She repositions herself on the bed, crossing her long bare legs. When she catches me staring at them she tugs at her skirt modestly. I look away, embarrassed. Busted.

"So," she says, "I heard you got all creepy and weird and went to jail. Then I heard that when you got out you were talking about Jesus and walking around the streets of downtown Seattle reading your poetry. My mother said you made a nuisance of yourself in church a couple of times. She said you gave away all your possessions and refused to wear shoes. I heard later you were living out of your car for a while."

More embarrassment. I was trying to put this part of my past behind me, and didn't want to talk about it. It's why I didn't mention it in earlier chapters and one of the reasons for my self-imposed exile. After I ruined my relationship with Linda and came out of jail identified as a stalker and creep, I tried to redeem myself through religion, but went on to screw that up just like everything else. I had been "born again" in jail, but when I got out, maybe to circumnavigate the jailbird stalker identity attributed to me by my peers and neighbors, an identity which I in fact deserved, I began making a spectacle of my faith. I fatuously and incorrectly quoted scripture. At my family's table when I said grace it went on and on, becoming a sermon instead of a brief expression of thankfulness. By my ludicrous example, I was corrupting the very message I wished to convey.

I still love Christ, but hope I am a better, more mature Christian. But I'm probably not. I'm sinful in my thoughts. I'm selfish and a failure at love. I neglect my Bible. My prayers are like begging. But at least I am celibate. I have that. It is my symbolic and actual demonstration of faith, a single act of redemption that I hope will make me worthy of the as yet undisclosed purpose for which God has brought me to Mexico.

"My mom said you had gone crazy, that you were on medication and your parents had you going to a therapist."

"This is why I don't want to go home. Everybody knows everybody else's business. Yes, I was prescribed medication but didn't take it and didn't need it. The meetings with the psychologist were a waste. They said I had an adjustment disorder. I was fine with that. I didn't want to adjust, didn't want to adapt, fit in or be the normal kind of man they wanted and thought I was supposed to be. My model of the perfect man was Christ. It still is. "

"Raymond, Raymond, Raymond. You always were a strange one."

"I suppose."

"Do you know what they used to call you in school?"

"A number of things."

"Weirdo Watson."

"I was probably called worse than that."

"You don't want to know."

"I can probably guess."

She moves to the edge of the bed, glances at a drawing in my sketchbook and says, "Jesus?"

"Maybe. I don't know yet."

"Hmm. Well, that certainly does sound like the kind of answer I would expect from our mysterious high school Poet Laureate."

"I think he is a beggar I met the first day I arrived here."

"I think he looks like you. But it's a crime, the terrible poverty and injustice down here. Begging is something I suppose we will never get used to and shouldn't. I wish there was something we could do. Well, actually there is; I have friends at the University who are working for social justice. I'll tell you more about that later. Do you have anything to drink?"

"I don't normally keep beverages here. I do have water, of course."

"Please tell me you don't drink the water."

"I don't drink the water."

"It doesn't look like you eat much either. When is the last time you had a meal?"

"I don't remember."

"Well, come on. We're going out for lunch."

She points to the bathroom door and adds, "But first take a shower. I'll wait. Take your time."

"Do you intend to bathe me?"

"Only if you have lye, rubber gloves and a surgical mask."

I shower quickly in the cold water, washing my face, crotch and underarms with the remaining sliver of bar soap. Hanging on the towel rack is a change of jeans and black shirt which, as luck would have it, I had scrubbed with bar soap and intended to wear when checking into a new hotel. Still damp, I put them on anyway, hoping they no longer smell.

Later, when we enter the lobby, Ricardo leers at us suggestively. I give him a disapproving glance on the way out. Smiling lasciviously, he shoves his middle finger in and out of his clenched fist in simulation of intercourse.

Captured

In the street outside of the hotel, Carla and I are met immediately with a succession of wind gusts. We lower our shoulders and wade slowly into them. Grit blows into our faces so that we must bow our heads against the wind and squint; it removes hats, inverts umbrellas; pedestrians stagger against it, fighting their way toward shelter. Several blocks later, passing the antiquated brownstone building that houses one of the city's two major newspapers, we turn onto another side street where, hemmed in by parallel buildings, the onrush of wind is less harsh. Here we are much less subject to airborne grit and can open our eyes fully again. The weak grey light of day is diminishing. It's getting late and turning dark.

"Hurry," says Carla. She summons a cab with the kind of loud, long, masculine whistle that is rarely heard from a woman, made with the index and middle finger in the mouth. It surprises and impresses me; I have never been able to accomplish it. We have a cab quickly.

Carla, giving directions in perfect Spanish, huddles beside me in the back seat and says, "You're cold. You have goose bumps, even. Here, let me warm you up."

She rubs her hands together to warm them, and then rubs my arms. It is the first time I have been touched by another human being since embraced by the beggar on the day of my arrival, and I recoil from the unexpected contact

"What's wrong," asks Carla?

"I'm not used to being touched."

"Yeah, well, I'm not surprised. I should be the one recoiling from contact, not you. Why are you wearing wet clothing, Raymond?'

"They were the only ones I had clean. I washed them with bar soap in the shower last night. They aren't completely dry."

"Well, they aren't completely clean either. You still smell."

It's a long ride to wherever it is Carla is taking us. A canopied military truck filled with helmeted soldiers passes. Others follow. I don't know where we are or remember having seen this part of the city before. I begin to see pedestrians stopped by soldiers, papers inspected, arrests. Carla explains the uniformed men are not patriotic soldiers, but Federal Police, adding that their prominence is not intended to assure one's safety, but rather to intimidate. Since the success of Castro's revolution in Cuba, Mexico's one party government is fearful of communism to a near psychotic degree, and intervention by police is haphazard, frequent, and seemingly without provocation. Apparently everyone is suspect of something, and fair game. What is more, she adds, Mexico City is engaged in an international competition to host the Olympic Games, and there is a citywide campaign to round up subversives and undesirables, empty the streets of criminals, remove unsightly prostitutes and generally make the city safe for everyone except its own citizens, who are more afraid of the federal police than any of these so-called criminals.

We arrive at a bottleneck of congested traffic for which there seems no visible explanation. The meter ticks off minutes and pesos.

"What's the holdup?"

The driver frowns, holds up his hands, shrugs.

"*Quien sabe?*"

The human shapes appearing in our headlights are like phantasmal dancing shadows. The highway becomes besieged with obstructive rings of children. They evade oncoming cars like skilled matadors against charging bulls. Our driver, holding steady on the horn, inches forward. Dirty young faces stare into the taxi windows with the dying eyes of old men. They begin pounding the fenders and shaking the door handles.

I reach for my recently acquired replacement wallet, but the driver shakes his head vigorously and speaks severely in Spanish to Carla, "No no. The sight of money is to them like the sight of blood to a school of sharks."

Our driver inches forward, bumping them gently with his fender. He seems not much older than the oldest of them, perhaps in his mid-teens, his features more Mestizo than Indian, his young face without a trace of moustache or beard.

We hear sirens in the darkness and then the children scatter into the night and we are on our way again, racing toward the twittering distant lights of the buildings of the University, the driver singing along with the radio.

"What the hell was that about?" I ask Carla.

"Orphaned children used to beg here, holding up traffic and sometimes breaking into cars and stealing from the occupants, but they were chased away by soldiers and for months there was no trouble. Now they have returned, but they are different than before. They seem to be more organized, and some are older. Newspaper editorials have speculated that young nihilist hooligans are being organized by revolutionaries. Government officials hold communist cells and student revolutionary groups responsible for the organizing."

A plastic Jesus swings back and forth on the dashboard as the cab weaves through traffic. The driver, shifting his gaze from the road to the rear-view mirror, races down the boulevard to our destination, a roomy, full-scale restaurant a few blocks off the main thoroughfare.

I don't want to go inside and face everyone. I'm too conspicuous, dirty and out of place. But it's too late. Carla, following the hostess, is already steering me through the tables in the main dining area to a small adjoining back room. We're seated near a corner window giving view to a sidewalk and street. Neither of us speak. I hear the rattle and clang of cookware, voices from the chefs and kitchen help. Waitresses carry steaming platters of food held aloft, bang in and out of the kitchen. I am the recipient of dirty looks from a party at a nearby table. Even without knowing Spanish I know they are talking about my dirty appearance and odor.

Carla breaks our silence and says, "You seemed to want to leave here before we even got all the way inside, Raymond. It's painful to even watch you. You're so obviously paranoid and awkward it's pitiful. You are your own curse. Why don't you do something to clean yourself up? People wouldn't stare at you so much and you'd be less paranoid."

I feel taken advantage of. It is as if she has trapped me here and is now attacking me.

"I'm not comfortable with the direction this conversation is taking, Carla. You're beginning to sound like my mother."

"All right. I'll change the subject. Tell me about your writing. What are you working on?"

"Good question, but a hard one to answer. I've filled a dozens of notebooks since arriving but don't know what I have. Maybe notes for a novel. I'm thinking I might call it, *A Holy Ghost in Mexico City*. How does that sound to you?"

"Poetic. I like it. I always did like your poetry, Ray."

We're interrupted by bus boys clearing an adjacent table. Carla obviously knows them and speaks to them. Their friendly exchange of Spanish is over quickly. When they leave, Carla says, "I'd like to see some of what you are writing if you want to show it to me sometime."

"I have some things I could give you. You'd have to understand they are rough drafts, though."

"I'd love to read them. But meanwhile, Raymond, we have to decide what to do about your parents. My mother is going to be asking about you. She will be seeing your parents, who are waiting for a report."

"Part of the reason I came here was to get away from my mother. The Bible says a prophet has no honor in his own home."

"Well you're no prophet and I promised my Mother that I'd check in on you. And really, Ray, don't you care that your Mom is worried sick? If you would just write them I wouldn't be put in the awkward position of playing spy."

Young boys with dirty faces outside the café windows press against the glass to watch steaming plates of *huevos rancheros* and platters of *arroz con pollo* carried by waiters from the kitchen into the dining area. From the expressions on their faces they might be discussing fabulously decorated parade floats with beautiful waving girls. The smallest of the boys might be crying. The others tease him, knock the hat off his head and affectionately muss his hair.

Kitchen workers wearing aprons and tall white chef's hats come banging out the back doors with baseball bats. The boys flee, dodging pedestrians and automobiles. One has a limp and is not fast enough. Struck across the back of the legs with the baseball bat, he falls to his knees. A kitchen worker stands over him. He shouts at the boy but does not again strike him, and the boy gets to his feet and limps off.

"Did you see that? They hurt that little boy."

"Yes but you don't know the half of it. You're not seeing the whole picture, Raymond. What you see can be deceptive here in Mexico. This is a restaurant with a conscience. They don't want to call the police. It's far better for the orphan boys to be chased off by the help than brutalized by the police or hired thugs. I know the staff and management here. At the end of the night, after the restaurant has closed, the staff wraps leftovers and leaves them in back. What they did with those boys was cruel, but Mexico is a cruel nation. There are too many poor to care for in Mexico City. Too many refugees cross the border to escape harsh economic policy and political persecution in Latin American dictatorships to the south. They want to find work but find only more subjugation, beatings, and hunger. Navio, my lover, can tell you more than I about this. He knows all about it. He cares deeply. You will see. I will take you to him one day soon."

She orders *huevos rancheros* and tequila and when it arrives applies to her platter a blistering rain of hot sauce that would put me in fetal position. I've lost my appetite because of the boys outside in the street, hungry and chased off.

Carla says, "Join me in a toast."

"Thanks but I tried tequila once and didn't like it."

"You should learn to. You are in Mexico, after all. There will be times in Mexico when you find yourself in situations where it is rude to refuse. Since I paid for the cab and the meal the least you can do is join me in a drink."

She raises her glass and says, "To old friends. To home."

We raise our glasses and clink them ceremoniously but my hand begins to shake and some of the liquid spills on my fingers. I'm having difficulty making myself swallow this stuff.

"Drink up, Raymond."

I take a tentative sip. The taste and odor of the tequila has briefly triggered the memory of the night of violence and flight from El Puño . The understanding frees me; I'm over it now. I take another polite sip. Carla tips her head back and downs her shot in one mighty swallow. She bangs the empty shot glass on the table a few times and playfully smacks her lips. They glisten with tequila, and she licks them with her tongue and smiles.

"That's how it's done, Ray. You need to slam it down in one quick swallow. You need to drink it with machismo. Yes! That's right," she says encouragingly as I comply. "That's how it's done." She orders two more shots. When they arrive I drink mine down machismo style.

She applauds and says, "Bravo!"

After her meal she sits back, lights a cigarette, and blows a perfect smoke ring. "So. Tell me, Ray. What brings you to Mexico City? Why are you here?"

"I came here to find suffering. I want to suffer greatly, magnificently, like the poor. "

"Oh please. Your bullshit could fertilize the entire state of Michoacán, Raymond. I think it's a way you have of pushing people away. In high school no one could talk to you because you always went off subject to talk about poetry or literature or theology or whatever you were into at the time, and even though you were talkative you were essentially private. I think many of us wanted to be your friend, but though you were friendly it was superficial and you really wouldn't make friends. You assumed we didn't like you and didn't respect you, but you kept us at a distance and it wasn't true. Do you *enjoy* being left alone and friendless?

"No."

"Then why do you act this way?"

"I don't expect you to understand, but sometimes it seems like my greatest satisfaction comes from denying myself the things that I want most."

"Well, your solitary confinement is over. I have found you and I'm not going to leave you alone to your misery, so you may as well drink up and resign yourself."

"I don't get it. What is in this for you, Carla? I don't understand why you even would take me out in public, the way I am. "

"Haven't you noticed how expatriates tend to seek out and congregate with their own kind? It's what people do when they are in a foreign country. But it's more than that too, Raymond. You're from home. In a way, you *are* home. We practically grew up together. We have a special bond, you and I."

My throat is burning; there's a lump in it and I'm having difficulty speaking. I force back a few tears, blinking them away, wiping my eyes with my sleeve. And then Linda's curse is upon me. I'm weeping openly now, and making a damn fool of myself. I hate myself! Linda was right about me. I'm not a man. I'm a sniveling little crybaby. Imagine what Carla must think. I can't face her. I never want to see her again. I weep all the harder because of it. I'm helpless. I don't know how long it lasts. When it's over I peek through my fingers expecting to see everyone staring at me, but everything seems normal. No one seems to have noticed. I'm still hiding my face in my arms though. The hard part now is facing Carla. I know how I must look, face mottled and flushed, eyes red and bleary from crying, nose running.

I have unfairly imposed my brokenness on an unsuspecting friend who, in her generosity and kindness, had intended no more than an uncomplicated afternoon of coffee and conversation. Now she is waiting for an explanation and I don't think I have one. I'm seriously thinking about leaping from this chair and making a break for it. Get a cab back to the hotel and check out. It had been my plan anyway.

"Talk to me," says Carla. She's staring at me oddly. "What just happened here? One minute we're chatting and I assumed getting along and then you start crying. Not that I mind, but I think you should at least try to offer some explanation. Did I say something to upset or offend you?"

"No, no. Nothing like that."

"What then?"

"Sometimes it just comes over me. If you knew me better you'd know that I cry easily. It's one of many things I hate about myself and want to change."

"You're not being honest, Raymond. There is always a reason for what we do."

"I'm sorry. I can't give you one."

"Well, you need to try. You owe me."

"I suppose I've been lonelier than I realize and, I don't know, I always did like you. You know that."

"But I didn't know that. You were always too private. Too proud. You need to lighten up, Ray. Have a little fun in life. You're way too serious. That's okay some of the time, but you need to get out of your head and into the world. We can make it happen, get you a life down here. We need to get you cleaned up so I can show you off to my friends at the University. You'd like them. They're interesting and intelligent—writers, artists and intellectuals, and social reformers. I especially want you to meet Navio Sanchez, my lover. You may have heard of him. He's a filmmaker and a leader of the student revolutionary council. And if you are clean, with some nice new clothes, if you trim your beard and get a haircut, I can introduce you to some available women friends of mine who would find you interesting and attractive."

"I really don't have much in the way of clothing other than what I am wearing, Carla."

"Buy some new ones, cheapskate."

"I'm on a pretty tight budget, Carla. "

"You're just making excuses. I think you're afraid. Clothing is inexpensive here, Raymond. At the very least you could wash the clothing you do have. But if you're short of funds right now, I'll front you the money. I know you're good for it. Your mother would give it to you, I know that. Anyway, you have no choice. I'm buying you some clothing, and then you will owe me. Since you won't take charge of your life, I'm taking it over."

She turns and shouts across the room for two more shots, then turns back to me. Smiling playfully, she says, "You are mine now, Raymond. Resistance is futile."

La Café Liberado

"Presents for Raymond," says Carla. She's carrying a shopping bag and looking good wearing tight blue jeans with short black boots and a tight red sweater under a brown jacket. Her hair is windblown, her face flushed. She kisses me on the cheek, her breath surprisingly warm. It's sweet too; she's been chewing gum. Did she sweeten her breath in preparation for a kiss? I should let her know right now that I'm celibate. But she'd laugh at me. Mock me.

She sits on the single chair in my room and fumbles in her handbag to find and apply dark ruby red lipstick, pursing her moist candy-red lips. This is beauty. This is entertainment. This is art. This is too much for me to take in. This is going to be trouble. I'd better look away.

Tossing the shopping bag on the bed, she says, "The receipt is in the bag with the clothing. You can pay me back when your next check arrives at American Express."

I had agreed to this, but now I'm worried about the money. Initially, when she insisted on taking me shopping I refused, but she persisted to the point where I weakened and "compromised," agreeing to her purchase of new clothing on my behalf, which I now remove from the shopping bag: lightweight blue trousers and a new white shirt. But I'm surprised to see wrapped scented soaps, underwear, a razor, shaving cream, aftershave lotion, deodorant, toothpaste and shampoo. This was not what we had agreed on. I did not ask for these additional items, certainly not the soaps, since generic hotel soaps are resupplied by the maids, and this is going to cost much of my monthly allotment.

"Don't look so surprised, Ray. Did I not tell you I intended to make you presentable and take you out? I want you to meet my friends at the University."

"Yes, so you keep saying. As if I existed in solitary confinement and didn't already have friends of my own, which I do, by the way. Many. As a matter of fact, Carla, I have a girlfriend. She's a reporter with the newspaper here who doesn't care how I look or dress."

"Why do you keep lying to me, Raymond? Ricardo says you're a sissy and hardly ever leave the building. He says you dine from the lobby vending machines because you're afraid to eat Mexican food or leave the hotel. Take a shower, Ray. We're going out."

She hands me scissors from her handbag and says, "Oh, and by the way. I'd love to see you without that beard. If you would you be willing to shave it, I think it would be a great improvement. You have such a nice face and it's hidden."

I cut it in in privacy, behind the closed bathroom door, first with the scissors before making use of the new razor. I don't mind, since I grew it more or less accidentally, when my razor blades ran out. But afterwards, rinsing the shaving cream, it's shocking to see my naked cheeks and startled buggy eyes. I don't look for long. Running my hands over my wet, cleanly shaven face in the shower, it feels strange, more like a woman's behind than the face of a man.

I soap my mop of hair with the shampoo and scrub my body from head to toe. There is plenty of hot water for a change. The small bathroom cubicle soon fills with steam. Standing under the spray of hot water, I find myself humming a tune. The realization startles me that I am happy for the first time in months.

I comb my hair straight back and brush my teeth. The shirt and pants fit, the pants loosely. When I leave the mirror and step out of the bathroom into the bedroom, Carla applauds and says, "Bravo! So handsome. You look wonderful, Ray. Do you have a belt? You really do need to put on some weight. Can I have a hug?"

Without waiting for an answer, she comes into my arms. The contact is electrifying. I feel the warmth of her stomach, thighs and voluptuous breasts pushing softly against me. It feels wonderful, but I'm relieved when it is over. I can only hope that what is happening in my pants will pass without her notice.

She briefly glances at the big bulge in my pants and says, "Ray, take it easy, honey. It's only a hug."

* * *

Moving paths of light from traffic on the opposite lanes of the highway briefly flashes across our faces in the dark back seat of the taxi as we are driven at a high rate of speed along a four-lane highway. Dangling silver rosaries dance and sway like ballerinas from our driver's rear view mirror, a battery operated Christ throbs on the dashboard, His wounds glowing blood- red. The blessed Virgin, her arms extending across the grill as if in a gesture of benediction, gestures from the taxi's airbrushed hood. We ride within in a fleet of these mobile air-brushed art exhibits as they glide through the jammed streets and broad open boulevards of Mexico City like gondolas through blue canals.

Pedro, our young driver, wearing jeans and a T shirt and Boston Red Sox cap turned backwards, has become a familiar sight around the hotel lately. He works in an unofficial capacity for Ricardo, running out to restaurants to comply with room service requests or driving guests to the airport and sometimes handling baggage. He is trying to grow a goatee but doesn't look like he is even old enough to shave. He has no trace of a beard. When he picked us up in front of the hotel, gallantly bowing and opening the back door for Carla, he reeked of marijuana, a scent I have become well familiar with in Mexico City.

He sings along with the Mexican rock and roll that blasts from the radio, takes a beer from the cooler on the front seat and opens it on a devise built into the radio consol. I glance at the speedometer. We're doing about 70-75, far too fast in this dense traffic, but he's just keeping up with the flow of traffic, not passing anyone. His radio is up so loud he probably doesn't even hear the siren behind us in the distance. I look out the back window to see whirling red light thrown from the roof of a police cruiser coming up fast behind us. Pedro ignores it without slowing down, and it passes us.

He pulls off the boulevard to negotiate a turn into a neighborhood of shops, kiosks, cantinas and bodegas. I count up to ten more turns before losing track. We are in what is called University City, the Colonia bordering the University of Mexico where Pedro drops us curbside at our destination, the *Café Liberado*. Smiling in recognition of an apparently generous gratuity, he tips his hat and drives off.

Carla and I enter the densely populated interior of the cafe, where the fragrance of bittersweet coffee and the raised, passionately angry voices of students who only recently clashed with police on the campus compete with the sound of clattering dishes and recorded American jazz.

"This is my favorite café," shouts Carla over the noise. "It's a popular spot for writers, intellectuals and students. Movie stars, poets, celebrities, you never know who might show up but you can always count on stimulating conversation. No one is ever bored here. Sometimes famous authors or distinguished visiting university professors arrive unexpectedly. I met Navio here, and through him Francisco, the consul from the Cuban Embassy."

Carla relates the news of a recent melee on campus in which several dozen university students were injured during a demonstration. There is concern that some of the suspected participants who have not been seen since are being held by the police. We navigate past patrons three deep at the bar and squeeze between cramped tables.

"There's Navio," she says. "He's saved us a place."

We maneuver through the crowded tables and chairs to his table, where he and Carla embrace and kiss one another on the mouths. Linda used to kiss me like this, deep and long, with her entire self, all her secrets, all that she was. Sometimes when she came she burst into joyous laughter and showered me with little kisses all over. I do sometimes miss Linda and what we had. I'm celibate but I know she's not, and it still hurts when I think of her with other men.

But I can't allow myself the indulgence of these memories of sexual love. It's too great a threat to my vow of celibacy, which is all I have remaining of my relationship with God. My celibacy may not redeem me or mitigate my sins but it is something. It is a demonstration of faith. Even when my prayers are empty and I feel no

Holy Presence, I have my vow. It validates me. It's what keeps me connected to Jesus and the world of the spirit that hides behind this one.

"This is my friend Raymond from home that I told you about," says Carla.

Navio, movie-star dark and handsome with thick black lustrous hair and expressive dark eyes, wears a neatly trimmed beard. His warm brown eyes are brooding and dreamy. He holds a cigarette in his left hand and wears a tailored suit over a Che Guevara tee shirt. When he shakes my hand his grip is firm and masculine, but welcoming.

"It's a pleasure to meet you," he says. "Please, have a seat."

I'm looking at his beard with envy. I wouldn't have shaved mine if I wasn't so easily manipulated by charming women. It's a problem I have. I let women boss me. In the past I trotted obediently to Linda's commands as domesticated and neutered as a housecat. Navio's beard is neatly trimmed and his hair is clean and neat. His English is articulate in the confident manner of a man who has become entirely at home with it after extensive higher education and time spent in the United States. Much of the ensuing conversation however is in Spanish and I can't follow it, so remain quiet.

A heated discussion at a nearby table has escalated to a degree suggesting a fight will break out at any moment. Am I the only one concerned about this? The debate has become a fist-banging, table-shaking shouting match, but no one but me seems to care or be giving the matter its due attention. Carla and Navio ignore them, chattering with the others at our table. Gesturing in the direction of the argument, I caution them.

"Those men have been arguing since we arrived, and their tone worries me. I think there is going to be trouble."

"It's nothing," assures Navio. "We Mexicans are passionate in our beliefs and love to debate."

"It sounds to me like much more than a debate."

"I assure you it is as I described. A friendly discussion, nothing more. It is not unusual behavior in this café. But welcome. Welcome to my besieged, struggling country. We are exploited by foreign interests, oppressed by corrupt officials, subjected to random police harassment and monitored by illegal surveillance, and yet we resist. We endure. We are Mexican."

He begins introducing me to the others at the table.

"This is Hector, who is studying economics. This is Romero, our sergeant at arms and publicist, and here is our esteemed comrade in arms Sonia Castellana, an exiled soldier of the revolution in Bolivia, now studying history, political science and military tactics at the University. I of course am Navio, guitarist, marksman, student film maker, editor of the besieged student newspaper and member of the Student Revolutionary Council. Please, be my guest. You are welcome here."

Hector gives me small smile that seems genuine and Romero lifts a glass in salute, but Sonia does not acknowledge either Carla or I and seems sullen and disapproving. Dark skinned, with Indian features, a faint scar under her left eye, she's dressed in a camouflage tee shirt, jeans and boots and wears a folded red bandana around her head. Her expression is intensely fierce. I extend my hand and she stares at it briefly before looking away without shaking it.

"Be nice," admonishes Navio. "Carla's friend Raymundo is our guest."

"Sonia does not like Americans," explains Hector.

"Nor would you if you studied your history," replies Sonia to Hector. "But no, you would rather drink and foolishly chirp like a parrot than study history or actively revolt. Talk talk talk like a parakeet, that is all you do. Talk foolishly, smoke marijuana and drink tequila."

Hector gives the impression that our identity as Americans is not particularly important to him one way or the other. As the night progresses, I decide he is mostly indiscriminately happy to be drinking and making conversation. His face is unfortunately pockmarked, but he has a nice smile. Romero regards me with inscrutable silence, as if deciding something about me.

The men at the adjoining table who only a moment ago had been arguing have inexplicably vanished, replaced by a strange man who seems to have materialized out of thin air. The observation is alarming. It is as if the rowdy, boisterous, quarreling men were suddenly vaporized.

But who is this peculiar man who has replaced them and how could he have done so without my noticing? He has a narrow Modigliani-like face and full beatnik style beard that one does not often see in Mexico, and hides behind the most ludicrous dark glasses I have ever seen. He is even more conspicuously out of place than I. In fact, he would look out of place in any context. There is something maddeningly satirical and disconcerting about this man, especially his absurdly oversized dark glasses. His ostentatious disguise is both presumptuous and offensive, because in his attempt to hide himself behind the enormous dark glasses and beard and loose clothing, he has achieved the opposite effect and become preposterously conspicuous.

He stares at me as if it is his sole purpose for being here. It's like he is watching me exclusively. A cup of coffee rests on the table, but he doesn't drink from it. He just stares at me intently. He writes something in a notebook on the table, sets down the pen and resumes watching me. Despite myself I cannot prevent repeatedly glancing in his direction. I begin to question whether I might know him from somewhere, if perhaps the beard and glasses are a recent addition to his appearance and responsible for my failure to recognize him. Maybe he finds me familiar as well, and is studying me in an effort toward recognition and remembrance.

"We must not let petty prejudices come between us," says Navio to Sonia. "Raymundo is to be welcomed as a friend of Carla's who, as you know, is important to our cause."

Sonia glances at me dismissively and glares at Carla with unabashed hatred.

To Navio she says, "She is important to you, not because of our revolution but because you are fucking her. This is why I have lost confidence in your leadership. You are far too trusting."

There is no mistaking that I am the object of the bearded man's attention and he intends for me to know it. The effect is agitating to the degree that I eventually give him a meek little wave hello. He doesn't return it.

"I'm sorry you don't trust me, Sonia, but our revolution is not about personalities and infighting. Here in Mexico mistrust is rampant," Navio says to me as if by way of explanation. "No one is beyond suspicion. Everyone is guilty until proven innocent, and the police act upon the belief that all are guilty of something, whether it can be proven or not. Men are arrested for no apparent reason and held for investigation. Mexico City is dangerous for University students now. We are subject to overt totalitarian fascism and the hysterical fear of communism. Soon we will no longer be able to meet openly as we do now, because as far as the Federales are concerned, to be a student in Mexico City is to be a revolutionary enemy of the government. They fear us because we intend to teach the poor the history and circumstances of their oppression. The government knows we are overdue for a revolution. This is the longest our country has gone in its entire post-Aztec history without one."

"Navio shouldn't even be here," explains Carla to me. "It's dangerous for him."

"*You* shouldn't be here," interrupts Sonia, the remark clearly intended for Carla and me.

Hector, a little drunk, slams his glass down on the table and proclaims, "Mexico is a conquered nation. Exploited Indian laborers make the indulgent lifestyles of the Spanish ruling class possible." It sounds like he is reading from a script.

Sonia regards him with an expression of contemptuous dismissal. Romero pours shots and passes around cigars.

"These are Cubans," he says. "Excellent quality."

Everyone accepts one, including Sonia. Romero lights us all around, and is correct. The cigar is smooth and flavorful. Because of the strange bearded man, I am having difficulty concentrating. If he is deliberately attempting to make me uncomfortable, he is succeeding.

"Indians in Mexico," explains Navio, "are like your Negros, or your own native American Indians, who also are a conquered nation. Here in Mexico, we are subjects of a one-party political system in which there is only the illusion of democracy and for Indians not even that. Here they are called *Los Desdichados*, which means in your language, The Unlucky Ones."

Romero, who has been mostly silent, spits on the floor and

says, "Luck has nothing to do with it. Their misfortune isn't a matter of bad luck; it is systemic because of an unjust political system and a ruling class that has invested in that system at their expense."

Carla excuses herself, pushes away from the table and walks toward the women's room. Sonia glares after her with hatred.

Hector, regarding me with curiosity, asks, "What is your position on this, Raymundo? Do you think Mexico is free, or oppressed by a ruling elite?"

The bearded man at the table slowly removes his glasses and places them on the notebook. His eyes lock on mine, but now that he has removed his glasses and exposed himself to me, I no longer feel at a disadvantage. I am fully prepared to meet his rude attempt at intimidation by staring directly into *his* eyes, until he looks away. But he does not look away. He meets my eyes confidently, without a trace of apprehension. What is more, he does not blink even once. The effect is highly disturbing. It seems impossible that he could stare at me with such uninterrupted intense focus for so great a time without blinking. I look away, lowering my gaze. When I next look up he smiles victoriously and returns the dark glasses to his face.

To Hector I reply, "I apologize for my lack of knowledge regarding the history and politics of your country. Most of my reading has been limited to fiction. The books I have read about Mexico are mostly travel books and works of fiction set in Mexico. I should explain however that I'm probably equally uninformed regarding United States history."

"There are no borders in this discussion, Señor Raymundo. It is not a matter of Mexico or the United States, of your country or mine, but of the rich against the poor. The struggle is global."

"As a follower of Christ it's my duty to care for and protect the poor. It's just that when discussing conditions unique to Mexico I don't know enough to comment."

"You should learn," snaps Sonia. "It is a matter of basic respect. You are in our country. For what purpose? I suspect for the usual. Like most American tourists, you probably regard Mexico as one vast brothel where you can violate our women and celebrate our dismal economy by living cheaply on the exploited labor of Mexican workers."

It is obvious that any reply I might give no matter how politically correct will not satisfy her, but I can't resist defending myself, if not to her then to the others at the table.

"I believe that all conflicts, whether political or personal, are spiritual. The way to eliminate poverty and strife is not through politics, but to follow the example of Christ. We need to let him work through us. We need to find Christ in ourselves and in each other."

Sonia says, "There has never been convincing evidence that Christ even existed. And we don't need to worship a God. History makes clear that if man is made in God's image, then God is cruel."

"It's not God who caused men to be cruel, but man's rebellion *from* God."

"There is no God. There has never been scientific evidence to support such a belief. It's time for mankind to become independent of these childish notions."

"I disagree. The fact is there is recent scientific evidence to support belief in God, but we who believe don't even need it. We know and believe on faith, not physical evidence."

Sonia, declining to answer, spits on the floor and blows cigar smoke in my face.

"This point of view is part of the ideology that keeps us oppressed," she decrees. "It is a control system. As communists, we reject the idea of God. We are atheistic. Mankind must take the place of God."

"You're an atheist, then."

"Of course."

"But atheism takes the cosmological position that there is no God. In this regard, it too is a religion because it is equally based on faith without indisputable scientific evidence. The agnostic is the true unbeliever, because he bases his belief on physical science and reason. Of course agnosticism fails when trying to understand the imperceptible world of spirit behind the material one we can see and measure. If there is no spiritual dimension to reality, what is it that animates matter? Science can't explain it to our understanding. According to recent theoretical physics the universe is a paradox, perhaps even many paradoxes all existing at the same time."

"Whether or not God exists, the church has always operated

in Mexico as a tool of oppression," says Romero.

"I can't speak for or defend the church in Mexico, but I believe in Christ as the savior of mankind. Even if you don't believe in Christ as God made flesh, how do you explain the appearance of an entity who seemed to be perfect, and who changed the entire face of human history and course of civilization? Was he sent here? Was he human or something more? He certainly wasn't like you or me, or anyone before or since."

"Raymundo does not believe as we do because he is not one of us," says Navio. "He is a product of a different culture. No one is to be held accountable for the circumstances of their birth. I tell you without shame that I come from a wealthy, educated family of land owners. It is what a man does after with his life that counts. Take Fidel Castro, for example. He too came from a family of wealth and influence. And Raymundo is perhaps correct to recognize a spiritual reality. My Uncle Pablo, after finishing medical school, suddenly and without explanation disappeared into the jungle of Chiapas where he put himself under the tutelage of a *curandero*. Who knows what spiritual entity compelled him to do this? My grandmother said he was under the influence of *Quetzalcoatl*. What is important for Raymundo to understand is that we already had our God before the arrival of European conquerors with theirs. The ancient ones are still strong here. Christ, if he exists, does not rule exclusively here in Mexico but must compete with powerful ancient Toltec, Mayan and Aztec deities."

"It's all delusion," retorts Sonia. "What Marx defined as the opium of the masses. This foolish American boy saying all we need to save humanity is to be awakened to the spirit of Christ within us is garbage. Why even listen to him? We have heard these lies before. Men are beasts and history has proven Christians the worst of them. You admit do not know history, gringo. You do not know anything. Men rape, murder, plunder and pillage in the name of God because they believe it is their right and they are entitled. The truth is they enjoy it. It is in their nature, what they are."

"I don't accept this, Sonia. We have a conscience to guide us in making a choice between good and evil. Most try to choose a path of goodness."

"You believe as you do because you are a frivolous, pampered American boy who has never, not even for a single day, experienced the world as Latino proletariat masses do every single tedious day of their miserable back-breaking lives, never experienced the slightest hardship. If you were to undergo what my people have, you would not be filled with this childish ideology you dare to carelessly espouse here. But it's easy for you. You can afford your delusions. Anyway I don't believe you are the Christian you say you are. Because your Christian principles have never been tested, you have no right to claim ownership of them. Go work in the fields and try to feed a family on these beliefs and see how long they remain important. Watch your children go hungry, see their bellies swell, their teeth fall out and lice crawl in their hair. Watch them weaken and become sick without medicine. Watch them literally die of poverty. See what results if you picket, strike, protest, or in any way draw attention to the plight of your people. Watch your brothers as they are killed by soldiers who laughingly shoot them in their faces. Watch as your mother and sisters are raped. And don't go to the church during these atrocities. They won't move from their golden thrones to give so much as a centavo to the poor and hungry. They ask *us* for alms when we have nothing. For the poor, the way to salvation is not through religion but through revolution."

"Your point is well taken," says Navio. "On the other hand Raymundo may be onto something when he says political and spiritual conflicts are related. There is a struggle here on Earth between good and evil, and in Mexico it is manifested between the rich and poor. If we are talking in spiritual terms the sin is one of omission when failing to recognize this and take a side. I am not a Christian, but I do regard Christ as a hero of oppressed peoples and the first historical communist. So you see, Raymundo, even Christ, as a Jew in Roman occupied Israel, was a subject of political and spiritual conditions. To be apolitical is an illusion and denial of fact. Here in Mexico it is complicated. Though we may not know or have influence on the hidden spiritual forces that shape history, we act on what is evident. We are a country which has evolved and made what progress it has not by democratic means through our government or prayers in church, but by revolution alone. Revolution is the only politics that has ever brought change in Mexico."

The bearded man at the neighboring table raises his hands and displays his palms so quickly that when he replaces them on the table I can no longer be certain there had been a flash of light emanating from them. Perhaps I only imagined this. His hands are folded on the table now, but a ruby red light that is like a laser beam emanates from a ring on his finger. Am I the only one who sees this? I close my eyes and blink rapidly. What have we been drinking here? What kind of cigars were these? When I look again the man nods at me knowingly. Miniscule sparks emanate from his ring.

"Mexico," says Navio, "has always been a place of conflicting spiritual forces. Quetzalcoatl was once Earth-bound. Death was the portal through which he rose to become immortal. Sacrifice was a means toward immortality. It is well known that here in what is now Mexico City but was once the capital of ancient Azteca, many thousands of captives of war were sacrificed. What is less known is there were men who gave their hearts to the priest's knife voluntarily. These men sought to become Gods. Your Christ also allowed himself to be sacrificed and immortalized. If he was a God, he could easily have saved himself but he did not. He allowed himself to be sacrificed."

"Rubbish," spits Sonia. "Men are not sacrificed to become immortal. They are murdered by puppet regimes supported by the United States. I don't believe in God. I believe in guns. There will be peace on earth only when we have killed every last one of the imperialist oppressors. All you men do here is talk. Meanwhile entire nations await liberation. Revolutionaries are the ones who make the sacrifices you speak of. You are not revolutionaries. You want to be but you are not. You are dilatants, pretenders, privileged students, hypocrites, children of the aristocracy. Which of you has been tested? Who among you has been broken and somehow managed to fight another day? There is no way of knowing if you are brave, if you are true soldiers. I alone among you have experienced the cruelty, the sadism of men. In my country cruelty was common.

"You might be seated at the table with your family. Maybe you are at dinner or at work. You are sleeping, it is the middle of

143

the night, your children are in bed, your lover beside you, and your dreams are pleasant. Then you wake to the stomping of boots up the stairs, the crash of rifle butts against the door. They beat you immediately. You face is made unrecognizable as your weeping family watches helplessly, and when you are a bloody sack of broken bones they drag you away. Your children chase after you, weeping as you are loaded in back of the police van. You see them for the last time.

"A black hood is placed over your face and you are taken across the city to where no one will ever find you. They push you out of the back of the van to the ground and remove the hood from your head. You feel the night air on your face, the gentle caress of wind, and hear the faint singing of birds. You inhale the fragrant blossoms of spring, the sweet odor of blooming bougainvillea, hibiscus and green lawn, and as they lead you into the prison you know that from this moment on none of this will ever again exist for you, nor you for it, because all beauty, all tenderness is to be eliminated. From now on there will be only fear and suffering and the only possible hope or wish that might come true for you is to die quickly.

"You are taken down a dimly lighted corridor where concrete walls and ceiling drip filthy water. There are fetid pools where you walk. Bare light bulbs shine along the narrow passageway, and you can hear someone screaming. They throw you into a windowless room with a cement floor stained with blood and feces, take your clothing and leave you there naked, broken and shivering.

"You lose track of days and nights, of where you are, who you are. Each night they take you down several flights of dark stairs to a large room where a table is set with dental tools, a hand saw, hatchet, and welding torch. There is a chair with restraints for your arms and legs and a bucket of water for your feet. An apparatus that looks like a radio with wires attached to it and an auto battery with jumper cables is nearby.

"They take their time. You beg them to stop, beg them to kill you. You are burned, electrocuted, raped hundreds of time, vaginally, anally, orally. They form a line and take turns. They come in your mouth and in your ass. The men who torture you enjoy it when you are new, but as the weeks pass they become bored with you. You have become so ugly with brutal beatings they no longer want to fuck you, hurt you or even look at you because you have become human garbage. They toss you aside and wait for you to die. If you do not die, they might take you out to be shot. Sometimes you are not even worthy of a bullet. They are confident you are already dead, broken and ruined beyond hope of repair. They push you out of the prison gates and watch you stagger away toward the irreversible damage of what remains of your life. You return to your family. But there is no family. They have disappeared. You know what has happened to them; know from experience what they have endured.

"How strong are you? How ready are you to fight another day? I was tested. I endured, found inner strength and joined the men in the mountains. I took up arms. I have killed men in battle. I shot a man execution style. I cut a man's throat. I dynamited government buildings. I fought for the revolution. But the revolution was betrayed by America. Now I am here in Mexico listening to you whine about oppression when you do not know hunger, do not know torture, and do not know suffering. I am more a man than any of you."

She spits on the table and slams down a shot of mescal.

I am greatly relieved to see Carla approach from the women's washroom. Even dressed down as she is in non-designer blue jeans with a white T-shirt, she is spectacular. She pulls up a chair next to me and takes my hand. Navio is talking now. Several students at tables around us have become quiet to listen to him. It is clear he is a student leader who is much more respected and admired than Sonia, who everyone seems to just fear. The bearded man in the dark glasses does not give the impression of listening to Navio or anyone else. His attention is fixed on me alone.

"That man has been staring at me all night."

"What man?"

He is inexplicably gone, replaced by an obese man wearing dress slacks, a white shirt and suspenders. Two fashionable younger women who might be his daughters and a much younger boy who might be a grandchild are with him.

Navio leans across the table and fills my shot glass. He looks into my eyes and says, "You still have not explained. Why have you come to our country? Carla has in the past tried to explain to me but I do not understand."

"Raymond has come for inspiration," replies Carla. "He's a poet. If he's hard to understand, that is part of the reason why. All poets are probably *un poco loco*, don't you agree? I mean, they tend to live too much in the word and not enough in the world. That is why he may seem to you politically naive."

"Politically naïve, yes, but a little crazy, as you say? I don't think so," replies Navio generously.

I wish I could be as sure. I keep looking over to the neighboring table but the setting is the same, two women, a man and child. No bearded man.

"He is a writer," explains Navio to Carla. "Artists are deeply thoughtful and empathetic men and women who are influenced by social conditions and spiritual events around them. No one can judge them. No one knows where their muse will lead them. Some will even become revolutionaries. Do you know Ernesto de Gomez, Raymundo? He is a famous and important Bolivian poet who left a Jesuit monastery to join the revolution. His poetry is beautiful because of his passion. His belief in his cause and the worth of his vision is absolute. He wears a silver cross, carries a pen and a rifle, and it is said he has used both to further his cause. A writer must have a cause. A writer without a cause is not a writer. The cause is what makes a writer. I think this is why you have come to Mexico, Raymundo. Mexico will lead to the discovery of your cause."

"He has come to fuck our women, exploit the cheap labor, and to assert his entitlement as an American," says Sonia. "*That* is his cause." She abruptly stands, glaring at us with hatred before turning and walking away.

"Try to understand," says Navio. "In her life she has endured great tribulation. But I can tell you this. She is sincere, a true revolutionary. It is not surprising that she resents your lack of attempt to understand the harshness of our oppression or the valor of the Latin American people's struggle. In this she has a point. Recently we have all been encouraged by the success of Fidel Castro in Cuba. I know that he is considered an enemy of your country, but we resent your government's attempt to overthrow him during the failed Bay of Pigs invasion. I think also that your government has implemented a specific propaganda campaign through your media to deliberately misrepresent him and the problems of Latin America in general. "

"I agree," says Carla. "If we had a Castro in America, he would be a national hero. You must read *History Will Absolve Me*, the statement Fidel gave at his sentencing before he was deported to Mexico after his failed first revolution. Do you still have a copy, Navio?"

"Only in Spanish. Promise me you will take Raymundo to the Cuban Embassy. They will give him an English translation there. Will you promise me this, Carlita?"

"I will."

"We will meet again," says Navio. "It has been a pleasure meeting you. I must go now but I suspect you and I will become good friends, Raymundo. Carla tells me that you give more than you can afford to the poor. She says that often you give so much to the beggars you meet in our streets that you go hungry and she has to loan you money or provide food. This shows heart, Raymundo. I admire this gesture, but ask you to understand that it is a gesture only. I appreciate your compassion and sacrifice for our people and believe your heart is right, but you do not understand the depths of our people's suffering or the degree of our problem. In the end, after you have given money to the poor beggar you meet on the street, what has changed? Nothing. He is still poor. Only our way is toward real change. Cuba has been an inspiration to all Latin America. Fidel has given hope to us all that one day, all Latin America will be free of capitalist imperialism. Here in Mexico and on the campus of our University specifically, we begin the transformation of our society. I want you to know that our movement is a people's movement. It is not exclusive, not solely Mexican. Carla is already with us. There is a place for everyone in our revolution. Carla was right about you. Your heart is good. I think if you remain with us, you will become one of us. You will become Mexican."

Is he flattering me or making fun of me?

I'm not sure.

Subjects and Principalities

The sensation of falling out of a dream from a great height wakes me to a silent darkness in which I sense I am being watched. Numerous tiny red lights dart through the room like fireflies. Tracing their flight takes me to the threshold of yet another dream, but then I snap awake again. The lights remain. They are like tiny red eyes spying on me in the darkness. I dare not lose track of them. Following their movement is exhausting. There is a quality in my attempt to track them that approximates rapid eye movement. I feel myself drifting again into a realm very like sleep, but not quite; it is as if the tenuous line between wakefulness and dream has been erased. I don't know; I haven't been here before. Pinpoints of light whirl around the room like frenzied hornets. I can't ignore them and can't close my eyes. I turn on the light switch on the wall. With the overhead light on, the phenomenon vanishes instantly, but now I am wide awake and restless. Something, or someone, is in my room. I have to get out.

I take the elevator to the quiet lobby and step up to the windows, open the lobby doors and step into the night. The silence tonight is a dominion. It is as if in the entire world I am the only one awake, the only one present, every living creature on the planet having evacuated, leaving me alone in a familiar yet utterly strange netherworld. The atmosphere seems subtly transformed, as if the very ground on which I walk has become rarefied, less dense and substantial. My footsteps, much lighter and less grounded than usual, are silent, almost without impact, as if the force of gravity has lifted in imperceptible increments in which I might begin to float slowly away. The air I breathe is a living thing. Each inhalation results in an enhanced sense of my own being.

Accommodating to this new, extraterrestrial atmosphere, my freedom from physical law is exhilarating. I feel psychically enhanced; a wonderful new sense of my own vitality as a sentient human being overcomes me. At the same time, I have the sensation of being not altogether within my own body but, much as the tide of the ocean is affected by the moon, adrift within it, oozing slightly in and out of my insubstantial shape as if influenced by an unseen gravitational force.

Is this still Mexico City or somewhere else? There is no smog cover here. Billions of stars are unusually numerous and brilliant, but viewed as if from a remote planet deep in space unobstructed by ground light. I am like an astronaut, drifting through them. One star in particular is brighter and more focused than the others and somehow peculiar. It seems to address me personally, calling for my attention. I have to close and rub my eyes. When I next open them it appears to have slightly moved position. I can't seem to stop watching it. My eyes begin to water from it.

I blink and look down to the pavement, shielding my eyes, and am engulfed in the center of a brilliance as abrupt and harsh as if I were illuminated in stadium floodlights. I am in the center of this beam and seem to be the momentary subject of its attention. From somewhere within this light, someone, or something, is studying me.

Light beams crisscross tenement buildings, pass over fire escapes, peer in windows and across neighborhood rooftops. Mothers shield their children's eyes and make the sign of the cross for protection. Some, as if warding off evil, hold forth family crucifixes. Men with cameras exit their buildings.

Many thousands of small phosphorescent lights fall like glittering fireflies from the sky. As quickly as the flicker of an eyelid, as fast as speed of thought, they renew themselves. They are like the lights I saw in my room earlier. They have fragmented into billions of dancing, weaving particles, making concentric circles and falling spirals. It is as if they are writing something in the sky with their movement. They merge, becoming a single pulsating ball of vibrating color. We are suspended inert in timelessness. We look into the sky, as still and silent as Easter Island statues.

* * *

I don't expect you to believe this. I can only report my experiences, not explain them. Maybe you think I am mentally unstable. I am not. Maybe you are. Maybe you think I was dreaming. If so what if anything does that clarify or explain? Dreams are not what you think they are. They are real. I should know. I almost died in one.

I was pursued by a grotesque drooling childhood monster that devoured young children. I ran from this horrifying creature as fast as my young legs would carry me, but always running in place, without making progress. Every night in my sleep this creature attacked me, its extended talon-like claws and wet glistening teeth ready to tear me to pieces and eat me. Each nightmare ended exactly the same. I escaped at the last moment by leaping off a cliff. My mother had told me I would wake before I hit the ground, and I always did.

But one night, unable to conjure the usual dreamscape precipice from which I leapt to wakefulness, it seemed certain this time I would die here, in this dream landscape. Then a psychic shift took place in which I was still asleep but knew within the dream I was dreaming. As if to verify the correctness of this, I willed my usual cliff-side escape into existence and stood at its precipice, back to the wind and the abyss. The monster that had hunted me for most of my childhood prepared to tear my psychic flesh into shreds of edible meat, its extended icepick claws glittering like daggers in the cruel dreamscape moonlight. I knew this would be a fight to the death and was ready.

I beat this creature mercilessly. It crumpled at my feet pitifully, begging for leniency. I dragged it to the edge of the cliff and threw it off. I heard it scream until its voice had become a diminishing whimper. I never dreamed of it again.

An event of profound consequence that would alter my life had taken place, but more importantly had been accomplished not while awake, but within a dream, which was the only way it *could* be accomplished. I understood the dream and its outcome to be a psychic and spiritual victory, but not yet the responsibility and challenge that came with it. I did not yet know, as I would learn later, that dreams are not exclusively a safe haven. The outcome of my repetitive nightmare could have been much different. Dreams do not guarantee safety or a successful outcome and can be dangerous. Not all dreamscape visitors are benevolent, and some hate us and want to destroy us. I needed protection.

In early adolescence I found it, and began dreaming of Christ. He did not speak to me so much as demonstrate his beauty and suffering with his presence. He had the most beautiful eyes I have ever seen. Somehow, it was difficult to look at him directly without crying. I was not yet a Christian, but I believe these dreams were guiding me toward Christ. As the years went on I dreamed of Him numerous times.

Once I dreamed that I was crucified. I was placed on a cross that lay on the ground while soldiers nailed spikes through my wrists and ankles. The gathering crowd cheered joyously through my screams. The cross was then hoisted and I faced the cruel bright sky and saw God in the sunlight. I wept happily. It was a triumphant moment of beauty and death. It was wonderful to be crucified like Christ, to vicariously experience his love and suffering.

I dreamed that I was sent by Angels into an astral realm to rescue a child from a sorceress. I swam through an inky darkness into an alternate dimension and then to a distant ringed planet lighted by three blood- orange moons. A psychic battle for the child ensued in which I emerged victorious.

I returned with the rescued child cradled in my arms. I fell through multiple astral layers to earth where I landed on an auditorium stage. Hundreds of robed adepts rose from their auditorium folding chairs and applauded my arrival.

I don't know what dreams are. I don't know where they are taking place. In my dreams I return again and again to a landscape and people unknown to me in my waking life, to cities where the foreign languages spoken are as familiar to me as my native tongue, cities that I have never seen while awake. I reunite with friends and lovers and dream-time relatives who have no connection with me in the life I know as "mine." Where are we? Who are they? Who am I?

* * *

"Wake up," says Ricardo. "The lobby is not for sleeping. You have a room for that purpose. Besides, you were snoring and talking in your sleep and disturbing other residents who were reading the morning paper and trying to enjoy their day."

I'm sitting in the hotel lobby on a cushioned chair facing the windows. I seem to have been drinking take-out coffee because there is an empty paper cup in my hand and a newspaper spread out across my lap. Though the lobby is empty, the presence of earlier tenants is evidenced by scattered empty coffee containers, discarded newspapers, overflowing ashtrays, and discarded unfinished pastries.

"I had the strangest dream," I reply. "At least I think it was a dream. It was one of those that seem so real you're not sure. Were there lights in the sky last night?"

He gives my foot a kick with his shoe and says, "Go to bed, Raymond. I think maybe you are *borracho*."

"What's borracho mean?"

"It means drunk. When you sleep your mouth hangs open and you drool."

"Thanks for notifying me of that, Ricardo. In the future I'll try to stuff my mouth with rags."

It's raining outside. People briskly pass the streaked lobby windows. Many carry umbrellas or hold newspapers over their heads against the rain. I have no plans, having decided it is a good day to remain indoors, do some reading and write in this journal. Maybe I'll write about the dream I had last night.

On my lap the newspaper's lead story is of rioting on the campus of the University, where there has been another student confrontation with the police. There are several photos of the melee. It looks pretty chaotic, with numerous fires, clouds of tear gas, mounted riot police and hailstorms of Molotov cocktails and other projectiles.

I have all but forgotten about Ricardo when, sneering, he points at the newspaper and says, "Some revolutionaries. They are clowns. I don't know whether to pity them or condemn them. If these students are the future of Mexico, then there is no hope.

They are hypocrites who should experience torture and jail. Then, if they survived, I might respect them."

His remark, oddly reminiscent of Sonia in tone, offends me.

"You should applaud these students, Ricardo. Unlike you, they have a cause greater than their own personal gain. They love this country and are your true patriots."

Ricardo wags his finger in my face and says, "They are like spoiled children with their games of politics and revolution. What do they know of our lives, the lives of the workers? They don't even work. They don't have to. Their families are wealthy. They know nothing of hardship, struggle or the people they claim to champion. Do you have any idea how much it costs to attend the University, or how out of reach it is for someone like me? They are the privileged children of the elite. The people they claim to liberate by their ineffective gestures of protest are in reality their personal servant class. And they are not my *true patriots*, as you erroneously and inarticulately declared. I am not Mexican. I am Cuban. I would not even be in Mexico if it were not for Fidel's betrayal of our own revolution, which forced a communist dictatorship upon the very people who fought for freedom and democracy."

He turns on his heels and strides back to his place behind the check-in desk where he begins sorting mail, throwing it into slots. Ignoring my better judgment and inner prompting to the contrary, I can't leave it alone. I approach him at the desk

"What is it about us, Ricardo, that whenever we attempt conversation we end up in a disagreement?"

"It's not important."

"I know that you don't like me, and I don't know why."

"You insist on encroaching on the boundaries of our circumstances. You are doing it now. Why complicate the situation with your American class consciousness and false sense of social equality? But I will tell you something. I do not dislike you despite what you may think. In fact, you rather intrigue me. You are not like other American tourists we have had here. But those protesters at the University want us to strike, and all we want is to work. But it's not new, this revolution. I have already experienced one in Cuba, and the demonstrations at the University have been going on for a long time, since before I came here. It's the same old story. I left my country and my home and still nothing has changed."

He leaves me to my newspaper, but it's a jigsaw puzzle of words I cannot put together despite my much improved Spanish because my tired mind will not cooperate. The effort fatigues me and I fall asleep again.

When I wake a man has pulled up a chair and is seated across from me so closely that his knees are touching mine. He stares at me with an expression so startling that I jump out of my chair to a standing position. Had my hair been able to comically stand up on end in fright, it might have. The newspaper falls to the floor.

He picks it up, places it on the table and says, "Please. Sit down. Ricardo tells me that you are an American. I thought I might introduce myself."

"We've met. You were in the restaurant last night. You kept staring at me. You were quite rude. Why are you following me? What do you want? Who told you that I was staying here, at the Hotel La Paz? "

"I'm sorry, but I think you may have confused me with someone else. I assure you, we have not met before."

He removes his rimless glasses to his pocket. He still wears the beard, but differently now, trimmed more in a Fu Manchu style. The dark glasses are gone. His manner of dress is different than it was in the restaurant too; he's wearing an out of date baggy suit with a white shirt, thin black tie and black oxford shoes and carries an attorney's attaché case.

"You kept staring at me in what seemed a deliberate attempt to intimidate me. It was at one of the restaurants near the University."

"I'm sorry, but this is not possible. I only arrived here in Mexico City this morning. See for yourself. I still have the airline boarding pass dated accordingly in my pocket."

It seems impossible for two men sharing his unique appearance to so much as walk the earth at the same time, much less in the same geographical location. If only he would just tell the truth it would be far less intimidating. And now there is a spherical flash of red light from the ring on his hand; it is not the reflective light off the facet of a jewel so much as an actual light beam. I remember it from before, when he was in the restaurant.

"I don't believe you."

He puts his hands in his pockets and takes them out again, his raised palms facing me. They flash like a neon light suddenly turned on and off. But it is only for an instant. Then again. All this happens so quickly that I cannot be sure of what I am seeing. Am I imagining this? The room in which we sit appears to blink. Twice. Is this even possible? In the corner of my eye I see the flicker of one of the red lights that had been flying around in my hotel room earlier. It bounces off the wall behind Ricardo at the desk and flickers across the ceiling. From there it begins flying around him madly, with such speed that I cannot altogether follow its movement. Can't Ricardo see this? Apparently not. It has just spun circles around him from head to foot.

"Who are you? What do you want from me?"

"I am Doctor Omar Mauk, an investigator of psychic and supernatural phenomenon. I'm here because of the lights you saw last night."

He blinks in and out of focus and seems to emit a faint, highly pitched, barely perceptible sound reminiscent of a hummingbird. Tiny red points of light swim around his face in an orbit so highly accelerated that it cannot be verified. The thought occurs to me that only when time is manipulated in this manner, slowed down to a lower vibratory range, does it becomes possible to outmaneuver immutable laws of physics and instantaneously transit from one location in the dimensional continuum to an adjoining one.

"Correct," says the bearded man. "But you will forget this because you are a human. Your mind is composed entirely of organic tissue. Well, that's oversimplifying. There are no "pure" humans anymore. All Earthlings, without their knowing, have been assimilated. You are all bionic to a degree. We should know. We designed you."

But did I even say anything? I'm floating along hundreds of flights of stairs. A door is opened to the sky and I feel the crisp morning air on my face. I hear the heartbeat of a city, an ocean of human voices and the mechanical mantra of machines. Above us is the passage of a silver jet airliner. Am I dreaming this? I hear automobiles and distant music. A chill in the air brings goose bumps to the surface of my bare arms. I'm shivering slightly. The flat roof on which we stand is bordered by a protective wall. I can hear the sound of windblown shirts and pants snapping fiercely on a clothesline. Several large wash basins are nearby. A black tomcat darts from out of the shadows. I stumble awkwardly in an attempt to prevent tripping over it. Something smells unpleasantly chemical, like burning wire. It is no longer raining and the sky is filled with holes.

"What are they?" I ask.

"Portals. Through them we leave and reenter this dimension."

"This isn't real. You aren't real. I must be dreaming this."

"Maybe there is no reality. Or maybe there are multiple. Whether or not this is a dream is irrelevant."

Beyond is the canopy of jungle, panthers prowl in search of living meat. Terrified shrieking monkeys leap through a canopy of jungle trees. Hundreds of startled birds rise from the branches, their flutter of wings thunderous. The earth itself trembles. I hear the swollen metronomic pulse of a single drumbeat, the heartbeat of Tenochtitlan. Through the canopy of forest, the peaks of several pyramids are visible. "Señor Watson, wake up, wake up!"

It's Ricardo. I'm on the couch in the lobby. It's broad daylight outside.

"You have been dreaming and shouting in your sleep," he says. "You have a telephone call." He hands me the receiver and says, "It is from that woman, Carla."

Her tone is sharp and accusatory. She sounds annoyed with me.

"Where are you, Raymond? You're supposed to meet me at the café, remember? I'm here now, waiting for you. Did you forget? We're going to the Cuban consulate today."

The Cuban Problem

The Embassy is located on a tree-lined street in a quiet residential neighborhood far from the city center. I would not be here today had Carla not indicated a willingness to reciprocate by attending church with me at an as yet unspecified date. Both she and Navio are out to convert me to Castro's version of National Socialism, which they insist is closer to Christ's teachings than what is practiced by the church. They are mistaken about this of course. Christ is the only way to peace and justice in the world.

Behind the high whitewashed stucco walls, the main wing of the hacienda is situated on the crest of a sloping lawn. Too distant and expensive for a cab, we have had to take three city busses to get here. We are cleared by the first set of guards and admitted through the front gates to an expansive freshly mowed lawn. A colonnade of trees flanks both sides of a wrap-around driveway leading to a parking area where limousines are parked. A ten-foot fountain spews foaming jets of water into a wide circular pond abundant with lazy exotic fish. Gardeners tend a succession of strategically placed flower beds in a series of moist gardens. Hedges are clipped to a uniform length.

A moderate breeze carries the scent of honeysuckle, grass, jacaranda, and hibiscus. Carla tells me about servant's quarters to the rear of the grounds beyond the tree line, adding there is even a small stable on this spacious, immaculately manicured landscape. The servants here, says Carla, are paid a fair wage, their children sent to private schools and given a trust fund for higher education. Most of the laborers are Mexican but many of the workers assigned to the Embassy are employed here from Cuba, rewarded for their service as soldiers for the revolution. They and their families live in the compounds in back.

Wide stone steps lead to the massive embassy front doors guarded by two rifle-bearing uniformed soldiers. Our identification and purpose verified, we are admitted into a central lobby where splendorous overhead chandeliers send pinpoints of light dancing on gleaming polished floors. The opulence of the Embassy is in my opinion representative of communist elitist hypocrisy. If you want a picture of true socialism at work, look at the life and teachings of Christ. Oh, I know the argument: Look at the Pope for an example of an opulent life style. Look at the Vatican for wealth and power. Look at the Inquisition for an illustration of Christian love in action. I know, I know. We live in a broken, fallen world. I don't need to be reminded of that. I am an example of it, as are you.

Carla, wearing sandals, is dressed in a loose Mexican skirt with a low-cut white peasant blouse. She carries a large woven Mexican bag while leading the way through the complex interior with the confidence of someone well acquainted with it. We are met by yet another soldier, this one wearing crisp military slacks and formal matching jacket with a holstered pistol belted over his shoulder, who greets her by name and then escorts us down a rear hallway to a large furnished room with a massive oak desk, comfortable couch, matching leather chairs and a small bar area. I see a carafe of water, several crystal glasses, and a decanter of what might be dark rum. Two small moving cameras positioned along the crown molding at opposite sides of the ceiling monitor our presence.

After a brief wait we are met, to my surprise, not by an adjunct but the consul himself, a tall, handsome, immaculately groomed man perhaps in his middle thirties. His neatly trimmed black hair is combed straight back and jelled perfectly in place. His clean white shirt is starched and crisp, his dark blue suit tailored to his trim physique. He knows he is good looking, knows he is in command. His hands are particularly elegant, with the manicured nails and long fingers of a concert pianist. Contrary to what Carla has told me about him, it's hard to imagine this man once crawled on his belly while carrying a rifle through steaming mosquito and snake infested swamps in the jungles of Cuba as a soldier of the revolution.

He takes Carla's hands in his with obvious fondness and says, "Carlita, my dear, what a pleasure to see you again. You are enduringly beautiful. If Diego Rivera were alive today, he would want to paint you."

Still holding her hands, he kisses them, then places them on his heart. Is this a Latin custom? This is hardly the officious greeting I expected, and it surprises me. It's corny in my opinion, but I can tell Carla loves it. She is near to swooning. I'm ambivalent and judgmental. I am not unaware that this man represents a nation hostile to the United States government.

"We have missed you," says the consul.

"I've been busy with my courses at the University but in good spirits and good health."

"I understand you and Navio both are doing important organizing at the University."

"Navio is still organizing, both at the University and in the factories. I less so. I'm here to introduce you to my friend, Raymond Watson. He wants to learn more about Cuba and the revolution. I want to get him started with Fidel's *History Will Absolve Me*."

"And that is an excellent place to begin. It's a pleasure to meet you Mr. Watson. May I call you Raymond?"

"Of course."

"And you may call me Francisco. Where is your home in the United States, Raymond?"

"A small northern suburb of Seattle, Washington."

"Ah, yes. The great Pacific Northwest. Nordic in appearance and mood, with many islands floating in the sea."

"In Puget Sound, yes."

"The Cascade Mountain Range. The Olympics. Gigantic fir and evergreen, their limbs bent with the weight of snow. Trees not indigenous to our tropical climate, suited more for a race of giants than men."

"Your description does it poetic justice. I couldn't describe it better myself. How do you know this?"

"I briefly attended the University of Washington, but when the revolution needed me, returned to Cuba. Now of course I cannot return because our countries have no diplomatic relations. It's a pity, because although our two nations are enemies, perhaps not our people. I believe we share a common sense of justice and the will to be free, a mutual appreciation of art, literature and music and, of course, baseball. Are you a baseball enthusiast, Raymond?"

"I'm not really a sports enthusiast generally, though when I was a boy I loved the game, played it and watched it on TV."

"And now that you are a man, Raymond, what is it that has replaced your love of baseball."

"God."

"You are a priest? A missionary perhaps?"

"I'm a believer and follower. A disciple of Christ."

"The man of character must at some time in his life reconcile with a truth greater and more important than himself. For you it is God. For us it is History and man's struggle against those who oppress him. What is it that you do in the United States, Raymond? How do you survive economically in a capitalist system?"

"Not very well, I'm afraid."

"Have you no skills?"

"I'm a writer, if that counts."

"In my country it counts for much. In yours, not so much. But either way it is a noble endeavor. What do you write? Are you a journalist or another kind of writer?"

"I write fiction mostly."

"Anything I might be familiar with?"

"Nothing you would know. I'm unpublished."

"This does not surprise me. Your country does not value fiction. Your authors are given recognition only if they generate large sums of money, or are already famous. The value of the work itself is determined not by the nobility of its intent, its effort or literary quality, but by the capital it produces. The actual process of communicating ideas of importance or creating a thing of beauty, this is of itself unimportant in your country, where literature is a commodity like chewing gum or laundry detergent. Art in your country is subject to what Lenin perceptively termed the cult of personality. What is revered in your country is not literature, music, or a work of art based on its own merit, but celebrity.

"Our writers are supported by the government. We nurture,

encourage, and subsidize them because we consider literature important. Everyone in Cuba writes poetry. Even Fidel writes an occasional poem, and of course his speeches have the cadence of the best poetry. You are probably aware that Hemingway wrote his masterpiece *The Old Man and the Sea* in our country?"

The telephone rings and the consul politely excuses himself.

"Miss Johansen is here, yes," he says into the phone. "Please bring the documents I requested. The English translation, yes, but also the other document. Thank you."

A female official wearing high black boots, military slacks and a loose blouse enters. Almost imperceptibly, the consul nods and she presents the documents and leaves. Left on the consul's desk is an English document but also an additional manila envelope stamped with a red star and lettering that looks Russian. The consul, briefly meeting my eyes, slides both into a desk drawer.

"Are you a Socialist, Raymond, as was Christ?"

"Christ the first socialist. I've heard that argument before. There is probably some theoretical basis for it but I don't think Christ was political. Render unto Caesar and all that."

"And you, Raymond? Do you render unto Caesar? Do you have a political ideology? In today's world, it is necessary. Either you represent freedom and equality for all men, or you do not."

"I represent nothing. I'm apolitical."

"Then you are an anarchist."

"You misunderstand. I simply do not have a political position."

"Everyone, Mr. Watson, has a political position, whether they care to acknowledge it or not. At the very least, everyone is subject to one. We are all part of a larger system. One's destiny, one's lot in life, is based on political realities. I appreciate your interest in Cuba. If only your government was as open-minded as its citizens. Are you aware that when Fidel first came to your country after the Revolution, he was accorded nothing in the way of the official diplomatic greeting or recognition due a great heroic leader and head of state of an independent nation? He was ridiculed in your press, which declined to interview him regarding his ideology, leadership, or aspirations for Cuba. They ridiculed his beard and rumpled fatigues while posting pictures of the remains of the chicken dinner taken in his hotel room. Editorials reported he picked the bones clean with his hands, that he wiped his mouth and beard with his sleeve, as if he was merely an uncouth, undisciplined, uneducated peasant guerilla soldier instead of the great educated liberator that he was. They mocked his appearance, his beard, army fatigues, even his cigars, perpetuating a racial stereotype insulting to not only a great world leader but an entire nation. This was a great affront to Fidel and to Cuba, but also a disservice to your own countrymen who deserve to know the truth about Cuba's revolution.

"This document, titled *History Will Absolve Me*, is a good starting place. The text consists of a speech given by Fidel and spontaneously recorded at his trial, at the time of his sentencing after the failure of his first revolution, just prior to his deportation and exile here in Mexico. The court recorder who made this document available was converted during Fidel's speech. It is the narrative of a true patriot and hero to the working class. Fidel loved his country, his people. He was a man of compassion, a man of purpose. It is Love, of course, that inspires men to great deeds and acts of heroism. But one needs a method. Love alone will not feed the world's hungry. Prior to our revolution, ninety percent of our natural resources were foreign owned. Fidel was not just fighting Batista and the puppet government in Havana, but powerful American corporate interests in the countryside such as our coffee and banana plantations, which were controlled by United States corporations. In Havana the Mafia owned all of the casinos. Cuba owned nothing. Among Cubans, only Batista and his family profited from the labor of Cuban workers. The world is governed by political and economic decisions that affect us all. Many of them are covert, immoral and illegal. Take Operation Mongoose, a CIA sponsored operation designed to overthrow Castro and the government of Cuba and ultimately control Latin American politics. The failed Bay of Pigs invasion was but one small component of it."

Where's a bathroom? I have to splash some cold water in my face. I'm falling asleep here. Is he finished? No, he goes on and on. God give me strength. He is a word machine, but the words are memoranda, recitations that do not engage. Carla looks like she wants to eat him for lunch. She's obviously crazy about him. My God, what a windbag. He goes on and on, a tape loop of political propaganda that never runs out. I'm bored and angry.

"At this very moment your government is training soldiers in Panama to prepare for yet another invasion. Why? What has the most powerful nation on Earth to fear from Cuba, a small, impoverished, struggling island-nation of banana and coffee farmers and poor fishermen that wishes only to be free to fulfill its own destiny? We are a poor land, a poor nation, and yet your government wants what little we have. And yet we have faith in the American people. We believe that if they knew of their government's covert activities in Latin America, they would oppose them. Read this document of Fidel's famous speech; read a history of Cuba from our point of view instead of the propaganda of your capitalist press. It is my hope that when you return to the United States, you will tell your people the truth about Fidel and Cuba. Tell them that contrary to what your government and press would have you believe, we love Fidel and love our revolution and how it is transforming our society."

The consul rises and extends his hand, which I reach across the desk to shake. His grip is assertive and decisive, masculine but without being aggressive. Is our meeting over? My hopes rise.

"It has been a pleasure meeting you, Raymond. And you, Carlita, do not stay away so long. I have missed you. I apologize to you both that I must adjourn our meeting so abruptly. Unfortunately, I have another obligation."

He comes around from behind the desk.

"It has been a pleasure meeting you, Raymond. Cuba wishes only to remain free and independent of American political intervention. We welcome inquiring, open-minded Americans who want to learn more about Cuba. It is your country, not ours, that forbids travel to Cuba. It is your country, not ours, that conducts covert operations around the world. We are proud of our country, of our Revolution. We believe that all men are brothers, and dream of a day when all can work together for economic and social justice."

Carla and the consul now converse in Spanish. Why the switch? They're talking too fast for me to assemble their Spanish phrases into a coherent narrative. I catch a few Spanish phrases, words here and there. I am being excluded, apparently. Carla doesn't reciprocate my eye contact and in fact seems to avoid it. The consul opens the desk drawer containing the Castro manuscript and hands it to Carla, who drops it into her oversize bag. But did he also include the document with red Russian lettering? I can't be certain, but I thought I saw a glimpse of it, under the Castro document. The Consul kisses her fleetingly on both cheeks and whispers something in her ear. She smiles demurely but her face is flushed. I believe there are secrets here, untold stories. When they embrace, it is more than the customary gesture of fond farewell, but from my perspective is more closely the embrace of conspirators and lovers.

Outside the main doors of the building, it's a beautiful sunny day. Beyond the compound walls, the glare of bright daylight reflects off the roofs of parked automobiles beyond the gates. Carla retrieves her dark glasses from her bag as we descend to the courtyard below. We pass through the main gates to a scramble of photographers exiting the side doors of a black unmarked van. We are temporarily blinded by the flashbulbs of their cameras. It is as if we are famous movie stars and they are paparazzi. There are probably a half-dozen of these photographers. Hiding her face from the cameras, Carla takes my hand and begins running.

"Quickly," she shouts.

We run to the end of the block, which is long and slightly inclined. Breathless we turn the corner. Doubled over, I begin to get my wind back.

"What was that all about?"

"It was the Americans," she explains. "The CIA takes pictures of everyone who enters and leaves the embassy. No telling what they do with them all."

On the Street of the Musicians

Hours later we sit under the shade of umbrellas at a sidewalk table on The Street of the Musicians in Garibaldi Square. Wearing elaborate costumes consisting of traditional enormous sombreros, embroidered black and silver spangled vests and matching pants with high black boots, strolling Mariachi musicians serenade diners at their tables. Their instruments consist of guitars and trumpets and the music has a ¾ waltz feel oddly reminiscent of polka, but with greater drama and sadness. The songs are beautiful but sorrowful and fated. The afternoon is breezy with conversation, tequila, and music.

"The Polka came to Mexico through Emperor Maximillian," explains Carla. "Mexico made it its own and transformed it. But like the Polka, much of this music is in ¾ time."

She orders beers for us both and pushes the English translation of Fidel Castro's speech across the table.

"This English copy is for you, Ray. It's a version I'm proud to say I helped translate, mostly improving on an earlier, less accurate translation. One of my professors at the University knew I needed to make some extra money. He introduced me to Francisco and I signed a contract and was given an advance. It was during the process of translating the document that I became a Fidelista. Until I came to Mexico and met Navio, I was like you. I had no idea of how American foreign policy contributed to the oppression and suffering of Latin America."

"I thought you had said it was Navio who introduced you to the Consul."

"No, you are mistaken. It was not Navio."

"But I'm sure you said it was Navio."

"I said no such thing, Raymond."

"Either way, Navio's activism concerns me. I worry that he will bring you trouble. This isn't the United States, Carla. The laws are different here. It's dangerous."

"Yes, but one has a responsibility to be brave, Raymond. History is an evolutionary process. We have a responsibility toward the many thousands of heroic men and women who sacrificed and suffered prison, torture and execution to bring positive change for the rest of us."

"And you see Navio as one of these heroes."

"Not exactly, though he would like to be. Navio is sincere, but I think he is not a genuine revolutionary like Francisco, or even Sonia, for that matter. Navio wants to be a hero and make sacrifices for his people, but he hasn't been tested and it bothers him that there is no active revolution in which he can be brave. He has been arrested and interrogated, but his father is rich and always rescues him while others are sent to prison. Navio resents it. He wants to be a genuine guerilla, to make an authentic sacrifice for his country. Navio needs a revolution for reasons that are personal, not solely for the political reforms needed by peasants. Sometimes I wonder to what extent his politics are not in some small part a reaction against his father, a rich landowner and powerful influential man with thousands of acres of plantations in Oaxaca. I met him once. He was rather intimidating. His mother, on the other hand, is part Indian and is from Columbia. His family is diverse. I think Navio has a bright future. I think in time, if there is no armed struggle in which he can prove his manhood to himself, his romance with revolution will pass. If there is no revolution, I think Navio will probably run for office one day and be a member of the government, though he would be angry to hear me say it. Not this government of course, but a future opposition party. He has high ambitions. Now Francisco, however, he actually fought in the jungle and mountains alongside Fidel and Che."

"And you admire that."

"Of course. Francisco is a real man, a true hero."

"Are you in love with him?"

"I didn't say that."

"You didn't have to. You were like a swooning schoolgirl."

"I most certainly was not! And you sound jealous."

"Not jealous, just surprised. I can't believe you are involved with communists and in the planning of a revolution. It frightens me."

"It's not a revolution, Raymond, not in its present form, anyway."

"What, then?"

"It's mostly student planned demonstrations and organizing labor strikes in the factories. I sympathize with the revolutionists, but unless they can overthrow the government with words, there isn't going to be any revolution here in Mexico because with the students it's all just rhetoric and University politics for the most part. Most of the students don't care about the workers as much as they want a real education, not just propaganda. University officials, in cooperation with the government, have been attempting to control curriculum. They've shut down the student newspaper and are trying to oust leftist professors and eliminate courses they consider radical. The government is afraid of an educated proletariat class. There is talk of organizing workers for a nationwide general strike, but it probably won't happen. People here are too poor and too frightened to strike, and the jackbooted Federales are too harsh and eager to arrest and brutalize them. I'm no soldier, but if there is a strike, I will march."

"What about Sonia? I'm not sure if she welcomes your participation."

"Sonia is genuine. No one really knows where she came from originally, but she has lived in Bolivia, Ecuador, Venezuela and Cuba. She's different from Navio and the rest of us. She wants a unification of all Central and South America under a communist led regime and has no scruples about the means to bring it about. Her loyalty is not to Mexico but to world communism, and I think in her heart she is a Stalinist. She is genuinely dangerous. I think even Navio is afraid of her. She hates me, and trusts no one. She and Navio were once lovers. I came between them."

An overweight, well-dressed drunk has collapsed in his chair, knocking several shot glasses and bottles of beer to the ground at his feet. He kicks them into the street and calls for a waiter.

"Bring me another tequila," he says in slurred English. "And mucho pronto." His accent is American.

"Our quintessential Ugly American," whispers Carla. "Is it any wonder Sonia hates us so? I don't blame her. I despise drunks and especially drunken American tourists."

"Just ignore him, Carla. I have to ask you something. At the Embassy, when the consul gave you the Castro document, it seemed surreptitious. I had the impression another document was hidden underneath the Castro papers."

"What other document?"

"The one with Russian writing stamped in red. I saw you put it in your bag when you received the Castro document. And then you immediately switched from English to Spanish. I had the impression you deliberately didn't want me to understand what you and the Consul were saying. You're not working with the Cubans on anything covert are you, Carla?"

"What exactly are you asking, Raymond? Are you inquiring as to whether I am a spy?"

"I wondered about it, frankly."

"That's a delightfully imaginative idea. So romantic and intriguing. Carla Johansen, international double agent. Well, we all have our secrets, don't we? You, for example. I haven't wanted to bring it up because I was hoping you would tell me about it on your own, but you haven't told me how you ended up in jail. Is it true what they say?"

"What do they say?"

"The story is you stalked and assaulted your high school girlfriend."

"It wasn't like that."

"I saw the newspaper clippings. They were horrific. You were convicted of assault, trespassing and voyeurism."

"There was a restraining order against me and I broke it. I threw a stone that had a poem wrapped around it through Linda's window. The window shattered and the shards of glass became imbedded in her cheek, nose and forehead and had to be surgically removed with tweezers. The photographs made it look worse than it really was. Linda was taking a lot of aspirin for headaches. The aspirin acted as a blood thinner, so she bled heavily. Her dad took sensational bloody pictures for the police report and sent copies to the newspaper, which made me out to look like an assassin. The editor printed them gladly. He was a golf friend to her father. So was the prosecuting attorney, for that matter. I didn't have a chance. I represented myself in court and got a year in the county jail."

"You must have been very afraid. A young, pretty boy like you in jail with hardened criminals."

"It wasn't like that. Most of the inmates were young kids who had made mistakes like me. There were a few career criminal types there, but they were mostly waiting to be transferred to maximum security penitentiaries and didn't mix with us. You learn that things aren't always as they seem in jail."

"So you weren't afraid."

"I was in the beginning. During the first few days I only felt safe in my cell. I was suspicious of everyone. I thought of them as criminals. I hadn't yet learned that I was a criminal too. I learned that later, in therapy. I hope I'm a better person now."

"I'm sure you are."

"I'm trying. I'm working on it. With God's help."

"God again. How the peasants of Mexico love their God. It's too bad he doesn't love them in return."

"But he does."

"The evidence is to the contrary. I could show you, take you to the slum beyond the city, or to the dump where indigent scavengers sift through enormous piles of garbage discarded by the rich. I could take you to the fields of hard labor where natives who love God as much as you work like mules tending crops they can't afford for themselves in return for a wage insufficient to put food on the table or pay their rent. If there is a God he has abandoned them."

"I've been to some of those places. There was love there too. A poor little girl living on the outskirts of the dump tried to give me a baby chick."

"And where do you suppose she is today? What do you suppose has become of her?"

"My point is that love is everywhere."

"But it is not a gift from God, Raymond. We create it. It is not

Divine, but part of our humanity."

A taxi arrives for the drunken American who had fallen earlier, but he waves it away and insists on still another tequila. The waiter at his table apologetically informs his patron that he has been cut off. The drunk objects with a string of curses, stands and wobbles unsteadily on his feet, his fists clenched threateningly. Management arrives promptly with two husky men wearing aprons and cook's hats, both carrying meat cleavers. The drunken man pays his bill and staggers to the cab. Carla lights cigarettes for both of us. I have not smoked in over a week and the cigarette makes me dizzy. I'm always quitting and starting again. It's a disgusting, dirty habit. I put it out in the ashtray and reach for Carla's hand.

"Come to church with me this Sunday."

She withdraws her hand from mine as if I had burned it.

"You persist in asking me this, and you know I don't want to."

"I kept my promise to you, Carla. I came to the Embassy and listened to that windbag communist hero of yours. You owe me. I'm not asking you to give your life to Christ, just to come to church with me one time. I don't understand your objection."

"I've explained this to you before. My attendance would be disrespectful. I wouldn't belong. I don't believe in God. There's too much suffering for that. It's like when Sonia says if there is a God he has created us to suffer. Sonia says there is no heaven, but there is a Hell, and it's Earth."

"And you agree with this?"

"Personally, I don't believe in hell in the punitive, biblical sense. I don't believe in God period. I already told you that. But I understand how she might feel that way."

"I know there is suffering and injustice. This is a fallen world, but you have to keep faith even when don't see or feel it, even during those times when in your heart you don't believe it."

"I believe man must save himself, not wait for God's mercy. Men must work together. I'm a humanist. Religion is not a solution, but a problem."

The strolling Mariachis, who have not stopped playing and singing since our arrival, now end an upbeat song and bow expansively. Applauding, snapshot-taking tourists enthusiastically reward their open guitar cases with a scattering of peso notes and coins. In my opinion a tape recorder would provide better documentation here than a camera. The musicians begin another song, a ballad.

"These are not ordinary love songs like at home," says Carla. "This music pays homage to the hardship of people's lives here. Because they reflect the lives of Mexican men and women, these songs recognize the inevitability of fate. You are listening to one of the best Mariachi bands in Mexico City. These musicians are accomplished, respected and successful, playing in a coveted location. Only the most highly esteemed musicians with established reputations can play here in Garibaldi Square, but music is everywhere in Mexico City. In my opinion the most exciting music is Cuban. You can hear it in the red zone's nightclubs and dance clubs where women will dance with you for a small fee or service you in a back room for a larger one. One of these nights, we'll go to one. I'll buy you some dances with some of the women there. Maybe you'd like to go in back rooms with one of them. That would be okay too. My treat."

"How can you even think this, Carla? That's exactly the kind of behavior by Americans in Mexico that Sonia objects to. What kind of socialist are you anyway, suggesting I exploit disadvantaged women by perpetuating prostitution?"

"But you've got it all wrong about prostitution here, Ray. That's the thing about Mexico; everything is turned around. It's not so easy any more to discern what is morally correct. Navio kept telling me that, and I didn't see it at first, but I do now. Prostitutes here are working girls with families to feed. They don't care about or need your respect. You would be doing far more to help their situation by paying for their services than by praying for their salvation. Besides, you need to get laid. I haven't seen you with a woman since you've been here."

"Well, you don't see everything I do or know everything about me. But you're right. I don't have a girlfriend. I don't want one. I'm still trying to come to terms with my last failed relationship."

"Whatever happened between you and your girlfriend, anyway? I wasn't around at the time, but I heard about it. My mother saved news clippings."

"Linda had an abortion without telling me. I didn't even know she was pregnant until it was too late to do anything about it. I began waking to nightmares in the middle of the night, and couldn't stop thinking about it during the day. I considered myself an accomplice to murder. I began having suicidal thoughts. I imagined writing a farewell love letter to Linda and then swimming out to sea beyond my ability to return. I thought of leaping from the Smith Tower, or standing on the railroad tracks until run down by a train. These thoughts were of brief duration, but persistent, and sometimes they scared me. I didn't want to die, but didn't want to live, at least not as the person I was. I was ashamed and hated myself."

"Raymond, it wasn't entirely your fault if Linda got pregnant. There were things she might have done to prevent it. Besides, it doesn't sound like she gave you any choice in her decision to abort and that was unfair of her."

"But she blamed me. Why? I would have married her. I would have done anything for her, whatever she asked. I couldn't understand why she wouldn't love me. It was obvious to me that no one would ever love her as much as I did. Surely she would come to her senses and take me back. I didn't understand why she didn't want me. I was obsessed with her. So much so that I began stalking her—oh, I didn't think of it as stalking at the time, but it was. I know that now. That's why I went to jail. I couldn't leave it alone. In retrospect, it's no wonder she became afraid of me. I was getting weird and creepy."

The Mariachi musicians have strolled far beyond us. We are approached by two men, one with a portable hand- cranked organ, the other with a trained monkey. They're not wearing the elaborate costumes of the mariachis and do not seem to me of same level of musicianship. Carla explains that they roam the streets of neighborhoods throughout the city.

"They're street musicians, but they're not supposed to be here, on the Street of the Musicians. When the Mariachis return, they'll chase them away. Surely you've seen them before. They're everywhere on the streets of Mexico City."

"How much do we give?"

"As little or as much as you want. The music is regional," Carla explains. "Like the harpists of Vera Cruz—not for everyone." I drop a few coins in their cup and they move on.

"So tell me more about your high school girlfriend. I remember her vaguely. You guys were freshmen when I was a senior, I think. She was pretty."

"It was a terrible time in my life, Carla. I don't like talking about it. When you fall in love the way I did, you lose yourself. I became someone I never wanted to be. Someone I didn't like. Linda didn't like me either, in the end. When you lose the person you love, it hurts more than I thought possible. You want to die. I hope and pray every night that I will never fall in love again."

I recognize the opportunity to let Carla know about my celibacy, but I don't want to. It's private, and she wouldn't understand.

"Maybe you were just with the wrong woman, Raymond."

"No. I was the wrong man. I'm not suited for that kind of love."

"There are other ways to love, Raymond. Mature, less exclusive ways."

"That's what I want, Carla. A love that is impersonal, but which encompasses all of humanity. The kind of love that Christ exemplified. A love that is Holy. You can't have it both ways. Or at least I can't. I've chosen to love God."

"I think you are just afraid. You will love again, Raymond, because love will find you. It will seek you out and send someone who will change your life. You're mistaken if you think that you can resist love indefinitely. But I understand. I was hurt, same as you. Many times. It's part of life, Raymond."

"It doesn't have to be. I've learned that we can make deliberate choices about what we want in our life."

"So then, why did you choose to come to Mexico?"

I had a story I could tell her about that, but the truth was I no longer knew why I had come. There were many explanations, but I didn't believe any of them.

"I came because of the dreams I was having in jail. The dreams were always the same. Christ was walking down a dusty road. I don't know how I knew that road was in Mexico, I just did. I knew I was supposed to follow him. I was being prepared for a mission that would be revealed to me over time. I didn't know what was wanted of me, but I was ready to accept the revelation and waited for it. I heard a voice. I can't begin to convey its inconceivable vastness. It was both terrifying and reassuring. I know that sounds paradoxical, but that's how it was. I knew this voice, Carla."

Carla removes a compact mirror, some tubes of lipstick, a small address book and several pens from her purse before finding what she was looking for, a crumpled package of cigarettes. She extricates a single cigarette and straightens it before lighting it. A small perfect flame leaps from her golden cigarette lighter.

"Earth to Raymond, Earth to Raymond. Newsflash. Hearing voices is a harbinger of schizophrenia. Maybe my mother was right. Maybe you really are crazy, after all."

"No, no. You don't understand. It's not like that. It's not like hearing a voice from outside of you. The voice is within you. It *is* you."

"I love it. Crazy talk from Reverend Weirdo Watson."

"It's not weirdo talk, it's Holy. You see, when Christ died on the cross his ghost was freed to enter us. We have his spirit within us if we chose to acknowledge and follow it."

Carla blows a smoke ring, winks and says, "They don't call religion the opiate of the masses for nothing."

"But how is one to know if one is on the right path? If I receive a telepathic message from God that I'm supposed to take a certain course, such as come to Mexico for example, but then when I try to put it into action everything works against me, what does it mean?"

"I'm trying to understand, Raymond, but I'm not sure what you are talking about."

"Everything changed, Carla. I became afraid of everyone and everything, reclusive and afraid to leave the hotel. I became obsessed with a beggar and got sick with dysentery. I wanted to follow Christ. I wanted Holiness. I went to Mexico in faith and was broken. I was not who I thought I was. Not who I wanted to be. There was nothing special about me. I was not chosen. I was a frightened boy who wanted to go home to his mother but couldn't because he was too proud."

Carla reaches across the table for my hands and says, "Honey, take it easy. Take a deep breath and relax. Remember, whatever it was that hurt you, it's over now. You're safe now. You're with me."

"And I'm grateful for your friendship, Carla."

"Then listen to my advice. I know what you need, Raymond. You need to come down to Earth. We have got to find you a woman. You need to get laid, my friend. It wouldn't be difficult to find a woman who would want you. I see the way women look at you. Women find you interesting and attractive."

"I doubt that."

"Oh? Look at those women on the corner."

Carla points to two stylish women on the corner across the street, both Castilian blonde, each with a crown of intricately fashioned golden hair probably maintained in an expensive upscale salon. Carla and I watch as they cross the street with the tall, confident, lengthy strides of models walking a runway. They are far, far out of my league.

"I'll bet you twenty dollars," says Carla, "that when they pass our table one of those women will look into your eyes suggestively."

"I don't have twenty dollars."

"Ray, a hundred dollars a month should easily cover you here in Mexico. You have got to stop giving so much money away. You can't give to everyone here that needs it. It's impossible."

She gives me a little kick under the table as they near. The taller of the two women stares boldly, right into my eyes, and does not look away. Averting my gaze, I look down at my table as she passes silently by. When I next look up, she is giving me a little backward glance. Carla wads a napkin and throws in my face.

"You should have said something to her, Ray."

"What am I supposed to say? I don't even know her."

She rolls her eyes in mock exasperation.

"You could try starting with the word *Hello*. Oh, and another thing. You might try smiling. You had the expression of someone who has just smelled dogshit on his shoes."

"It doesn't matter. Those women weren't my type."

"What's wrong with you? Do you need to have your eyes examined? Those women were beautiful and elegant."

"Carla, to me you are more beautiful in jeans and a tee shirt than the most glamorous movie star in designer clothing. You are far more elegant without even trying."

She throws another napkin at me and says, "Liar. But thank you."

"But I'm not lying, Carla. In fact, I'm even starting to worry I might fall in love with you. Would that be a problem for you?"

She smiles and says, "Not as much as it would be a problem for you."

PART FOUR

El Federales

Why did I say these things to her? I can only imagine what Carla thinks of me now. Probably I will never know. She'll probably stay far away from me. I can't blame her for that. I talked too much and said things I regret, things I couldn't expect her to understand. It's just that when I get on the subject of the Holy Ghost, the spirit comes over me and I lose myself. I have to learn to be careful.

But no, she calls the very next night, invites me to the Café Liberado. We arrive in separate cabs to find it crowded and noisy as always. We have to shout over the loud recorded American jazz that plays continuously. The usual poets and writers and leftist intelligentsia are in evidence, but also controversial leftist University professors and their radicalized students. Chain smoking students and angry disillusioned dropout intellectuals drink endless cups of coffee and argue politics in raised voices while waiting hopefully for the first rifle shots of the revolution. In my capacity as an American tourist, my presence is at best tolerated here, anti-American sentiment being what it is these days in Latin America, and without Carla on my arm I would likely be met with open hostility, from which I am not altogether spared even now. Carla, however, knows everyone here and is warmly accepted. We wade through the smoke-thick congested interior, where Hector and Romero wave us to their table. Hector manages to find unoccupied chairs and we somehow all squeeze around our table, elbows touching

"Nice to see you again," says Romero to Carla. "Hello, Raymundo. I see you are still with us here in Mexico. Welcome."

Hector and Romero are normally civil to me to the degree they include me in their discussions but often, as an American tourist,

I am the subject of their teasing. Again, without the support of Carla, and especially Navio, I would be shunned here, where to be an American is an offense. I find it ironic that amid the expression of so much anti-American ideology the musical preference here is for American jazz and the most popular menu items consist of hamburgers and French fried potatoes, but I mostly endure my role here as the tolerated Ugly American in silence. Meanwhile I can't help but notice, despite all the talk about social justice and expressions of concern for the poor, everyone seems to have plenty of money to waste on alcohol, which in my opinion could be better spent.

"Have you seen Navio? He is supposed to meet me here."

"No, Carla. Not at all this week."

"Perhaps he is with Sonia," offers Romero.

"Sonia," says Hector mirthfully. "She is likely with some unfortunate man, cutting his balls off with a butcher knife."

"Or a machete", offers Romero.

"Yes, a machete. She wears a string of men's cohones around her neck like an amulet."

"No," corrects Romero, "like a Rosary. She worships the Goddess of Castration."

Hector laughs so hard he spits beer across the table. Some of it comes shooting out of his nose. He recovers and says, "She *is* the Goddess of Castration. Armies of militant lesbians salute her."

"She decrees that all men will bequeath their gonads in tribute."

"Not bequeath. She will take them by force."

"With her bare hands."

"No, with her teeth."

"She eats them for breakfast. She douses them with hot sauce and chases them with Mescal."

"She finds them delectable. She is preparing a gonad cookbook for publication."

Both Hector and Romero are spasmodic with laughter. Romero has tears of laughter in his eyes. Hector pounds both fists on the table and kicks his legs in and out like someone being electrocuted.

Carla says, "I don't think either of you would be talking this way if she was here."

"Only if I was very drunk and foolish," agrees Hector. "My own gonads remain precious to me. I wish to keep them."

"There are limits to Machismo," concedes Romero. "Sonia is a formidable opponent. On the other hand, we are only joking here. We respect Sonia and consider her a comrade in arms and our equal in every way. It's just that our tongues are loose with the tequila. Our foolishness is only a way of showing affection."

"I don't like it," says Carla.

"I'm surprised that you of all people would defend her. You should hear some of the things she says about you. We can joke about her, but you never. She would beat you like a dog and enjoy every minute of it."

"Let's just drop it," says Hector. "I don't want to talk about Sonia any longer. Carla is right; it's not fair to discuss people when they are not here to defend themselves."

"Agreed," says Romero.

He turns his attention to me and says, "And what of you, Raymundo? How are you enjoying your vacation in Mexico? Have you been able to find enough suffering here in Mexico to make you happy?"

"That's not fair," protests Carla.

"Suffering is plentiful here in Mexico," says Romero, ignoring her. "Keep looking, Raymundo. You will find much of it. It is Mexico's gross national product."

"We would like very much to export it to America," adds Hector.

"Yes," agrees Romero. "They have already stolen California, Utah, Arizona, New Mexico, Colorado, Nevada and Texas. They might as well steal our national identity as well."

"What are we supposed to do with this conversation," asks Carla. "Are we supposed to apologize for being Americans?"

"We meant no offense. You know we love you, Carla. As for you, Raymundo, we enjoy teasing you and assume you take no offense."

"Frankly, I'm weary of it. I won't apologize for being an American and you misunderstand me. If I once spoke that I sometimes feel ashamed that I have made so little of the advantages that being an American has given me, I never meant to say that I was looking for suffering, only that I was seeking atonement and redemption."

"But through suffering. That is what you have said, that you wish suffering upon yourself. You have said so."

"I have, yes."

"I don't think you will accomplish this. No one suffers willingly. When the moment of one's suffering arrives, one endeavors to overcome it. No one accepts pain and suffering willingly."

"Christ did."

Romero says, "That is debatable. What choice did he have? He was condemned to death as a criminal. Even his own father would not save him."

"It was his destiny," adds Hector.

"I do not believe there even was a Christ," says Romero. "Where is the evidence? The priests cannot offer it. Have faith, they say. On what basis? But you, Raymundo, because you are a wealthy American I don't think you can ever truly know suffering except vicariously, never experience it firsthand, profoundly and personally the way we do in Mexico."

"That's just distorted nationalist pride," interrupts Carla. "No nation has a monopoly on suffering. As a communist you should know this. Secondly, Raymond is not a wealthy American. He probably has less money in his pocket than you do."

"But Raymundo is here on vacation. We live here."

"Yes," says Carla, "and you live well, dining in restaurants, drinking tequila, smoking expensive American cigarettes, taking taxi cabs."

"I'm not a rich American and it doesn't matter. No human being, rich or poor, is exempted from the law of suffering. Read the Book of Job. The rich may not go hungry or homeless, but they will suffer in a manner less visible and obvious. A wealthy, trouble-free man might live his entire life without hardship. He may have a wife, a family, status, prestige, a warm secure home and family life. Then his only son kills a man and goes to prison. His wife becomes stricken with a fatal disease and dies. He loses the loss of his legs to diabetes and goes blind. All that remains is his money, and he

would gladly return it to have his family and his health returned
to him. As long as we love and have a heart, as long as we are human and feel empathy, we suffer. No one escapes the facts of life,
Romero. Everyone at some point in their life eventually shares in
experiencing disappointment, grief, or loneliness."

"I understand what you are saying, Raymundo, but if you were
more widely experienced with other cultures, you would know this
is not suffering. It's not your fault but you are young and American and don't understand. This disappointment, grief, loneliness
and failing health you define as suffering we simply regard as the
cost of living. Everyone eventually becomes ill and dies. Everyone
loses people they love. This is life. What we call the cost of living.
How is this suffering when compared to conditions of hunger, political oppression, subjugation and systemic poverty? The poor cannot concern themselves with examination of their feelings. They
cannot afford a life of introspection. They are too hungry for such
speculation."

"I'm not immune to unfortunate conditions, Navio. I have
experienced hunger at least to the degree that I know what it is. I
may not have been subjected to political repression but I have been
incarcerated, and I could probably teach you a thing or two about
loneliness. Try moving to a country where you don't have a single
friend and can't even speak the language to make one."

I'm being careful with myself, avoiding further discussion of
Christ and faith because of the mistake yesterday with Carla. Now
is not the time to reveal myself or what I believe to be our true purpose. We must rise. We must ascend. All of us are meant to become
Holy. But I cannot say these things. Now is not the time or place. If
these revolutionary students are to become Christian, then Christ
will have to bring them to me. And he will. I know that one day,
one of these men, maybe Navio, Romero or Hector, or maybe even
Sonia will be sent to me.

As the night wears on we are continuously interrupted by
handsome young men seeking courtship with Carla. An art student
has sketched her and asks if she would agree to model in his studio.
A student film maker wants her to play a part in his film project. A
bearded professor introduces himself as a guidance counselor and

mentions that his office is always open for advice and fellowship. A young man kneels theatrically at her feet to present a poem and single long stemmed rose. Another performs a song in her honor on guitar. Carla smiles graciously and takes it all in stride, all the while keeping watch for Navio, who does not arrive.

Because of recent demonstrations, a curfew has been implemented in this busy neighborhood on the fringe of the University, but the curfew is not legal, has not been strictly enforced, and everyone ignores it. The discussion continues and we stay late.

We hear the army trucks before actually seeing the soldiers. They barricade the street and post sentries at the front and rear doors of the café. Soldiers storm the interior of the café and herd patrons from the bathrooms, employees from behind the bar and the kitchen. The rest of us are ordered to remain seated at our tables. No one is allowed to leave. The soldiers stand in silent formation, holding their rifles against their chests. They are a ragtag group mostly, some of them fat and misshapen, many wearing ill-fitting shabby fatigues. All carry military issue carbines.

In charge is an officer who cannot be more than five feet five inches tall. He wears a neatly pressed officer's uniform consisting of a formal military jacket with epaulets on the shoulders and medals on the breast. His handsome black riding boots rise to his knees and are shined to a high gloss. He carries no rifle but wears a pistol in a leather shoulder holster. He is young, probably no older than Carla and I, but his authority is evident to all.

"Turn off the music immediately," he commands. "No talking." When the room goes silent he says, "My name is Colonel Garcia and I am here under the authority of the federal government. This is a federal security action and I demand and expect your absolute silence. You will now commence preparing your identification papers for inspection."

No one talks. I hear only the shuffle of identification papers being presented and the sound of the Colonel's boots as he paces back and forth, assessing us all. I hear his riding crop snap, and watch as soldiers begin routinely collecting identification papers. The Colonel barely glances at them. A distinguished, elderly liberal University professor is arrested and led outside to the trucks.

Others soon follow.

Suddenly a male student wearing an Army field jacket similar to the ones worn by the soldiers hurdles over chairs and tables. He's agile and fast as an Olympic hurdler in a track and field competition. He manages to vault numerous tables, overturning chairs, beer glasses and coffee cups while making a break for the kitchen and back door. With the exception of the soldiers, everyone applauds his effort.

"Silence!" shouts the Colonel. "What did I tell you?"

But no one obeys. We are all inspired by the escapee. But then soldiers drag him back in by the feet. He is unconscious and his face is smashed in. The room goes silent. The soldiers continue collecting identification, working their way toward us in the back of the room.

"This is illegal," whispers Carla. "They completely ignore the law. I don't know if this is an authorized search or if this tinhorn is acting independently."

She goes on to explain there is no law requiring citizens to provide identification papers on command, but failure to do so is grounds for holding one for investigation until identity can be confirmed, adding that anyone can be detained on a number of charges, such as the widely utilized "suspicion" charge, which can mean nothing or everything, depending on one's point of view. Conspiracy is another popular charge.

"Conspiracy to do what," sneers Carla. "Conspiracy to conspire, perhaps. They don't know. They make it up as they go along."

The colonel glares at us and shouts "Silence!"

He slams his riding crop across a table top and kicks away a chair with his high, glossy black boots. He stands over us, his expression fierce.

"What did I tell you about remaining quiet?"

He strikes the crop on our table with such force that it overturns a half dozen beer bottles.

"You need to learn obedience. You need to learn to respect men in uniform who are here to protect you from anarchists and communists. But then, that is the point, isn't it? You are probably communists yourselves, seditious University students who hate your own country and would like to replace its flag with a red star, hammer and sickle."

"I love my country as much as you do," replies Romero boldly. "More, probably."

The colonel brings the full force of the blunt end of riding crop down on Romero's hand and screams in his face.

"Arrest this communist. Take him out of my sight."

Romero, clutching his injured hand, is led to the trucks.

The colonel turns next to Hector and says, "You. Your papers."

Hector presents his passport but the colonel doesn't even open it.

"Arrest him too," he says.

Hector is pulled from his chair and taken to the trucks. The colonel points at Carla and I with his riding crop and says, "Arrest them too."

Carla calmly removes her U.S. passport from her purse and opens it to her photograph and the U.S. seal.

"We are American citizens. You have no right. I will report you to the American Consul, a personal friend of mine, who in turn will notify your commander of this intervention, which I am willing to bet is probably unauthorized."

The colonel, frowning and taking his time, examines both my passport and Carla's. He hands them back and scowls at us hatefully. My hands are shaking under the table. Carla calmly lights a cigarette. The Colonel addresses us in perfect, educated English.

"Why are you here in Mexico?"

"I am an exchange student at the University," replies Carla.

"I see. What is your course of study?"

"Spanish language and Latin American Studies."

"And you?"

"I'm a writer."

"Are you also a student at the University?"

"I am not."

"I apologize for your inconvenience," he says, his tone cordial and acquiescent. "We welcome the United States and its citizens as friends of our country and allies in the fight against world communism. It is our wish that you will enjoy your stay in Mexico."

When we leave, much later, long after the soldiers have made their arrests and loaded their prisoners, we are met with accusatory glares from those who remain. My response is conflicted and perhaps typical of advantaged and protected Americans abroad in a repressive third world country: I am both embarrassed and grateful to be an American.

Crisis

Navio and I were supposed to have met yesterday after-noon in Garibaldi Square but I ended up falling asleep with a headache and never made it. His telephone call has wakened me from a sleep without rest. I dreamed deeply in the night, but have not slept well, waking often and having difficulty falling back to sleep. I clear my throat and speak into the phone, my voice hoarse with sleep and too many cigarettes.

"I'm sorry about yesterday, Navio. I might be coming down with something, maybe the flu, I don't know. I had a headache and stayed in bed most of the day."

"I waited for you but it's all right and not why I'm calling. Carla is missing. I'm worried she may have been picked up by the Federales."

"This is Mexico, Navio, not Bolivia. People here do not disap-pear, especially not American citizens."

"But you don't understand how the secret police work here. Elite renegade factions operate independently outside of the law. They do whatever they want, Raymundo."

This may in fact be true, but what I do not say is I happen to know, by her own recent admission, that Carla has been trying to slowly and gently disengage from her romantic entanglement with Navio, and I have reason to suspect she has begun seeing someone else. Also, it is not unusual for Carla to mysteriously "disappear," if only for a few days, a week at most, always to return with a plau-sible if perhaps suspect explanation. My guess is Navio is jealous and suspicious.

"Are you worried she is with another man, Navio?"

"I am worried for her safety. What reason do you have for saying this?"

"Navio, I'm sorry. You are a friend and I'm being insensitive. Please accept my apology."

"But I think you are right, Raymundo. Carla has been fucking the Cuban consul."

"I seriously doubt that."

"They were seen together, splendidly dressed in an exclusive restaurant on the Paseo de la Reforma."

"Sometimes she takes translating work from the Embassy. It might have been a business meeting."

"A violinist serenaded their table. The consul purchased roses from a flower peddler. They were said to drink champagne with interlocking arms. The two of them left together by limousine."

"That's a lot of information, Navio. How could you know all this?"

"I know one of the waiters there."

"The Consul is married. If he was having an affair, don't you think he would be more discreet?"

"Latin American men do not need discretion."

After agreeing to meet him at the café, I call the desk to request a cab. Minutes later Pedro is weaving us expertly through thick traffic. My stomach rumbles and I have a vague headache and am irritable. The University district turns out to be unusually quiet. Shops that would be normally open are closed with their shutters pulled down. I'm starting to think today must be some kind of national holiday. Pedro drops me a block from the café Liberado, but it turns out to be chained and locked. Official bulletins posted on the front windows announce its temporary closure by order of the Federal Police.

The drone of many hundreds of voices reminiscent of those made by a large crowd in a sporting event is vaguely discernable in the distance. Is a parade in progress? A university soccer match? There is no sign of Navio. I wait a half hour before giving up on him.

There's not a cab or bus in sight that might return me to the hotel. There's little traffic of any kind. Where is everyone? The streets are empty. Walking toward the University campus, I begin seeing columns of gray smoke. Hundreds of shouting students are in in full charge. Demonstrators carry anti-American posters, baseball bats, chains and bags of stones. Bottles with flaming gasoline-soaked rag tails fly from windows and rooftops, exploding on impact when hitting the ground. The air is poisoned with drifting clouds of smoke from homemade incendiary explosives and the remnants of police tear gas. My eyes burn and water profusely. Men stagger bloody and limping; one is being helped along by two others. He is soaked with blood. I can't even see his face through it. Mounted police trample screaming students fleeing in every direction.

A student is viciously beaten by police with nightsticks. He drops to the ground and is kicked repeatedly, then dragged off. Policemen charge through the smoke; one of them swings his nightstick in my face. I turn my head away from it, but too late. I drop to my knees from the force of nightstick against my head. I curl into a fetal position while a dozen black police boots repeatedly kick me. I feel someone grabbing my feet, dragging me out of position. I'm screaming over and over, *Americano, Americano,* but I can hardly hear my own voice over the roar of rioting. I manage to extricate my passport and wave it at the police. They release me and move on.

Twice I try to rise to my feet only to fall to my knees again. On the third attempt I manage it, staggering toward what I hope is a way off campus. My head pounds and my vision is blurred. All I want is safe passage but I'm still in the thick of the fighting, stumbling along with my U.S. passport held in front of my face like a small shield. A student protester points me out accusingly and shouts, "*Americano!*"

A wine bottle sails through the air, breaks against my head and shatters. Blood runs down my face. I wipe it away and begin running, chased by a mob of angry, cursing, rock-throwing anti-American students. I'm hurt, but my adrenaline is pumping so hard I barely feel it. Eyes watering and vision blurred, I emerge from the smoke to find myself safely beyond the University campus. My ear throbs. My clothing is stained with blood. My heart pounds furiously. I'm hurting all over. I'm limping and my mouth tastes like blood. I crouch in the street to vomit.

No taxi will stop for me. I board a city bus, passengers recoiling at the sight of me. One of them takes pity and offers his seat, which I gratefully accept. I have no idea where the bus is going. It ends up taking me through an upscale commercial neighborhood of hotels and restaurants. An English speaking hotel desk clerk sympathizes with my story and lets me use the lobby facilities to wash. I fill the basin and rinse my face, the water turning pink with blood while I remove pieces of glass imbedded in my face and hands. My nose throbs and might be broken but I still have all my teeth and the cuts on my face are mostly superficial.

When I return to the La Paz the lobby is crowded with guests gathered around the television. Everyone watches without speaking, their expressions grim. President Kennedy is on television giving a speech reporting the presence of Soviet missile bases in Cuba. He calls for a naval blockade, an act of war he euphemistically refers to as a "quarantine." Shipping lanes to Cuba are to be cut off, and freighters boarded at sea and searched for arms.

Khrushchev denounces the blockade as "an act of aggression" and instructs his ships to ignore it. The 1st Armored Division prepares for a possible invasion of Cuba. Kennedy issues a Security Action Memorandum to authorize the loading of nuclear missiles into aircraft. Short range B17 bombers are deployed to civilian airports to position for aerial raids on Cuban missile sites. A U-2 spy plane "accidentally" entering Soviet airspace is intercepted by MIG fighters. Another is shot down over Cuba by a surface to air missile and crashes in the jungle. Four Crusader jets pass over the San Cristóbal and Sagua la Grande missile sites. Cuban ground forces fire with anti-aircraft guns and small arms and one plane is hit. NORAD goes into full alert. Soviet vessels slice through open waters en route to Cuba.

We have reached what used to be called a Mexican Standoff, which television commentators and journalists refer to as The Cuban Missile Crisis. Everyone knows this war will be a nuclear Apocalypse of unimaginable, ultimate, mega death. President Kennedy would kill us all to save us from communism. Khrushchev bangs his shoe on the U.N. conference table. Who can save us from these madmen?

I walk for hours, aimlessly through the city during what might be the last day of life on earth. The entire planet is imperiled. The sky will burn, the ocean boil. Every living thing will die. Our fate is out of our hands. It probably always has been. Navio, Romero, Hector, Sonia, Carla, Francisco the Cuban consul, everyone has been trying to tell me that whether or not we choose to acknowledge it we are global subjects of a political system, and they were right. Until now I have acted as if by disavowing a political position I could be free of one. I did not listen. I thought I was above politics. Now I know that it is irresponsible to ignore political reality. The imposed geopolitical systems that regulate economic and social life have failed us. The leaders of the world are insane. Now we are all about to die. And what do I do? I write in this notebook. Pitiful. I can't even pray. I'm too pissed off and frightened even for that.

I wander down to the Zocalo to find the great Cathedral swollen with worshipers. Why am I not among these reverent, hopeful men and women of faith? Where are my prayers? Why am I not on my knees? I'm too angry to be in God's presence right now, too angry to come before him, angry at everyone, even Carla.

Because where is she? Why isn't she here, with me, during what might be our last days? I imagine a Cuernavaca hacienda where a green manicured lawn slopes downward toward tennis courts. The sound of a spewing fountain rises from a cobblestoned courtyard below. A breeze sweetened with fragrant bougainvillea and lavender caresses a wrought iron balcony where Carla stands overlooking a shimmering blue swimming pool. She wears a sheer white negligee through which her voluptuous naked body is visible. The Consul watches her from where he reclines under the gauze canopy of their bed. He's naked and smoking a cigar. There is a flash of light in the distance and then the atomic blast of fire consumes them.

Good. Serves them right. To hell with them.

I can't believe I even thought that. I'm ashamed. I didn't mean it. Forgive me. I'm sick with this. I wander aimlessly through Mercado, through Chapultepec Park and the upscale neighborhoods of Insurgents and the Paseo de la Reforma. Will we live another day, another hour? I find myself hoofing through my own neighborhood again, but can't stop this aimless, nervous pacing and wandering. Even though my legs are throbbing and my feet burn and I'm exhausted I don't want to go back inside the hotel. I want to keep moving, keep shuffling along, eyes upward toward the incoming missiles. Do I see them? Not yet. They're at rest in their silos. We're trapped like shivering hamsters in the laboratory cages of deranged scientists.

I manage a few hours of fitful sleep and open my eyes in the morning to a terrible new day. It's like I am already in my coffin. It's bad enough to face the imminence of Death by natural causes but the horror of nuclear war is an evil too hideous to consider. I want to call Carla but I don't know where she is. Navio doesn't answer his phone either. Where the hell is everyone? I don't want to be alone. I want to get out of here, out of this bed, out of this room, deep into city streets overflowing with the daily activity of human life.

I shave and brush my teeth but in the shower can't avoid thinking of the death chambers of Treblinka and Auschwitz. Half dead men with skeletal bodies and haunted eyes; children with dead parents and ruined lives. To those in power, we are nothing, hostages, mere commodities useful only for exploitation, work, and killing.

Ricardo is reading a magazine behind the check-in desk, but not a girlie magazine this morning; he's reading the newspaper. We are all famished for news. But Ricardo doesn't look up. He's reading with intense focus and concentration. His expression is grim. His mouth and jaw are clenched as tensely as if biting a railroad spike.

"Good morning, Ricardo."

"Good morning. Are you going out?"

"Yes, but I don't know where."

"Well, have a nice day. It may be your last."

The construction noise, blare of automobile horns and grinding mechanics of the city at work, usually such an annoyance, is welcome this morning, as I walk. Even the pollution is welcome. I'm grateful just to breathe, for the odors that usually annoy me, the stench of stale beer and garbage and smoke, the dog shit and piss. I'm grateful for all these people around me, the women, each uniquely beautiful and sweet, the young girls with their dark fragile beauty—their dear mothers with them, protective and secretive—sometimes looking up to meet your eyes, and you fall in love instantly. And the men, smelling of work, of hard drinking and hard living, let's welcome them too. Welcome the sweet stinky funk of humankind; bring it on, all of it good, all of it announcing the presence of abundant life. Thank you. We remain. These old brownstone buildings and seething adobe tenement apartment buildings still proudly stand. Maids hang freshly laundered white sheets on rooftop clotheslines. The familiar, inviting, gumball-blue and bright canary yellow interiors of cantinas and restaurants remain active. The chatty sidewalk cafés and crowded trolleys, quaint little picturesque shops, storefronts, busy newsstand kiosks and sidewalk markets and kitchens continue. The city remains and is still beautiful. I'm seeing with a renewed clarity and appreciation, a sharper focus.

The city is quieter today than normal. It's as if it has been unanimously decided that if this is to be our last day on Earth, if our lives are to end here, today, then let this day be gentle. Let it be beautiful. Let us be kind to one another.

Men and women acknowledge one another deferentially in considerate acquiescence to the needs of others. Usually there are millions of automobile horns all sounding at once, but today they are less numerous and without the usual aggressiveness. Street vendors, kiosk proprietors, and roving young shoeshine boys who sell lottery tickets and Chiclet gum seem to do so without shouting; everyone speaks at a softer volume and more slowly. It's the opposite of what I might have expected. I anticipated that activity in the city would be frantic, that they'd be scrambling around for supplies, stocking up on bags of flour, bottled water and medicines needed to survive and endure the coming end of civilization and subsequent reversion to global savagery. But people in the markets are not fighting to be first in line; no one is maneuvering aggressively for advantageous position or shouting over others for service.

Trucks continue to pick up the morning garbage in refuse barrels along the street as they do every Wednesday morning at this hour, but today it seems mythical and heroic. The usual mobile fleets of bright decorous airbrushed taxis continue to crisscross the grid of city streets, taking passengers to work, to weddings and funerals, to movies and restaurants, to meetings or music lessons or luncheons or rendezvous with lovers; its business as usual but today the busy drivers and their passengers have added value.

Flower vendors roam neighborhood streets, their bundles of gladiolas, roses, passion flowers and baby's breath stacked neatly in wooden mobile carts or carried in baskets; their contribution seems enormous. Teenage boys walk to school or places of work. Shop keepers rhythmically sweep the sidewalks of debris. Fruit vendors stack oranges, mangoes, papayas and bananas on display stands; organ grinders play their happy music. It's all ordinary, all part of the daily life of the city, and somehow it all seems miraculous this morning.

The trolleys are running, the kiosks are open, the bus has stopped at the corner, the window washers are out, the waiters and waitresses glide between tables of diners, and why? Why do they work, why do they bother when everything that presently exists might come to an end at any given moment? It seems a magnificent act of heroism that these people continue their lives as if nothing has changed, as if they do not know they are going to die. If you think it is because they are in denial of the danger they are in, then you are wrong. They know that they are doomed. They know that they do not own their own destiny. They know that they are not in control of the historical events that determine their future. They know that others control them and will decide their fate. And yet they continue. They are a brave and faithful people, and I love them. I love this city. I buy a dozen candles from a vendor and light them in my room, fall to my knees and pray at last, grateful for this one day of life, whether or not it is to be our last.

* * *

The glamorous woman in the raincoat who paces the La Paz lobby carries a newspaper under her arm and wears a scarf over her head and large dark sunglasses over her face. Her manner and appearance suggest a famous person evading recognition, someone like Jackie Kennedy for example, or perhaps a famous movie star traveling incognito to elude the press. But no, it's Carla, in disguise for reasons unknown and returned from locations as yet unidentified, though I have my ugly suspicions.

Do I even know this woman? I thought I did. I once knew the Carla Johansen of Edmonds High School, the straight A student we all admired and of whom we expected so much. But who is this version? I know nothing of her life over the past three or four years since high school. I would love to see her passport. Is it stamped with passage to Cuba? The USSR? Is her true connection with the Cuban consul political, romantic, or both? And which possibility bothers me more? And why?

She whips off her glasses upon seeing me enter. Her expression is angry. She quickly replaces the glasses and I can't see her eyes, but her mouth is tense. Near her is a suitcase.

"Leaving or returning," I ask, indicating the luggage.

"I can't stay at the University right now, there's too much fighting. As an American I'm a target."

I reach out and impulsively remove her sunglasses; her eyes are red and swollen. She waves the newspaper in my face and says, "Khrushchev the Russian shoe-banger versus Kennedy the Irish crime boss. Either would prefer to annihilate us than lose face."

She tosses the newspapers into the trash as if the gesture might put an end to the matter.

"I'm disillusioned with politics and the men who engage in them. No one has the right to control another's destiny, even if it is for their own betterment. I'm disappointed in Fidel's manipulation by Khrushchev. Why doesn't he take the lead and demand the missiles be removed? It's insane."

"I know it is, Carla. The events of the past week have taught me that Navio was right. Politics are a necessary evil. We can't just stand by and let ambitious men of power take possession of our lives. Passivity is not an option."

Ricardo, eavesdropping as usual from behind the check-in desk, looks up from his newspaper and says, "Mexico City is not strategically important except as a staging area for an invasion of Cuba, and there won't be time for that. Of course there is always the possibility a missile will go astray. Who can gauge the accuracy of these missile systems? No one really knows. They have never been tested. A rogue missile could miss Miami or Havana and deliver a direct hit. If that happens, most of us will die instantly in a firestorm. They will be the lucky ones. The rest of us will die slowly of radioactive poisoning. You will see children with puss oozing from open sores on their faces, people doubled up vomiting in the street from eating poisoned food, rabid feral killer dogs devouring corpses, people leaping from tall buildings to end the horror. There will be murder and madness everywhere as men fight to survive. None of us will. The fallout will kill all of us over a period of time if the violence of others doesn't kill us first."

"You sound happy about it," I observe.

He shrugs indifferently and resumes silently reading.

"So what will you do now, Carla?"

"If we get out of this crisis intact, I'll wait for the anti-American climate to settle down at the University and finish classes. After that maybe take some time off. I want to do some kind of honest work that can't be exploited by ambitious politicians. I might do some honest labor in the fields in a third world nation. Or I could teach in an American ghetto, a third world country or even Cuba, provided Fidel remains true to the people's revolution and backs away from Soviet coercion. Cuba seems the last hope for a communism I can endorse, if only it frees itself from Russia. I don't know what to do next. I don't know, Raymond. I'm confused and discouraged. I've even thought of going away with Sonia, taking up arms in the mountains somewhere, but that is crazy and just my anger talking. Meanwhile, until the hostilities simmer down at the University, I'm checking into a hotel. In fact, I was going to check in here at the La Paz, but there are no rooms available."

"Carla, you know you can stay with me. I'll always make room for you."

"That would be complicated and confusing, Raymond, and not a good idea considering."

"Considering what?"

"You really are naïve sometimes, Raymond. You know that, right? But it doesn't matter. I've already found another. I just called them. But thank you for offering."

"And what of your Cuban diplomat friend?"

"Francisco? What about him?"

"It's rumored that you two are having an affair."

"Francisco is married."

"You have been seen dining together in romantic settings. You have been away during this entire crisis. I looked for you in the Café Liberado. No one there had any idea where you were."

"And you are waiting for an explanation."

"I would like one, yes."

"If you must know, I was away on a field trip to the Yucatan as an assistant to my anthropology professor, but why do you need to know this, Raymond? I'm back now. Isn't that all that matters?"

"I thought you might want to be forewarned as to what people are saying."

"Let them say whatever they want about me. I don't care. I never have. It doesn't matter what they think."

"What about me? Does it matter what I think?"

"Of course it does, Raymond. You are my best friend and ally. Now more than ever. Are we quarreling? This hardly seems the time for it. Where's my hug?"

She smiles and steps toward me, and then she is in my arms, or I am in hers, it's difficult to discern, because we are like one body, and it no longer matters what the world does or even if the missiles are already on their way, because if it is going to end, this is how I want it to be.

* * *

But we are saved. Khrushchev and President Kennedy make a deal. Russia will withdraw missiles from Cuba in return for removal of ours from Turkey. Thus begins a world-wide, media-fueled propaganda campaign designed to reassure a skeptical world populace that the catastrophe was not as close as we feared, that we need not worry, the geopolitical system is failsafe and the leadership of Khrushchev and Kennedy, in which we can safely put our unreserved confidence and faith, will assuredly continue to protect us from catastrophe. But we know how close we came to annihilation, know our helplessness to prevent a future holocaust which might come at any time at the whim of world leaders. Everything and nothing has changed. The truth is eternal. Our salvation is not given us by world leaders, but because of the mercy and divine intervention of Jesus Christ.

Ghosts in the Cathedral

My father, a down-to-earth practical man not given to philosophical, spiritual, or mystical contemplation, once came home from the sea with the expression of a man haunted by a bewildering, life-altering experience. His facial expression was reminiscent of photographs I had seen of battle-shocked men at war in the jungles of the Pacific, men with haunted eyes fixed in what was commonly referred to as "the thousand-yard stare." Dad had always been quiet, but on this occasion was preoccupied, brooding. Emily, my mother, remarked on it during dinner.

"What's wrong with you," she finally inquired, exasperated. "Why aren't you eating? Is there something wrong with the roast?"

"No, of course not. You know I love your cooking."

"Well, you may as well be back on the ship for all the company you are."

Dad set down his knife and fork and paused for what seemed an inordinately long time, staring down at his plate of barely touched dinner without speaking or making eye contact with any of us. We knew him well enough to know he was considering his reply.

"I've been having strange dreams at sea," whispered Dad. "Sometimes I'm not sure they even are dreams. I'd rather not talk about it."

My mother made light of it and said, "Are you dreaming of me, Frank? Were you dreaming of this pot roast?"

"It's not funny," he replied. "I'm serious."

"Well, you usually are. A sense of humor has never been your strong point."

"The dreams were strange and disturbing. I couldn't describe them even if I wanted to. But they seemed real. In some ways more real than this moment with you."

Dad fell silent. It was as if he was no longer with us. There were tears in his eyes. This was not my father, not the man I knew. Over the years I asked him about his dreams several different times, but he refused to speak of it again. Whenever the subject came up he became withdrawn, with a far-away expression on his face that was unlike any other, and I knew that something had happened to him at sea which I would never understand and more importantly, he would never understand. Sometimes strange events beyond our comprehension happen to us. They happened to me, torn from the fabric that holds our world together as if in a paradigm shift, and as instantaneously as a shaft of slanting light through a stained glass window.

For me, those windows are in the Great Cathedral. I remember how happy I was that morning to at last be taking Carla. I remember how the warm sun felt on my face and arms, the sweet singing of morning birds and the rhymes of children skipping rope, dogs barking in courtyards, bright laundry fluttering on clotheslines. As we walked, Carla locked her arm through mine. Occasionally she gave me little kisses on the cheek. She had never done that before. It made me feel normal and deliriously happy, as if we were a couple.

Vendors hawked tropical talking birds in cages, handwritten prayers, straw baskets and paper flowers, miniature ceramic statues of Jesus and the Virgin Mary. Smoke drifted from open air sidewalk kitchens. The lingering odor of cooking was everywhere. Huge pots of beans were stirred. Men ate chilies drowning in hot sauce and wrapped in corn tortillas. I bought a beef taco at a stand, doused it with hot sauce, and ate it as we walked. I don't know why I did this, I wasn't really hungry. There was something compelling about the woman who sold it to me. Her dark glinting eyes both frightened and seduced me into buying a taco I didn't even want. Carla ended up eating more of it than I did.

When we faced the great Cathedral it was like standing on the threshold of the ancient world. We stood before a historic architecture worthy of ancient Rome, Carthage, or Alexandria. Never had I witnessed anything remotely similar in size, scope or ambition as this. Its enormity cast a huge shadow over the square. We stood before it in silence, holding our breath before its massive and elaborate architectural details.

I had come to worship, but Carla as a tourist. Reading aloud from her guidebook, I learned it contained sixteen chapels, each dedicated to a different saint, with one hundred and fifty windows, seventy-four arches, and forty columns. It had taken three centuries from its inception to completion, and many thousands of men labored all their lives in building it.

The procession we joined varied from solemn to celebratory as we began our ascent of its broad whitewashed steps. A group of pre-adolescent girls in clean white dresses wore ribbons tied through their hair. Their little ears were pierced with small golden hoops and they wore gold crosses around their necks. Their faces shone with the untarnished optimism and joyousness of a clean and innocent youth not yet tainted with the hardship, suffering, and cruelty of Mexico. They were pretty, innocent, and precious to the mothers who watched over them protectively. Their brothers, young boys who would be men long before they reached their teens, carried straw hats and wore white shirts and denim trousers like their fathers. Their faces were already stoic beyond their years. I knew from talking with Navio, Hector, and others that boys such as these came from large families that were poor, and were born and bred for labor. They loved their sisters, their fathers and mothers. They would not go on to college or even graduate from high school. They would sacrifice and work for the families they loved. It wasn't fair. They deserved better. I knew they loved God as much as I. More, probably. Where was the justice?

Mexican men and women came to have their children baptized or to petition for loved ones who were sick and could not come themselves. All generations were represented, parents, grandparents, children, orphans. They walked, they crawled on penitent knees or if infirmed were carried by others. They brought photographs of sick relatives or unrepentant deceased loved ones, begging for their mercy. They carried offerings of glass beads, coins and peso notes, candles and incense. I began to feel sick. Quite suddenly and without warning my stomach began cramping violently.

I doubled up and held my stomach, helpless and afraid that I might vomit on these sacred Cathedral steps.

"What's wrong?"

"I don't know. I think I am going to be sick. Maybe it was that taco I ate."

The blazing sun seemed cruel and punishing; it was cooking me alive.

"You look terrible. Are you going to be all right?"

"Yes, just let me rest here a minute."

I remained on my knees. I was drenched in sweat. My clothing clung to me. Rivulets of perspiration ran down my face. I was afraid to move; my stomach was in agony. We waited. Perhaps ten minutes passed. The cramps remained but became less violent, of less duration and infrequent.

"I think I can go in," I said.

"You're on your knees, Raymond. Are you going to do it penitent style?"

"No, I'm getting up."

"Do you need help?"

"No, I can do it."

We entered a shrouded cavern lighted by thousands of votive candles. The solemn statues of dead saints loomed in the dense smoke of burning incense. I was chilled, my body speckled with goose bumps. The bumps were itchy and feathery. There had been something in that taco. I was sweating despite the cold. I don't know how long I stood, unable to continue down the aisle. Everything appeared viscous, as if my world was in a process of evaporation.

I saw a shaft of light fall from stained glass windows. The light illuminated us and I believed this light anointed us. High along the domed gilded ceiling, the intricate webbing of a hierarchy of delicately carved cherubs, seraphim and other angels moved along the ceiling like spiders in an ethereal web. I heard them, whispering among themselves, discussing us.

I was sweating and verged on fainting. Tens of thousands of flickering votive candles cast shadows against the stone walls. The entire chamber was adrift in huge clouds of smoky incense. Everything I saw appeared to me tenuous and wavering, as if the substance of experience that we thought was our existence was only a reflection, and flimsy as a soap bubble. Feathers seemed to be sprouting from my under arms. I examined them with my fingertips, small feathery bumps that seemed to be growing. Some had tiny sprouts, like newly budding plants. I felt them budding on my back and legs and chest.

I saw Jesus. He was illuminated in a light so bright that I had to cover my eyes and not look at him directly. The light was coming from his face, but He could not see me because of the blood. He was wounded and suffering greatly. A golden crown was around his head, but it was a crown of barbed wire and cut glass. Blood poured from it down his face. His hands and feet were like raw bleeding meat. His legs were broken, his chest crisscrossed with bleeding whiplashes and there was a gaping wound in his side.

A bare-chested, feathered native danced around him to repetitive drumbeats. Someone was blowing a whistle. I heard the laws of physical reality torn like a veil and felt a convergence of clashing paradigms.

I saw feathers growing out of my hands. My nails had become like talons. I think I may have screamed. I remember that I rose to my feet and began running through smoke and shafts of light. I was alone in space; there was nothing under my feet, nothing below or above me. This time I know I screamed because the sound brought me back. I stumbled up the aisle for the massive doors. Outside the sun was fierce and I began running.

Many Mansions

I saw Carla sitting in one of the lobby chairs facing the front windows when I entered. I wanted to turn back but it was too late because she had already seen me. She was dressed as she had been for church, in a black skirt and white blouse with comfortable flat shoes. Her expression was angry when I entered. She rose abruptly from the lobby chair and crushed out a cigarette in the ashtray. I could see in her eyes how I must have looked to her. My white shirt was perspiration-stained under the arms and wet across my chest, my dirty face was sweaty, and I was drunk.

I'd gone from the Church to a cantina where I drank several shots of tequila, spilling much of it over my trembling fingers in the process of raising the shot glass to my lips. Later I bought a pint bottle and took a taxi to a movie theatre on Insurgentes to try to get my mind off what had happened in the Cathedral, but I fell asleep and woke with a headache and left the movie—a Hollywood western with Spanish subtitles—before it had ended.

I kept flashing on the memory of the taco I had eaten and the face of the old woman who had sold it to me. I kept seeing her cunning smile, her sloping long nose and high cheekbones, but most of all her penetrating stare. My head continued to hurt from processing what had happened, and I was no closer to coming to an understanding. I kept examining my body for feathers. But I was not a bird, or a birdman. I was flesh.

I was exhausted and longed for sleep.

Carla wanted and was owed an explanation, but I had none.

"What happened to you today, Raymond? You went running out of there like someone had poured gasoline on you and lighted it. I've never seen anything like it. You went positively white. You looked like you saw a ghost."

Not *a* ghost, but three. I could see them now, indistinctly hovering like mist behind an illusory separation. What was happening to me? I had to get alone someplace and think this through. And I had to apologize and somehow explain to Carla.

"I'm sorry, Carla, but I had to find a toilet, and quickly. I became suddenly feverish, dizzy and weak. I felt I had to lie down quickly or I would faint. It was all I could do to make it outside and find a cab."

"You were fine on the bus ride over. And now you reek of alcohol."

"It's from the medicine that the pharmacist recommended. In fact, I'm pretty woozy from it. I really need to just lie down and go to sleep."

"I ate as much of your taco as you and it didn't upset me at all. Have you been drinking the water again?" She touched my forehead with the flat of her palm and said, "You do feel feverish. Do you need me to stay with you?"

"No, I'll manage. The way I feel, I'm likely to sleep through the night."

"Well if you need me, I'm staying temporarily at the Hotel Franco."

Did she say Hotel *Franco*? Did she mean *Francisco*?

I would find out later. I escorted her out of the hotel to the corner intersection, deposited her in a cab and returned, instructing Ricardo to hold my calls. I almost fell asleep standing up in elevator I was so exhausted. The air conditioning in the room gave me a chill but my shirt was soaking wet, so as soon as I got in my room I removed it and dried my back and upper body with a hotel towel. Maybe Carla was onto something. Maybe I really was feverish and didn't realize it. That would explain everything. I fell asleep immediately.

* * *

Notebook entry, present time: I wake to a great massive throbbing headache and phenomenal unrelenting thirst. Buttoning my shirt as I go, I stagger down the hall for the elevator. The soft drink dispenser in the lobby alcove is humming and thankfully well-stocked. My thirst is absolute and compulsive. I drink two colas quickly. The streets outside of the hotel are wet and glimmering. It has recently rained, and the lighting is unfamiliar, neither night or day, and a bluish shade of gray I have not seen here before. It's eerily quiet, an effort to move through this strange liquid twilight.

Jesus the Beggar glows under a lamp post. He is barefoot and wears the same dirty rags as the day I met him. I close my eyes, squeezing them shut tightly, but still see his illumination through my eyelids. Am I dreaming this? It begins to rain, a fine, light drizzle. I feel the first few tiny drops on my arms and face, then taste it on my tongue. I feel the cool rainwater in my hair. It trickles down the back of my neck. Walking toward him, I seem to make no progress—we remain equally distant with each of my footsteps.

I follow him down an alley but he eludes me. I call to him, my voice echoing down the empty passageway. It is an eerie, forlorn, disembodied voice which leaves the impression of not belonging to me but someone else. My feet are without sound on the cobblestoned alley. It's narrow and without light here, littered with enamel wash basins, charred dirty cookware, dirty diapers and the remains of smoldering fires extinguished by rain. The cobblestones are uneven under my boots; my footsteps precarious in the darkness. I stumble, and it feels as if I am falling for thousands of miles, falling forever. I land on my knees in the darkness on some wet cardboard.

The passageway has narrowed. There is barely room for me to stand. Damp laundry brushes against my face as I make my way slowly into the darkness. There is a stink of human and animal excrement and spoiled rotten flesh. Something grunts that sounds like a pig. I hear garbage cans being overturned, the patter of hooves. Something brushes against me. Was that me who screamed? I do not see the beggar.

* * *

Damp and shivering, I pull the blankets around me and drift in and out of sleep. Carla calls, concerned. She wants to take me to a clinic in the University. No, I tell her, it is nothing. A slight fever at most. I'm probably just coming down with a cold. I'll go tomorrow to the Pharmacia for some antibiotics and cold medicine. Some sleeping medication as well.

Promise me, she says.

I promise, Carla. Not to worry. I will sleep this little fever away.

When she hangs up I get out of my damp clothing and into the shower but there is little hot water. Now I am really shivering, and have to put back on the damp clothing and wet boots. At least I have dry socks.

When I arrive in the lobby Ricardo says, "You don't look well, Raymundo." He actually sounds concerned. Even offers to send Pedro to the Pharmacy.

It's afternoon, the sun indistinct in the haze of city smog and exhaust. There are no puddles, no evidence of any rain of the night before. I board a bus with no idea of where I am going or where it will take me, get off at random, walk and board another. Something outside of my will seems to be leading me. I board yet another bus. I don't know how many times I do this, perhaps four or five.

Get off the bus, says a voice inside of me.

I step off into an unfamiliar neighborhood of tenement buildings surrounded by high walls with gates to inner courtyards. I have never seen this barrio before. It is almost entirely Indian. The high-rise buildings of downtown Mexico City are barely visible from here. There are no tourists here; it's off the map, probably unknown to them. I see very few inhabitants who even look Mexican. Other than a few traditionally dressed Chinese men with long white beards, the population here is a mix of Mexican Indian races.

Hand painted barely legible weather- beaten signs creak in the wind. A proprietor thrusts a live duck in my face. Its wings beat violently against its owner's grip as it twists in an effort to free itself. It hawks insistently in my face, its hoarse vocalese strident and annoying. A man across the street sits outside his shop, watching. He sells large gunnysacks of charcoal. They're stacked to the ceiling. No wonder he is sitting outside. He probably coughs up gobs of black dust all night. He's black with its soot. His hands are like coal, his black face reminiscent of a vaudeville minstrel.

Doors open to rooms kept mostly dark. Many have small portable fans. Their merchandise is mostly damaged. A man with sad hazel eyes, a gray beard and thick white moustache tries to sell me a fistful of shoelaces, all used. His straw hat is unraveling; remnants of it shoot out of its brim and peaked crown, giving him the appearance of a scarecrow. A woman pulls a wagon heaped with maize and corn husks. She crosses the street, stepping into a road riddled with deep potholes filled with dirty puddle water. Another woman sells scraps of paper on which prayers are written. She smiles broadly, displaying her three or four remaining teeth. The prayer is written in a language I have never seen before. It's not in Spanish, not in any language familiar to me. A traditionally dressed Chinese man with a long pointed white beard sits in a rocking chair where he smokes a long-stemmed pipe. He offers opium and dreams.

But I thought I was dreaming already, I reply.

No, he says, no, no, this is only the surface—only a ripple on an endless sea of dreaming, a shattered fragment of dreaming, a distant melody that has played in your unconscious from the moment of your conception until now, a single leaf falling from the tree of life, a cosmic breath taken when rising to the glimmer of sunshine on the surface of the sea , a . . . His voice fades, becomes a whisper, then fades into nothingness.

A hunchbacked woman sitting behind the counter of her herb store smokes tobacco out of a corncob pipe. A sign over the counter reads *Curandera*. Her shelves are lined with glass jars containing plant cuttings, mushrooms, and dead toads floating in formaldehyde. Huge wicker baskets overflow with broken dolls, some with missing heads or arms. She smiles, showing a black misshapen tooth in the front of her mouth. She is dressed in a patched together burlap sack dress and wears a black bandana over her messy gray hair. Something is wrong with one of her eyes, which is filmed over with a white liquid substance that obscures its pupil. She looks exactly like the woman who sold me the bad taco outside of the Cathedral. She addresses me in Mayan. Why do I understand it? I don't speak or understand Mayan. Maybe it's not Mayan. It doesn't sound like Spanish. What is it?

I hear the croaking of toads, the chatter of talking birds and exotic parrots. Lizards scatter across the counter. Beetles and spiders scurry across a bamboo ceiling packed tightly with straw. A dead black cat floats in a jar of formaldehyde. There is a smaller jar of what look like eyeballs. A beaded curtain separates a back room from the shop. Through the beads I see a man dressed in feathers shaking a rattle and dancing. The woman takes down a huge jar of what turns out to be chicken feet strung together in necklaces. She places one around my neck. I feel the scratching of toenails. They seem to be writing something with their claws. The necklace clings to me and fights my effort to remove it. I yank it off, toss it on the shop woman's counter. It curls into the shape of a coiled snake ready to strike and seems alive. The shopkeeper takes some tissues and wipes my neck where the claws had been; there is blood on the tissue. She lights it afire and watches the tiny specs of burned tissue float upward. She makes strange signals with her hands as if drawing in the air with her fingers, says I have been guided to her by a spirit. She wants me to lick the sweat off the back of a toad.

"No, no, I say. "I am a Christian. *Christos! Christos!*"

She wants to sell me what she calls a lucky bone, a rib bone of a virgin who was killed by a venomous snake. If you place this bone in a stream, contrary to natural law it will drift upstream. That is how you know it is magic. You make a wish as it floats away.

She scoops parts of broken dolls out of a bin, spreads them out across the counter like a deck of tarot cards, moves them in a circle at dazzling speed, changing their positions like in a carnival shell game. Feathers brush against my cheek. I feel myself weaken; my eyesight becomes blurred and I become faint. I stagger and fall into a case of what looks like pig embryos in glass jars. I am falling and falling.

You are in danger. Leave at once.

Who has said this? Was it Jesus? I think it was. I think I saw him riding past on a donkey. Outside the sun is like a brutal hammer than brings me to my knees. I cannot see anything but light. A little girl with large expressive brown eyes emerges from within it. She carries an obsidian cross bordered with hammered silver, holds it forward in both hands as if warding off a spirit. Christ is affixed to it, drenched in crimson blood. His grimacing face bears an expression of raw agony. It is grotesque and brutal, a passionate and accurately Mexican representation of the Crucifixion. The girl vanishes in mist.

I board a bus, mute passengers staring at me knowingly. Their faces, as if carved in limestone, are utterly without expression, their fathomless brown eyes selfishly guarding dark secrets.

* * *

My sheets are flung all across the dirty floor, the pillows on my bed spattered with blood stains. A pile of fresh animal scat is steaming in an ungodly reeking pile under the air vent. I kneel to examine it. What kind of animal might have left this? By what means did it enter? Why does the picture of a jaguar come to mind?

Something flies from the closet, moving so fast it's a blur. I have to duck my head to prevent being struck. I hear the flutter of wings, feel and hear the whoosh of animal flight. A large black crow settles on the dresser and stares at me with a hostile, sentient expression that makes me shiver. Its damp, iridescent feathers glisten. Its eyes are disturbing, its gaze fixed on me, probing my mind. It watches my every thought as I go into the bathroom to vomit. I can feel something inside of my mind altering my thoughts, inserting imagery, editing and rearranging my memories. I'm not nauseous from indigestion as much as from fear. I can't stop shaking.

I look horrible in the bathroom mirror, my face distorted with fear. Perspiration drips down my face. My eyes sting with the effort of perceiving. The mirror steams over with moisture. It's like a hothouse in here. I stare into the mirror and glimpse the indistinct movement of dim presences. A water glass falls off the sink and shatters into hundreds of small pieces. Millions of reflections within the shards reveal a multicolored kaleidoscope of ever-changing fragmented images—dense emerald jungles and high mountain desert fortresses, the migration of birds, strange little monkeys in tight little suits with short pants and conical hats, scores of cartwheeling giants, jugglers and whirling dervishes, exotic dancers with exposed breasts and jewels in their navels, costumed accordionist dwarfs. A camel-driven caravan departs for infinite metaphysical deserts. Magical beings on winged animals pass, the furled sails of ships, the eternal march of successive oceanic waves crashing against craggy shores. Tall spires of ancient Moorish cities collapse into dust. My feet are cut and bleeding on the broken glass surface of an alien planet. The water in the sink is overflowing. I turn off the faucet and return to the bedroom.

Damp clothing adheres to my flesh like blood-soaked bandages. I'm almost too tired to make it to bed, but somehow manage it, collapsing like an armored knight wounded in battle, spiraling into vertigo, delirium and dreaming. Carla raises a glass of cool water to my lips to sooth my raw, parched throat. Carla, my guardian, my guide through this maze. I stare at her adoringly, lost in her angelic soft face, her kind friendly eyes, her soft golden hair and cunning malevolent eyes, ugly warts and wrinkled evil face.

She looks identical to the old woman who sold me the taco outside of the Great Cathedral. I recognize her now. She is the Curandera who wanted me to a lick a toad. She is holding the toad now, a large ugly creature with an abnormally long flickering tongue. It perches in her cupped palms as if on a throne, shouting in my face. It's the largest toad I have ever seen, a sickening shade of mottled green and grey. It leaps out of her cupped hands and lands on my bed. It croaks in my face insistently and spits up something like bile that burns a hole in the sheets. The hag smiles insidiously as she retrieves it and places it on the bureau next to the crow.

"Listen carefully," she says. "The Mayan world was not entirely destroyed by its conquest. The intersection of conflicting European and Toltec realities during the arrival of Cortez was a collision of two alternate dimensions that were never supposed to converge. *We were never meant to inhabit the same reality.* You have come here by a similar accident. Mexico is a dimensional vortex where alternate realities are shuffled like a deck of cards, a psychic and spiritual intersection where inexperienced travelers who become lost are subject to mischievous trickster entities who will lead them into dark, non-linear realms of no return. The hospitals are filled with these dreamers. They are said to be catatonic but have themselves become dream entities."

The crow agrees with her. It squawks in my face, flaps its long black wings and seems angry with me. The bloated toad croaks and jumps up and down in a frenzy of agreement. Faintly visible beings gather around me. They want me to understand, but what? I can't think, can't breathe. The hag's breath is sickening. She takes a deep inhalation of the putrid air and blows it in my face. Her exhalation is a force capable of bending trees. Wind roars from her mouth, an audible onrush of terrible cyclonic energy and power. Pages of my notebooks are tossed through the air like confetti. Bedsheets hover against the ceiling. Discarded clothing rises like resurrected ghosts. The shaking bed rises. Comb, bar of soap, pens, spare change, wallet, passport, journals, everything airborne and whirling. The room spinning...

I hear Carla calling me but she's far far away and I can't find my way back to her.

The bathroom door opens and then I see her. She wears a white nursing uniform with small white buttons and a stethoscope around her neck. Places a thermometer in my mouth and stands over me adjusting a stocking. Her legs are spectacular. Wars have been fought over legs like hers. She's wearing nylons and a garter belt, but no panties. She gently takes my head in both hands, pushes my face hard against her crotch.

But I wake alone in my room. Sexual fantasies are rampant in my mind, a kaleidoscope of high-speed pornographic newsreel images. I'm splashing cold water in my face from the bathroom sink. My legs are weak, folding in on themselves, my equilibrium off kilter, the room floating and making me seasick. I grasp the sink with both hands to steady myself and look into the mirror. My face is damp with sweat, my long hair matted to my face, my eyes rheumy, jaundiced and vaguely bloodshot.

In the mirror, behind the image of my face, the Curandera stares back at me. Behind her in the mirror is an endless column of replicated doubles, each one slightly smaller than the next in a genetic chain of faintly visible beings incrementally diminished in size and clarity until becoming tiny specs indiscernible to the human eye. In the great unfathomable distance, far into the mist where these ghosts have vanished, beyond the ringing in my ears, out in the silence beyond this room and the visible world, high along the crest of a volcanic mountain range, a naked, dark-skinned shaman with white circles painted on his face, arms and buttocks, steps out of the mouth of a cave. This cave has been his home since the beginning.

He stands high on a ledge and gazes out into the loop of

time itself, off into a primordial landscape of smoldering volcanic mountain chains and vibrant throbbing green jungle. He sees beyond this to glowing red deserts where luminous blinking messages are sent by invisible beings scattered through millions of stars to traverse vast cosmic oceans where floating crystal cities drift like inconceivable ships across eons of time. But there is no time, no past, no future.

This shaman looks out across eternity from the mouth of his cave as if through a telescopic lens and sees it all happening as he always has, everything at once, everything that has ever made a ripple in the fabric of the great cosmic mind of the universe. Everything that has happened in time has always happened and is happening now. Over his left shoulder is a leather quiver filled with magical feathered arrows. He draws one from his quiver and inserts it into the thread of his bow. He pulls the bow string, releases it, and the arrow begins its long journey. There is no escape from it. It will travel through time and find its target. I am that target. I hear ritualistic singing in an ancient lost language. I hear the sound of someone striking a drum and the ritualistic footsteps of someone dancing in place. I hear the shaking of a rattle. I smell white sage burning, cedar, and pine. It is our ghost who leads us through life. Maybe we are already dead.

* * *

Carla returns from the pharmacy, places a palm on my forehead and says, "You're still warm but I think your fever may have broken."

Her pretty undulating breasts are filled with expensive champagne. I try to touch them but she slaps my hand away.

"Stop it," she says. "What's the matter with you?"

She sits on the edge of the bed, her skirt rising up her legs, a flash of silk panties visible. She wipes my face with a damp cloth, brushes wet hair from my eyes. I have never even tried to kiss her. If I kissed her, there would be no going back, no stopping. I can't stop watching her, but my eyelids are heavy and it's a struggle to keep my eyes open.

When I wake she says, "You were talking in your sleep."

"What was I saying?"

"I don't know. It was like you were talking in tongues. I didn't understand a word of it. It frightened me."

"I was dreaming again."

"I know. You're dreaming now. We both are."

She leads me up a spiral staircase, lifts a steel door upward to stars and a full moon. The night air on the roof sobers me. Standing on the balcony, facing the wind that sweeps up from the abyss, the view of the lighted city is spectacular. Carla leaps first. I next, into the vortex. The sensation is exhilarating. I have not flown like this for a long time. Carla is beautiful in flight, her hair streaming behind her, her long white gown shifting in wind currents.

We could picnic on the craters of the moon but it's only a dream, and I awaken. Carla dampens my perspiring face, removes the sleep from my eyes, washes under my arms, my chest, stomach and legs. Naked, I feel myself become erect under the clean white sheet that covers me. She smiles and gives me a knowing look and a matronly kiss on the cheek.

"It's good to see you awake, Raymond. If not for your tossing and turning and talking in your sleep, I might have thought you had died. I took your temperature and you were burning up. I went out for antibiotics and made you sit up and take your medicine with mineral water but you went right back to sleep. You slept fourteen hours."

"I think that taco I bought from the old woman when we were in the Zocalo made me sick."

"When were we in the Zocalo?"

"When we went to the Great Cathedral."

"Raymond, whatever are you talking about?"

"Don't you remember?"

"No."

"We walked to the Zocalo on the way to the Great Cathedral. I had a taco that made me sick. I left you alone in the Great Cathedral without explanation. I'm sorry for that, Carla."

"Raymond, you should know by now that I would never so much as step foot in the Cathedral. You asked me a hundred times and each time I refused. I have never in my life visited a Catholic Church and I don't intend to. You must have been dreaming."

"Am I dreaming now?"

"Raymond, you're scaring me. Of course you're not dreaming. What's the matter with you? Why would you think that? Take your pills, Raymond. Your morning dose is on the nightstand."

"What kind of pills are they?"

"Antibiotics, and aspirin for your fever."

"I thought maybe they were magic. Maybe some kind of love potion. I'm falling in love with you, Carla."

"Don't be silly, Raymond. That's just your fever talking."

She goes to the chair in the corner to read, sometimes looking at me with an expression I can't quite read, as if she might be trying to decide something about me. When I wake I am alone, the radio tuned to a soothing classical station.

Flesh

I'm with Carla in a Mexican movie theatre showing an American film with Spanish subtitles. I place my hand on her bare knee. Absorbed in the movie, she doesn't remove it. She hardly seems aware of it. The movie is a story about adultery in which a woman is in love with a married man. On screen they yield to temptation for the first time. I move my hand under Carla's skirt, my fingers ever so slowly inching toward her hidden treasure and my heart's desire. She swats my hand away without so much as a glance away from the screen and continues eating popcorn. I have an erection and hate myself for it.

Later, in a restaurant after the movie, we both drink too much wine. Her blouse has come slightly unbuttoned at the throat. I understand now why the neck is the favorite blood site of vampires. The tease of cleavage is tantalizing and ultimately irresistible. Her ear, peeking shyly out from where her hair is tucked, also looks delicious.

Later, in the back seat of the cab, I resist the urge to kiss her. And later still, in the hotel elevator, I find myself literally swooning and want her so bad I have to grab onto the railing. I wish I could stop this but I can't. I have an erection and can't seem to stop gawking at her.

I fumble for the key to my room, open the door, turn on the light and reach for her, two dear friends in a friendly hug. But I want more. I am determined to kiss her. I will not release her. My intentions are clear. She knows, fights my embrace which has continued far beyond our comfort zone. I try to find her mouth with mine but she tilts her head evasively, exposing her unprotected neck, which I kiss and suck.

Her frightened blue eyes are inspiring. I impale her against the door and kiss her decisively. I suck on her lips, put my tongue in her mouth and hands between her legs. She can't escape even if she wants to. Her body won't let her. My hands stroke her face, her breasts and the curve of her buttocks.

When we release one another, our hearts are pounding. She steps out of my reach, pushes some locks of hair out of her eyes. Her face is flushed and she is breathing heavily. One of her breasts is faintly visible from where I had partially unbuttoned her blouse.

"That was definitely not our usual hug, Raymond."

"Carla, I didn't intend this, but I've fallen in love with you."

She frowns, purses moist lips that only moments ago I kissed. I want to kiss them again. She takes another small step backward.

"Oh, Raymond. Oh dear. This is a worry. This might not be good. Please don't misunderstand. I have feelings for you, but not in that way. I don't think we should pursue this. Even if I wanted to, it's too soon. We have to think carefully about this and not rush into it."

"I already have thought about it, Carla. I can't *stop* thinking about it. I'm in love with you. It changes everything and I don't know if I can go back to being just friends. It's too late. "

"Ray, you're lonely, young, inexperienced and probably just horny. You may have thought this through, but not me. I didn't expect this."

"I didn't either. But I love you."

"I love you too, Raymond. You are my dearest friend."

"But it's no longer enough to be just your friend. I want more. I want you to love me the way I love you."

I pull her into my arms and kiss her. This time there is no resistance from her, no expression of her feelings except for a sigh of resignation. We end up on my bed. Her face has softened, become younger. The room takes on a quality of moistness. The entire moment has become liquefied. We have entered another, softer dimension of being. She whispers my name.

Raymond. Raymond, please ...

This is not her voice, not a voice I have heard from her before. It is small and weak, trembling, vulnerable and endangered. But please what? Please yes, or please no?

My hands find their way under her blouse; her nipples are hard as pebbles. I push my hands down her pants and find her to be wet down there. She rolls away and says no, retreats into the bathroom and locks the door. I stand on the other side of it, my heart pounding. I hear water running and the sound of her washing.

When she returns her face is clean and her hair back in place. The flush in her cheeks is gone. She sits next to me on the bed and says, "Ray, we have to think about this. We have to be sure."

"I'm sure I love and want you more than anything else in my life. You wanted me too, Carla. I felt it. What's holding you back? Are you in love with the Cuban Consul?"

"What? Why bring him up?"

"Are you sleeping with him?"

"That's private and irrelevant Raymond. I don't think you should ask."

"Are you sleeping with Navio too? "

"Sometimes, yes. But we're not exclusive, Navio and I. He considers monogamy to be bourgeois and counter-revolutionary. I ended up agreeing, and we've kind of drifted apart. Navio's great love will always be Mexico and his revolution."

"But do you love him?"

"Of course I love him, but this is not about Navio or Francisco either, for that matter, so let's keep them out of it. It's about us, you and me. If we take this step there is no going back from it. I want us to be sure. If we have a love affair it might end our friendship. I don't think you and I can have it both ways. I don't think we can be lasting friends and lovers, and I can't stand the idea of losing your friendship. I don't know which to choose."

"I want both."

"Trust me; it doesn't work that way. I'm experienced and know about this. Besides, I'm really not in a position to begin a serious, committed love affair right now."

"I want to kiss you again, Carla. Our kisses are real. All this talk is only evasion."

She pushes me away and says, "Ray, Ray, Ray, slow it down, okay? Now is not the time. I'm weak and if I kiss you again, I'll end up in your bed. I can't stay here any longer. I have to go. Right now."

She hesitates at the door, purse slung over her arm, and says, "I don't know where we go from here, you and I. I need some time to think, Ray. If I am going sleep with you and become your lover, I don't want it to be because of a weak moment I will regret later. I want it to be a deliberate act that I can own. I want it to be a clear decision. Let's both think about this when we've cooled off a little, and we'll talk about it next time."

"And when will that be?"

"Probably not soon. I've been falling behind in my classes and need some time alone, both to study and to think this over. You really surprised me, Raymond. I wasn't prepared for this."

Perhaps neither of us were. Something elemental has changed. Carla is no longer the orchestrator of this dance. I feel both tender and brutal. I have found my inner machismo.

* * *

But what a difference a week makes. I'm powerless again. I fall to my knees right there in the hallway. I don't care who sees it. I'm on my knees, clinging to her, my arms wrapped around her perfect long legs, my tear-streaked cheek against her adorable bare knees. Her tanned bare feet are in sandals, the toenails painted red. I'm all but drooling on them.

"Where have you *been?*" I cry. "I thought you were *never* coming back."

When I look up I see that she is braless, her nipples visible through her delicate cotton blouse. It's hard not to stare. I don't even try.

She smiles and says, "But Raymond, I told you I needed to take some time to study and to think about us."

It's obvious by her smile she's as happy at this moment as I. She looks down upon me on my knees as if I was the most beautiful thing in this world. Her hands stroke my hair. I take them in mine, tenderly kissing each one before rising to kiss her hard on the mouth. There is no reluctance, no hesitation. We belong together. Our bodies know this. Mine does, at least.

She backs off and says, "We need to talk, Raymond. I needed time to myself to think things through, and now that I have, here is what I know. The temptation of sex will always be between us unless we make up our minds right now whether we want to be friends or lovers and swear to abide by it."

"But I've already decided, Carla. I know you don't want me to, but I love you. I can't stop thinking of you. I can't sleep from wanting you. I don't care if it is dangerous and unwise for us to fall in love. It's too late. I already have. I know you think if we become lovers our friendship would somehow be damaged, but I think if we don't it will always be between us, always on our minds."

"It's on my mind right now," says Carla.

Our mouths find each other in a kiss so urgent it is as if we want to inhabit one another. Our imperative to merge possesses us beyond even a thought of resistance. Her hands are all over me. When I reach under her skirt she doesn't stop me. We tear at buttons, snaps and zippers in a delirious urgency to feel body against body, flesh against warm flesh. Our excitement is self-defeating; we can't stop pawing and kissing one another long enough to get our clothes off. I manage to lift the blouse over her head and her beautiful full breasts come free, round and soft and wonderful to touch. Her left breast has a small beauty mark the size of a pea. Her nipples are darker than the rest of her, her breasts white as pillows.

"Do you like them?" she whispers.

"They're beautiful. I love them."

"They love you, Ray. They love your hands on them. See how the nipples harden? You may kiss them if you like."

Each breast responds differently to my lips. Both taste faintly of salt and powdered sugar. I'm rock hard and pulsating. Her hands find the zipper of my pants. She sits on me and puts me inside of her. She's coming almost immediately. I can't tell where her mouth begins and mine ends. We are two separate organisms fused into one for the sole purpose of pleasure. Her face is the most beautiful thing I have ever seen. I know absolutely that this is the most beautiful moment of my life. She shouts my name. I think I might be crying. She comes again, and I feel her moisture, warm and salty, wet and inexplicably Mediterranean. Everything has led to this moment, this climactic release. I come and come.

Afterwards we sprawl gasping in my disheveled bed, our legs entangled in the twisted sheets. Perspiration drips down our grateful, satiated bodies.

Carla exhales a long stream of warm breath toward the ceiling and says, "You surprised me, Raymond. You're usually so cautious. You don't have any regrets about this, do you?"

"Of course not. I'm excruciatingly happy."

"Do you have something strong to drink?"

"Tequila."

"Perfect. Do you think we can make love again? Not now, but later."

"I can do it right now, Carla. I want to."

"No, let's wait a bit longer and have some of your Tequila. It will relax us. The next time will be even better. I mean, the first time was wonderful, but the next will be even better, less urgent, more deliberate and relaxed. We'll take our time. We'll sit here and drink tequila until we're drunk and pet each other until we can't stand it. We'll taste each other."

"I love you, Carla."

"I know," she replies softly. "And guess what? You are going to love me a lot more before this afternoon is over."

And she is right about that. It's even better the next time and I love her even more. I fall asleep happily in her arms.

* * *

And wake to this message:

My Dearest Raymond,

That was wonderful. We will do it again many times. For the next few days I have finals in several classes, but I'll try to get in to see you again soon, if only briefly, for a sweet kiss. Until then, you will be in my thoughts and in my heart.

Love and kisses,

Carla.

I clench her note in my fist like a stolen treasure map to a fabled lost city. I hold my fingers under my nostrils and breathe deeply. As long as her scent remains, I will not wash my hands. The message she has left me is greater than any poem I might ever have written. It is my most valued possession.

We'll do it again, many times.

Yes.

That is what I want to hear and want to do. I want her wet soapy body in the steamy shower stall, the warm water cascading down our backs like a tropical waterfall in Eden. I want her on the desk where I write this, her slender long legs wrapped tightly around my face, her crotch pressed against my mouth in a ravenous kiss. I want her in my bed, in the hasty tangle of sheets, on the hard bare floor. I want her straddling me. I want her in the hotel elevator, in her dorm room, on the rooftop of this hotel, in sequestered alcoves of the University library. I want to hear her say fuck me, fuck me. I want to watch us in a mirror. I want her on top, on bottom, from behind, on my face. I want her everywhere; I want to do everything.

We are all Beggars

I know I have contributed to Christ's suffering as surely as a Roman soldier lashing him at the crucifixion. I remember what we did, Carla and I. How we fornicated under the cross like possessed drunken satyrs at a Roman orgy. I raise my hands to pray for forgiveness, but smell Carla's sex on them. I stagger barefoot to the bathroom, run cool water in the sink and splash it on my face. The face of a traitor stares back at me. I might as well be staring at the face of Judas. But I don't want to walk in Christ's footsteps anymore. I don't want to carry his cross. It's Carla I want. Stop testing me. I can't even carry my own cross, let alone yours. I'm ready to be punished, cast out of the Garden, exiled to a psychic ghetto in a bad neighborhood East of Eden. So be it. I don't know if I even care any longer. I'm leaving, headed there right now in fulfillment of prophesy on city streets I have come to love. Well, that's probably overstated. The truth is I have long been known to relieve certain mental disorders with long walks instead of the medications that in the past have been advised. It is my hope now the clear air might restore me. But of course there is no clear air. This is Mexico City, smog capital of the world.

The rains have relented for now. The leaves on shrubs and trees glisten. And now the sun passes from behind scattered clouds. For the next several hours everything appears bright and fresh, renewed in the morning sunlight. Somehow it seems a hopeful message of forgiveness. My sight is directed to beauty. Vivid tropical flowers blossom in tenement window boxes. Birds sing from cages on balconies. Vendors are out early. Why is this pretty Mexican girl probably no more than thirteen years old not in school? Where is her mother?

Mexico City birds sing from their perches on the branches of trees that border a wide tiled pathway in Chapultepec Park. A stone bench faces a green terraced flower beds in at the edge of a still murky frog pond with floating water hyacinth and lilies. The mating of regal swans is in process. A spectacular group of white birds ascend from the reeds and take flight. Doves? The sight would thrill Carla if only she were here to see it. Carla, who taught me to love this city, to open myself to its beauty and, more importantly to not interpret everything that I see but just let it be, to get out of my own head and into the splendor of the world around me. Carla, who I also betrayed. I empty my mind into the frog pond and remain vacant for hours.

Later the smog becomes a terrible presence; my eyes burn and water with it. Tenements shimmer as if being cooked in a cosmic oven. If only I had been out here earlier this morning, when it rained. I miss the Seattle rain. I wish it would rain now. I wish it would wash away my troubles. I wish that I did not hold myself to a standard of obedience and holiness that only Christ was able to maintain in his lifetime. Why can't I free myself from this need for righteousness? Why can't I simply be a man like any other, without covenant or vow, without need for holiness and transcendence?

Well, no rest for the wicked, as they say. The fragrance of strong coffee is in the air. My mouth waters. I am in a body and this body I inhabit controls me. I want food, I want sex. I want Carla. I want to suck on her and hear her sigh and moan and beg. I want it right now.

Remember the cowboy I met at the Woolworth's lunch counter in El Paso? Ate my French fries without asking and called himself Jive Jerry or something like that? Well, he was right. We're already damned, so why not party in Hell like he said?

Eight million living persons in Mexico City and it feels like they are all driving and honking their horns at the same time. Damn I want a beer. Yes, why not a beer, and a double shot of tequila too. I don't care if it costs my last centavo. I am a man now. I have a man's desire. I have a man's heart. This is what we do, we broken men in this broken world; this is how we survive. *Una cerveza por fucking favor* and pour in a shot of tequila while you're at it. Una fucking mas. Thank you and I'll be on my way.

Keep walking, Raymond, keep moving. Damn but it's crowded out here; too many people. Get away you; I don't want any damn Chiclets. And you! Do I look like I have the money to waste on a lottery ticket? Get away. Excuse me, excuse me, yes I stepped on your foot, so what, can't be helped, what do you expect in this crowded midtown street?

A dissonant symphony of automobile horns reaches what sounds like its final, climactic movement. Where are the tympani drums, the clash of cymbals? An American tour bus pulls to the curb. Tourists disembark. Luggage handlers load heaps of leather suitcases onto gleaming brass luggage carts. A stooped elderly woman wearing a large white sunhat while holding a small, professionally groomed white dog in her lap is pushed in a wheelchair by two identically uniformed bellboys.

An aproned waiter sweeping his sidewalk chases a young panhandler away with his broom. Begging is bad for business. It suppresses the appetites of the rich. I'm hungry but can't afford these prices. I had expected Mexico to be cheap. I thought I would get by easily on my hundred dollars a month allotment. I was supposed to have been the rich American, living and dining in opulent hotels. I am often hungry and short of funds. I can't seem to keep track of my money or budget, and have difficulty refusing the roving beggars who seem to size me up on sight as someone with a deep pocket and generous heart.

The young man about my own age who appears before me wearing a white button-down shirt under a sports jacket, clutches my sleeve. He looks more Spanish than Mexican I notice he has a slight limp. His eyes are excessively bloodshot, his face vaguely yellowish in appearance. His blue polyester slacks are expensive looking and perfectly fitted to his lean build. His hair is fashionably cut, if a little shaggy and in need of a trim. He's asking for money, clutching my sleeve so tightly I can't move without it tearing, and brings his face so close to mine I briefly think he intends to kiss me. He has a shadow of rough beard; the faint scent of alcohol and cheap cologne pervades. A closer look exposes his fancy European shoes as scuffed and worn down lopsidedly at the heels. The collar of his white shirt reveals a crusty ring of dirt, a tiny burn hole is visible in the knee of his fancy trousers. His clothing reeks of cigarettes and his eyes look jaundiced.

"I am very hungry," he says in English. "Can you please spare a few pesos so that I may dine?"

Dine? This is not street vocabulary. What the hell type of beggar is this guy? His hand still clutches my sleeve. I see now that he wears a wrist watch probably worthy of pawning. I'm guessing he comes from a good family, perhaps once with a promising future. All over now.

He's on his way down, but has a long way to go. He doesn't even know yet what deep shit he is in. Of course, I have my own troubles. I give him some money, but very little, a few centavos basically, less even than I normally give the city organ grinders, and shake him off. He limps behind me, trying to keep up, but I easily evade him. He gives up the chase, turns and limps off, looking for another prospect.

In a way, you're like a medic doing triage. You can't give to them all; it's impossible. It's difficult, but you have to choose. Besides, I myself am in miserable shape. Life is not easy. We possess a multitude of hungers. There is more than one way to starve, more than one kind of hunger, and many expressions of need and begging. Sometimes it seems as if all of us are begging for something in one way or another. You who read this are probably begging for something right now, if not actively beseeching in the street then in your heart. Maybe you are not even aware of it. Maybe when you pray you are begging. Maybe you beg for forgiveness and redemption as I do. Maybe you beg for love, charity, healing, or deliverance from circumstances. Maybe you beg for food and shelter. For money. Sex. I am begging for Jesus to release me from our covenant. I am begging for Carla to forgive me, to fuck me and love me. I don't know what you are begging for, but I can't help you. I'm down here with you, fallen.

Children run alongside me like small nipping dogs. One child in particular is especially persistent. *Please,* he pleads in English, *please please please señor.* He can't be more than ten or eleven, a stunted, scrawny little runt of a kid, short, bony and grimy, with the dirt-smudged face of an otherwise pretty child and the resigned paradoxical eyes of someone who has seen too much suffering, cruelty, and death. Please is probably the only English word he knows and he won't let up on it, keeps repeating it over and over, please please please please please. He wears a pair of shredded dirty white sneakers with holes in them. His big toe is partly exposed. His shirt is buttoned to the neck but missing some buttons so that his hard distended stomach shows through. His arm is in a dirty sling, a filthy bandage wrapped around his head.

People around us are convivial and happily chatty. They don't even see us. Life goes on for them while less fortunate die in the indifferent streets around them. There is nothing to be done about it. Not even our generosity is sufficient. We live in a fallen world. I give some money to this boy and then watch as older, bigger boys move in to take away what was given him.

A businessman lunching at a sidewalk café table belches and flicks a lighted cigarette butt to the street. An alert young boy with a gimp leg and amputated arm scurries like a broken tarantula into the traffic to retrieve it. A dozen more follow, leaping into the on-coming traffic in pursuit of the prized cigarette butt. They are too late. The one-armed boy has already retrieved it and is smoking from it happily. He holds it in his lips and takes several deep puffs in succession while rubbing his tummy happily with his remaining arm.

A little girl probably no older than ten, takes my sleeve and begins singing.

"Eye Yi Yi Yi, come to my weendo...."

It's a cornball song, probably not even Mexican in origin, pop-ular with tourists for its recognition factor rather than its musical-ity. She can't sing at all. She's trying, but alternately sharp and flat and at the pre-adolescent age where her voice might be changing because it abruptly jumps octaves and changes key without har-monic or melodic logic. If she cannot successfully beg from you she will try selling you something, but all she has to sell is this pitiful song. I give her a few pesos and leave her to fight those who will take them from her.

As many as two dozen shouting children who have witnessed this cling to me as I chase after a bus that has stopped at the corner. I have to fight my way through them, dragging them with me while pushing, cursing, shoving. Some have their hands in my pockets. I have to grab their little arms and twist them forcefully to free myself. They hang on me like monkeys, almost pulling off my pants. I'd be torn apart like a piñata in the ensuing frenzy if I gave to even one of them.

I have to kick a young boy hard with my motorcycle boot. Where is my shame? When did begging children become less a sight of heartbreaking pathos than an aggravation? Is this what the city does to us? Does it make us impervious to the suffering of others? Does it numb us in the face of others' misery, disease, and desperation? Is this what it means to become a man on this Earth? To become cold, selfish, and blind to the misery and need of those around us? I don't know. I try to give, to have an open heart, but it's difficult if not impossible in this city.

The bus windows open to a breeze, but offer little relief as I ride looking out the window at the changing neighborhoods. The crowded streets seethe with activity. Music is everywhere. I step off the bus into the odor of marijuana fumes drifting from the double doors of a cantina. Mariachi music blares from a juke box. It sounds like the people inside are having a good time. Maybe that's next for me. Maybe I'll start smoking dope, drinking heavily, hanging out in whorehouses.

A pretty little brown-eyed girl with golden ear-rings who could be no more than ten holds the hand of her little brother, a sickly kid with a lame leg. She tells me that he needs medicine. I give her a few peso notes. A lady wants to sell me fresh cut flowers. I shake my head no but she gives me one anyway, so I run back and give it to the little girl and her brother. An old man bursts out laughing on the street for no discernible reason. A teen-aged boy inquires whether I want to fuck his mother or sister. Says she is "cheep" and *muy bueno*. How about my little brother? You want to fuck heem? No? How about me, señor? You want me? Ten pesos for my tight young *culo?*

A black Ford van receives a casket. In a tenement window above, a young woman dressed in black weeps into her hands. But she is so young, too young to be a widow. Maybe it is her father who is dead. Maybe an older brother. Who knows, with so many dying around us?

The human scarecrow who steps barefoot out of an alley is the present day equivalent of a leper. His dirty bare feet are bloody with running sores. His soiled clothing hangs like rags from his emaciated frame. He reeks of alcohol and vomit. I fill his hands with peso notes. Maybe he wants to buy something to eat with this money. Maybe he wants to waste it on drink. I don't mind at all. I could use one or two myself. We need these comforts, we who are exiled here in this harsh broken world of error, misfortune and shame. But the man vanishes like an apparition. Maybe he is already dead. Maybe it was his ghost I saw. Or maybe I am dead. Maybe it is I who am the ghost.

It's been a long day and I'm tired, weary from all this walking. My feet hurt. I'm thirsty and famished. I want some goat meat, beans, tortillas, chicken and rice. I'm counting my money, but there's not much left. A large cast iron cook pot hangs over a charcoal fire. Slowly, the Indian woman stirs, slowly. She has a wash basin and water, plates, bowls, and tarnished metal utensils. I bend over the pot and inhale the rising steam. It smells delicious, thick and meaty, a kind of casserole or mole stew of some kind that makes my mouth water.

We count my coins together. There is enough. In fact, a little more than enough. She gives me five coins back. The bowl is filled generously to the brim, almost to the point of spilling over, and anointed liberally with hot sauce. I take my first few spoonsful and it's delicious and restorative, as good as it smelled and even better than I had hoped. Chicken or maybe goat, cornmeal, a chocolate mole, it's just what I need. I'm happy, peaceful and in the moment. Not even the thought of Carla or my broken covenant interferes with my pleasure.

But let me ask you this. Imagine that you are dining with a friend who has a dog, and this dog, during the meal when you are eating, watches your every gesture with its round wet earnest eyes. Suppose that you know this dog, know it's loved, valued and properly fed. This dog knows its place. It is obedient. This dog knows it is not allowed to approach the table. It stays in its place. But it never loses hope or ceases for even an instant to watch intently for any gesture that might suggest the unlikely possibility a scrap might be thrown in its direction. Its hangdog facial expression is so false and overtly manipulative that sometimes you just have to laugh.

I tell you this because the gray-haired brown-skinned man wearing sandals, torn jeans and a serape who slouches nearby has exactly that expression. He reminds me of Jesus the Beggar, but it's not him. He can't take his eyes off my food. It's impossible to determine his age. His wears a gray beard and straw hat and his wrinkled face is old, but it's hard to tell, here where lives can be hard and age one quickly. He has the same eyes, the same frowning mouth and hanging jaw line, the same expression of the begging dog. But there is nothing humorous or cute about it. He is not a dog. He is a man. Because he has no hope, no expectations, he does not beg. He only watches. He doesn't speak, just gazes at my bowl of warm mole as if it is a beautiful reminder of something that once was in his life, but is no more and never again will be. I count my coins and have just enough for another bowl of the woman's mole and bring it to this man, who is not a dog, but a human being. He regards me at first in bewilderment but then, gradually comprehending, accepts the dish with trembling hands.

"*Muchas gracias, señor.*"

His voice is less than a whisper, so weak and tenuous I might have imagined it. His eyes are faintly moist with a trace of tears. After several spoonsful he turns to me and smiles happily. And later, walking deeper into this fellaheen neighborhood of tenements and traffic, I know that sharing this meal has given it more power to restore and give me strength than if I had eaten all of it myself. I sense a new lightness in my step, a spring to my legs and swing to my arms that had not been there before. I feel like I could walk all the way to the hotel and back again without stopping. My visual acuity is enhanced; I can see for blocks and blocks where before I saw only what was before me. My hearing is amplified where before I was not listening. I hear the sweet chirping of birds, the delighted voices of shouting young children at play where there is a playground, swings, teeter-totters and a basketball court. There's even a big municipal wading pool with children splashing. Picnic blankets are spread on patches of lawn. Someone softly strums a guitar. Mothers nurse their infants. Men nap listening to the sounds of their children playing. I hear singing from a church across the street.

Hundreds of small flickering votive candles cast shadows on the cool adobe walls in the dark interior of the Chapel of Maria de la Luz. Narrow paths of light stream through stained glass windows. Women bow before a Christ crucified on a gilded cross. Somehow a dove has gotten into the chapel and flutters around the ceiling and stained glass windows in search of an exit. A robed priest recites from the Holy Bible. We fall to our knees. Prayers of gratitude and petition are whispered. The presence of God is with us. I feel Him here. It's been so long since I have felt His Presence like this. I can't hide, can't lie.

I join the queue of parishioners waiting to enter the confessional. Take my place on the kneeler. It's cramped but pleasant in here, the thick oak walls utterly without décor. A wooden slide opens a window where a priest presents himself for my confession. I had expected an older man, someone wise, perhaps with a grey beard, not this clean-shaven young man probably not much older than me.

"Forgive me, father, for I have sinned."

"How long has it been since your last confession?"

"I'm sorry. I've never done this before. I've never even been in a Catholic church before, except once, in the Great Cathedral. It was terrifying. I barely got out with my mind intact. I'm afraid *now*."

"Then why are you here? What troubles your heart?"

"I am in love."

"That is no sin."

"I had been celibate for almost a year. I was honoring a vow I made to Christ to be chaste until married. I broke that vow."

"Sex outside of marriage is a sin, but God forgives those who repent."

"Yes, but my confession is that it's not God's forgiveness I want but Carla's."

"I don't understand."

"She didn't know anything about my covenant and vow. I should have told her if we were going to have sex. She had a right to know. I kept it from her because I was afraid if she knew she would refuse me. I wanted her more than God. I still do."

"Listen to me. You already know what is right and what you must do. Confess to Christ and repent. Go to this woman; confess to her as you have to me. Tell her what is in your heart. Confess your covenant with Christ, and how it came to be broken. Have faith that He will be with you always. Wherever you go, He will be. Everywhere you are, He is. Let him guide you."

When I leave the darkness of the chapel the world outside is beautiful. I am renewed with confidence. I know what I must do, and God will help me do it.

* * *

How had this happened? How had I fallen in love? I certainly never expected it. Carla's hair is braided into a crown on the top of her head like Frieda Kahlo's. Her pendulous silver earrings capture flickering light. She wears sandals, silver bracelets, black beads and ruby red nail polish. A faint lingering fragrance on her neck is what I would imagine opium to smell like. It intoxicates me with fantasy.

I don't think I can stand to see her cry because of something I have done, but I know she will. She gazes into my eyes with the unsuspecting love and trust I'm about to take away from her. What I am about to confess to her will break her heart. If only I could have been satisfied with just her friendship. But no, I wanted consummation. I wanted flesh. I want it even now. I want to fall to my knees and kiss her tanned feet. She smiles beautifully, happy to see me.

"Did you miss me, Raymond?"

"More than you know. I thought about you endlessly. I couldn't sleep."

"Poor, Ray. He is in love."

"Yes. Hopelessly in love."

"It's not hopeless, Raymond. It's beautiful. I couldn't wait to get back here. Come here, Raymond. Don't you want to kiss me? What's wrong? You seem distant."

How do they know? I have been told women have a superior intuition. I tend to believe this. Women are smarter than we are, and more dangerous.

"There's a secret about me I haven't told you because of fear you wouldn't love or respect me anymore."

"Don't worry. We all have our secrets, Raymond. Keep your secret to yourself if you wish. In the big picture it's not important. We have to love each other the best we can now, because the momentum of history is insurmountable. We are participants in a greater historical process, Raymond."

I have no idea what she is talking about. I want to slap her, make her listen. This is important, damn it.

"I have to tell you this and I don't know how."

Carla slips off her shoes, puts out her cigarette, and yawns. She unzips her skirt, which falls to her ankles. Stepping out of the fallen garment gracefully, standing in her panties, she unfastens the top buttons of her blouse and begins working her way down the row. Without taking her eyes off me, Carla lifts both arms above her head and pulls off her blouse.

"My secret is that I made a promise to God. We broke it when we had sex. I'm so sorry and ashamed, Carla."

She unhooks her bra, presenting her pearl-white naked breasts. Gracefully she steps one long leg at a time out of her panties. Naked, she pulls back the sheets on my bed and gets in.

Patting the empty space in bed beside her she says, "Is that your big secret, Raymond? You know I don't believe in God. Come to bed, honey. You know you want to and there is no harm in it. Besides, what's done is done."

And so we make love, and I give up all notions of sainthood to become an ordinary man, and am relieved and grateful. I feel a burdensome weight lifted from me.

PART FIVE

Deception

Ricardo's back is turned to me but I know even without seeing his face he is scowling. He's behind the check-in desk, going through the mail for the third time today at my insistence, clearly not happy about it. He's throwing mail around like a crazed, angry postal worker.

"There's no message here for you here from Carla, just as I said. She has probably found someone else," he says. "Just as well, too. I never did like her. She had a nice ass but was far too bossy."

Three weeks earlier, on the telephone, Carla had been abrupt and impatient, as if having called out of obligation and not really wanting to talk, and I wondered what was up. I asked, and not for the first time, when I might see her again but she kept putting me off.

"What is the matter with you, Raymond? Don't you listen? You keep asking me this and I have repeatedly told you I have to sequester myself in the University library to study."

Something was wrong. I could feel it. I wanted to be supportive and say all the right things, but her tone worried me. I backed off awhile, giving her space, thinking it was the right thing to do. Later I began calling her dorm. Always someone different picked up from the common phone in the lobby, and the answer was invariably the same: they didn't know her. Said they had never heard of her. They had no idea who she was.

Ricardo smokes a cigarette from an ivory holder. The cigarette is wrapped in golden foil, not his usual brand, the holder also a new affectation. On the desk are a file and emery board, and he alternates between smoking and filing his pointed long fingernails. He wears a black shirt and black slacks, has lost even more weight, and has begun to resemble a malnourished vampire.

"Personally," says Ricardo—not that anyone is asking—"I prefer professional women. They enjoy a good fuck like anyone else, but they're in it for the money with no ulterior motive. Women who want you to love them end up trying to control you. They want to suck away your manhood and leave you neutered as a housecat. A good, professional whore, however, is another matter. She is working for a fee, and for a gratuity will let you do whatever you want. And speaking of whores, Raymond, you know of course I am in a position to supply you with professional women with advanced sexual skills. I personally guarantee their ability to make you no longer care whether Carla returns or not. You *need* this. You need to fuck your troubles away. That is what we do in here in Mexico."

Will he never shut up? His voice is a like an annoying mosquito, something to swat and silence. I don't need another woman and don't want one. But I'm angry with Carla. Her strange habit of disappearing without adequate explanation, the way she seems to live separate, unconnected lives—Carla the student, Carla the communist, Carla the friend, Carla the lover—I've had enough of it. She definitely has some explaining to do. No more secrets. I'm going to demand she explain everything.

On the other hand, it's possible Carla might be in real trouble somewhere, locked away in a Federal prison or kidnapped by extortionists. So what does that make me? Cuckold, jilted lover, or paranoid creep? I don't know whether to be angry at or afraid for her safety. I have only my imagination to guide me and my imagination is not my friend.

Ricardo is still talking when I abruptly turn to leave the hotel. He's talking when I stride out the door. Once outside, I glance through the lobby windows and see his lips are still moving in speech. Lately he has been hyperkinetic and compulsively talkative to the degree I suspect he has been taking some kind of stimulant, Benzedrine or even cocaine. You can get anything in Mexico, most of it over the counter.

I end up taking a series of crowded busses to the University, which takes three transfers and over an hour to reach because of all the stops. Appropriately named University City, the campus is enormous, with the population of a small city. It is too much to hope that I might by chance encounter Carla among the thousands of students swarming the campus like busy ants, but sometimes fate intervenes on our behalf and I'm out of options. I don't know what else to do; I'm just shuffling along, going through the motions, meandering aimlessly through the library, the student union building and cafeteria and identical high rise student housing buildings.

I intercept students between classes, inquiring as to whether they happen to know a beautiful American student named Carla Johansen who is majoring in Latin American Studies, but everyone is in a hurry and no one seems to know her. I am made to wait forty-five minutes in the student affairs office of the administration building to see a woman administrator who is a caricature of an old fashioned librarian, her gray hair in a bun, outdated rhinestone -decorated dime store glasses hanging around her neck by a thin beaded chain, and a forbidding, no-nonsense face that looks like it has not smiled in a decade. A plaque on her desk identifies her as Juanita Pacheco.

"Thank you for seeing me on short notice without an appointment, Mrs. Pacheco."

"Yes, happy to oblige but unfortunately, we will have to keep this brief under the circumstances."

"Of course. And I assure you it is of the utmost importance. I am here to find my sister, an American student," I explain. "Her name is Carla Johansen. She is enrolled in Latin American Studies here at the University. She's stopped writing or calling, which is highly uncharacteristic of her. We worry that she might be sick. Or even kidnapped. It's not like her not to contact us. But her mother is very ill, maybe dying. For this reason it is urgent my sister return to our mother's bedside immediately."

"Did you say her name was Carla Johansen?"

"Yes."

The woman squints suspiciously, taps her pen on the desk top and says, "And you are?"

"Raymond Johansen."

"And you have identification to verify this?"

"I'm sorry, I don't carry any."

She drops the pen as if the matter is ended and says, "Verification of identity would lend credibility and reassurance of your kinship but it doesn't matter, really. Our policy prohibits giving out information regarding our students. Not that I even know whether or not she *is* a student. But I assure you, we will look into the matter. You can leave your contact information, and if Miss Johansen does turn out to be enrolled here, we will deliver it to her."

"But by then it may be too late. My mother may be already dead."

"On the other hand, you might not be who you say you are. We have to be careful, here at the university. Our students' safety is our number one priority."

"Yeah, right. That's why your campus police beat them with nightsticks."

"I believe this meeting is adjourned, Mr. Johansen. If indeed that is even your name."

It's late afternoon outside the building, crisp and breezy turning dark early. The streets around this neighborhood are quiet this time of day. The Café Liberado is within easy walking distance, but I know I'm unwanted there. Too many times lately, I've made a nuisance of myself there.

But here I am, spying through the dirty café windows like a cuckolded husband intent on obtaining evidence of infidelity. I recognize a few patrons at the congested bar where not a single stool is available. No one says hello or nods in recognition when I enter, but they know who I am. Everyone here does. And they don't like me.

I begin squeezing between crowed tables without seeing Carla at any of them.

Returning to the bar, I find I'm in luck. A man in process of paying his check has left his stool, which I seize. The bartender, Chico, name probably fake, glances down the length of the bar in recognition of me and frowns. He ignores me for as long as he can but when a couple next to me shout for service he has no choice but to drift down to where we sit. He serves them shots of tequila and ignores my order for a beer.

He frowns and asks, "Why are you even here?"

"I'm looking for my friends."

"What friends?"

"You know what friends. Carla Johansen, Navio, Romero, Hector, even Sonia. Where is everyone?"

"How many times do I have to say it? Your friends are all in hiding, Raymond."

"Hiding from whom?"

"From you. You have become pain in their culos."

Eavesdroppers nearby break into laughter in recognition of his cleverness at my expense.

"Just tell me if you have seen them. If they are alive."

He pours two shots of tequila, but drinks them both himself.

I watch him walk away, and know he won't serve me tonight. To him I am just a gringo who asks too many questions.

Danger

Until now, Sonia has never called me before. She usually doesn't even acknowledge my presence except to insult or belittle me in front of others. Nobody trusts her and everyone fears her, even Navio. I can't imagine why she would be calling me now and don't welcome it.

"Meet me in front of the hotel in fifteen minutes," she says.

She's bossy and unpleasant about it, her tone closer to a demand than an invitation. I have no intention of giving into her for several reasons. For one, I don't like her. Another is I am as afraid of her as everyone else.

"I don't think so," I reply.

"Are you afraid of me?"

"Not at all," I lie. "It's just that I know you hate me."

"I don't hate you, Raymond. You're far too weak and ignorant to hate. But I do pity you as a victim of a capitalist educational system based on lies and misinformation. I'll bet you don't even know about your own revolution because they don't teach you about it in your schools."

"The American revolution is covered in elementary school, Sonia."

"But I'm talking about the American worker's labor revolution. You don't even know your own soldier heroes—Samuel Gompers, John L. Lewis, Walter Reuther, Big Bill Haywood, Mary Harris Jones, Emma Goldman. It's pathetic. I know more about worker's struggles in your country than you do. What you need is a lengthy internment in a reeducation camp. But I have a generous, forgiving nature. I forgive you for being a United States citizen and wish you no harm."

"Well, I'm touched."

"I promise you, Raymond, after the revolution, when you face the firing squad, I will honor you by respectfully attending your execution."

"Great. It's been nice talking with you, Sonia. I'm going to hang up now."

"Have you heard from Carla lately?"

"No, not that it's any of your business."

"You won't either. Carla is in deep serious trouble beyond your comprehension. So are you, for that matter."

"I don't trust anything you say, Sonia."

"You're wise not to trust me. In your position you should trust no one. On the other hand, you had better believe me when I say you are in danger. You had better prepare for what is coming, Raymond."

"Why are you telling me this? I would think any threat to Carla or to me would bring you great happiness."

"You would be wrong, but I can't explain because I don't trust the man who answered the hotel telephone."

"Ricardo? Why not? He's harmless."

"His accent was Cuban."

"He's the desk clerk and yes, he is Cuban. What of it?"

"Cubans who fled their homeland after the revolution are counter revolutionary. Do you know who these people were who left? Oppressive rich land owners who fled to escape reprisal. Cowards, traitors, and worse. Officers of the secret police who tortured and murdered their own citizens."

"Your rhetoric is tiresome, Sonia."

"Do you want to meet me or not? Or do you not care about Carla after all?"

"Of course I care."

"Well then?"

"I'll meet you in two hours at La Liberado."

"No, that's out. I can't be seen there any longer and neither would you if were smart. If you think your status as an American citizen guarantees your safety you are making a big mistake, Raymond. Listen carefully. We are in a position to help each other. You have something I need, and I have important information about Carla. It's probably too late for Carla, but not for you. I'm just four blocks from you at a pay phone. Meet me in front of the hotel in five minutes."

She hangs up abruptly. I'm not sure what to do. I'm unprepared for the challenge of dealing with Sonia at this early hour, but can't risk disregarding the possibility she has important information about Carla.

It's a slow, lazy Sunday morning outside. The sluggish, breezeless air is oppressive, weighted with the usual smog. The Chinese laundry across the street is closed. Cars are quietly parked along the curbs on both sides of the narrow street, with almost no moving traffic. Damp laundry hangs from tenement clotheslines and wrought iron railings of small terraces. Pigeons strut around doorwells or perch on balconies. A small dog lifts its rear leg to pee on the tire of a parked car.

It's just chilly enough this morning not to want to stand around. I keep moving in place from foot to foot like a prizefighter warming up, dancing and blowing breath into my hands, rubbing them together. Maybe ten minutes pass. There's no sign of Sonia. She's not coming and probably never was.

I'm walking toward a café three blocks up when an old four-door Buick sedan with a sputtering leaky muffler approaches. It's at least fifteen years old and looks like it has been through a war. Its mismatched junkyard front fenders are painted different colors and its front bumper hangs loose and rattles. I have a bad feeling about this. Lately there has been an increase in crime against foreigners, Americans especially—robberies, beatings and recently, kidnappings by revolutionary cadres who use the money for weapons and wider criminal activities. I'm hoping the Buick will pass but it doesn't. It's clearly stalking me.

Both doors on the passenger side are smashed in. The windshield is cracked and side windows tinted. I can't see anyone inside. Then, when the front passenger window rolls down, a man I do not know gestures with a fat hand- rolled cigar that smells suspiciously unlike tobacco.

"Get in," he says.

His appearance is anything but reassuring. He's probably in his thirties and has an acne-pitted complexion and ugly scar running down the length of his cheek. It's a face that inspires paranoia and makes you immediately look away. The back window rolls down and it's Sonia.

"It's me," she says, opening the back door. "Come on, get in."

The man with the scar in the front seat leans out and spits. His spittle, stained with the juice of his cigar, dangles in an elongated yellowish gelatinous strand and splatters to the pavement. Marijuana smoke drifts out of the open window. The inside of the car is hazy with it. The scarred man turns to say something to Sonia and I see for the first time he is missing an ear. In its place is a mass of discolored scar tissue.

"Forget about it, Sonia. I'm not getting in the car with you."

Sonia's laugh is a derisive, mocking snort.

"You'll do whatever we say you will," says the one-eared man. He flashes a stiletto and says, "Don't push your luck, gringo motherfucker."

Sonia says, "Don't make him angry, Raymond. If Hernando should be made to lose his temper, I can't protect you. But we do need to talk. There is no other way, Raymond. It must be done."

"We could have *talked* on the telephone, Sonia. I told you, I'm not getting into your car."

"We can do this in the hotel if you prefer."

"Only if you leave your friends here behind."

One ear spits again. Gesturing with his knife he says, "You aren't in a position to dictate terms, gringo motherfucker."

Sonia turns to him and says, "It's all right, Hernando. I can handle Raymond."

I can't stop staring at the blade of his knife. I always had a knife as a boy, when I didn't need one. Now that I am a man I need one. A man needs a knife in this world.

Sonia opens the car door, gets out and takes me by the arm into the hotel elevator. When we get to my room she paces around, looking behind the bathroom shower curtains, in my closet, and even briefly under the bed. I wish she would settle down and tell me why she is here, what it is she wants. She's wearing fatigue pants tucked into boots, an army-green tee shirt with no bra. I see the hilt of a knife tucked into a boot. She wears her raven black hair short like a boy's, with no makeup, jewelry or adornments other than pierced ears, but her oval face is pretty and she cannot altogether disguise her femininity. Her firm breasts are small but perfect for her figure, which is as powerfully compact and utilitarian as a gymnast's. She moves with a lithe elegance that cannot be mistaken for grace or poise—more like the predatory intent of a hunter. When she moves there is no sound from her. It's like she's walking on air. She is a female jaguar stalking prey. I have never seen her smile; there is no warmth from her. Her eyes betray nothing of what she keeps inside of her. When she speaks, it is like memorized monotonic recitation.

"Do you have your passport. Raymond?"

"Yes, of course. Why? Are we going somewhere? Because if you think we are, forget about it."

"Not you, me. I want your passport. Give it to me."

"Absolutely not. You of all people should know how important it is to have papers for the police. Without it, I'd no longer be "a protected American," as you are so fond of saying. But you already know this. Without a passport, I'd be at risk."

"For you an arrest on Mexican soil would be at most a minor inconvenience. Your embassy would intervene. They would manage your release and issue temporary identification papers until the passport can be replaced."

"It's anyone's guess how long it would be before the Mexican authorities would report my arrest or contact the Embassy."

"But you won't be arrested. All you have to do is go to the Embassy and report your passport stolen or lost. They will issue temporary papers until it can be replaced."

"Without papers verifying my identity I'm not sure that the Embassy would comply. Not that it matters, because I'm not giving it to you. The answer is no, Sonia, absolutely not."

She pulls the knife from her boot so quickly it's an obviously practiced and perfected move accomplished with the precision of one who has performed it many times before.

"Listen, Raymond, I don't want to hurt you but I'm not leaving here without that passport."

"I'm not giving it to you. Get out, Sonia. Get out and don't come back. I don't ever want to see you again or hear your voice again."

She throws the knife, which narrowly misses my face and lodges into the wall behind me. I walk over and remove it. It's heavy, with a large bone handle, the blade sharpened on one side and serrated on the other. I wonder if she has used it as a weapon before. I wonder if it has killed anyone. I turn it over in my palm, examining it. I run my finger over the blade. It's cold and beautiful.

"You're too good to have missed," I acknowledge, "so you must have done so on purpose. That was a mistake. Now I have the knife and you are left unarmed. How does that make you feel, Sonia, to have the situation reversed?"

"Ha. I could take it from you easily. I have done it many times before. "

The recognition of how badly I want this knife makes me shiver.

I hand it back to her and say, "Here, take it."

But I already miss the way it felt in my hand and want it back. My covetousness for this knife, of all imaginable objects, unsettles me. My first knife was a Swiss Army knife. I had been, briefly, a very young, failed Boy Scout. I once carved a heart with a girl's name in it into a tree. She never knew. Once, when I was angry with her, I practiced throwing the knife again and again into the heart that I had carved. I imagined it was her heart. I once had a whole collection of knives. I don't remember what happened to them, why I gave them up. They were lost now, like my baseball card collection, toy soldiers, comic books, my youth, my innocence.

"All right," says Sonia. "I could separate your head from your body as easily as coconut from a palm tree but I won't. You're not the enemy, I know that. You care about the poor. You may be politically uneducated and childish, but your heart is in the right place. I wouldn't have come otherwise. I didn't come here to hurt you. I came because you are the only one who can help me. I'm in trouble, Raymond. I need to change my identity. As an American, with an American passport, I would be safe. I need to leave the country. I can alter the name and photo. I'm afraid, Raymond. I'm afraid of Mexico. I'm even afraid of my friends, the people you saw outside in the car. All that talk earlier on the telephone about firing squads? That was for their benefit. I don't know who to trust, who is my friend. If I stay here, I will be killed or kidnapped and deported, tortured and put in prison. I don't know if I can go through that again. You're my only hope, the only possibility I have to free myself."

To my astonishment, her eyes fill with tears. I would have thought her incapable of them. She looks up at me, her face wet, her eyes filled with tears. Who is this person who cries? She looks like she is about twelve years old.

"I want to go away where it's safe, Raymundo. You are the only one who can help me."

And she comes into my arms. Where she weeps. She weeps like a child in her father's arms.

"Please," she says, sobbing into my shoulder. "You're my last hope. Please."

"Don't cry, Sonia. Of course I'll help you. I didn't know. Here, take it. Take my passport; it's yours."

She snatches it out of my hand, stuffs it in her boot beside her knife. She smiles briefly, but it is the cunning smile of someone who has just won something from me.

"You said you had information about Carla."

"It is better for you if you don't know. Carla is not who she seems. For that matter, neither am I. Here is what I will tell you. Here is what I give you in exchange for the passport. Listen carefully because this is the last warning you will receive from me. It is not safe for you here. You are in danger already. You will be having some visitors, Raymond. Some very unpleasant visitors. If I were you, I would leave Mexico immediately. Go home. At the very least, leave the hotel. Move away from this neighborhood where they will be looking for you. Forget about Carla. You can't help her. You are out of your element here, Raymond. There are things you don't know about Carla and are better off not knowing. That is all I will tell you. Keep your eyes open. Trust no one."

"Not even you."

"That's right," agrees Sonia. "Not even me. If I were you, Raymond, I would leave the hotel right now and not return. Better yet, go home. Go back to the United States while you still can."

Last Meeting with Navio

A week later I sat on a bench waiting for Navio in Chapultepec Park, a newspaper spread across my lap. The weather was pleasant, balmy and breezy, the recently quenched shrubbery grateful for the earlier rain. A sweet fragrance of damp quivering jasmine lingered in the air. Two park employees wearing identical faded overalls squatted in the damp earth to work a flowerbed. Another unloaded fresh sod from a city dump truck. Families strolled along a path from the children's petting zoo and bird sanctuary. In the grassy field, boys in short pants played with toy boats in a small wading pool while their younger sisters played mother to elaborately dressed dolls. Far across the field, a soccer game was in progress. Fathers watching on the sidelines shouted encouragements from lawn chairs.

The bombing of a government records office by sabotage was the lead story in the newspaper. Sensational front page photographs showed broken furniture, trashed drywall, concrete and twisted iron framing. Floating sheets of documents drifted like large white moths over exploded debris. The damage was attributed to a student revolutionary group held responsible for an earlier attempted sabotage of an American embassy official's limousine in which an explosive device attached to the undercarriage failed to detonate. These were not isolated incidents. There had been a sudden increase in bombings of late, with various degrees of damage. Protests on the university campus occurred almost weekly now. There had been walk-outs and strikes in many of the factories.

As I waited, I wondered about Navio. I hoped he was not involved in this. I had been waiting for close to an hour now, and though he was habitually late I was beginning to suspect he wasn't going to show. I worried that he had been picked up by the police. If

Navio was involved in this escalation of revolutionary activity, not even his father would be able to rescue him.

I had forgotten my dark glasses and the position of the sun now made me squint while watching a distant elderly blind man slowly tapping his way toward me with a white cane. His beard and hair were gray; he wore a baseball hat and dark glasses and walked with a limp. When he reached my bench he tapped it with his cane and sat quietly beside me.

"Buenos Dias," I said politely.

"It's me," he replied.

He removed his dark glasses and winked.

"A stooped gait, a few streaks of gray combined with a cane and dark glasses and, voila, I am no longer Navio but someone's sweet old blind grandfather."

He pointed to the newspaper, tapping it with his index finger.

"As you can see, it's not safe for me these days to be identifiable."

"If you are in any way connected with this, then you are in deep, serious trouble. They will hunt you and eventually find you, Navio. Not even your father will be able to extricate you from the trouble you will find yourself in."

"But we had nothing to do with it. We believe the sabotage and attempted assassination to have been staged by the Federales as a means to criminalise and imprison us."

Some of the gray flaked from his hair when he removed his hat; particles fell across his shirt and into his lap. He quickly swept them away.

"Where have you been, Navio? I've been looking for you. Carla has pulled one of her disappearing acts, but to make it worse, I couldn't find you, Hector or Romero or anyone else that usually frequents the Liberado. I've made such a nuisance of myself there asking about you they won't even serve me anymore."

"Everyone has split up, Raymundo. Even I don't know where the others are located. It's not safe for any of us. What we don't know can't be tortured out of us."

A group of three little girls in their Sunday best carried bundles of balloons. Behind them a boy struggled to keep his arms around a huge stuffed lion. Their father, dressed in a suit and tie, pushed a child in a stroller. His wife, tall and elegant, carried a parasol and wore awkward heels that sounded on the pavement.

"Behold," said Navio. "Mexico's so-called emerging middle class that its government is trying so desperately to create. The ruling class knows the country is divided between its wealthy minority elite and its poor masses. Unless a middle class is created and assimilated, the poor will rise up in revolt."

"Christ said the poor will always be with us."

"Yes, because the rich need their cheap labor to maintain their lives of insulated comfort."

"I need to see Carla, Navio. She left me, and owes an explanation."

"I don't know where she is. No one does."

About twenty yards behind the Mexican family, a uniformed guide leading a group of tourists spoke in German. The men wore pressed khaki shorts and tennis shoes and appeared fit. Their bare legs were muscled and hairy. Their women wore sun hats and dark glasses and carried umbrellas. Their voices were high-pitched and somewhat louder than the men's.

"Today I went to a Curandera," said Navio. "I had my fortune told by a woman who looked a hundred years old."

"What did she say?"

Navio laughed and said, "She said I was going to die. As if I had to pay her for *that* information. We are Death's children. It is our common fate. Even Christ experienced it."

"And defeated it," I replied. "For all of us."

"I doubt it. But who can say? Here in Mexico we accept the mystery of death and life. We know that spiritual forces in Mexico exert a powerful influence on events. Things happen to people here that defy explanation."

"Yes, I agree. Mexico has taught me this to be true. Did I ever tell you that during my very first day in Mexico City I was accosted by a beggar? He was the very first human being that I encountered here. I gave to him, but not sufficiently, not enough to help him and not enough that I sacrificed anything on his behalf. In fact, I think I gave initially just to get away from him."

"Raymundo, we have discussed this before. Mexico City has many of these beggars. Those who can give just a little. You can't give much and you can't give to them all because then you will have nothing."

"But I think that is what God wants of us, to give all. Anyway, that was a test for me about giving, but I failed it. And there was something special about this man. I began to think of him as a supernatural being. I saw him once in the street and followed him but he just vanished. I even saw him once in my hotel room. There was a mirror on my bureau and he stepped out of it. Maybe I was dreaming. But I don't know what dreams are, here in Mexico. I once saw thousands of tiny dancing lights make geometric patterns on my ceiling and walls. I met an absurd man who may or may not have been a hummingbird. I had a mystical experience in the Great Cathedral that haunts me to this day."

"My uncle would tell you that Mexico is a place of magic, supernatural power and danger, Raymundo. This beggar that you saw the day you first came to the city, who later entered your dreams and appeared in your room, I suspect he was a *Bruho*."

"No, the beggar was a man, Navio, and he was dying. Perhaps it was his ghost that I saw. What is this *Bruho* you mention? I don't know this word."

"A sorcerer, Ray. We have many of them in Mexico. You should know the Great Cathedral is built over the ruins of an Aztec temple where many thousands of human sacrifices were performed. It is thought that as many as seven hundred thousand sacrifices a year were performed in Tenochtitlan. Also, the Zocalo where the cathedral is located is the site of the last stand of the Aztec nation. Many thousands of dead warriors who fought Cortez are buried beneath the Zocalo. Later it was the site where Catholic priests tortured Aztecs who refused to worship Christ. The Catholics proved themselves to be as cruel and bloodthirsty as the Aztecs. Not that they didn't have it coming. I don't believe in God, but your Christian God would be a better one to follow than Huitzilopochtli."

"I thought the Aztec god was Quetzalcoatl?"

"Quetzalcoatl was a benevolent god of peace opposed to human sacrifice. Huitzilopochtli was a rival, a blood- thirsting war

God. His symbol is the Hummingbird. Mexico itself is a supernatural battleground in which opposing spiritual energies exist. We Mexicans have mostly learned to coexist with them but when foreigners experience these energies, it sometimes has a profound, lasting effect. It is possible that you do not act on free will but in accord with powerful ancient forces that have conscripted you."

"I take sole responsibility for what happens to me."

"That is because you are not entirely Mexican. Not yet, anyway, though you are on your way to becoming one. I understand your conflict, Raymundo. I know what Christian values are. I know why you resist a violent revolution. Many of the Catholic priests here want social justice the same as we. But I don't believe they can accomplish it their way. At this very moment, as we speak here, while Mexican men and women toil under the sun like overworked mules, how does faith restore them when hungry and beaten into submission? They will die as paupers in corporate fields. If you believe in justice, then you must believe in revolution. We must and we will take back our country. If we fail, if we die in the struggle, our deaths will be an inspiration to those who will follow us. I am willing to die for the weak and subjugated, for those who cannot fight for themselves. Isn't this what Christ did?"

"If you are talking about a revolution with violence, Navio, the answer is no. That is not Christian behavior no matter how well intended."

"I am a Mexican. You are becoming one. The way of machismo is to stand tall and take what life has to give. Come, let's walk. There is a café across the boulevard on the other side of the park. Let's have a drink. I have something for you from Carla."

"I thought you didn't know where she is?"

"I don't. Come. Take my elbow. I'm blind, remember?"

We ambled along the concrete path through the park to the opposite side of the petting zoo, where we faced a wide boulevard busy with traffic, crossed to the other side and settled at a sidewalk café. Navio ordered tequila with beer chasers, then reached into his jacket for an envelope and placed it on my lap.

"This was given to me by a third party who wishes to remain anonymous. I apologize that it has taken this long to bring this to you, but I have been in hiding. We all have. I rarely come into the city these days and when I do it's in disguise, as you can see. As I have said, Hector, Romero, Sonia, we are all split up now. It's become too dangerous for us here."

But I was no longer listening. I urgently opened the envelope addressed to me in Carla's handwriting, my hands trembling in anticipation.

My Dear Raymond,

I always knew that at some future point in time I would have to abandon present circumstances and leave the country without preparation, and that time has come. Events here in Mexico beyond my control have converged suddenly, leaving no time to say goodbye properly.

But I didn't want to leave without telling you one last time that I love you. I'm sorry I can't explain in full why it has to be this way or answer all the questions you surely must have, but it is for your own protection. I will say only that certain activities in which I was involved here in Mexico had consequences I had not foreseen. Perhaps no one could have. I know now how a small involvement, a small event, can grow into a much larger, more serious situation beyond anyone's expectation. Not that I have any regrets. There is still the chance that a greater good can come of these things. But not for us, unfortunately. I have to say goodbye, and I am sorry.

I can't tell you where I am going and can't promise that we will ever see one another again, or even that you will receive another letter from me. It is my hope that you will believe me and understand when I say that this is not solely for my own safety, but also for yours.

I had to keep my relationship with you somewhat less than honest and forthright, Raymond, because I did not want to compromise your safety. That is why I did not take you as a lover sooner than I did, although I wanted to, and it is why I never took you to my apartment near the University and why, when we became lovers I tried to keep us sequestered away in your hotel room.

These precautions may not have been sufficient. I may have placed you in danger, and I am sorry for this. It is possible that you will be intercepted by men who will question you as to my location. Show them this letter. They are not pleasant men, but they are not without reason. They will see that I have left you, that you have no information they seek.

But Ray, I think you should return home to the United States and I hope you do this. It will be safe for you there, where legal and political protocols and safeguards such as Habeas Corpus prevail, and you can go back to the life meant for you. I think you should go back to school, maybe fall in love with a woman who values you greater than social or political causes, who places you first, and who does not make trouble for you as I have.

I hope you will do this, Raymond. You are a beautiful person, conflicted but beautiful and kind and gentle, and I will always remember you that way. Please don't judge me harshly but think of me fondly, and take care of yourself. Don't worry about me, Raymond. I can take care of myself. I'll be fine, though I will miss you terribly.

Take care and farewell,
Carla.

I carefully placed the folded letter in my pocket, turned to Navio and said, "Carla is in danger. Tell me what you know."

"I think you had best leave this alone, Raymundo. Your interference might only put her in jeopardy. And I know nothing that will help you find her. But let me say that I'm sorry for you and Carla. She told me about your vow, and how it came to be broken. You were willing even to give up your God for her if it was the only way that you could have her. How much more can a man give? When she told me this I knew that you loved her more than I. I for example would never abandon my revolution. You are a very unusual and sometimes foolish man, Raymundo, but I do not judge you. This is Mexico. In Mexico we believe that those who love deeply are forgiven all things. Men here behave passionately when in love."

He began scratching his beard again, then removed his hat to work on his scalp, also streaked with gray. Glancing nervously around the café, he adjusted his dark glasses and said, "If one is to have a beard in Mexico City, it has to be gray. The police are randomly stopping young men with beards without provocation these days. Young bearded men are suspected of being Fidelista."

Two uniformed Federales leading a large German shepherd police dog crossed the boulevard in our direction. Navio began to rise but then apparently thought better of it because he quickly sat down again and said, "If we go rushing out of here we might arouse suspicion. We will finish our beverages normally, as if unconcerned."

The Federales—small, rumpled, portly men dressed in wrinkled fatigues and scuffed black boots—arranged themselves under the umbrella of a sidewalk table near us and rested their rifles against the table. The waiter arrived with our beers and placed them on our table. To my surprise, Navio bought a round for the soldiers. They raised their glasses to us in salute. Later they left without incident. Navio visibly relaxed and lighted a cigar. He leaned back in his chair and exhaled a cloud of smoke.

"Tell me what you know, Navio. Tell me everything; don't leave anything out."

"You want me to explain Carla's duplicity and vanishing acts, her secret life and the circumstances leading to her flight from our lives."

"Please"

"Well, I can't do that. This letter that I have delivered was given to me by a third party. I promised not to reveal his identity, but frankly I think he was just a courier without a personal connection to Carla. I don't know why the letter wasn't just mailed. Maybe for your sake Carla didn't want to post it with your address. Maybe she was afraid it would be intercepted. I was instructed to deliver it to you and have done so, out of friendship. My obligation both to you and Carla is now fulfilled. I wash my hands of the matter. Of her as well. She may have betrayed us both. Do not forget, I was in love with her the same as you. Now I believe I was in love with an imposter. I don't know if I ever knew who the real Carla was. She had too many secrets."

"It was no secret that she loved me. That's what is important to me."

"Perhaps she did, but first she loved me, and then the Cuban official. She was fucking him, you know."

"I suspected it."

"Some of us believe her relationship with the consul was not what it seemed."

"If you're suggesting Carla is a spy, I asked her about that once and she found the suggestion hilarious. She laughed in my face."

Navio removed his hat and scratched angrily.

"Damn paint. I may be allergic to it. It's sad, I am a patriot who loves his country and yet must hide himself from its attention. Circumstances have changed for the worse. We are being hunted and arrested. I don't know where my friends are hiding. I don't know who my friends *are*."

"I fear for you, Navio."

Our voices were lost in a cacophony of sirens from a fleet of vehicles from which our conversation became briefly impossible. A speeding group of police cars and ambulances passed, and then Navio continued.

"I will tell you this, Raymond. Carla became increasingly allied to communism as it is practiced in Cuba, while for me it has always been Mexico. Not Cuba, not a unified Latin American or world communist movement, but Mexico. Our differences escalated to the degree that she left me for a politically uneducated American boy. Yes, Raymundo, you. You think she loved you, don't you? That's what I thought too. In hindsight I wonder if she was using me as a means to gain credence within the Cuban Embassy. It was I who took her there, initially. It's possible this was her agenda all along. It is also possible that she was using the consul the same way. Maybe she was a double agent, working both sides. Of course all this is mere speculation. We may never know the truth."

"I don't think Carla was a spy."

"Perhaps not. In fact, probably not. I'm just speculating, but these suspicions are not unfair. By her strange behavior and sudden departure, she herself is to blame for them."

"How do you know I'm not an informant or CIA agent?"

"The possibility was discussed. We ultimately dismissed it. People, circumstances and events here in Mexico are rarely what they seem but you, Raymundo, are in some respects an exception. Some of us laughed at you, some, because of your uninformed politics and misguided Christianity, did not respect you, but except for Sonia we all came to regard you as sincere and genuinely yourself. You were what you appeared to be. Sonia, on the other hand, until she had possession of your passport, was convinced you were a CIA operative. She was furious when it turned out that your passport was not an official diplomatic one."

"So now I'm left wondering if I am a fool in love with an imposter."

"You are a man recovering from a love affair that ended prematurely. There is no shame in this. Love is a very powerful force. But I worry about you. You have no passport and are in a dangerous country illegally. You should return to your own country."

Navio's cigar had gone out, and while he paused to light it with difficulty in the wind I said, "I intend to find Carla and take her back to the United States with me, Navio."

"Hope that you do not find her, Raymundo. Do you think you will then live happily ever after, like in the movies? You are not prepared for the kind of men you will encounter."

"Your reply tells me that you know more than you are telling me, Navio."

"I know we are all in danger. All of us who associated with Carla, whoever she may turn out to be."

"I'm not afraid."

"Then you are becoming more Mexican than I realized."

"I intend to see this to the end, whatever it may be."

"Consider this, my friend. Suppose Carla does not want to be found. Suppose she deceives us even now."

"Then I will know. I have to know the truth, Navio."

"I think I have underestimated you, Raymond. I think you will accept your destiny and follow your heart even if leads into danger. That is the way of machismo. That is the Mexican way. I think you have become one of us. Let us embrace in friendship and know that we are men who differ, but who respect one another and share a common love of Mexico."

And so we did, rising from our chairs, and then, tapping his white cane like the blind man he pretended to be, he walked off without looking back or saying goodbye. I never saw him again.

Guests of the La Paz

I picked up my mail at the American Express, cashed a traveler's check and returned to the hotel. Piles of luggage on carts blocked the elevator, with more being unloaded from taxi cabs and buses parked in front of the building. Newly arrived parties crowded noisily around the check-in desk. Many were low- income tourists like me but some, because they carried meters, telescopes, Geiger counters and other quasi-scientific equipment, were identifiable as ufologists arrived to investigate recent sightings.

The increased hotel occupancy had apparently been anticipated, because Ricardo had extra help. Pedro and two other young men served in the capacity of bellboys, assisting with the luggage, loading it onto carts and into the elevator. A female employee I had not seen before helped Ricardo behind the check-in desk. Every chair in the lobby was taken. I couldn't even maneuver to the elevator because of the piles of luggage waiting to be taken to rooms upstairs.

One family in particular had a small mountain of luggage, two large trunks, a half dozen suitcases and strollers for their children, one of whom cried loudly. Their ugly small dog barked incessantly. Something held up the check-in process; a short jowly bald man pounded a cane on the desk in complaint. His language was indecipherable and may have been Russian or Slavic.

Two men who were identical twins spoke Spanish with an indeterminable accent, making it difficult to ascertain their origin, whether or not they were tourists, or if they were Mexican which, based on their accents, I doubted. They were handsome but faintly feminine men who wore their glistening jet-black hair combed

straight back and heavily coated with pomade. They dressed identically, in tight black pants and pearl-buttoned black western shirts
with silver bolo ties. Their black leather belts were adorned with
silver, and their black leather boots with large silver buckles.

It remained impossible to get through the piles of baggage
to the elevator or stairs, so I decided to wait it out in a neighborhood cantina where I was known if not by name, at least as a familiar face and person of the neighborhood. I took an empty stool
facing the wide horizontal mirror that ran the length of the bar
and ordered a beer. The bartender made some small talk regarding
the World Cup soccer tournament, which was being televised and
in which Mexico was a participant. I hadn't been following these
matches, and mostly listened politely. He ambled down the bar and
went about washing glasses in the sink behind him.

I was on my second beer when the twins settled in a booth
behind me. Whenever I looked up from my beer into the mirror
one or both were staring at me. Probably they were just watching
the soccer match on the TV behind the bar, but I was jumpy, my
nerves ragged from the warning from Sonia and the letter from
Carla. One of the twins left the booth and sauntered to the counter. He ordered two tequilas. Like his brother, he was tall and lithe
and carried himself with the slow graceful movement of someone
who might practice Tai Chi. His narrow, Modigliani-like face was
inexpressive, the extreme thinness of his lips enhanced by a narrow pencil-line moustache. His cold glazed eyes suggested drugs.

A couple of beers later, upon leaving the bar, the lighting outside was bright and glaring. I turned and saw the glint of the silver
belts and boot buckles of the twins. Both men wore dark glasses.
Their stride was choreographed to keep up with me, yet distant
enough that it would not appear suspicious.

I was within sight of the hotel when it occurred to me they
were staying in the same hotel. It was no wonder they were "following" me. Case of nerves was all. The warnings from Navio, Sonia,
and in Carla's letter had me more on edge than I realized, apparently.

My preoccupation with this matter caused me to overlook the
two men in the lobby who had been waiting for me. Broad shoul-

dered professional men wearing suits and ties and carrying attaché cases, they followed me to the elevator doors. Each took an arm with a determined grip that was firm but not overtly hostile.

"Excuse me. Mr. Raymond Watson?'

"Yes?"

The man who said this spoke in unaccented English. His voice was pleasantly modulated with the flawless diction of a radio or television announcer. Clean shaven and redolent of aftershave that smelled like rum-soaked cigars, his hair was graying at the temples and neatly trimmed, his suit neatly pressed. He wore a beige knee length raincoat and grey felt Stetson hat with a gray suit

"My name is Lloyd Berenson," he said. "I'm one of the attachés to the American consul here in Mexico City."

He handed me a business card with an embossed U.S. government seal, then offered his hand, which I shook. His grip was strong, his fingernails clean and trimmed. He wore a gold wedding band and expensive looking watch. His gaze was engaging and direct, but non-threatening.

"I wonder if I might have a word with you."

"Regarding what? Am I in some kind of trouble?"

"No, no. Of course not, Mr. Watson. This is about Miss Carla Johansen."

"What about her?"

"We hoped you might provide information regarding her location. She might be in need of our assistance."

"I don't understand. What kind of assistance are you referring to?"

"In regard to Miss Johansen.'s present location"

"Is she in trouble?"

His beefy partner had the build and body language of a man who might have at one time wrestled or played college football, but who over the years had gone pudgy. He reeked of cigarettes and his rumpled suit looked as if he had slept in it. His nose may have at one time been broken and reset unevenly. He seemed to have a perspiration problem and kept wiping his damp face with a wrinkled white handkerchief. His balding hair was patchy and cut short.

"Matt Sullivan," he said, introducing himself.

He too handed me a business card, also with an official U.S. seal. I briefly glimpsed a holstered pistol under his jacket when he reached to shake my hand. "I'm assigned as security to the Embassy," he explained. "I'm assisting Mr. Berenson with an investigation. When was the last time you saw Miss Johansen, Raymond?"

"I haven't said that I even know her."

"But you do. You and Miss Johansen were quite close. We know for a fact you spent many nights together here in the hotel. Do you deny it?"

Sullivan's accusatory tone put me off. His cop manners reminded me of the police who had arrested me and taken me to the Snohomish County Jail in what now seemed like another lifetime. I was someone else now. I was no longer that person, no longer Raymond. I was Raymundo now. The troubled boy in my past who had been in love with Linda Grigsby, who had agonized, gone to jail, fallen to his knees in shame and sworn obedience to a path of righteousness was but a distant memory.

"I don't see how that could be any of your business," I said.

"Take it easy," replied Sullivan. "We're here to help Carla."

"Help her with what, exactly?

He offered me an American cigarette, which I declined.

"I'm going to level with you, Raymond. Your friend Carla is in danger. If you care about her and know where she is, you need to tell us without delay. For her sake."

"I don't know where she is."

"That's unfortunate."

"Unfortunate for who?"

"For her of course. For you, if it turns out you're withholding information. I suggest you think a little harder, Watson. Surely you at least have suggestions as to where we might inquire. Names of friends, places she might hide out, that sort of thing."

"I have no idea where she is. I've been looking for her too."

"You have my card with my number," said Berenson. He had removed his hat. Unlike Sullivan, he had a full head of light brown hair. He ran his fingers through it, then replaced the Stetson.

"If you hear or remember anything at all that might be a lead, no matter how trivial, please call. I assure you it's important and in

Carla's best interest."

"This is a matter of importance to the government of the United States," said Sullivan. "It's imperative to get it cleared up quickly."

"I already told you, I don't know anything."

Sullivan backed off, his tone more conciliatory.

"You have our business cards. Keep them handy. Remember, Raymond, we're on your side. Yours and Carla's."

"I'll take it under advisement," I said. I don't know where that came from. It was a phrase I had never used before and had never heard outside of the movies.

"Thanks for your cooperation, Mr. Watson. Again, please call if you happen to remember something that might be helpful."

* * *

Days later I sat on the bed debating whether to call the numbers on the cards left by the Embassy officials. I had been thinking of little else ever since they had contacted me. I didn't know what kind of trouble Carla might be in, but I wanted to find her, and they might be able to help. I picked up the phone and dialed, then changed my mind, hung up and placed the two calling cards inside the pages of this journal. I lighted a cigarette and smoked it down to the filter and put it out. The sound of a television turned up loud came through the wall from next door. The hotel was close to full occupancy. A woman occupied the room across the hall, and two male guests I had never seen the room next to mine. Their radio was always on, and loud. I once had a glimpse of the person across the hall. She wore a long raincoat with high heel shoes and styled her straight blonde hair short as a boy's. I figured her for a German or perhaps a Dane.

Later I met her in the lobby. Initially friendly and inquisitive, she became evasive regarding her circumstances. She spoke with a French accent and rolled her own cigarettes. I sat across from her, by the lobby windows with a view to the street. Guests came in and out of the front doors but mostly we had the lobby to ourselves. She wore a short skirt that rode far up her legs, which were pale and exceptionally long. Her breasts were small but pretty, her long legs extremely provocative, as was her posture. I figured her for somewhere between twenty-five and thirty.

"Are you an American?" she inquired.

"I used to be. I'm Mexican now."

"Interesting. How did that come about?"

"I don't know. It just happened. Maybe that's what comes of staying here too long. You can't go back."

"I think I understand that. I'm not going back to Canada, but I doubt that I will stay here. I consider myself an international. I like to keep moving. I'm thinking maybe next to Ibiza or Corfu. On the other hand, I find my skills more in demand in Latin America. It's a blonde thing."

I didn't understand this but didn't pursue it.

"Did you arrive here from Canada?"

"No. From Lima, Peru. Don't ever go there. The food is disgusting, the buildings are infested, and the streets are crowded with peddlers, stray dogs and lewd soldiers."

"Sounds pretty dismal."

"You don't know the half of it, and don't want to. The beaches stink and are littered with fly-swarmed fish heads. The fascist government is repressive and the people are submissive and passive. I knew almost as soon as I arrived I had made a mistake. Flew out of there and came here three days later."

"Why Mexico City?"

"Why not? It can't be any worse than Lima."

She lighted a cigarette and regarded me with a lingering, assessing gaze, as if deciding something about me. I did not avert my gaze in return; she was pretty and sexy, with a quality of honesty and directness about her, a frankness both disconcerting and engaging. I liked her blue eyes, which sparkled and were peculiarly child-like.

"What do they call you here?"

"Raymundo."

"I'm Michelle. What's your name back in the states?"

"Raymond."

"How long have you been here, Raymond?"

"Long enough not to remember."

"Why do you stay?"

"I like it here."

"Are you a student?"

"Not really. A writer, I suppose."

"If you are a writer, you should not suppose. You should know it above all else. You should doubt everything but that. Tell me something, Raymond. Do you like to spend money on memorable experiences of beauty and exquisite pleasure? After all, experience is a writer's greatest tool."

"I don't have money to spend on much of anything. I receive a small monthly allotment from home in return for attending the University."

"I thought you said you weren't a student."

"I'm not. I haven't attended a single class."

"How small is your allotment, Raymond? And are you flush or waiting on its arrival?"

She put out her cigarette and raised her legs higher on the chair. She wore no panties, and I had a glimpse of trimmed blonde pubic hair and her vagina.

"Would you like to come to my room, Raymond? I may cost more than Mexican whores, but I'm a professional and highly skilled. Weirdness and satisfaction guaranteed."

"Nothing personal, but I'm with someone."

"Of course you are. No problem. I get plenty of work. Mexican men just love natural blondes for some reason. All the better for me, because there are few of them to be had here in Mexico. But see me when you get your next allotment, Raymond."

A long black limousine pulled up and double parked in front of the hotel.

"There's my ride," said Michelle. "See you later, Raymundo."

She hurried to the curbside limousine where a chauffeur came around and opened the back door. When she got in the back seat I saw again that her long legs were spectacular. The limo pulled away and I was left to wonder. Carla had been gone only weeks, was possibly in trouble, and yet I wanted this woman and had been tempted. What kind of man was I becoming? How far would I fall? Maybe there was no bottom.

Back in my room I fingered the embossed consulate cards and

considered my limited options. These men could find Carla better than I. I needed their help. What the hell, I decided. I picked up telephone. At least maybe I can get some new information. I thought better of it, however, put the cards in my wallet, and did not call.

Ambush

The elevator doors were already closing when the tall man who followed me into the hotel hurried to them, throwing his body between the closing panels and pushing his way inside. Lately there had been far too many new faces in the hotel. I had a particularly bad feeling about this man. He wore large dark glasses and gloves with a wide-brimmed hat pulled down almost to the bridge of his nose and carried a rolled up newspaper. I considered whether the newspaper might conceal a weapon. He stood behind me and I didn't like it. I changed position in the elevator so we were side by side. He rode with me all the way to the top floor where we both waited for the other to exit. He stepped out of the elevator and strode down the carpeted hallway in the opposite direction of my room. I watched him fumble with his key, saw his door open and close.

A mere case of paranoia, then. The recent warnings from Navio, Sonia, and in Carla's letter would not let me rest. I extracted my key and inserted it. At that exact moment I briefly glimpsed the two tenants exiting the adjacent room. One of them grabbed me by the neck and slammed my face into the door. My face made a sound like a rotten cantaloupe smashed with a hammer. It was sickening to hear. I might have broken my nose. There was blood all over the door. Someone flipped me around and began hitting me in the stomach with expert precision to maximum effect. I doubled over and felt a knee impact with my face. I tasted blood in my mouth and dropped to my knees.

They dragged me into my room and sat me in the single chair. I wiped my face and my hand came away red with blood. My nose bled profusely. I recognized these two men now— twins with jet black oily hair, long sloping noses, cold eyes and cruel faces. They were dressed as before, entirely in black with bolo ties and silver buckles on their belts and boots. One was wrapping his belt around his fist, the large silver buckle over his knuckles. He hit me in the face three times and then his brother kicked the chair out from under me. I remained on the floor, aching with each breath and unable to get up.

I may have lost consciousness for a moment. I remember being on the floor and seeing only their boots, which were kicking me repeatedly. It went on for what seemed a long time. The men spoke Spanish, but with an unusual accent I could not immediately place, though I had heard it before somewhere. They didn't stop kicking until they were winded. Then they were quiet. One went into the bathroom and came back with a wet towel.

"Wet your face," he said. "Clean yourself up. We have some questions for you."

His twin brother wiped my blood off his belt buckle and threaded the belt through his pants loops and said, "Get up. Go sit in the chair."

The chair had been kicked across the room. I heard myself cry out as I managed to get to my feet. It was difficult to stand. I thought I might fall during the few steps to the chair. I reached it and collapsed. They began duct taping me to it.

One of the twins removed my dresser drawers and turned them upside down, shaking loose their contents. Discarded notebooks, matches, cigarettes, pencils and loose change clattered to the floor. They were looking for something, but what? My radio was smashed and gutted, my closet emptied of my few clothes and the painting of the conquistador. My pillow was slashed, its feathers removed, the mattress pulled off the bed, flipped over and gutted. The twin in the bathroom was cutting towels with a knife.

"Where's your whore girlfriend?"

"Carla?"

I was given a blow to my temple for this answer. The force of the impact knocked the chair over, me duct-taped to it. It felt like the man who had struck me had brass knuckles or maybe sap of some kind. It didn't seem possible a fist could hurt so much otherwise.

One of the twins turned me upright again.

"Don't play dumb with us."

"If it's Carla you want I haven't seen or heard from her in weeks. No one knows where she is."

I was trying to place the accented Spanish. Norte Americano? Mexican? Salvadoran?

One of the twins stood reading Carla's letter. It seemed to make him angry. He tore it into pieces, wadded it into a ball and threw it into the accumulated clutter. He went through my wallet but showed no interest in my money. He examined the business cards from the American Embassy, tore them into tiny pieces and tossed them in my face. His brother removed a package of cigarettes from his shirt pocket, took two from the pack, placed both in his mouth and lighted them with a zippo styled silver lighter.

He exhaled a huge cloud of smoke into my face and said, "Let's start over. We seem to have started badly. Please accept my apology and this cigarette."

His brother seized my face, forced open my jaws and shoved the towels he had been cutting into my mouth while his twin placed both lighted cigarettes into my nostrils. The pain was immediate and consuming. I began writhing and kicking in the chair, screaming through the towel. The cigarettes extinguished for lack of oxygen. I snorted furiously until they were dislodged from my nostrils and fought back tears. Both nostrils throbbed.

"This gringo fuck needs to learn that smoking is bad for his health," said the twin with the cigarettes.

"Let him enjoy his smoke," said his brother.

He produced a small canister shaped lighter and ignited it. A thin jet-stream of blue flame appeared. I watched in horror as he inserted the flame into my nostrils. I was choking on the rags stuffed in my mouth, but still screaming. I gagged on the rags in my mouth until I thought I would vomit. I knew no one would hear my screams. The twins were so doubled up with laughter they had trouble standing and had to hang onto one another. One was laughing so hard he had tears running down his face.

I saw the flash of a knife blade, and then felt it pushing hard under my nose.

"I have often suspected," said the twin with the knife, "that in the high altitude and thin air of Mexico City, one larger nostril would be an advantage over two smaller ones."

He held the lighter's flame under the knife blade and said, "It's important always to sterilize surgical implements for prevention of infection."

The other twin said, "My brother once wanted to be a doctor. Today he's an amateur surgeon. It's a hobby, but he's passionate about it."

I passed out. When I came to they had removed the strips of towel from my mouth. A trickle of blood ran from where the tip of the searing hot knife had entered my nostril. I tasted blood on my lips and licked it away with my tongue. It tasted salty and bitter. It tasted of fear.

"This is your chance. Where is Carla?"

"I told you, I don't know. That's the truth. If I did I wouldn't tell you, but it doesn't matter because I don't."

He lighted another cigarette, only one this time. I saw him stare a long time at the lighter flame, which he did not extinguish, and then an equally long time at me. By his expression I knew what was coming. Again the rags were stuffed in my mouth.

I began thrashing wildly, aiming kicks while trying to break free of the restraints binding me to the chair. The lighter was placed about an inch under my ear and gradually brought closer until I could feel the direct flame. He held it against my ear a long time during which I did not stop screaming. I fainted, and was beaten for it. When I came to I could smell burnt flesh. My pain was un-imaginable. It was my entire world. They removed the rags from my mouth and I vomited yellow bile streaked with blood.

"What did you tell the two men who questioned you the day we saw you in the lobby?"

"What two men?"

"You know what two men. You have their business cards. You spoke with them at the elevators. What did you tell them?"

"There was nothing I *could* tell them. They wanted to know about Carla, same as you, same as me, but I don't know where she is."

"Did you see them again? Have you had any further telephone contact with them?"

"No."

"This gringo knows nothing," said one brother to the other. "He is of no use to us."

He shoved the rags back in my mouth and I braced for more punishment.

"Well," he said. "This hasn't been particularly informative but it's been fun. Not as much fun as when we find Carla, of course. We have something special in store for her."

"Oh yes," agreed his brother. "We'll keep her as a pet. Take it slow and practice our skills. But what about this *cabrone* here? Let's cut his dick off. Take it to Carla as a gift."

His twin smirked and said, "Not today. I'm already bored with him. I'm hungry. Let's get something to eat."

Hatred

I could hear the twins in the hall outside my door, their voices sounding angry. I heard phrases here and there as they argued. One of the twins wanted to continue torturing me until I told them what they wanted to know. The other said it was better to let me live because I might lead them to Carla. I was bound to the chair with duct tape without a way to call for help because my mouth was stuffed with rags. It wouldn't take much to finish me. I couldn't take another beating. It seemed imperative to lock the door but I didn't know if I could even get to it. I couldn't even move because either the chair was too heavy or I was too weak. I couldn't lift it. I rocked back and forth until I had successfully toppled it, the spill to the floor eliciting a cry from deep within me. A rib may have been cracked or broken during the beating. Maybe it was breaking now, in my agonized attempt to drag myself with the chair to the door. I managed to get to my knees and push the lock button on the door handle with my nose. Under different circumstances the sight might have been funny. I wasn't laughing. My pain was excruciating. Pain was my world now.

My right arm, under the duct tape, had loosened, with a possibility of freeing, but pinned beneath me. Somehow I would have to make myself upright in the chair again, but brute strength was not going to work. I was on short supply of it anyway. I would have to think my way out of this. I slithered to the dresser, dragging the chair with me, and got to my knees. I worked my arms like chicken wings under the duct tape until they became loose enough to allow insertion of both elbows inside an empty drawer and used the leverage to pull myself upright. It took what seemed about an hour to free myself. The effort exhausted me.

My legs felt incapable of supporting me. I crawled to the bed, sat and tried to light a cigarette. My hands trembled holding the flame. From now forward, I would see a cigarette lighter as a weapon, and a cigarette as an instrument of torture. The cigarette tasted terrible but I smoked it anyway. My jaw ached, my left ear seemed on fire, and the inside of my nose was shooting rockets of pain into my head. I touched my lips with my fingertips. They were puffy and sore to the touch and my fingers came away with blood.

I limped to the bathroom and ran cold water in the sink. I looked in the bureau mirror, relieved to see both bloody nostrils intact. Blood was encrusted around my nostrils, but probably as much from the beating as the knife. I ran the water a long time, making it cold as possible. My gums and lips were bloody and my eyes were swelling and turning blue. I knew they would look much worse tomorrow. I soaked a washcloth and patted my swollen lip, but it hurt to do so. I needed an icepack. There was an ice machine in the lobby but I didn't know if I could make it down to the elevator and back.

I urinated blood into the toilet and took four leftover codeine tablets from a long forgotten bottle in the medicine cabinet, turned on the shower and sat on the shower's wet tiles. I screamed when the warm water hit my severely burned ear and turned the nozzle to cold. The water in the drain was tinted with blood. I washed my hair, also bloody. I sat shivering on the wet shower tiles, remembering having been in a fetal position while being methodically kicked in the head, groin and kidneys. I kept seeing their faces in my mind, their sneering lips and cold snake-like eyes. I burst into tears. I honestly don't think that until this moment I had ever hated anyone before, never wished harm on another human being, but I hated these men.

I wrapped a towel around my body and called the lobby. Ricardo answered.

"Yes, what is it, Raymond?"

"I need room service."

"Pedro is out right now."

"I'm hurt, Ricardo. I've been in an accident and need help. "

"Do you need an ambulance?"

"No. Just someone to run to the pharmacy."

"I suppose I could send a maid, but you will be charged a service fee. What is it you need?"

I recited a list of supplies and hung up, falling asleep almost immediately. There was a knock on the door.

"We have your *medicina*, señor."

"Leave it outside the door."

"*Si, señor.*"

I listened for her footsteps to diminish and fought my way to a sitting position. The effort brought tears to my eyes. It was an ordeal to make it to the door and pick up the shopping bag. I sat on the bed and removed a bottle of ninety Percocet tablets, a dozen morphine ampules and syringes, Vaseline, 4 by 4 gauze bandages and a six pack of beer. I injected a morphine ampule in my thigh, swallowed three Percocet tabs with a beer and coated my throbbing ear with Vaseline, then applied the bandage. Afterwards I called information for the number of the embassy, which I called.

"Hello," answered a receptionist. "You have reached the American Embassy. How may I direct your call?"

"I would like to speak with Lloyd Berenson. It regards Carla Johansen."

"I'm sorry. Who did you say you wished to speak with?"

"Mr. Lloyd Berenson, one of the assistants to the consul."

"Sir, we have no Lloyd Berenson here."

"Of course you do. He left his business card. It was an official embassy card, embossed with the U.S. eagle and stars."

"Our embassy business cards don't have the seal you describe, but I have consulted the directory and can assure you, sir, no Lloyd Berenson is attached to this embassy."

* * *

I don't remember much after that. I don't know how many days passed. I couldn't breathe out of my nose because of blisters from the ignited cigarettes. Everything hurt, but my throbbing ear was the worst. Sometimes I cried in anger. Hatred festered in me. I kept seeing the cruel dark faces of the men who had beaten me, their cold brown eyes, sneering mouths and mocking expressions. They had taken such pleasure in torturing me, I shuddered to think of what they might do to Carla. They had said it would be worse for her.

I entertained daydream fantasies of hunting them down and killing them until it became an obsession from which I could not release myself. The obsession progressed from revenge fantasy to actual possibility. Twin brothers who looked like movie star gauchos couldn't be too hard to find, even in Mexico City. If I killed them, I would be doing the world a favor. They were the kind of men the world would not miss. Whether or not these thoughts were delusional, they gave me hope. They were something to live for.

How long had it been since the beating? I had lost track of the days and nights. But I was now beginning to feel the first stirrings of hunger. I called the lobby but Ricardo was off for the day. I paid a maid to run out for food and she returned with some tacos, juice, and chocolate. I ate most of it, took some more Percocet, rinsed my mouth with bottled water and spat into the sink. There were still traces of blood in the spittle. I showered, injected a morphine ampule, dressed and began the long arduous walk down the hall to the elevator. It might have taken as long as twenty minutes to get there. My legs were weak and I thought I might not make it. The pain in my side was excruciating. I found myself hanging onto the wall all the way down to the lobby, where I flopped into a chair.

"What happened?" asked the desk clerk.

"Where's Ricardo?"

"Do you need a doctor?"

"I need Pedro's cab."

"Pedro is out. I'll telephone for one."

By the time the cab arrived the morphine and Percocet were kicking in and I was able to walk without hanging on to anything. I was limping and looked like I had been run over by a car but the taxi driver's expression gave away nothing and he asked no questions.

I stretched out in the back seat and closed my eyes but the sneering faces of the men who had beaten me were staring at me inside my mind. I opened my eyes to the oncoming traffic and gazed out the window at passing buildings.

"I want to purchase a gun," I told the driver.

"But they are illegal in Mexico. Gun laws here are very strict and rigorously enforced. I'm sorry, señor, I cannot help with this."

I knew about the prohibitive gun laws but the driver was probably lying when he implied he didn't know where I could get one. Maybe my bruised face frightened him. Maybe he thought I was going to rob him. Maybe he was just watching out for me because something in me had changed. I knew for the first time in my life what it was to have an enemy, to thirst for revenge. The twins had beaten hatred into me. I closed my eyes in the back seat but the men were still there, in my mind. The driver pulled over without explanation and parked in front of a neighborhood chapel.

"Señor," he said, "I think you should go in and pray. I can sense that you are troubled."

What kind of cabbie was this? I was losing patience. If I was going to pray, it would be to Huitzilopochtli, the Aztec god of war. Certainly not to Christ. I didn't want to love my enemies. I wanted them dead.

"Praying will help you, señor."

"No. It won't. Take me to the thieves' market."

We were nearby, and five minutes later I was there. The busy aisles were crowded with Mexicans of all ages. I wandered among the stalls, found some young toughs wearing gang jackets, gave one of them fifty pesos and asked if he could take me someplace where I might buy a gun.

"Si, but they won't open the door for you, gringo "

The kid got in the taxi with me and gave an address to the driver. The location was on a back street not far away. We parked and I instructed the driver to wait.

It was windy outside of the cab, with a lot of dust and grit in the air irritating my wounded nostrils. Windblown grit stung my eyes, collecting on my tongue and in my mouth. There wasn't much traffic. People walked with their heads down, some of them holding onto their hats with both hands in the wind. Everyone seemed in a hurry.

The shop had a steel door with no window. The kid rapped a complex rhythmic code on the door, which was opened a crack by a scowling man with a cigar clamped between his teeth. There was brief exchange in Spanish I couldn't quite follow and then I was inside being frisked. Two men, presumably the owners, stood behind a long metal counter. The low-ceilinged windowless room was cramped with display cases, metal file cabinets and aluminum tables placed closely together and piled high with merchandise. The men who presided over the merchandise seemed to take the idea of theft very personally. A tall wiry man probably in his fifties with an enormous inverted handlebar moustache watched everyone suspiciously. The other proprietor was probably not much over five-foot-eight, with large broad shoulders, thick muscular arms and an enormous hard stomach. He wore dress slacks and a short sleeve white shirt. A sidearm was strapped in a holster across his shoulder. A teenage boy, probably a stock clerk, came in and out of a storage area in back.

A rack of some two dozen mounted riles were displayed behind the sales counter. I had no use for a rifle and wouldn't even know how to load a handgun, much less fire one accurately. Pistols were in open display in the locking glass showcases, some in shoulder holsters with only their handles visible. I saw what I knew from the movies were silencers, which I knew to be illegal in the United States. It didn't seem like it could be too difficult or complicated, learning to fire a pistol, not like learning a musical instrument or foreign language for example. How much skill could it take, after all? Where was the difficulty? You simply walked up to your adversary, stuck a gun barrel in his chest or to the back of his head, and pulled the trigger.

I wandered through tables piled with canteens and army fatigues, combat boots, dog tags, ammo pouches and ration kits. Much of the merchandise was damaged. The canteens were dented; moth-eaten uniforms had bullet holes in them. The place was a treasury of memorabilia and curiosity. Metal filing cabinets contained drawers of letters written during the Revolution. There were stacks of photographs taken at battle stations, old Life magazine articles with war photography, diaries, and maps. The place reminded me of the many old curiosity shops along waterfront Seattle. I used to spend hours in them as a kid who was supposed to be looking for work. I was a miserable boy then. Now I didn't know who I was.

I browsed a martial arts section displaying a dozen or more modern Samurai swords and weapons I had never seen before:

golden disks with saw tooth blades, wooden cylindrical blocks connected by a length of chain, and articles of weaponry not even remotely familiar to me. These were of no use to me. I paused briefly at display case of brass knuckles and saps. I couldn't see myself using these either. I was beginning to give up the idea of buying a weapon. The idea of me carrying a gun was crazy and dangerous. I hadn't sought a firearm for personal protection. I wanted to be the perpetrator, the instrument of justice and revenge. I wanted first strike.

I was about to give it up when I saw the knife case. I don't know how long I stared. I remembered my first knife as a boy, a Swiss Army knife with multiple small blades for multiple purposes, and my first hunting knife, how I sharpened and polished it, how I sometimes sat on my bed just looking at it. I remembered throwing a knife into a tree in the woods behind the house in Edmonds. I had maybe a dozen or so knives at one time. During the summer, just before entering high school, I lost interest in them and put them away except to take out every now and then along with the baseball cards, comic books, board games, yo-yos, and other souvenirs of youth. I don't know what became of my knives; I think my little brother may have gotten them.

"May I help you?"

His intrusion startled me. One of the owners had left his place behind the sales counter.

"Possibly you would like a closer look."

He unlocked the display case and waited while I examined several switchblades. Most felt flimsy, unreliable and vaguely effeminate. I moved on to some sheathed knives. These were better. There were many, and I handled several of them. One fit in my palm perfectly. The blade looked to be around two inches in width and maybe five in length, serrated on one side and razor sharp on the other. I tested it for sharpness, running the blade across my fingertip, and drew a bead of blood.

"Careful," said the clerk. "These are sharp."

"Sharp is good," I replied.

"That is a good knife for cutting, one of the best of its kind."

"What other kinds are there, if not for cutting?"

"There are knives for slicing, for thrusting, deboning, and for throwing."

He demonstrated a knife with a smaller, thinner blade but a heavier handle, throwing it into a bull's eye drawn on a dummy.

"I'll take that one," I said. "What else do you have?"

"Here is one designed for a very specific purpose."

He reached in the case and retrieved a knife with a button on the handle that ejected its blade, which became a lethal projectile.

"This knife is accurate only from a few feet," he said. "But very effective at close range."

It was mostly a novelty item, but I bought it anyway, along with two others.

"I need sleeping bags and large rolls of tape."

"What kind of tape?"

"Masking tape, duct tape, electrical, it doesn't matter,"

"We have many sleeping bags. We do not carry tape, but I will send our stock boy. How many rolls do you need?"

"A dozen thick rolls."

The owner guided me away from a pile of cheap used sleeping bags to a table of new, scientifically designed bags said to be warm and dry in all kinds of weather, suitable for sleeping in the mountains and comparatively impenetrable to snakes. I bought four of the cheapest used bags I could find. I had other purposes for these bags and no intention of sleeping in them.

Vengeance

Fueled on Percocet and tequila, I drew a bull's eye on the wall in my room. I duct-taped the sleeping bags around the clothes tree into the likeness of a human shape, slashed and stabbed it, testing the knives and my throwing ability until my arms ached with the effort. I missed the target more often than not. I woke late the next morning, every bone in my body still aching from the beating I had taken. My ear resembled a lump of burning coal and felt like it was on fire. I washed my swollen face, dressed and limped down to the check- in desk and leaned on the counter. I almost missed it. My depth perception was off because my right eye was mostly swollen closed.

No wonder my knife throwing was so inaccurate. My left eye was black and blue, my lips puffy and split, my left cheek bruised. Outside, a fire truck, its siren wailing, shook the lobby windows. It seemed there was always a building burning somewhere in Mexico City.

"Answer me this," said Ricardo. "Are you fucking that dummy you made of the clothes tree? Because if you are, you sick pervert, you now disgust me, in addition to frightening me. Here is a bill for the damages to your room. Management is holding me responsible for repairs they insist must be paid. That's all they ever really care about, of course. Not that you go naked in your room, that you throw knives into the walls, cigarette butts on the floor, vomit in the bidet, destroy your room. As long as you can pay for it they will tolerate it. And you *will* pay. I have assured them of that. Meanwhile, I will hold your passport."

"I don't have a passport."

"You are lying. I have seen it."

"I no longer have it. It was stolen."

"Then you must pay me without delay."

"I will. I promise."

"Immediately. Right now."

I tapped the register book on the check-in desk counter.

"The men that checked into the room next to mine. Who were they?"

"How should I know who they were?"

His telephone rang and he picked up.

"Hello, Hotel la Paz, Ricardo speaking. How may I help you? Yes, we have vacancies. No, we do not have a restaurant but there are several within easy walking distance. No señor, we do not have a pool but we do have roaches, drug addicts and perverts, insufficient hot water, malfunctioning fire alarms and faulty wiring."

He hung up the phone and said, "A pool. Imagine."

I tapped the register book in disbelief and said, "Don't you have the names of the twins on the registry?"

"Yes, I have their names, but the registry is confidential."

"Look at me, Ricardo. Those men did this to me. "

"I know this and I am sorry for your suffering. But I am not authorized to give you the information you seek. If you want to file a police report, however, I can give the information you request to the police."

"No. No police. I want their names for my own purposes."

The phone rang again but he ignored it.

"I would not make trouble with men such as these, Raymond."

"They are the ones who made trouble with me."

"Why did you suppose they did this? Did they rob you?"

"No."

"Then why?"

"Please, Ricardo, I need your help."

He sighed and said, "I will give you the twin's names, but I doubt that it will help you find them, if that is your intent. You did not get these names from me. Perhaps you stole them from the registry. Perhaps you hired an independent investigator. Do you understand, Raymond? I took their names from their passports. They registered as Claude Luis Hernandez and Roberto José Hernandez. I had misgivings about these men from the start. They were Cuban.

I knew men such as these in Cuba. Professional criminals without loyalty or scruples, freelance enforcers on hire to anyone who will pay them. I don't own this hotel, Raymond. I had no cause or for that matter authority to turn these men away."

"I understand that."

"We are a small, well acquainted community of Cuban exiles here in Mexico City. Most of us live in a specific neighborhood and know one another. Cuban twins should be easy to identify if they remain in the city. I will ask my friends to watch for them and report back to me."

"Thank you."

"But I would rather you engage the police."

"This is a personal matter, Ricardo. No police."

He shook his head and said, "You have changed, Raymond."

"I know."

"I don't know if I like this side of you. "

"You never liked me before."

"It is true," replied Ricardo, smiling, "but before I was not afraid of you."

* * *

I spent the rest of the day in bed. Early the next morning I staggered to a chair facing the lobby windows, hurting with each step. I saw Michelle in the middle of the narrow street, cars swerving as she got out of a limousine to fumble in her purse for a cigarette. It was seven in the morning and I figured she had been out all night and just getting in. I don't know if she was aware all of us were watching her, but I suspect so. Everyone the lobby stopped talking as this defiant creature entered, her high heels clattering on the tiles as she went to the desk for her key. A new clerk was on, working the final hours of the night shift. He seemed flustered and dropped the key. He retrieved it and apologized. It appeared he was smitten. We all were. She started toward the elevator but changed course when she saw me in the lobby and sat down next to me. A small magazine table separated us. She wore a short black satin skirt with a long slit up the side and a white blouse through which the shape of her breasts were discernible. She wore no bra. Her speech was slightly slurred.

"Were you in an auto accident?"

She regarded me with an expression that made me believe her question was not intended for the sole purpose of satisfying her curiosity. Disheveled, her blouse untucked, her hair a bit messy, I could smell alcohol on her breath, but she was still pretty. She seemed the type who would wake up pretty.

"That eye looks bad. You should be soaking it. That's a nasty cut on your lip, too. It looks like it's on the verge of becoming infected. And what happened to your ear? It's the same shade as my lipstick. Come on, let's get you to bed. I'll come over with a compress and some ointments. Don't worry; I'm not coming on to you. You're not in shape and I'm tired and not in the mood."

She extended her hand to help me out of my chair, but when I rose it was as if I had been stabbed. I pressed on my side and must have winced because she said, "You are really hurting, I can see that. We may have to tape those ribs. Did you go to the hospital for X-rays?"

I didn't answer. There was no way I could check in at a hospital. I had no passport, my student Visa had long since expired, and I was in the country illegally. We went to the elevator and I tried not to hang onto her as we staggered down the hall to my room. She opened her door across the hall from mine and said, "I'll be right back."

It had been hours since I had had pain medication and it hurt to even reply. I nodded assent, went to my room, closed the door and flopped into the single chair. Michelle entered later, carrying towels, sheets, and a large bucket of ice.

She froze suddenly and said, "What the fuck?"

The gutted mattress was bleeding matting and the sleeping bag which enveloped the clothes tree had been slashed into long hanging shreds. The wall behind it was riddled with puncture holes made from throwing knives, one of which was still embedded. Michelle looked at me inquisitively a long time as if deciding something.

"Should I be afraid of you?"

"You have nothing at all to fear from me, Michelle."

"You promise? Because in my business you run across a lot of sick people."

"I have enemies who wish me harm, but you're safe from me."

She seemed to make up her mind and said, "All right, then. Let's get you patched up, if possible. Do you have a scissors or a small knife?"

"In the wall," I replied.

She removed a knife from the wall, held it to the light and said, "I said a knife, Ray, not a hatchet. What are you doing with this?"

"You don't want to know."

"You're right. I don't."

She found a sheet in the closet, cut it into lengths and began wrapping them tightly around my ribcage.

"We want to make these as tight as possible."

She began cinching the sheets, then tied them off.

"This will have to do until we can get some proper tape. I was a nurse once," she explained. "I wasn't suited for it. I liked the medication too much. Latin American drug laws are so much more humane than ours, don't you agree? Morphine tablets at discount prices, no prescription necessary. One of several reasons I mostly restrict myself to living in this part of the world."

She brought four Percocet tabs and a glass of water, and two tablets I did not recognize, which she said were sleeping pills. I was too tired to argue about it. She began cleaning my wounds with hydrogen peroxide and applying antibiotic ointment to my ear and the cut over my eye. Afterwards she ordered me to lie down. I quickly passed out.

* * *

There were hundreds of listings in the directory for Roberto Hernandez and I wrote down the address for each one in a notebook. I bought a street map of Mexico City at a neighborhood kiosk, then squatted on the floor in my room and spread the map, searching for the Hernandez addresses written in my notebook. I circled each one with a thick black marking pen and went to each address, eliminating those that did not belong to the twins. I interviewed shopkeepers, bar keepers, restaurant hostesses, vendors, street kids, anyone who might stop and listen to inquiries regarding Cuban twins. Some wouldn't talk to me. Those who did gave little information.

I canvassed neighborhoods systematically, widening my circle of investigation methodically until the distances were too far to cover on foot and I had to take busses. I did this every day. Entire neighborhoods were crossed off the map and eliminated.

I did not inquire for long in the Cuban barrio, where the mistrusting population was suspicious of outsiders and protective of their own. For that I relied on Ricardo, who had forewarned me the Cuban barrio would assume I was with immigration or the police. But I hoped the word would get out that I was looking for Cuban twins and they would hear of it and come after me.

I practiced knife throwing on the roof, targeting the wooden posts that supported the maid's clotheslines, increasing speed, distance, and accuracy. I did this at night, with only moonlight to guide the flight of my throwing knife. My accuracy improved and I became deadly with it. Occasionally Michelle came up and watched, smoked, and did yoga stretching exercises on a mat.

There were nights when I couldn't sleep and walked the streets or sat in neighborhood cantinas drinking shots of mescal with beer chaser. Sometimes I thought I was being followed. I hoped it was the Cubans. I wanted to face these men again. They would not be prepared for me, not expect me to fight them. I would benefit from their surprise. I intended to kill them both.

Some nights I just sat in the lobby of the hotel. I saw Michelle come and go, often in the black limousine. She sometimes left by cab, and I knew then she was not going to her usual john, who always sent the limousine, but to someone else. These outings were not without risk; once she returned with a bruise on her cheek, and sometimes she came into the lobby in tears. She once confided that the man who sent the limousine was her favorite. She wished she could service him exclusively but he sent for others on a rotating basis and saw her only intermittently, and she could not provide for herself on his generosity alone. Once or twice she had to walk the streets soliciting and this was particularly dangerous and she was often afraid. I worried for her safety.

One morning I came downstairs into the lobby and Ricardo

said, "I think I have found your Cubans." He had the newspaper spread open on the counter, where he was drinking coffee and smoking a small black cigar.

"Here," he said, offering the newspaper. "Take a look."

The front page showed two men in a pool of blood on the pavement in front of a popular Cuban nightclub. They had been shot dead. They were Claude Luis Hernandez and Roberto Pablo Hernandez, the Cubans twins. One had died on the site, the other in the ambulance on the way to the hospital. There were no witnesses who would speak of what they had seen, but I suspected the killers had been the two men who called themselves Lloyd Berenson and Matt Sullivan.

Last Days in the Hotel La Paz

I began to spend more time with Michelle, whether in the lobby, on the roof, or in my room. We sometimes went to a movie theatre on Insurgentes during the day or drank together in one of the local cantinas. She introduced me to marijuana cigarettes, of which she was very fond. She smoked a joint down until it was but a tiny red glowing dot, a minuscule red fragment that seemed impossible to hold between one's fingers. She said that was the best part. The roach, as she called it. Marijuana proved to be a solace during the time I was recovering from the beating at the hands of the Cuban brothers, but I later gave it up. Michelle and I didn't have sex, though we talked about the possibility and kept the option open. She said if we were ever to sleep together, it was to mutually comfort one another, without any great declarations of romantic love or promises of fidelity or a future together. We would be friends with no entanglements or expectations. I told her I was surprised and confused by this, because Carla had always said sex changed a friendship between a man and woman and transformed it into something else, which usually ruined the friendship. Michelle said that was nonsense; you just had to keep a clear head and keep it real.

She told me about her life as a nurse in Canada, saying it now seemed to her like another life belonging to another person, a mindset I readily understood and shared. Over a period of time I told her about my life in Mexico and about Carla, though nothing of my life in Seattle, which seemed to no longer belong to me but to a dimly remembered relation, perhaps deceased.

Here, recently picked up at American Express, is a copy of the most recent letter from home:

Dear Raymond,

We have contacted the University and learned that you are not enrolled. There is no record of you ever having enrolled. You lied to us. You have broken our hearts, but your father and I are too worried right now to be angry.

What have you been doing there these past fourteen months? Why have you stopped writing us? If you are in trouble down there, if you are having some kind of legal difficulty, are in jail or a hospital, we are ready to put all our resources into getting you out and bringing you home. You are an American citizen. That gives you certain international rights.

There can be nothing in your life that is so serious or shameful that you cannot face us, cannot come home. We are your parents and love you no matter what. That is the one constant in your life, the one thing that will never change.

Let me tell you this too, Ray. I have never seen your father the way he is now in all our married life. He has always been a quiet man, as you know, but now he rarely speaks at all, mostly only when I initiate it, and then he always seems to be startled, as if he had been so lost in his thoughts that he forgot anyone else was even around. He doesn't say so, because you know how he is, a pillar of strength and reliability, and he's keeping it together, keeping it inside, because he thinks he has to be strong for me, but he is worried sick about you. His smoking has picked up; he is drinking alone late at night after I have gone to bed, and has taken to nervous gestures that I have never seen in him before such as rubbing his palms together or cracking his knuckles or tapping his fingers on the tabletop, and I don't have to tell you how out of character that is for him. One night I heard him crying, though I would never mention it to him because he is such a proud man and would not want me to know.

Don't even for a moment think that your father doesn't love you or wouldn't sacrifice anything for you to help you no matter what.

As you have probably noticed, enclosed within this envelope is a bus ticket home. The money order that accompanies it is the last we will be sending you. We want you to come home and that is why we are stopping your funds. I know this will make you angry with us, but your time in Mexico must come to an end and is only a small segment of what we hope will be a very long and productive life. You can't see that now, but in time you will, I know that you will.

Please spend this money wisely; save enough for food and whatever else you might need for the trip home. When you get here we can have a long talk and try to get you what you need. I've spoken with your old boss and told him you are coming home and he has even said he will give you your old job back. But if you want to go back to school, that is fine too. If you want to attend church, we will go with you. If you have questions we will try to get you to the right people to answer them. The important thing is for you to take this bus ticket, get on a bus and come home. It's time, Ray. I'm tired from crying and tired from writing and I'm going to sign off and go pray now for your safe return to your home and family.

Love,
Mom and Dad

Even Carla, from whom I recently received a maddeningly brief, newsy letter care of American Express that I will exhibit here shortly, advises me to leave Mexico and return "home." But this is my home now. It feels right for me to be here.

Here is a copy of the letter from Carla sent from Lisbon, Portugal:

Dear Raymond,

I'm sorry I had to leave the way I did, suddenly and without explanation, but by now you probably know the extent of the danger I was putting us both in, and the urgent need to circumvent it. I hope you know that I did love you. I still do, but this is not a time for love, and it's probably too late for me to become the kind of person I would want to be for you, unencumbered with circumstances, duties, complications, obligations and debts. I know I am being evasive about exactly what those are, but that is the way it has to be. Don't write me back at this address, because I won't be here and am not a position to leave a forwarding address.

I will never forget you,
Love,
Carla

Was that all I was worth to her, a single paragraph?

Michelle read the letter. She shrugged and said it didn't matter. I was fucking lucky to be alive. Her husband had been killed in an automobile accident on the trans-Canada highway while en route from Montreal to Vancouver, British Columbia. She told me this without tears, without remorse, but as a sad part of her life that was over, with scant relevance to the present.

As time went on I began to care less, and Carla began to fade in my memory. There is a place in my heart where it sometimes still hurts when I remember her, but it is far away, and basically she is all but dead to me.

* * *

I was now behind in the rent and without funds, reduced to hiding from Ricardo. I tried to make myself invisible, creeping through the hotel hallways, evasive and quiet as a jewel thief while on the alert for Ricardo to suddenly spring from an unoccupied room or janitor's closet with the overdue bill. I had no money to pay him. Nothing. Each morning I woke further behind in the rent with no prospects of ever being able to pay. I avoided the front entrance as much as possible, leaving by the fire exit, which led into an alley in back. But the fire exit door locked from the inside when closed. There was no way back other than by the front entrance where I had to crouch outside the lobby windows like a peeping tom, waiting for an opportunity to enter the hotel unseen, then making a break for the back stairs.

One night I found a padlock on the door to my room. I slept a couple of nights on the roof, and once in Michelle's bed when she was away for the night with a trick.

Her room was a duplicate of mine, but feminine. It was almost equally minimal. Her few framed photographs looked impersonal, as if fabricated, cut out of a magazine with no real connection to Michelle's life as I imagined it. A lonely windswept prairie made me wonder if it was a representation of her inner landscape. A small framed picture on the dresser showed a deer drinking from a brook while standing in a moonlit pine forest. Michelle later told me the deer was her token animal—wise and gentle, but also untamed, a hunted creature of the wild with a tendency to anticipate trouble and run.

A seashell framed picture mounted between two tall candles by her bed looked professionally taken and appeared to be the sole personal touch. A pretty little blonde girl, perhaps four years of age, smiled out at the photographer. Was it Michelle at a younger age? I didn't think so.

* * *

Ricardo's windowless office in which I was being held against my will reeked of nasty carpeting and stale cigarettes. The municipal policeman who had ten minutes earlier apprehended me in the alley now stood arms akimbo, legs spread, a police baton clenched in his fist. The baton hurt. The policeman had used it on me effectively, dropping me to my knees. Ricardo leaned back in the reclining chair and raised his feet on the desk. His Italian shoes were almost in my face. I could see him studying his reflection in them.

Fanning himself with my hotel bill Ricardo said, "Here are two possible resolutions to our problem, Raymond. The first is you can pay this bill, right now, and we will set you free. That would be the preferable course."

"What's the second option?"

"The second is I turn you over to the police and consider the matter closed. It's your choice. What will it be?"

"I'd gladly pay you, but I don't have any money, Ricardo. My funds have been cut off."

"Not my problem. On the other hand, I do have a problem of my own, and there may be a third option. Pedro will be spending some time away. Maybe three or four years, depending on the judge and sentencing. I need someone to resume in his place."

"But I don't have a cab, or even a driver's license."

"Mostly you wouldn't need it. Your duties would consist of filling room service requests. Most of these you could do on foot. Sometimes you would run an errand for me. Deliver packages, that sort of thing. If the errand required cab fare, I would pay for it. In exchange you would have your room free of charge and keep your tips. Of course it's entirely up to you. If you prefer, I can evict you in care of this police officer as of right now."

This is how I ended up working delivery for Ricardo. I ran to local restaurants and or pharmacies, picked up dry cleaning and laundry from cleaners, and was sometimes entrusted to drive a rented automobile to pick up a guest at the airport. Often these pickups were mistresses, but sometimes wives and children. Sometimes Ricardo sent me on mysterious late night package deliveries. The tip money for these late night deliveries was often generous. I soon found that I was working room service deliveries less, and package delivery and pick up for Ricardo more. I never knew what was inside these packages, but because of Ricardo's evasiveness had every reason to suspect their contents would land me in jail if examined by the police.

Later I began carrying sealed manila envelopes to a storefront laundry in Mexico City's Chinatown. I never opened these bulky envelopes, but it felt like bundles of cash were enclosed. The envelopes were received by an old Chinese man in traditional dress who wore a long white beard that came to his waist. I found him to be tenuous and insubstantial, and he never spoke to me.

* * *

One night I answered a soft tapping at my door to find a barefoot Michelle in the hallway, smoking a joint and holding a bottle of wine, and wearing only a white satin slip. She said she was having "one of those nights" and did not want to be alone. She asked if I would mind sharing some time with her in her room.

We sat on her bed. She said to take off my boots and relax. She passed me the joint, which is the last time I ever smoked marijuana. Later she lighted the two candles on her dresser and turned out the light. I could see her naked body through the slip, the shape of her long legs, her small pretty breasts.

I had seen her naked before. I had once towel dried her back when she had come out of the shower. Her back and buttocks were red from a spanking inflicted by a customer with a tasseled riding crop, and I had been instructed not to rub but to pat her dry carefully. There was nothing seductive or suggestive about it at the time because she made it clear there was to be no "funny business." Red lash marks crisscrossed her back and her buttocks. I had been afraid to touch her for fear of hurting her. Now she sat with me on the bed, sexier wearing the slip than she had been when naked, though there was nothing overtly seductive about her exhibitionism.

She pointed to the picture of the little girl in the framed picture on the dresser and said, "Do you know who this is? That's Julie, my daughter. She's ten now. After Julie's father Mark was killed in the automobile accident, I began abusing valium and later became addicted to heroin. That's how I lost my nursing license and first started tricking—to raise money for drugs. I got arrested twice for prostitution, and then a third time for drugs. Julie was put in a foster home and later adopted. I don't know where she is now."

She was tearful, not openly crying, but brushing away a few teardrops.

"Today is her birthday", she said. She raised her wine glass to the picture and said, "Happy Birthday, Julie. Mommy loves you."

"Some mommy," she added, and then said, "Well, I suppose she's better off."

She attempted a weak smile which didn't quite work and we clinked glasses and drank. She rose and went to the bathroom. She was a pleasure to watch, pretty and poised, and a friend I liked very much. She left the door slightly open; a shaft of slanted light from the bathroom made a path toward the bed and I could hear her pee. I heard the toilet flush and saw the light go out. She came back to the bed and started unbuttoning my pants.

"You did know we were going to have sex tonight, didn't you?"

"No, I did not know that, Michelle. Are we? Do you want to?"

She lifted my shirt over my head.

"You're as thin as I am," she said. "Smooth too. None of that thick body hair of so many of my tricks. I like that. You want this, Raymond. I know because I feel you getting hard. This is going to help us both. Me because I'm lonely and sad and you because it will help put closure between yourself and Carla."

She took me in her mouth and said, "I like the way you smell and taste."

She pushed me back on the bed, sat on my lap and put me inside of her. We were a little drunk, the marijuana having intensified the effects of the wine. She talked to me almost the entire time in a low whisper, telling me how much she liked me, what a nice boy I was, what a naughty girl she was, a lot of crazy talk I don't remember.

Afterwards she opened another bottle of wine. We talked awhile and then started kissing again. She pulled me on top of her and I came so hard I think I may have screamed. Spent, I held her and thought I might weep with relief.

* * *

Michelle was right, as it turned out. Making love with her liberated me from the last remaining painful memories of Carla. I rarely now spent a night across the hall in my own room. I stayed with Michelle.

I ran errands for Ricardo during the late afternoons and evenings, while Michelle continued to turn tricks at night. She came home to me late at night or early in the morning, when she curled naked beside me in bed. In the beginning she would shower before coming to bed after turning a trick, but I told her she didn't have to, I didn't mind if she smelled of another man, I welcomed her as she was; it was up to her. Sometimes we showered together, and I loved to rub lotion into her skin before brushing out her hair. We had breakfasts together in one of the city cafes and then went for long walks. We were friends. There was never a question of a future between us; there were no expectations or conditions. The black limousine continued to come for her twice a week. If she had other work she had the hotel call a cab, or one was sent for her. She gave up walking the street. It was the one request I made of her.

One night she came home late from the man in the limousine and said she had something important to tell me. She ran the shower and came back to bed with a towel wrapped around her and sat on the bed with her back to me.

"It's easier for me to tell you this when I'm not looking at you," she said.

I dried her back and her hair, and kissed the back of her neck.

What she told me is this:

The man in the limousine, whose name she now told me for the first time was Sergio Camacho, had offered her a job. He was a wealthy influential man with connections, part owner of a passenger ship leased by a reputable, well known luxury cruise line. His offer of employment was as an assistant to the ship's activities director, a salaried position with a legal contract protecting her. She would have a printed, notarized job description. Her duties would consist primarily of assisting in the scheduling and organizing of ballroom dances, bridge and snooker tournaments, birthday parties for children, weddings and other cruise functions. Her room would be provided free of charge, and she would be able to save money. The ship was scheduled to sail at the end of the week from Vera Cruz for Rio de Janeiro and from there to Cape Town, South Africa and then on to Istanbul with stops in Casablanca, Barcelona and Marseille. Her passport was in order, and she had savings sufficient to fly back from any of these ports should the job not turn out as promised.

I said that I would miss her, but if it turned out as described, I would be happy for her and relieved that she had found a better way of life.

"What about your way of life, Raymond? Do you intend to live this way forever?"

She said she worried about me a little, that I should go home to America, and offered to pay my air fare. I said I had a bus ticket home if it came to that, but for now I would remain in the hotel working for Ricardo.

We spent the next three nights together and then she was gone. I was happy for her. I hoped things would work out for her and liked to think they would.

I began spending my days idly sitting in the lobby, waiting for room service calls to come in, or for night errands to the Chinese laundry.

One day, sitting in one of the large wingback chairs in front of the lobby windows, I saw a canopied military police vehicle pull up and double park in front of the hotel. Soldiers with rifles exited the rear and entered the hotel's front entrance. There was little time to leave the lobby for the hotel's back exit, and it seemed likely an attempt to do so would only draw attention to myself and result in the demand for identification papers and passport, or a substantial bribe, and I had none. I hid behind a trembling open newspaper that I pretended to read while the soldiers congregated around the desk. I didn't know if Ricardo would point me out or not. He was legally required to, and my name was in the hotel registry. At best he might be able to buy me some time by saying I was out of the building.

But it was Ricardo they had come for.

Ricardo was arrested, handcuffed and taken outside. The soldiers did not manhandle him and were not rough with him. One of the soldiers gave him a cigarette, placing it between his lips and lighting it for him. I thought I might have even seen this soldier put his hand on Ricardo's shoulder, resting it there as if in sympathy and friendship, as if they knew each other or were distantly related.

Ricardo stood with his hands cuffed behind his back while smoking and then one of the soldiers removed the cigarette from his lips and threw it to the street. Ricardo stepped into the back of the truck and looked out from within the canopy, an expression of stoic resignation on his face, as if he was now committing to memory everything that had been his life as he had known it. The hotel he had managed, the money he had made, his wife, mistress, all of it. The canopy was closed and I saw Ricardo no more.

The soldier who had taken the cigarette from him stared toward the hotel windows and for a brief moment I thought our eyes locked. It startled me. I quickly returned to hiding behind my trembling newspaper, not looking up from it until the truck drove off.

I didn't know why the soldiers had taken Ricardo, but strongly suspected it had something to do with the packages I had been delivering. If so, I was an accomplice. It was no longer safe for me at the Hotel. In addition to complicity in whatever Ricardo was involved in, I was in the country illegally without a passport or source of income.

I returned to my room and sat on the bed and counted my money. There wasn't much of it. I flopped back on the bed with my head on the pillow and hands behind my head and stared at the water-stained ceiling. I kept thinking of the pre-paid bus ticket from Mexico City to Seattle tucked safely in my boot.

I might have dozed, but not for long. I woke remembering the stoic expression on Ricardo's face as they led him into the police van, as if he had always known this day was coming; now it was here and for him it was all over, everything that his life had been and might have been.

One moment you're immersed in the activities of the life you have made for yourself and in the next your life as you know it is suddenly no more, taken from you. Your freedom, your plans and hopes for the future, snuffed out as quickly as a burning match dropped in toilet. It could happen to me. It could happen to you. It's the same everywhere. You think you are free. You are not. We are all subjects.

I gathered up the lined notebooks and loose pages that you read now—whoever and wherever you may be—and packed them in my seaman's bag with a change of clothing, candles and matches, pencils, knives and The Bible. I collected hotel towels, soap and wash cloths from the bathroom and stripped the bed. Sat on the bed with my knife and cut a hole in the blanket's center, looping it over my head to wear it draped over my shoulders like a serape.

I closed the door on the room that had been my refuge for well over a year and took the stairs to the lobby, which was empty. No one was behind the check-in desk. Only I had witnessed Ricardo's arrest. It was possible that management had not yet learned of it. I went behind the desk, found my name in a registry book, and tore it out. I intended to leave no evidence of ever having resided here.

In one of two cash drawers I found Ricardo's watch, his wedding ring, and eight hundred pesos, which I pocketed. He rarely wore the ring. I had seen his wife only once during my entire time in the hotel. I wondered if she knew he had been taken. Maybe they arrested her too. I took the ring and wore it on my right hand, along with his watch on the left. The second cash drawer contained a loaded snub nose .38, a palm sized .25 caliber Beretta, and small flashlight. I took everything, zipped up my bag, and strode through the front doors without looking back.

Seventh Inning Stretch

I took the first bus that passed and began transferring until I was on the far outskirts of the city where bus service was no longer available. Neighborhoods declined until I was on dirt roads in sight of volcanic mountains in the far distance. Spontaneous gusts of harsh wind swept dust along the street and into my nostrils, eyes, and mouth. The bandana over my face offered minimal protection. The wind kept blowing it loose. I tasted dirt in my mouth and my teeth were gritty.

There were many beggars on these roads, and I gave to most. Volcanic Popocatepetl and Izataccitiuatl cast their ominous shadows across the thirsty landscape, while the descending orange sun spilled the last vestiges of its diminishing light into the city below. Storefronts pulled down their gratings. It would be dark soon, and cold. Everyone seemed to be scurrying off to shelter, fleeing the night's encroachment.

I walked until I found myself staggering. My swollen feet ached inside my unevenly worn motorcycle boots. I huddled on a stoop to count my money. Not much was left. I had given most of it away. The sun drowned in an ocean of amber light, then extinguished itself on the horizon, replaced by a slowly rising blood-red moon. Stragglers began to appear. They were different from those who had been present during the day. A new shift had taken over. These were nocturnal creatures. The volcanic mountains under the moon seemed to be advancing determinedly toward me, as if for a meeting of great consequence.

Except for the hazy moonlight it was dark. I was looking for a hotel or hostel but the surroundings were unpromising. I wandered ahead, the rundown tenement neighborhood becoming worse instead of better. Men in small groups gathered in vacant lots or on street corners, most of them drinking, some watching me with predation. A group of three began following me. I lost them in a maze of narrow alleys and dirt side streets.

I opened a rusted lopsided gate to follow a dark, litter-strewn dark pathway leading to yet another littered courtyard and entrance into a shabby building. I walked along an enclosed hallway as dark as a train tunnel. At the end of this tunnel, beneath a single dangling light bulb, an enormous man stood guard holding a shotgun. Another man sat on a stool behind a card table that supported a cigar box containing petty cash. He wore a greasy black stingy-brim hat and had a big bushy moustache that seemed ill fitted to his narrow, weasel-like face. He was so short he may have been a dwarf. His feet did not quite reach the ground.

The shotgun-bearing man was massive, with huge shoulders, a nose that looked like it had been broken many times, and the broad well-defined chest, shoulders and arms of a weight lifter. His enormous head was shaved clean. In addition to the shotgun he carried a machete in a leather sheath attached to a wide leather belt. Another machete lay across the card table. Behind these men was a steel door.

"The sign says you have beds."

"Si. Beds. Twenty pesos."

I paid the twenty pesos and the man behind the desk opened a tackle box and took my name, which I gave as Raymundo Martinez. The seated man who had taken my money issued a mortise key attached by chain to a large padlock and recited house rules in a bored, disengaged monotone. No one was permitted to leave the premises until the key and lock were turned back in, but it was mandatory to leave the premises each morning, when the entire place was hosed down.

After an explanation of these rules the man with the shotgun banged the gun butt on the steel door, which was opened by an extraordinarily thin and frail man with a large hump on his back, who escorted me down yet another long dark windowless corridor. There was no circulation and the damp fetid air stung with a pervasive odor of urine, body odor and sour clothing. The long hallway was inadequately lighted every twenty feet or so by a wire encased bulb. The man I followed was so tall that he had to duck to avoid hitting his head. Many of the light bulbs were flickering or burned out as we trudged along the dim corridor. My feet became wet from sloshing through puddles that reeked of urine. I was shown two foul toilets and one cold-water shower for up to fifty men. The toilets consisted of fly-swarmed holes in the ground that stank horribly. The "rooms" turned out to be adjoining wood frame storage cages separated by chicken wire. They provided no privacy, leaving occupants exposed. A few men hung blankets to compensate. The "beds" were army-issue cots. Mine was in a cage almost at the very end of the corridor.

"You be careful," said my stooped escort. "Watch your gear, lock your cage, and don't open it for anyone. This place sleeps some good men, but also some very bad ones. Men recently released from the prison down the road."

I secured the flimsy door with the lock, and sat down on the cot. It was a struggle to remove my boots because my feet had swollen from the long hard walk. I managed it, and felt inside for the bus ticket home. Maybe the time had come to finally use it. When the little money I had left was gone, how would I earn more? Where would I sleep? How would I eat? Would I become a beggar like Jesus? It was too dark to see clearly, but I put the bus ticket inside the stocking on my left foot where it could not be taken from me in my sleep.

I'm writing this by candlelight, with a pencil worn to a stub. The light bulb in the hall is burned out. Men in cages down the aisle groan in fitful sleep. I hear men cry, cough, call for Jesus, their mothers, or women from their past. Oddly disconcerting is the prevalent sound of men stomping on the concrete floor. What could this possibly mean? It's like fifty men are doing the Mexican Hat Dance.

The lighting plays trickster. Shadows dance on the wooden door frame, floor and walls. The flicker of my candle is hypnotic. I blow it out and manage finally to fall asleep.

* * *

A gorilla is screaming obscenities through my cage. It has

grasped the wooden door frame and is shaking it violently. My trembling flashlight beam, pointed in its direction, illuminates a hairy sasquatch-like beast, its frame wide as a refrigerator, its shadowed ghoulish face illuminated in a manner reminiscent of the old campfire trick performed during ghost tales. Whoever this creature is, he is too big to be entirely human, and looks insane. It may have been years since he has had a haircut or trimmed his bushy beard. He is shirtless, his massive hairy chest shaped like an oil drum. His dirty tangled hair and beard are like a briar patch. I can smell him from where I lie. He has the door frame in his meaty hands and is trying to tear it from the cage.

"Let me in," he shouts. His voice is like steel wool, gravelly and hoarse, as if he might have had throat cancer.

"This is my cage, motherfucker!" He's shaking the door frame violently.

"Go away. This is not your cage."

"You lie! You are a thief and a liar. It's my cage you bastard."

My flashlight beams lands on something glinting, and then I see a large hunting knife. He's cutting through the flimsy chicken wire.

"I will kill you," he shouts. "I will cut your throat and fuck you in your quivering ass while you die."

"Wait! I will let you in. You can have this cage but first you must put your knife away because I don't trust you."

"All right then," the man replies, putting away his knife, "but hurry it up goddamn you."

I extinguish the flashlight and the cage is enveloped in darkness.

I smell the man before reaching the locked door of the cage. He reeks of alcohol. It's like he sweats alcohol. His breath is putrid too, as if having recently vomited.

He's cut a fairly large hole in the wire, enabling me to reach through and grab a clump of his beard and pull his face up to the mesh. I shove the barrel of the .38 deep into his mouth. He's choking and gagging on it.

"Do you know what this is I have in your mouth?"

He tries to answer but is choking on the gun barrel.

"Si señor."

"Then listen carefully. You are drunk. This is not your cage. The cage on your right is empty. Maybe that is your cage. Take your key and see if it fits the lock."

I release his beard and the man staggers to the adjoining cage and unlocks it. He stumbles to his cot and falls asleep instantly. Now men on both sides of me are snoring. I'm so angry I can't stop trembling. The man sleeping next to me threatened to kill me. Worse than that, he threatened to rape me. The idea of even being touched by such a foul beast fills me with revulsion. I lay awake, thinking of the bus ticket in my stocking. Somehow, thankfully, I too fall asleep.

I wake and suddenly know why men were stomping their feet earlier. A large cockroach is crawling on my face. Hundreds of them swarm the walls and cot where I lie. Some have found their way up my pants leg. I can feel them crawling in my hair and on my bare flesh. I pull my pants down and brush them loose, jumping up and down to shake them off. I can hear myself screaming. Someone in a neighboring cage down the hall laughs mockingly.

I fasten the buttons on my shirt with emphasis on the sleeves and tie off my pants legs at the ankles. Using a hotel towel from my bag, which is itself seething, I begin sweeping the walls of the cage. Roaches fall from the walls. They dart across the concrete floor in frantic escape. I can hear their crustacean shells crunch under my boots as I crush them underfoot.

But it ultimately doesn't seem right to kill them. They belong to this darkness. They were created to be what they are, and in this regard are innocent. That makes me the killer, the hideous one. I tie the towel over my face and enclose myself as much as possible in my blanket and finally, exhausted, fall back to sleep. Later I am wakened by a high pitched squeal of a rat.

* * *

The hunchbacked man who had escorted me to my cage ambles down the corridor early in the morning, rattling cage doors and demanding everyone to rise. We are all to leave while the cages and corridor are hosed down. I wake and rub my eyes. The cockroaches are gone. Their pulverized remains are littered everywhere.

The man who had tried to force entry into my cage is still asleep in the adjoining cage. The hunchback is having trouble rousing him.

"Get up," he shouts. "Time to leave, José."

"*Si. Un momento.*"

He rises to a sitting position on the cot, glances at me briefly and places his meaty hands on his head in classic hangover pose. I slip the .38 into the back of my pants, grab my seaman's bag and head down the hall with a deep thirst for justice and retribution. The man called José who frightened me will apologize.

The dwarf with the stingy-brim hat is behind the card table as before, but a new man tends shotgun. I turn in the lock and key and leave the dark interior for the bright morning daylight. The scrubby, weed-choked courtyard is littered with rusted tin cans and food cartons, empty beer and wine bottles, and windblown newspaper. It's cold. The morning sun, low in the sky and partly obscured by clouds, provides minimal warmth. Morning songbirds preen on the adobe walls that enclose the area. More alight on the limbs of trees and laundry lines. I wait on a stone bench for José.

Men come staggering from the building into the courtyard, squinting in the daylight, shielding their eyes against the contrasting brightness. Some do not make it far, but fall into the dust and sleep right there. Others continue down the narrow pathway beyond the high walls to stagger into the unnamed dirt street, where an occasional automobile passes.

José is one of the last to leave. I recognize him immediately because of his hair and beard, and sheer size. He wears blue overalls without an undershirt, and shoes with missing laces. His fly is open, and he seems to be having trouble walking while fumbling with the metal buttons. He is talking to himself, very softly. He urinates on the ground, squinting in the brightness and staggering as if still slightly drunk. I shift the .38 from the back of my pants to the front. I intend to frighten him the way he did me. Make him beg on his knees for his life.

"Hey! You there, José." He stops and gazes at me curiously.

"*Si señor.*"

"Do you recognize me?"

"Si señor. I think I saw you this morning as you were preparing to leave."

"No, José. That's not what I mean. Do you recognize me from last night?"

"I don't know. I don't think so, señor."

"Let me refresh your memory. You threatened to kill me. You said you were going to fuck me in the ass."

"I said this?"

"Yes."

"Then I am very sorry, señor. Some men should not drink. I am one of them. It is what put me in the prison beyond this court-yard, and three years later landed me here, in this stinking shithole where I must live like a caged animal. I am ashamed and apologize sincerely. Please accept my apology, señor. If only I could quit drinking, but I can't. In fact, I already thirst for tequila and I have only just risen. The drink is killing me, and yet I want it this morning more than I do food."

"Come then. I will buy you a drink."

"I do not deserve it, after what you have told me of my behavior last night, but I will gratefully accept."

I am grateful to him. He has reminded me that forgiveness is Holiness. I will sell my guns at first opportunity. I should sell everything and give the money away. This is the way to true freedom. To Holiness, maybe. That is our mission in this world. We are all supposed to become Holy.

The lopsided heels of my boots make walking on unleveled ground difficult. There is little automobile traffic here, where there is no demarcation between the street for driving and pedestrian walking area.

José takes my arm and pulls me out of the path of a passing car and says, "You won't find this neighborhood on a city map. This is not even officially a part of Mexico City. The shacks you see here are made from scrap salvaged from the dump. This is how we live here, señor. We have nothing, and yet even here we are not left in peace. There are no police, but once every few weeks the Federales arrive in trucks and arrest people and take them away. Sometimes they come into the rooming house demanding identification papers. Who among us has such papers?"

We step into the open doorway of an unnamed cantina where men are already drinking at this early hour. Inside are two tables, both taken, but no stools. We drink standing up.

"Salute," says José. His hands tremble when raising his shot glass of tequila.

"Salute."

"What is your name, señor?"

"They call me Raymundo."

"You might not believe it, Raymundo, but I was once a man with a better life than I have now. I had a wife, children, a respectable job as a clerk. All gone."

"I do believe you and I'm sorry for your loss, José."

"It's not your fault. It was a long time ago. It hardly seems real today. It's like something I may once have read, or saw on television. Anyway, my fall from grace was my own mistake. I have no one else to blame. I stole from my employers and went to prison."

"Again, I'm sorry."

"As am I, señor. But it was a long time ago. In another life, as it were. Before my oldest son died and my dear little daughter ran off and became a whore. Before my wife died slowly of cancer and I took to the tequila for solace."

"I too have a life that is lost to me, José. It seems there is no way to prepare for what the future holds for us. In an instant our lives can be taken, or unfavorably impacted by circumstance."

"It is true," replied José. "We adapt or die. But sometimes I think death would be better."

"I sometimes think this life *is* death. We are the dead waiting for resurrection."

"Then let us drink," he replies. "To death," he says, raising his glass. "To *El Muerto*. But not today. Today we can live, and we can drink."

"I have unfinished business in the city, but the heels of my boots are so worn I'm having trouble walking. Is there a cobbler within walking distance?"

"Si. Rafael Sanchez. He is easy to find. Turn left after leaving the cantina and go two blocks. There on the corner you will see an old gray-haired man sitting on a tall stool. Beside him will be a small mangy dog. That man is a cobbler and much else."

"Thank you, José. Good luck to you."

I see that his glass is empty and call out to the bartender.

"Two more shots for my friend here."

"*Muchas gracias*," exclaims José. To my surprise and revulsion, he embraces me in a bear hug, from which I immediately try to extricate myself.

"You know, I'm sorry to say this, but you do not smell so good, José."

"I know. I am sorry. I should wash. Perhaps later, in the rooming house."

"If I were you, José, I would find shelter outside of the rooming house. Even an alley or empty building would be preferable. Anything is better than returning to the cages."

"It is not safe. There are many gangs. It's dangerous in the parks even during the day, and suicide to enter them at night."

"Parks? I didn't see any parks."

"Well, there are none, but there are many vacant lots and open fields. Gangs have taken them over."

I glance at Ricardo's watch and say, "I must go. Take care, José. *Via con Dios*."

"Yes, always. *Via con Dios*."

He's looking appreciatively at the wristwatch. I take it off my wrist and give it to him.

"Here, take it. I saw you admiring it."

"It would be wasted on me, señor. I would probably sell it for strong drink."

"Do with it as you like, José. It is a burden to me, and not really mine anyway."

* * *

I find the cobbler exactly where José had said he would be, perched on a tall backless stool in front of his shop. The man is so frail he might shatter into a million pieces should he fall. I guess him to be probably in his late seventies, though it is hard to tell in Mexico where hard lives age one quickly. His dog, some kind of mongrel, its mangy coat layered with dust, twitches and whimpers in its sleep, scratching itself, maybe dreaming. The whiskers on the dog's face are as gray as the man's scruffy beard, who the dog strongly resembles. Steadying himself with his cane, the cobbler rises slowly from his stool. It almost seems like I can hear his bones creak as he limps into the tin shack that serves as his workshop.

Leather working tools and various small hammers are scattered across a large wooden workbench inside the shaded interior. I sit on a bench and remove my left boot, but when I feel inside for my bus ticket it is gone. My heart pounding, I remove my right boot, groping around inside, but no bus ticket is there either. I turn both boots upside down and shake them vigorously but nothing comes out. My fingers prowl the damp interior of my boots again and again, but no ticket. I am near to tears with worry and grief. It has to be in one of my boots as before. How could it have been taken from me without my knowing?

But then I remember having put the ticket in my stocking and, to my great relief, there it is, damp and worse for wear, but intact. I hold it up to the cobbler's fan to dry it. I won't wear it in my sock any longer. The perspiration and sandpaper calluses of my feet are too damaging. Better to have it in my boot than against my bare foot.

The cobbler works quickly and expertly, removing what remains of both heels and replacing them. He reinforces the soles of each boot using glue and stitching with leather thread. He then shines the boots on a foot operated buffing wheel. The boots when presented to me are conspicuously like new. He holds up ten fingers four times and I and pay the cobbler and put the bus ticket back in my boot. Not a word has passed between us during the entire procedure. I glance outside to the street, shocked to see two uniformed soldiers walk past.

"I want to sell two handguns. I also need a bus back to the city."

The cobbler nods and scratches his face.

"Si, señor. Then you need to see my brother-in-law, Juan Mendoza. Everyone knows him. He buys and sells many things."

"How do I find this Mendoza?"

"There are no street names here, señor. I cannot give you an address, but will draw you a map."

He produces a sheet of paper and marking pen, expediently drawing the map as if having done so many times before, with the outline of a small shoe to indicate the location of his shop, then a series of intersecting straight lines that I understand to be streets, and finally an X contained by a square over which he writes Mendoza.

"Mendoza's spread is one of the few surrounded by a fence. He carries everything you might need. If you cannot find his place, ask anyone. Everyone knows him."

"Thank you, señor. I will go to him. What are these other roads, with all the curves?"

"Those are not roads, señor. One is a creek, the other an open sewer. Do not drink from these or you will become very sick. If you need water, children with wagons will sell it to you."

He makes two large squares on the map and says, "This is a field that you must pass to reach the prison, which is here."

He points to a crudely drawn representation of a castle, a square box with awkwardly rendered battlements and gun turrets.

"There is only one bus to this district. It brings the women to the prison once a week to visit their spouses and returns them late in the afternoon. You are in luck because today is the day spouses are allowed for conjugal visits. This bus will take you back to the city, but you have to cross this open field to reach it. It can be dangerous. Stay to the edge of the field. Do not enter its interior. Gangs congregate there. Sometimes they play soccer, or baseball. The games always end up with arguments and fighting, sometimes to the death. If you should encounter someone along the way, do not make eye contact. Keep your eyes on the prison, look at no one, and keep walking."

* * *

Men with rifles sit on metal folding chairs placed outside of the Mendoza compound, a complex network of welded interconnected railroad boxcars. The high adobe walls surrounding the infrastructure are topped with nails, broken glass, concertina wire and razor blades. Behind the fencing is a wasteland of discarded tires, broken refrigerators, stoves and toilets, box springs and mattresses, and rusted washing machines. Scrap metal and damaged merchandise are strewn over the filthy oil-stained grounds as if an explosion had landed them there. Dogs patrol a maze of narrow trails between piles of rusted, abandoned appliances and automobile body parts.

Two armed men escort me through a network of intersecting boxcars leading into a large warehouse-like interior cramped with tables of merchandise. Fat, iridescent blue flies circle the stagnant air. A shimmering arc of light through the building's single window creates a surreal stairway of illuminated drifting dust motes. The man behind the counter, presumably Mendoza, has a shaggy, inverted handlebar moustache. He wears a straw hat, white shirt, and greasy denim overalls. A revolver sits on the table in front of him.

He regards me without expression.

"Your brother-in-law the cobbler sent me. I have some things for sale that might interest you."

I place the seaman's bag on the table and shake its contents onto the table. Mendoza studies the guns and knives and flashlight, then me. He whistles for a man with a shadow of beard and a broad flat nose. He wears an ammunition belt and holstered pistol and carries a rifle with a hand hammered silver design on the stalk. The rife is a thing of beauty, and so old it might have been used in Villa's revolution.

Mendoza counts out pesos, a transaction witnessed by swarms of annoying flies and engorged mosquitoes. I swat them away. Mendoza doesn't bother, ignoring a tiny black fly that has settled on his ear. The sound of their circling dominates the stifling air. It is a maddening, unrelenting presence, a mechanized noise from hell. Overhead fans do nothing to cool the air, but provide a landing pad while blowing the hot air around. The lack of circulation and stagnant humidity inside the building have combined to drench my face in perspiration.

Mendoza stops counting, pushes the bills to my side of the table and stares at me with his face of stone. I take the money without counting and put some of it in my pocket, some in my bag. The man with the rifle grabs my arm and gives me a long hard stare.

"So how will you protect yourself, now that you have sold me your weapons? Only fools walk these streets unarmed."

"I am protected by God."

"I am sorry, señor, but you are not. There is nothing special about you. Any man can be killed. All of us are all susceptible to violence and death. There are no exceptions. God made us all the same."

"Yes. He made us the same in that he made us Holy in his image."

"No. He made us perishable and in need of protection. Didn't my brother-in-law warn you? You are a stranger here. They will rob you. Kill or rape you."

I shrug, unconcerned.

The man with the rifle says, "If I were to cut your balls off with this knife, you would bleed. If I slit your throat with it, you would die."

"It doesn't matter what happens to me."

"Sometimes mountain lions come down from the mountains and drag away stragglers and eat them."

I shrug again.

Mendoza points to my right hand and says, "I want to buy this ring on your finger."

"It is not mine to sell," I reply.

* * *

The path I walk is so narrow two men cannot pass abreast. Which man will give way? Me. I will. I no longer want or need my inner machismo.

I'm in a neighborhood of squat ramshackle houses made out of Coca-Cola cans, fence posts, scrap metal and whatever random material might be available. None have fans, electricity or running water. A few are comprised of pieced together wooden garage doors. There had been a stack of these garage doors at Mendoza's.

Families far too numerous for their confined living space inhabit dark single rooms where children sleep on scraps of cardboard or on newspaper on dirt floors. The faces that stare out of these hovels are black with soot. The smoke of burning charcoal hangs inside with no circulation. I want to give to these people until I have nothing left, until I have become one of them.

The high sun reflects off tin roofs. The bright shining reveals luminous beings of pure light who, just beyond our range of perception, sparkle, dance and glitter. If you look very closely and remain very still you can see them. Ghosts and flitting disembodied spirits abound.

The singing of morning birds is exquisitely poignant and personal. I love everyone, the living and the dead alike. Love is everywhere around me, inside and out. I wander the streets, crying, giving money to all who ask. I love you, I love you. Here, take it, I say. Where I am going I won't need it. God loves me and provides for me. Everything and everyone I behold is tender, beautiful and blessed. My own Holiness is blessing it. I radiate Holiness. Light surrounds me.

The dust in my eyes is like pulverized gold, each individual glittering facet of each minuscule unique particle geometrically distinct and inconceivably perfect. I see so much beauty and love that I think I might die of it, that it might bring me to my knees under its weight and crush me. I have to close my eyes to it. Illuminated ancient writing flickers against my closed eyelids. Trapezoids, mandalas, hieroglyphs and mathematical equations burst in my mind, a softly drifting confetti all about me. There are messages everywhere, in everything. Nothing is without profound significance and importance.

In the open doorway of a cantina, I rub my eyes in disbelief. My dad sits on a barstool, his shoulders erect, his chin slightly lifted, I know beyond any doubt that it's Dad, here in Mexico. It's got to be him.

I stagger to the dusty windows. It's his characteristic posture, his slope of broad shoulders and unique manner of staring at his cigarette when smoking. It's him. Why is he here? Am I supposed to go home? Do I want to? I enter the cantina and tap the man on the stool on his shoulder. He swivels on the stool, smiles and raises his glass in salute. It's Dad, but a Mexican version of him, and he doesn't know me.

My mother crosses the street, her characteristic stride so familiar to me and specific to her alone that my heart rejoices at the sight of her. But she does not know me. The woman I see is her

Mexican version and she does not know me. No one does, not even my little brother Mickey. He walks right past me, eating a banana while languidly kicking a soccer ball. His big liquid brown eyes and goofy little gap between his front teeth—it's got to be Mickey. But he doesn't see me. He walks on by, without acknowledging my presence.

I'm stumbling along, my heart breaking. I miss my little brother Mickey's cherubic smile and unconditional love. I want a hot bath, clean clothing and my own warm bed with freshly washed crisp sheets. I want Mom's perfectly cooked salmon with fresh asparagus, the tranquil afternoon naps and mindless entertainment of evening television. But mostly I want Mom, Dad, and my little brother. I want to read poems to my mom like I used to, toss a softball back and forth in the front yard with Dad, wrestle with little Mickey and tickle him until he begs me to stop. I clutch the cobbler's map tightly in my fist. It is my treasure map. It will lead me to the municipal bus outside the prison gates, and then to the inner-city Greyhound station and bus home.

* * *

A creaking rickety board no more than three feet wide wobbles slightly under my boots as I bridge the first of the two creeks drawn on the cobbler's map. In the murky water below, a large black snake does not seem to be swimming so much as drifting with the motion of the creek. At first I think it's dead but then it raises its viperous head and flicks its tongue at me.

The wooden plank leads me into a field of waist high grass with a narrow path leading through it. I hear the rustle of bushes and tall grass. Something is moving in there. I remember the warning about mountain lions concealed in high grass and shrubbery.

I smell the sewage canal before reaching it. The air is heavy and thick with the pungent stench of sulfur and excrement. Here the water is extremely sluggish. A foul coating of sludge foams on its surface. The plank crossing the canal is so narrow one can cross only by very carefully and slowly putting one foot ahead of the other.

In the distance is the imposing presence of the enormous prison, a formidable concrete rectangular bunker with gun turrets and high walls crested with concertina wire. I wonder if Ricardo is in there. I see also the bus that waits at the gates. Soon I will board that bus. It will take me back to the city, and from there to another bus, this one to Seattle, Mom and Dad, and little Mickey.

Floating cumulous clouds cast dark shadows over the landscape where some of the field is cut clear, probably to provide an open plain from which guards at the prison watchtowers might sight and fire at attempted escapees. In the center of this clearing a large group of young men gather. The bus is parked some two hundred yards further, at the prison gates, but the men in the clearing are already approaching, striding across the field. Some carry baseball bats, others machetes.

I break into a run, but it is too late. They soon have me in a circle and will not let me out. Each time I try to exit, I am pushed back inside. Many are mere boys, the youngest probably no older than thirteen. Some hold rags that reek of chemical intoxicants to their faces. Their eyes are glassy, lifeless and bloodshot. An older boy who seems to be their leader breaks the circle and approaches me. He carries a baseball bat and wears no shirt, his hairless chest a gallery of gang scars and crude black prison tattoos. He spits on the ground and walks slowly around me three times, looking me up and down as if assessing whether I am a worthy opponent. He spits again and mumbles something in Spanish slang that sounds derogatory. The others laugh in agreement.

A boy with a machete holds the blade to my throat while others go through my pockets and seaman's bag, which they have tipped upside down, spilling the contents to the ground. They kick through my spilled possessions, towels, wash clothes, soap, notebooks. Finding nothing of value, the boy with the machete looks angry.

"Give me your ring," says their leader, "or my friend here with the machete will take your entire hand."

I remove it, hand it over and watch as he puts it on his own finger.

"You cannot pass through our territory without paying tribute," he says.

"I'm sorry. I didn't know."

"You are Americano! I can hear it in your accent."

"Yes, I am. Or used to be."

Suddenly all the boys are crowding around me, firing off questions.

"Have you ever been to Oregon? I have a cousin there. Do you know him? Antonio Chavez?"

"Do you know Los Angeles? My brother went there. Perhaps you have met him. His name is Octavio. He swam across the Rio Grande."

"My brother died trying to cross it."

"My uncle was murdered in Los Angeles."

"My older sister was killed by a rattlesnake in the Arizona desert. I was there at the time."

"I have a friend who lost his legs on the railroad tracks outside of San Diego."

"My father went to Kansas City when I was still young. He sends money. I hope to someday to surprise him there."

"I have a father who may as well be in Kansas City for all the help I get from him."

"I have an Aunt in Cincinnati. Her name is Gloria Vasquez. Do you know her? She has a job there."

"Texas is the largest state. I learned that in school. I should have stayed there. In school I mean. Then I might have been able to get a good job instead of just playing baseball and sniffing glue."

"I want to see the New York Yankees."

"Yes," others agree. "Mickey Mantle, Roger Maris, Yogi Berra."

"No, no. I want to see Hank Aaron. He hit more home runs than any of them."

"Red Sox," says another.

"They have no pitching."

"I like Willie Mays."

"He's not a pitcher."

"I know that."

"Have you ever eaten a hot dog like the ones they sell at the ball park?"

"Yes."

"Why did the Brooklyn Dodgers move to Los Angeles?"

"I don't know," I reply.

"I cannot imagine this. No more Brooklyn Dodgers."

"Is nothing sacred?" asks another.

"My name is Ernesto," says the leader. "We came here this morning to play baseball but are short a player. Do you play?"

"I haven't in a long time."

"We need someone in center field. Can you run? Can you catch?"

But he is already leading me by the arm into the clearing. About thirty yards in I see where someone has laid down trails of lime to delineate baselines. Burlap sacks filled with dirt serve as bases. Machetes and baseball bats are piled behind home plate.

"The other team is up first," says Ernesto. "We need you in center field."

"Where is my glove, Ernesto?"

"We are Mexicans. Few of us have gloves, gringo. We are poor. Only our catcher and first baseman have gloves. Take your position."

I trot out to center field. Our team is called *Los Rebeldes Negro*. We have a good pitcher who yields no hits for three innings. I catch a couple of pop-ups, easy catches which seem to please the team. They have me last in the batting order and when it comes my turn to bat we have a man on third base. I want to knock in a run but receive no good pitches and walk to first. Ernesto, our catcher and team captain, calls time out and comes out from behind home plate to talk with me.

"Don't even think about stealing second, but if Tino should miraculously get a hit, then run like the Devil himself is chasing you and hold up at second."

The prospect of Tino getting a hit seems dubious at best. He is one of the smallest players in the group, probably barely thirteen, and before stepping up to the plate squirts a gob of glue from a tube onto a handkerchief and inhales three times in rapid succession. His legs buckling, he wobbles at the plate, blinking, sometimes staring off into space instead of at the pitcher or ball. His swings are weak, lazy, and randomly haphazard, as if he were having difficulty holding up the bat. Once he half-heartedly swung when the pitcher hadn't yet even released the ball.

Ernesto is furious.

"What are you swinging at *idiota*? Just stand there and don't swing at anything. Maybe we will get lucky and the pitcher will hit you in the head with the ball and you can walk to first base."

Tino smiles stupidly and swings at nothing. The pitcher hadn't even finished his windup. Three outs. I trot back to center field. The wind has picked up in favor of the batter, adding velocity to fly balls and making it difficult to predict their flight. Our pitcher strikes out the first two batters but the other team is at the top of their lineup. The man who steps confidently to the plate looks capable of knocking a ball all the way back to El Paso. He is smart and patient, waiting for the pitch he favors. When it comes, a fastball right down the middle of the plate, I see him bring the bat up under the ball, hear the crack of wood as the bat connects, and see the ball rise high into the sky. The sun shines in my eyes and I have trouble tracking it. It sails over my head, hits the ground and rolls off the cleared section of the field into some high grass. There is still a chance to retrieve it, and with a good accurate throw, maybe stop the batter at third base.

I chase the ball into the grass but find it next to what at first looks like a dislodged beehive, but it moves and is no bee hive. It's a large diamondback rattlesnake. I back off quickly.

"Snake!"

The batter is rounding third for home plate.

"Time out," shouts Ernesto.

Carrying a machete, he heads out toward center field toward me. I think he is going to kill me but he walks right by and quickly and efficiently chops the head off the snake. Far downfield, in front of the prison walls, the bus pulls away, leaving a cloud of dust. There will not be another for a week. I have no money, nowhere to go.

Ernesto raises the decapitated snake in his fist like a war trophy and shouts into the wind.

"Play ball."

The Father, the Son, and the Holy Ghost

F rank Watson still sometimes dropped in at the Sailors of the Pacific Union Hall in downtown Seattle, but it was not easy for him. Frank, more at home in the company of working men than anywhere else, was always welcomed by former shipmates, but their camaraderie under the present circumstances remained difficult because it enhanced his bereavement and longing for his life at sea.

Usually they pulled out a chair to deal him in at the poker table. Frank was a first rate poker player who during past voyages had taken their money more often than not, and they joked that he owed them a chance to win it back. Everyone eventually asked when he was going to sign on for another ship. The inevitable inquiry was like a knife blade thrust in his abdomen. He ached for the sea, its vastness, isolation, quietude, and bracing wind. It was a place where a man could choose to be either alone with his thoughts, or in the company of seafaring men who understood. The freshest air on the planet was at sea and he longed to feel it on his face, hear his clothing flutter in its gusts, to breathe its salty nutrients deep into his soul. He wanted to stand again on the ship's bow, gazing into nights at sea as if into eternity itself, where jeweled stars glimmered in a darkness so absolute that without them you couldn't tell up from down. He longed to hear the familiar lullaby of ocean waves breaking against the bow, to succumb to the gentle listing of a ship rocking him to sleep.

But he missed the work too—monitoring the ship's inventory, logging in cargo, updating time cards, issuing allotments and paying off the crew. In his officer's role as purser he had been responsible for all of it. And he could have it again. All he had to do was sign his name in the union logbook.

So why didn't he?

Raymond was why.

He did not tell his former shipmates about his wife Emily or his estranged wayward son, Raymond. He did not reveal how, upon returning from his last voyage, he had found the bills unpaid, the unwashed laundry piled in a neglected heap in the garage, the housekeeping a mess, dirty dishes and pots and pans stacked high in the sink, the yard, bushes and flowers dead or gone to weed, and Emily in bed with an empty bottle at one-thirty in the afternoon. He did not confide how, from that day on, it had been up to him to pull their house together, pay the bills, get their finances in order, call in housekeeping and lawn services, get Mickey off to school in the mornings, and generally manage their affairs until the mess with their son Raymond could be resolved. Meanwhile, his grief stricken wife was deteriorating ever more deeply. He hoped she would soon pull out of it and he could go back to work, but he doubted it.

So now, at home on the morning of his important meeting with the Mexican Consul in downtown Seattle, he hoped the day might finally provide answers to the mystery of his son's disappearance. On the telephone they would tell him only that they had relevant new information. They would not discuss it except in person. The meeting was not scheduled for two more hours and he was trying with difficulty to be patient.

He put on the coffee, listening to it perk while reading the morning newspaper, which gave confirmation the country was spinning out of control and going down the toilet. President Kennedy was dead, supposedly shot by Lee Harvey Oswald, who himself was shot dead by Jack Ruby on live television. In his opinion the unconvincing investigative Warren Commission's interpretation of events was suspect at best. The lone assassin theory stunk of coup d'état and cover-up, the American people were proven to be gullible fools for accepting it, and the country was probably screwed. Meanwhile, as if that wasn't bad enough, on the Eastern Front of his own personal war, Raymond remained colossal in his absence, gone missing in Mexico and probably in some kind of trouble beyond his comprehension. Oh yeah. Raymond. Who had always been a problem. His first born son. Who he had always loved.

Frank Watson had fought bravely in two wars, but how did you fight this? He could manage the household during Emily's breakdown, but could not repair his broken family. Only Raymond could help them now, and he wouldn't. Or couldn't. And that was the most vexing of all, the not knowing which. Either his son was somehow incapacitated and unable to come home, or he just didn't want to.

Raymond had always been different from other boys. The boy read too much, thought too much. His room was jammed with cases of books. Bertrand Russell, Jean Paul Sartre, Rudolph Steiner, Kerouac. Philosophy, comparative religion, theosophy, and of course, Mexico. Had his son actually read all these books? The entire family read widely, but Raymond, in this as in everything he undertook, was excessive.

He did not understand his son. He never had. He had been at sea more often than at home. He had failed as a father and now wanted to rescue a boy who probably didn't want to be rescued. He should have listened to Emily, who understood Raymond better than he ever could. Emily had insisted Raymond should not leave home, had said so repeatedly, adamantly, as far back as when Raymond's expatriation was still in the early planning stages. Emily, his dear wife and great love, who now had a formal diagnosis: depression. Emily who had once adored and admired him, but who now seemed to regard him with contempt. Who had screamed at him accusingly, her face distorted almost beyond recognition with rage, spittle flying from her mouth as she cursed him, weeping bitterly, blaming him, screaming into his face it was all his fault, he should have known, he should have listened to her when she had said Raymond needed family intervention and psychiatric help, not a quixotic adventure to some steaming God forsaken hellhole like Mexico, of all places.

But he had argued that an experience as a young man in a foreign country might provide their son with a much needed rite of passage into manhood, instilling in him a sense of competency and a worldly perspective that might serve him well throughout his life. What he did not say was that it seemed important his son cut the apron strings. Emily had always coddled the boy.

Once when Raymond was a little boy Frank had come home from the sea to find Emily, her sister and four of the women from the neighborhood standing in a circle, doubled up practically convulsing with laughter. In the center of these women was Raymond, about five or six years old at the time, made up in a frilly dress with pearls and dangling ear rings, a purse hanging ludicrously from his arm. They had even put nail polish and lipstick on the boy. Fuming with silent anger, he took his son from their midst and carried him upstairs to wash away the makeup and lipstick. When he came back downstairs, he ordered the women out of the house.

The next morning, he enrolled Raymond at the local YMCA and signed him up for basketball, wrestling, swimming, even judo. But it didn't take. Raymond was not competitive, not a fighter. The boy had no killer instinct.

"Of course not," Emily had said. "Your son is not a warrior, he's an angel."

Raymond may have been a good boy, but he was no angel.

He tried to focus on the newspaper again but could not. The importance of the day ahead loomed large in his mind. He tossed the paper aside and began to focus on his impending appointment at the Mexican consulate in downtown Seattle. He looked at his watch but it was still too early, so he drank two more cups of coffee, thereby stimulating a heightened wakefulness necessary to meet the difficulties of the day, which he expected to demand much of him. He poured a bowl of Cheerios for Mickey and made the boy's lunch with an apple, cheese sandwich and Hostess cupcake.

"Better hurry it up, son. It's getting late."

Mickey, age 11, emerged from down the hall, dressed for school in a clean shirt and jeans, his hair uncombed, its antenna-like cowlick comically pointing upward as if to receive radio signals from outer space, but his hands were washed and teeth brushed. The boy ate the Cheerios quietly and quickly, milk dripping from his spoon to the countertop.

"Your bus will be here soon, Mickey. Your lunch is in the fridge."

"Thanks, Dad."

Mickey hurried out the back door with a backward wave, schoolbooks tucked under his arm. Frank watched from the back porch window until he was safely on the school bus: Mickey, his remaining son, who kept asking when his big brother Raymond was coming home. Who wanted to know why his Mother was so often crying, and would not get out of bed.

In the bathroom, Frank shaved the old fashioned way, with a mug of lather, brush and straight-edge razor, then washed up and opened a new long sleeved white shirt still in its cellophane package. His dark blue suit, in the zip-up bag from the cleaners, fit as perfectly as when he had purchased it years earlier for a shipmate's funeral. He looked in the mirror briefly, with minimally interested satisfaction. He was trim, without the bulging stomach of so many men his age, and had he not lost his hair, would have looked much younger than his fifty-five years.

He knotted his tie, straightened his collar, and returned to his sleeping wife in the bedroom. She used to be shapely. Now she was far too thin, wasting away, her face troubled even in sleep. It was recommended she sleep with a cushion between her teeth. She couldn't sleep without medication, but the drugs prescribed for her caused her to grind her teeth violently. He wished with all his heart there was something he could do for her, some way he could help her, but he was powerless. It was all about Raymond, who failed the courtesy of so much as a postcard while his mother languished in bed too depressed to get up and take a shower and come to breakfast. He kissed her on the cheek and left her to her troubled sleep.

He took the back door from the kitchen to the garage, got behind the wheel of his Plymouth, backed out slowly and drove into the early morning daylight where the Seattle mist was just starting to break. A faint promise of sunlight was present, unusual for this time of year. When the mist lifted, he was given a brief view to the Cascade mountain range and then a spectacular view of the great snowcapped Mt. Rainier, which dominated Seattle's skyline. Even after all these years it took his breath away.

Arriving downtown, he parked in a pay station, locked the car and walked two city blocks to the high rise office building housing the Mexican consulate. Revolving plate glass doors framed in gleaming copper opened to an immaculate expansive mezzanine. He located the directory near a bank of elevators. The consulate office was on the 15th floor, its massive double doors to its inner offices elaborately carved with the national emblem of Mexico, an eagle killing a snake. It was an appropriate avatar, in his opinion: Welcome to Mexico, where innocent boys routinely disappeared and the icon representing the country was emblematic of murder. The door, hand carved, was impressive. He imagined it weighed several hundred pounds and had probably been shipped north from Mexico. It opened to a pleasantly lighted, deeply carpeted reception room smartly furnished with comfortable leather chairs and a large oak coffee table. A youthful female receptionist sat behind a handsome reception desk. Behind her, the Mexican flag bore the same eagle and snake insignia.

He was meeting today not only with the consul but with a Senator flown up from Mexico City for the sole purpose of this meeting. Frank announced his appointment to the receptionist, which she confirmed, offering a seat in the adjoining waiting area, where he browsed magazines on the table and magazine rack. Most were travel magazines featuring enticing photographs and articles about Mexico. The view out the window was busy and picturesque, with a pleasant view to Puget Sound.

The consul arrived promptly to greet him.

"Good morning, Mr. Watson."

Balding slightly, with warm brown eyes, dark skin, thick lips and moustache, he wore pressed blue slacks with a matching vest and starched white shirt with cufflinks. Frank accepted his handshake, noting the man's soft hands and gold watch.

The consul escorted him past several small offices to a spacious conference room furnished with a long mahogany table that might comfortably sit a dozen or more people. Large picture windows overlooked the city below. A man Frank took to be the senator, waiting at the table, rose and shook his hand vigorously.

"Good morning, Mr. Watson. I am Senator Franco Sanchez. It's a pleasure to meet you."

The consul said, "Would you like something to drink, Mr. Watson? We can offer coffee, tea or, if you prefer, an alcoholic beverage."

Frank shook his head negatively and wasted no time getting to the point.

"I believe you know why I am here," he said to the senator. "My son is missing. He has disappeared in Mexico. We cut off his funding and sent him a bus ticket to come home and never heard from him again. I read the papers, Mr. Sanchez. I know of the crime problem in Mexico City. Robbery, kidnappings, murder, it's a mess down there. I want to know first-hand, from you personally, exactly, what *recent* action your government has taken to find my son."

Frank heard his voice break slightly with anger. He reined it in, recognizing it as unreasonable and premature. But he was angry. Not with this man, who he found to be polite and accommodating, but with Mexico itself.

"We are aware of your situation and we sympathize, Mr. Watson. The documents filed with the Director of Overseas Citizens Missing Persons at the U.S. State Department were procedurally forwarded to Mexico City. The search for your son has been ongoing but complicated. We believe your son does not want to be found and returned to the United States. It is unfortunate, but these things sometimes happen."

"Not to my family they don't."

Sanchez smiled gently and said, "Mr. Watson, I do not wish to argue the point, though an argument could be made. Please understand. If you are concerned Mexico is not actively pursuing an investigation, I assure you that is not at all the case. We have found, however, often young men away from home for the first time in a foreign land with no one to answer to, do not behave with the same discretionary prudence as in their own country. Young men do sometimes go missing in Mexico but are almost always found eventually and sent home, frequently over their objections."

"Are you saying there is something so dysfunctional about our family that Raymond would not want to come home?"

"I think we are misunderstanding each other here, Mister Watson. All families have their troubles from time to time."

Outside the large picture windows, the weather, typical of Seattle, was already changing; large gray rain clouds were sweeping in over the Sound.

"Please try not to take offense, Mr. Watson. But there are certain sensitive and difficult facts in this case which must be addressed. We know your son was troubled before he arrived in our country. He had been convicted of a crime for which he was incarcerated. He had emotional problems. He had been treated for depression. I'm sorry, these are the facts. Please understand. We must by necessity ask difficult questions, investigate every possibility."

Sanchez presented a bundle of mail and said, "Perhaps you can explain why your son would not pick up his mail at American Express. There are several traveler's checks here. Wouldn't your son want possession of these checks? They were never cashed, never picked up."

"Raymond was under the impression we had discontinued his funding. We sent him a bus ticket and told him to come home, adding there would be no further checks to pick up. Later we thought better of it and resumed his funding, but we didn't know if he ever received our letters or knew money was still being sent."

"I see. I know this is difficult for you, Mr. Watson. Perhaps it would help to assure you that the United States consul in Mexico is procedurally notified whenever a US citizen is hospitalized, arrested or, heaven forbid, turns up in the morgue. This is required by international law."

"Yes," replied Frank impatiently. "This has been explained to me many times before."

"So in this regard we know that your son is most probably alive and well. I am optimistic he will be found in good health. His passport photograph has been widely circulated. Any visas or tourist permits he may have had would have long since expired. If stopped for any reason whatsoever by a police official and asked for papers, your son would be immediately arrested and handed over to immigration. Of course, in that event your consulate would be notified immediately."

"And if he was kidnapped?"

"We think it unlikely. No one has been contacted for ransom, and these travelers' checks, which he might have used for bartering, were never cashed. I am confident your son will eventually be located".

But Frank remembered how Raymond had once falsified his driver's license to buy alcohol when underage, created a false social security number and other false identification. If Raymond didn't want to be found and was determined to remain in Mexico, he might have altered his identification. And who could say what he may have done to alter his appearance.

"I was told over the phone you had some new information. So far this is all old news. I've heard it all before."

"It's very complicated, Mr. Watson. I don't have all the details but officials from your government are to arrive here shortly and will explain further."

It began to rain heavily. Rivulets ran down the windowpane outside. From time to time the windows shook with sudden gusts of wind. The consul answered his telephone.

"My receptionist," he explained apologetically

"Yes," he said into the telephone, "thank you, Inez. Please, send them in."

Two men wearing identical black suits and raincoats entered. They removed their dripping wet hats, shook them free of excess water and hung them with the rain gear on the corner coat stand. One of the men immediately came over, shook Frank's hand and announced himself.

"I'm Henry Williston and this is my associate, field agent Bill Reilly. We're from the Central Intelligence Agency. We have some information regarding your son."

Frank braced himself for the worst.

"Is he dead?"

"We don't think so."

"Why is the CIA involved?"

"We believe your son may have been involved in seditious activities unfriendly to the government of Mexico, and by association, to the United States. Mexico is a friend and ally to the United States, Mr. Watson. As you know, Latin America is of strategic and ideological importance, what with Castro and all."

"What has any of this to do with my son? Surely you aren't suggesting he is some kind of spy?"

"Perhaps not willingly, not with full cognizance perhaps, but we suspect at the very least he became associated with and perhaps was taken advantage of and manipulated by a politically seditious illegal communist cell in Mexico City. He is associated with a group dedicated to the overthrow of the Mexican government and the unification of all of Latin America under communist rule."

"That's ridiculous. My son doesn't give a hoot about politics."

Agent Williston unsnapped the latches of his attaché case, retrieved a large sheaf of documents and said, "We would like you to look at some photographs."

Frank examined a photo showing a gated brownstone building where high concrete walls and a series of terraced steps led to doors guarded by two uniformed sentries. Descending the steps were two indistinct individuals, their heads bowed as if to avoid having their photographs taken.

"The building you see in this photograph is the Cuban Embassy. Do you have any idea what kind of business your son might have at the Cuban Embassy, Mr. Watson?"

"Absolutely not. As I said, my son is not politically minded."

"But that is your son. We know this, Mr. Watson. Do you recognize this other person?"

"No."

"Her name is Carla Johansen."

"Oh. Yes. I recognize her now. She went to high school with Raymond. Emily has mentioned her. I recall meeting her, but she looks different here."

"Do you have any information that might help us to contact her, Mr. Watson?"

"Is she also missing?"

"Not exactly.

"Is she with my son?"

"We don't know. We don't think so. At least not any longer."

"Is she in some kind of trouble?'

"Miss Johansen is a subject of interest in a confidential matter of concern to the United States. That is all the information we are allowed to provide. I must warn you however that withholding information regarding this matter could result in possible federal prosecution."

Frank heard his voice rise.

"How dare you threaten me. I know my rights and won't tolerate it. Anyway, I have no idea where Carla Johansen might be."

Williston produced yet another photograph, this one of a handsome, dark young man who appeared to be in his middle twenties.

"This was taken at University of Mexico. The man is Ernesto Navio, a communist leader of an organized student insurrectionist movement and participant in illegal campus rioting. He is believed to be responsible for sabotage of several government buildings. He is charged with sedition, conspiracy, sabotage, and treason. Both your son and Miss Johansen were very close to him. We have many pictures of them together. They were at times nearly inseparable. Some believe the three of them comprised a triumvirate of political conspiracy and revolutionary activity."

"My son is not a criminal. If you knew Raymond at all you would know he is not even slightly political."

"Your son, Mr. Watson, is not who you think he is. If you believe your son is not political, perhaps you can explain this photograph."

The photograph showed Raymond making an obscene gesture to the cameras.

"This," said agent Williston, "certainly looks like a political statement to me. It's your son expressing his gratitude and loyalty toward the U.S. government. The men to whom he is making the obscene gesture are agents of our government assigned to watch the Cuban Embassy in Mexico City. Do you see the other two men in the background? You can't see their faces very clearly here, but we suspect one of them to be Lee Harvey Oswald. We don't think your son is connected to Oswald, and believe your son's presence at the Cuban Embassy at the same was coincidental, but the CIA is interested to know more."

Frank rose from his seat and stood facing the two agents. His voice rose angrily. He forced himself to control it and not shout.

"This is preposterous. The man in the picture doesn't even look like Oswald to me. If Raymond stumbled into the Cuban Embassy it was probably accidental, or out of mere curiosity. I tell you my son is not political. He never has been. I expect your full cooperation in the rescue of my son, not an investigation into his personal life based on tangential circumstance and political paranoia."

He sat back down, shaking slightly and angry to the point of being out of breath. "I know my rights and your obligations and won't be bullied. I want you to tell me exactly what your intentions and methods are toward finding my son and nothing else."

"We are only trying to determine the fate of your son, Mr. Watson. We are aware this is difficult for you, but this line of inquiry is necessary. It is important you understand the Cuban Embassy is legally and politically regarded as Cuban soil. It is illegal for an American to enter Cuba, and the State Department is not issuing passports for travel in Cuba. Technically then, at the very least, by visiting the Cuban embassy your son is guilty of illegal entry into a nation hostile to the United States."

"I'm sorry I lost my temper but it's my son we're talking about here. You would understand if you had a son."

"I do have a son and I am sorry for your circumstances, Mr. Watson."

"Okay, but no more accusations based on suppositions. I didn't come here for that."

"Mr. Watson," inquired Senator Sanchez, "can you tell us for what purpose your son entered Mexico? Was it as a tourist, merchant, or student?"

"You know very well he entered with a student visa."

"His visa has long since expired. Are you aware that he never did enroll in the University and as such was in Mexico under false pretenses?"

"An innocent mistake. My son probably intended to enroll. He's like that. He wants to be a writer. A novelist. I doubt he is even aware his visa expired. He's not efficient with organizational details, and I'm afraid his mother spoiled him and fostered a dependency somewhat in that regard."

Sanchez nodded and deferred to agent Reilly who sighed and

said, "Mister Watson ... may I call you Frank?"

"I prefer you address me as Mr. Watson."

"Very well then, Mr. Watson. I 'm sorry, but there are certain facts that implicate your son in serious charges. One of our agents working undercover was assassinated. Your son knew this agent. His name was Hector Garcia. He had successfully infiltrated a seditious and illegal student organization led by your son's friend, the student leader Ernesto Navio. Agent Garcia was important to us and a good man with three children. In connection with this case, we arrested an operative who was using your son's altered passport. It is possible your son's passport was lost or stolen, but its status was never officially reported as required by law and if your son willingly gave his passport to the suspect he is complicit. If the passport was instead either sold or given away, it is still illegal and serious. And your son's lack of communication with his family and former associates arouses our suspicion. If your son is hiding, why? We believe he is deliberately incommunicado and hiding to avoid prosecution."

He opened an attaché case on the table and removed a folder.

"Property belonging to your son was recently found in a remote peasant neighborhood of Mexico City known for its indigent population and poverty, where one seldom sees outsiders. As an American, your son was rather conspicuous. We are told he wore his hair long like a girl's and had a beard. He was seen as recently as three months ago."

"Where exactly," inquired Frank. "What is the name of the section of the city where my son was seen?"

"It is called Netzahualcoyotl," the Senator replied. "It's an Aztec name. I'm not sure I am pronouncing it correctly." The Senator shook his head despairingly and said, "It is not really part of the city. Not officially. Squatters abide there illegally in shacks. It has an estimated population of around two million, though census taking there is difficult and unreliable. We hope to clear it out and clean it up one day."

"Spell it for me," said Frank.

The consul complied, spelling it out slowly, while Frank copied the letters onto the cover of the travel magazine he found on the rack.

Agent Williston produced a tattered nylon duffle bag with a broken zipper from which he removed a large bundle of hand written pages and said, "Do you recognize your son's handwriting, Mr. Watson?"

"Yes! Where did you find this?"

"In Netzahualcoyotl. This is a copy, actually. We are keeping the original document. You may keep this one. But frankly, Mr. Watson, we don't know what this is. Some is definitely diary, some memorabilia, and some we suspect is just plain fiction. What is important to us are the written descriptions of meetings with undercover officer Hector Garcia, Ernesto Navio, Sergio Romero, and Sonia Castellana, who are wanted by the Mexican Federal Police. Since your son appeared to be working on a novel, we have no way of knowing how reliable these accounts are from a factual standpoint. There is no direct mention of seditious acts by your son, but we do suspect his complicity in some capacity, and at the very least believe he is in possession of information helpful to us."

"What kind of information?"

"Regarding Carla Johansen."

"Regarding political crimes against Mexico as well," said the consul. "This is not just about United States' interests."

"Your son may be in trouble," said agent Williston to the consul as much as Frank, "but he is still a U.S. citizen, with all the rights and protection that affords him."

"I appreciate anything you can do to find him and protect his rights," said Frank weakly. He was so angry and depressed he could barely speak. They were interested in his son only for interrogation and possible prosecution.

"Please keep me informed of any progress toward his apprehension."

"Of course."

The men shook hands, the interview apparently over.

Frank, on his way out, stopped to tear the cover page from the magazine on which he had written the name Netzahualcoyotl. He left quickly afterward, shutting the office door behind him. Seething with anger, he hurried past the receptionist. Waiting for the elevator in the hallway outside of the consulate, he began shaking.

The federal agents were right when they said his son was not who he thought he was. He did not know his own son. But he knew this: He loved him more than anything he could name. And Raymond was no criminal or revolutionary. Raymond was a good boy. Troubled maybe, but kind hearted.

The elevator descended to the lobby and he strode over the marble floors through the revolving glass front doors to the street in front of the building. Everyone wore hats or carried umbrellas. The wind was gusty and chilly; it was raining, and he had forgotten his own umbrella, useless now in the back seat of the Plymouth.

He was cold and soaking wet when he reached his car. He placed the keys in the ignition but then thought of his sedated wife sick with worry, his son gone, possibly dead, or at the very least in trouble with the law in both Mexico and the United States. He sat motionless behind the wheel, wet and shaking, without the slightest gesture toward starting the car and driving home. He lighted a cigarette with trembling hands but did not start the engine.

He replayed the meeting in his mind, trying to make sense of it. It seemed the CIA was interested in his son only to the extent he might lead them to Carla Johansen, the real subject of their investigation, while the Mexican interest was in locating the student radical. Both were interested in his son only for interrogation regarding their whereabouts. If indeed the Mexicans were even looking.

He pulled out of the pay lot and began to merge with traffic. The rain came down hard and spattered against his windshield. Turning the wipers to a high speed and driving slowly along the congested expressway, he could not help but repeatedly glance at his son's duffle bag beside him on the front seat. It had a tear in the vinyl, its zipper was broken, the manuscript cover page in plain view: *A Holy Ghost in Mexico City*.

* * *

He drove home without incident, parked the car in the enclosed garage and locked the manuscript and duffle bag in the trunk. Emily was already waiting. When he came into the house from the garage, she almost collided with him in her eagerness to open the door. Frank imagined she had been at the front windows for hours, anticipating the sight of the Plymouth descending Hummingbird Hill. She wore the same unwashed robe and slippers, a cigarette in her hand, and her hair a mess.

"Well?"

"They believe he is alive and report he was seen recently," said Frank.

He did not mention the duffle bag, or the manuscript.

"Thank God," replied Emily.

* * *

Late that night, long after Emily had taken her sleeping pills with a glass of bourbon and water and had been asleep for hours, Frank opened his son's manuscript and began reading *A Holy Ghost in Mexico City.*

He was still reading when daylight appeared out the windows. He had not finished the book, but had seen enough. His eyes were blurry, his stomach sour and his mouth foul from the cigarettes he had chain smoked with too much black coffee. It was 5:20 on a Saturday morning in which the Seattle rain, more of a drizzle than a downpour, did not so much fall as hang shrouded in the air. Fog misted over the wooded hillside below their house. The leaves on the trees were bare. Whitecaps marched across the Sound.

He was packing his sea bag when Emily woke.

She sat up in bed, groped on the night table and said, "Don't tell me you've signed on for a ship."

"Airplane," he replied.

She found her cigarettes in a mostly wadded pack and lighted the one remaining, which was bent. She had taken up smoking again when Raymond went missing. Ashes fell on her nightgown. God but he hated that rag of a nightgown, hated seeing her in it, and it seemed she was always in it. It had a cigarette burn adjacent to her left nipple. You'd think she would have gotten rid of it by now. The old Emily would have. She would have been mortified. She wouldn't have been caught dead in the thing.

"But you hate air travel."

"I'm going to Mexico to find Raymond. I'm going to end this, Emily."

"Without discussing it with me first?"

"You no longer discuss, Emily. You react. It always ends with you crying."

"Who will take care of me while you're away, Frank?"

"You will. I expect you to take care of both yourself and little Mickey. I want you to get out of bed, Emily. Right now. Get up, take a shower and clean yourself up. And I'll tell you something else. I don't ever want to see you in that particular nightgown again. After you've showered, throw it away."

"What's gotten into you, Frank? You've never talked to me this way before. Who do you think you are, bossing me around? I'm not one of your deckhands, you know."

"Marriage is supposed to be a partnership and you're not doing your part. We may have lost one son, but we still have Mickey, and he needs you. We *both* need you. When I'm away I expect you to do the shopping and cooking, pack Mickey's lunches and get him off to school and check his homework. I want you to water the flowers and plants and keep the yard neatly trimmed."

"But I don't know if I *can*, Frank. I'm *sick*, remember?"

"You have medication, therapy. Do whatever you need to but when I come back with Raymond, I expect to return to a clean house and the wife I married instead of this frumpy bagwoman in a rag of a nightgown. This has gone far enough. If I come back and find you in bed, the house a mess and Mickey improperly cared for, then I'm moving out and taking him with me. I'll sue for divorce and custody if necessary. Now please, Emily, get up and get in the shower."

"All right, Frank. I'm going. You don't have to threaten. I didn't know you felt this way. I'll try to do better. I love you, Frank."

"I love you too, Emily."

"I'll clean myself up and drive you to the airport."

* * *

Transportation by air was not at all like sailing into exotic ports, where identity was determined by architecture, temperature, sound and odor. International airports were uniformly the same everywhere. One arrived with no sense of having journeyed.

Carrying his single bag, Frank strode through the Mexico City airport and fought his way through harried, luggage-laden travelers who bumped shoulders in ticket lines, hurried for their gates, or just lingered with time on their hands while waiting for flights. Overcome with an immediate need to get out of the building, he took the first exit to the exterior and held himself still, listening to his heart pound. Frank hated crowds. Their cacophonous jumbled conversation, the piped in public address announcements, odors and human encroachment combined to agitate him.

He lighted a cigarette and stood outside of the building, calming himself and watching automobiles pull to curbside for baggage check. The roar of jet airlines taking off was pervasive. It was breezy outside, with a slight chill in the air. He was on edge, he knew, because of the aggravating flight, but also in anticipation of trouble he expected to find in the days to come. He recognized but did not altogether welcome the familiar but disturbing conversion in his perception and attitude. He felt himself gradually shifting from his usual officer and gentleman perspective to that of the combat veteran he had been in the past. It was not a side of himself he favored, but it was there when he needed it. Frank considered himself a peaceful and reasonable man, but it wasn't always possible, and like many quiet men, he was slow to anger but explosive when pushed to the breaking point.

Once, in a Subic Bay port in the Philippines, two men had tried to roll a shipmate who was too drunk to defend himself. There was no time for negotiation or Frank would have bought them off. He was on them before they knew what they were getting into, striking the larger of the two with a blow that sent him sprawling. The second man pulled a knife but Frank broke his arm and pushed him through a plate glass store window.

Everyone made a big deal about it on the ship and later word got out in the Union Hall, people slapping him on the back and boasting on his behalf, but he told them not to speak of it again. He was not proud of what he had done, though it had been necessary. Even Raymond learned of it and had been proud of him. Why? Where was the honor in violence? It was a last resort. Why not instead be proud of a father who went to work every day, was faithful to his wife, paid the bills and put food on the table and made personal sacrifices for his family?

Taxi cabs waited three abreast on the far side of the roadway. Their drivers, shouting in competition for fares, ran up and down the loading area, their voices often lost in the thunderous roar of passenger planes during takeoff. Dressed down in loose fitting khakis, boots and a brown leather bomber jacket, Frank was not entirely immune to their solicitations, but mostly the cabbies here pursued families encumbered with piles of luggage, bewildered tourists with dazed uncomprehending expressions, or harried individual executives in suits and ties. Frank paced the queue of parked taxis until he had stridden almost to the end. For what he had in mind none of the drivers quite looked suitable.

He had almost reached the end of the taxi queue when he saw the kind of taxi driver he was both looking for and knew from his world travels would be here. The man was built for trouble, barrel-chested with broad shoulders and thick arms, and leaned against his cab without hawking fares. His unmarked cab was unidentifiable except for an amateurish cardboard sign in the window with the single word "Taxi" written in both English and Spanish without care for artistry or precision. He wore his Hawaiian shirt unbuttoned almost to the naval with slacks and a sports coat and polished black shoes. His nose was slightly crooked and had been broken probably more than once, thought Frank, and probably not from any auto accident. He wore a gold chain around his neck and rings on both hands. His radio was turned up loud, blaring music sung in Spanish.

Frank knew the type. In his life as a seaman he had slammed down shots of the local poison elbow-to-elbow with men in run-down waterfront dives as distant as Cairo and Cape Town, Saigon and too many exotic places to name. He was familiar with waterfront toughs all over the world. Approaching the man now, Frank could see that the driver had sized him up as well.

The driver seized his luggage without consent and was putting it in the trunk when Frank took it from him.

"This stays with me," he said.

The taxi driver shrugged and opened the back door but Frank, after sliding in his suitcase, got in the front. He wasn't falling for it—lock your mark in the back, take him to a warehouse or abandoned building and call the family for ransom. It had happened to one of his shipmates, and it wasn't going to happen to him.

"Do you speak English?"

"English, Spanish and a little German," the cabbie replied.

"I need a guide," said Frank. "But not just any guide, and not one for transportation to the usual tourist attractions."

He was looking at the volcanoes in the distance out the windshield. They were driving down a four lane highway into a valley. ablaze with lights.

"The driver I'm looking for has familiarity with remote areas of the city infrequently shown to tourists. I need a man who is connected, unafraid, and who knows how to handle himself in trouble."

"You've already found him," the driver replied. "You have just described me."

The cab stunk of stale beer. They had to shout over the volume of the music on his radio.

Frank removed the page he had torn from the consul's office and handed it over.

"I can't pronounce it, but my missing son was last seen here. I've come to find him and bring him home."

"I know the place well," the driver replied. "Netzahualcoyotl. At one time in my life, before I had my cab, I lived there. We call it Cuidad Nez. Is that where we are going?"

"Tomorrow morning. I need to rest and clean up. Take me first to the Hotel la Paz."

"Whatever you say, but that's a pretty shitty hotel. I know the place. You can do better for less money. "

"No. For now I want the Hotel la Paz."

They arrived forty minutes later and pulled to the curb, Frank removing his seaman's bag.

"Meet me here tomorrow morning at eight o'clock," said Frank. "I'll be waiting."

He strode into the lobby, which smelled of stale cigarettes and old carpeting, and approached the desk.

"I need a room. Do you speak English?"

"Yes, and I have a room available on the third floor."

"I don't want just any room. I want the room previously occupied by my son, Raymond Watson."

"I can assure you all the rooms here are basically identical."

Yeah, thought Frank upon entering his own, identically overpriced and sleazy. It stank of cigarettes, and there was no window other than to an air shaft. He sat on the mushy, too-soft bed and bounced up and down on it a couple of times. He wouldn't stay here long. Just long enough to get a feel for the place, and maybe ask some of the other residents if they had known his son. It had been a long day and he was tired. He showered with lukewarm water in the grimy shower stall, then sat at the desk reading Raymond's manuscript of A Holy Ghost in Mexico City. He finished early in the morning, discouraged. The book suggested it was probably too late to save his son.

Last Journal Entries

The indifferent sun watches as I stumble and fall to the ground. It's not a problem. Not a big deal. I simply pick myself up, brush it off and keep walking. It's the third time I have fallen down this morning. I don't know where I am going. I never do. I have no intention, but take what the day offers. Earlier someone proffered an orange, which was delicious. Presently I have this blemished brown banana, which turns mushy under my fingers. Did I eat yesterday? I don't remember. Probably. Am I hungry now? Of course. But because my hunger is self-imposed, it is inauthentic. I don't fool myself about that. I have a bus ticket tucked safely in my boot. I can return to warm, lovingly prepared healthy meals at any time of my choosing. The circumstances in which I now find myself are entirely of my own making; I chose this. If I'm hungry it doesn't matter, and it's not important.

It's an old story you've probably heard before: A wrinkled old man watches a youth walk on a beach littered with thousands of starfish dying in the sand after a storm. As the young man picks them up, tossing them back into the sea, the old man scoffs, shakes his head and says, "Why do you even bother? There are far too many to make a difference."

The young man picks up another, flings it into the sea and says, "I made a difference to that one."

But what about the rest of us, the ones who don't get picked up? What about the *Desdichados*, those whose lives are defined by misfortune? Are they not deserving? Are they not, in fact heroic? Is there not affirmation and strength in their laughter, genuine tragedy in their weeping? Even those most afflicted with crushing poverty, rampant illness, brazen corporate exploitation and political subjugation embrace their lives earnestly and hopefully, and I would say heroically for making the best of their circumstances regardless of unceasing hardship.

There are consolations for these hardships, and we sometimes avail ourselves of them to excess. We drink ourselves into numbness, smoke, shoot or snort dope, lay between the legs of women we don't love, gamble, fight, fuck, or whatever else might give temporary comfort. And why not? Why shouldn't we, since most of us are born into circumstances not of our choosing and we're going to die anyway? That is the one promise we can still believe in. When all else is lost, or has been exposed as lies, we are sustained by the promise of Death. We leap from tall buildings, drink poisonous beverages, swim out to sea, eat our guns, steer our cars into oncoming traffic, get ourselves shot. You don't have to look far to know why. Disease, hunger, slavery, exploitation, suicide, missing children, war and prison, destroyed lives, destroyed families, should I go on? It's a long list. And no matter what endeavor or ambition we might pursue, whether successful or not, whether chosen for us by a higher power or undertaken by our own free will and volition, the ending will always be the same: certain death. There's no arguing with that, is there? We're going to die, all of us. That means you, Mom and Dad, and Carla and Linda, and you who, for whatever reason, may happen to be reading this.

So here we lie, in our existential death beds. But I'm not dead yet. Not as long as I'm writing. I may be by the time you read this, but I'm alive now, while writing it. And yes, I could take the bus ticket out of my boot and go home to a warm bed, freshly washed clean sheets, hot soapy baths and a refrigerator stocked tight with delicious healthy food. I'm a bus ticket away from the simple pleasures of a good, ordinary life, a decent job with a fair wage, a loving wife, kids, home cooked meals, a mother's love and the American dream. But how to go back to abundance, to the dream of America, and leave the wounded behind? I love these people, here in Mexico City. They inspire me because they love greatly despite insurmountable difficulty. I love them because they are beautiful, Holy and doomed.

Weed-choked dirt lots and high adobe walls hiding family secrets surround me. I am led by impulses and subliminal messages—go where I am directed and do what I am told. I follow the commands of my intuition. I know, for example, that my present direction is incorrect. I should turn north, opposite of where I am now. I don't know how I know this, but am directed by a kind of intuitive guidance system inside of me. I don't exactly hear a voice telling me what direction to take, but experience either a feeling of correctness or its absence. It's a matter of cultivating and trusting a certain sensitivity to inner signals.

I obey, passing through a concrete archway into a dusty courtyard strewn with plastic tricycles, rusted worn bikes, toys, scattered tin cans, empty bottles and windblown sheets of newspaper where silent men with thick white hair and deeply lined faces play dominoes at a rickety card table. Except for their eyes, their faces are expressionless as granite. Beside them, three fat pigs lie sleeping in the dust. A few dozen chicken coops are at the far end of the courtyard. A young Indian woman hums a lullaby while tending a nursing infant under a small tree to which a goat is tethered. Her chocolate mole brown breasts are swollen with *leche*. She looks up from her child and smiles at me sweetly. Her expression is maternal and warm, her beatific face worthy of adoration. I know I am where I am supposed to be. I have not come here in error. When one is in tune and obedient to commands, there are no errors.

A young helmeted man on a motor scooter pulls into the courtyard. He gets off the scooter, takes off his helmet and strides across the courtyard toward a woman who, stepping away from her wash basin, kisses him on the mouth. Their kiss goes on a long time. The other women watch approvingly.

At least a half dozen skinny listless dogs lie in the dirt, but none bark at my trespass on their territory. Probably exhausted from unrelieved heat and malnourishment, they barely look up in acknowledgment from where they doze. Competing with street noise outside the high courtyard walls, shirtless boys playing soccer kick up pools of dust. From an open upper window, someone sings a declarative ballad while below, in the shadowed door well of a tenement building, two boys smoke a marijuana cigarette. Men in the courtyard men seem to be in the middle of a disagreement, but it turns out only to be machismo braggadocio because they are apparently friends and begin laughing loudly. Young mothers and old women wash heaps of wet laundry at huge cast iron washtubs. A bare-chested boy uses his shirt to play matador with his dog. Old folks drink beer while listening to music on a portable radio. They glance at me briefly as I pass, but I am nothing to them.

A man has the neck of a chicken across a stump and holds a machete. With one swift motion he brings down the machete and the chicken's head falls off and rolls in the dirt. The decapitated chicken, spewing a crimson geyser of blood from its butchered neck, runs headless through the courtyard. Does it not know it is dead?

The nursing girl under the shade tree walks barefoot through the dusty courtyard into the dark shadows of a narrow passageway. She sings a lullaby in a beautifully tender voice, cradling her nursing child, enters the building. A beautiful moment interrupted. But a moment I had been waiting for. When she is gone I urinate against the adobe wall enclosing the courtyard. The goat watches. No one else pays any attention to me. I am as ragged and brown and every bit as poor as the rest of them now. No one suspects that I am not one of them, but an American. Only my accent gives me away.

Jesus the Beggar stands on the second floor landing of the tenement at the far end of the courtyard. I know now that this is why I have come, why I have been led here. He is dressed in Mexican cotton whites, his hair grown even longer than mine. Shimmering like an apparition on the precarious wooden staircase outside of the building, he looks like an older version of me.

His beauty takes my breath away. He waves to me with his right hand and smiles. When he waves, emanations of light fly from his fingers. *Come*, he seems to say, *follow me*. The creaky wooden steps under my feet are littered with diaper pails, dirty and clean laundry, plastic toys, dog and cat dishes and other debris. The handrail wobbles when I lean against it.

A paunchy, unshaven man with a bottle of beer in his hand and a quizzical expression on his face answers the door at the top of the landing. His hair is unwashed and disheveled, his shirt is open to the naval, and he wears a silver cross against his perspiring bare chest. I can see into the tiny apartment where people are seated at a dining room table. There are many of them, probably an extended family. They probably all live here, wife, mother-in-law, children, sister, nieces and nephews, grandchildren. The table is set with platters of fried chicken, beans and rice and dishes of tortillas. A radio plays Mexican love songs and ballads. Teenaged girls at the table sing along. At a small space by the window, a couple is dancing.

"Is Jesus here?"

The man of the house scratches his bare stomach and points to a portrait of a lurid bleeding Christ on blue velvet. His wife regards me with a puzzled expression, and then looks to her husband, who shrugs.

"I'm sorry to have interrupted your family," I say, turning to leave.

"No, no," the wife protests, gesturing toward the table, "Come. Eat. Please, sit." Behind her on the mantelpiece are several dozen burning candles.

"Yes," the children agree. "Please."

"It would be our honor," says the man of the house.

His wife offers a ceramic platter holding rolled tortillas, some beans and a chicken leg. Come, says the woman. Christ winks at me from the blue velvet painting. Am I dreaming this?

What does it matter, the woman replies? Mexico is a place of magic, where reality and dream overlap.

***

Life is ironic, contradictory, sacred and beautiful; we are holy but our imperative to obey the needs of the flesh is sometimes profane. Everything is connected. Heaven is distantly related to earth, angels to human beings, humans to the animal kingdom to the insect kingdom and microscopic life forms. My signals are weak this morning. I stumble ahead, waiting for instruction. My feet sweat inside my motorcycle boots, the most valuable item I own, still in good condition, but clumsy and cumbersome on the ravaged roadway.

Salvaged trucks and junkyard automobiles without mufflers sputter slowly up the unpaved dirt street. None of these vehicles appear to have air conditioning, because all the windows are down; all have radios, with the music turned up full volume. It's cold this morning, but in another few hours it will be hot and everyone will be looking for shade. I'm wearing the blanket from the Hotel La Paz over my tee shirt. Many of the shops on these streets have not yet opened and have their protective steel shutters pulled down over the entrances. Proprietors sweep the stoops to their shop entrances, some singing softly as they work.

A tall thin Mexican wearing huaraches on his bare feet and a torn straw hat on his head leads two burros carrying an enormous, precarious, shifting load of goods. The animals take up most of the sidewalk, move slowly and ignore their master's futile admonitions. They unpredictably urinate on the ground or emit huge noisy rank farts. The burros continue, but then stop again, stubbornly refusing to continue. One of them leaves an enormous pile of steaming dung on the unpaved walkway.

A gray-haired Mexican woman wearing braids and a black shapeless dress chases a squealing piglet that darts between the legs of pedestrians, some of whom are made to lose their balance. Oblivious penned chickens in the bed of a pickup truck are being transported to a horrible ignoble death and the subsequent naked ignominy of a butcher shop. A dozen bearded goats are herded along by a similarly bearded old man. Crossing the street and turning left, the signals come in stronger. I'm on the right track now.

A thin Mexican man wearing torn pants and baseball cap bearing the logo of a brand of Mexican beer stumbles toward the battered swinging half-doors of a cantina resembling a saloon in a western movie. His eyes are red and bloodshot, his hat askew. He pushes open the swinging half doors, stumbles, falls first into me, then face down to the ground. Fortunately for him, I have somewhat broken his fall. This is why I was led here, to shield this man's fall and minimize his injury. He gets to his knees and looks at me with red dazed bloodshot eyes, gropes for my pants leg to pull himself up, but can't manage it. He smiles foolishly, exposing yellow stubby teeth, apologizes and crawls on his hands and knees back inside the cantina. There are no accidents. I am supposed to follow and do.

The cantina is cool and dark, shaded and quiet. Less than a dozen men are inside. All but the proprietor wear faded denim pants and wide brimmed straw hats. The proprietor is bald and hatless. Most congregate around the makeshift bar, a mere wooden plank balanced on oil drums on a dirt floor. There is no music in here; only the buzzing of flies breaks the silence in the smoke-thick interior. A large man wearing dirty cowboy boots and a baseball cap drags the man who had fallen earlier to a chair at a table, but the man's head crashes into the table top and he falls out of the chair onto the ground again. They leave him there.

No one at the bar during this time has taken their eyes off me for more than a few seconds. Men wear thick moustaches, their eyes squinty and expressions unreadable, perfect for poker. Their faces are deeply lined. A fearful man might find a sinister, dangerous quality to their appearance. Back before I became Raymundo, when I was still Raymond, they would have frightened me. I have learned since that in Mexico appearances mean nothing.

Whispers of *Americano* rise among the men when I ask in accented Spanish for a toilet. The proprietor points to a narrow passage flanked with cardboard boxes and wooden crates. A ragged sheet of burlap insufficiently conceals the toilet at the end of the cramped hallway. While I squat over a hole in the ground and release a stinking mess that makes a plopping sound, I can see right through the burlap. Only a few pages of torn newspaper remain for wiping.

We angels have fallen into imperfect human bodies. There is humiliation in this. We need this, we proud humans. The proprietor, when I have returned, points to a glass of mescal on the bar.

"*No dinero,*" I explain.

I turn my pockets inside out and shrug.

"No problema, señor. *Para nada.*"

The others smile in what feels like genuine camaraderie.

It would be rude to the point of insulting to refuse. I drink it down and pound the bar with my fist: I am one of you. Like you, I find solace in strong drink.

Men nod approvingly, one of them clapping me on the back in camaraderie.

One man, not participating in this ritual, has watched throughout without speaking. I'm offended. He has no right to judge me. Such men need to be corrected.

"What do you want? Why do you stare at me?"

My tone is accusatory. I am not afraid of him. I'm not afraid of anyone. I am free.

He points to my motorcycle boots, my last remaining possession of value and all that remains of my former life, my life as Raymond. I bought them in the U.S. shortly before leaving. They have served me well, and still have plenty of good rubber and leather remaining. Given a fair price, I can buy cheap huaraches and have money remaining for food and other necessities. The man who had made this inquiry slowly ambles down to where I am sitting at the bar. He takes a wallet out of his back pocket and begins removing bills, places them face down, one at a time, counting them off, stopping at 1800 pesos.

It's a fair price and I need the money. The first boot removes easily but I am deliberately slow and cautious with the second, because it has the bus ticket inside of it, not wanting the ticket to tear. The bus ticket is intact, but an illegible scrap, disintegrated, faded, unrecognizable and worthless. There is no way it could be identified as a bus ticket.

"What's so funny, señor?"

Tears run down my face. Am I laughing or crying?

"I don't understand," he says."

"We're not supposed to. We are just supposed to obey."

"I still do not understand."

"Faith, my friend. It's about faith."

The man examines both boots carefully, turning them over, inspecting the soles and heels, shakes my hand, closes the deal. He points to my duffle bag, disappointment visible on his face when I unzip it. The bag contains only these pages, one change of clothes, and what remains of a bar of soap I took from the hotel when I checked out so many months ago now I don't even remember when. I had a bed then, hot water, clean sheets and towels. I sometimes ate in restaurants, took taxi cabs, and went to movies.

I open a notebook to sketches of Jesus. The men express admiration. I accept money for the boots and a few beers for the drawings and toss the cash into my bag and zip it back up. As usual, my obedience to signals has been rewarded. I am instructed to leave now, and do.

The day is warming with the rising sun, but it's still chilly. The clouds have moved away; the sunlight piercing after the dark respite of the cantina. The combination of mescal, beer and heat threaten a headache. I have no shoes and my stockings are so threadbare my feet are exposed to the surface of the road. I have to skip like a girl and hop like a fool because the soles of my bare feet are tormented by pebbles, broken glass and other debris. But I am encouraged. Huaraches will require only a few pesos, and even less if I can find used ones. Their thick protective rubber soles made from automobile tires are cheap, but durable. While they may not provide comfort from cold and rain, my feet will be safe from cuts. The steel shutters of entrances to shops are rising now, and I expect one of them will have huaraches for sale.

My mood is cheerful and optimistic now that I have money in my pocket. How easy it is, this life, when one obeys. Because I listened, because I obeyed the impulse that led me into the cantina, I have been rewarded and affirmed. How liberating it is to live like the birds of the field spoken of by Jesus. I follow my promptings, with no thought for tomorrow, and am given all that I need.

* * *

I walk all morning. The smog cover has lifted, the sun high in the sky and fierce now. There is no wind whatsoever here to offer relief and I'm thirsty. The sun's reflection off passing automobiles is so fierce that it is painful. If only I had some sunglasses, or even a sombrero to keep the sun out my eyes. And yet, also, the glare is inexplicably beautiful, because everything it touches is shimmering with light and I think this is what heaven will look like. It will be illuminated, exploding with light, but we will be able to look at it directly without squinting because we will be at one with it. We will be the light and the light will be us.

Laughing children point me out as I monkey dance over the hot pavement. They scratch under their armpits, jump up and down and make monkey noises. I show them the rotted bottoms of my stockings and bare feet in explanation, but they only laugh all the harder. I'm happy to be entertainment for them. My feet disagree. If Jesus was here with me in the flesh he would give me his sandals. Maybe he would pick me up and carry me. I wonder how he would do it? Would he carry me in his arms, or would he give me a piggyback ride? Forgive me. Crazy thinking. I'm dehydrated, undernourished and vaguely delirious.

Where am I going? I have no idea. I just walk. Human suffering and need is everywhere. So is joy, so is happiness. None of it lasts, but it's good while it is here and only fools and penitents don't seize it. Men get married, have children, go to work and come home to the comforting arms of their women. They take the sweet moments of happiness that life has to offer. For many of us, it doesn't work out. Wives tire of us and leave or get sick and die; men make foolish mistakes and run off with a younger or prettier woman who will not love them and will treat them badly and make their lives miserable. They long for their former wives, too late now. Children endure disappointment and misfortune or get in trouble and go to prison. I understand why men drink, why they seek the company of whores, why they fight and go to jail or ride freight trains or go to sea. Either you live hard like a man, or you try to soften your heart and live with gratitude, obedience and love.

I understand why men die young too. Eventually, at some point in our lives, in spite of or perhaps even *because* of moments of almost unendurable beauty, some of us just want to. We've seen too much. We can no longer withstand so much beauty and dying around us. I'm just walking the streets aimlessly, waiting for further instruction. I don't know yet why I am here or where I am being sent, but remain vigilant to vibratory promptings. Usually these nonverbal messages are a subtle, gentle prodding I feel inside of me. This one is different.

I recognize it as one of the rare, much more powerful emanations from a great silent inconceivable distance outside of me. I have no choice but to submit to it. It owns me and will do what it wishes with me. I feel it in my body and hear it in my mind. It is a surging, incrementally mounting vibratory wave that breaks over me and sweeps me along its shore like so much driftwood. I abandon myself to it, surrendering command of my legs, my footsteps, my eyesight, relinquishing the operation of this broken, fallen body I have inhabited for my brief, borrowed time on this Earth, plunging into ocean waves of being and nothingness. The waves break at the mouth of a narrow alley between tenements. The message is clear. I am to enter this mouth, and do. The message recedes, the waves returning to sea. I am where I am supposed to be, treading spiritual waters, waiting further instruction, sensitive and alert to significance.

Shards of broken glass glitter in the sand. My feet bleed on the beach. I pass overturned garbage cans. Feral cats pick through spilled egg shells, discarded milk cartons, chicken bones, coffee grounds and tin cans. Where the alley opens up to a small square and an area of grass and a bench under a few shade trees, I see the movement of traffic.

A smattering of tiny, dark red droplets is spattered where I walk. They are so miniscule I might have missed them without prompting. This is why I have been sent. It's a blood trail. As I follow it, the droplets become larger, brighter. They lead to some concrete steps descending to a tavern's back door delivery entrance. The stairwell is steep, with a metal handrail. The steps number exactly twelve; I count them as I descend. A young boy about the age of my brother Mickey squats at the very last one. He's sloped against the concrete wall, which is streaked with bright crimson smears of blood. He wears a baseball cap, khaki pants with a hole in the knee, a tee shirt and converse sneakers. He glances at me briefly, grimacing, with fear in his eyes. When I reach the crawl space where he is slumped in front of the basement door, he scurries like a spider on his hands and knees and curls into a fetal ball as if for protection, leaving a wide swath of blood in his wake. I kneel to place a hand gently on his shoulder. He clutches his stomach with both hands, blood oozing from between his fingers. His stomach has a large hole in it.

"I've been shot," he says.

Darkness is coming for him, but at this moment there is a light inside of him, a lantern that illuminates his soul. His face is made Holy by death; it's an angelic face, one worthy of a Renaissance painting. Shivering with fear and loss of blood, he gazes up at me hopefully.

"There was a policeman on the corner earlier. I'll go to him for help."

"No. Please. No police. They are the ones who did this to me.'

"You need an ambulance."

"It's too late. I am dying, señor."

And it's true. I can see the color draining from his face, the life force ebbing with the flow of blood from between his fingers.

"Yes," I reply. "I know. I'm sorry."

He begins crying and says, "I'm too young to die. I want to live."

"I'm sorry. There is nothing I can do to save you."

He's shivering so hard I can hear his teeth are chattering. He's trembling all over.

"I'm so ... so ... c-c-cold ..."

"Here, let me help you."

He lifts both arms for me to remove his bloody tee shirt. The wound in his stomach pumps a thick jet of crimson blood. I tear his tee shirt into strips and stuff some of it into the hole to stop the bleeding, but it doesn't seem to work. I give him my shirt to wear and put the hotel blanket over his trembling shoulders. I may now be without a shirt or shoes, but unlike him, I at least have my life. All he has now is the nearness of his death. We the living can give what we have to prolong another's life, but of what help is it, if it only prolongs suffering? But it is not for me to decide this boy's fate, or to wish for him the relief that his death might offer.

The sun slips behind some clouds, bringing some blessed, shaded relief. A declaratory, soothing breeze sweeps the alley.

"Please," he says. "Don't leave me."

"I won't."

"Promise me."

"I promise."

"I wish I had lived differently," he says. "I wish I had been a better person. I wasted my life."

I don't know what to say, how to comfort him.

"Life is complicated and for many it is difficult," I reply. "Don't blame yourself for what isn't your fault."

"Thank you for staying with me. I'm still cold, though. Will you hold me?"

His shivering body is damp and weak. There is no resistance from him. We lie together, entwined on the blood soaked concrete, he with his head on my chest. The boy's labored breathing is unnaturally rapid and audible, as if each breath is fought for. I can feel his chest moving with each inhalation. His blood soaks my trousers. I stroke his hair, his face. I can feel his breathing come more slowly now, as he stares up at me with trust in his eyes. His beautiful eyes.

But what is left for him to hope for, this boy with the beautiful eyes who looks up at me, knowing that he is going to die? He is hoping for what yet remains. For Love. For mercy. For one more breath. If I was like Jesus I could touch this boy and he would be restored but I am only a man and this is Mexico where life and death coexist like darkness and light and there is nothing I can do for anyone who suffers but give a brief moment of empathy. My love for this boy, for Mexico, and for life itself is helpless to alter fate.

A small bird of a species I cannot identify flutters down from a rooftop. It perches on the staircase railing above us and walks the rail. We are surprised by its fearlessness, by how close it comes to us. It's a pretty little bird, not uncommon, but delicate and pretty nevertheless, with a beige body and yellow wings, its dark brown beak speckled with yellow. It cocks its small tufted head and stares at us as if having deliberately singled us out for a specific unknown purpose. Its moist brown eyes engage us. It earns our acknowledgement and appreciation. We are in the presence of sentient intelligence and cognition. It's like this bird knows us. Our attention is commanded entirely. We both are silenced, the boy and I.

The whole world waits. There are no human voices, no radios, no construction noise, nothing. Not a single horn is sounded; not even the sound of automobile tires in the street. Only the wind blowing down the alley. The lighting seems to soften, becoming muted and tender. The bird moves closer to us on the rail, lifts it perfect small face to us and begins singing. Its song is so perfect, so melodic, affirmative and strangely familiar that we are both transported, the boy and I. We forget our troubles and the troubles of the world. The song it sings is a gift for this moment in time. We exist in a universe of unutterable beauty and love. There are tears of gratitude in my eyes but also a smile on my face. The boy too is moved, even manages a smile and laughs a little, softly through his tears. The bird's tender melody is poignant with love and understanding. It knows what lies beyond. It reassures us.

I don't know what kind of bird it is, maybe some kind of finch, I'm no ornithologist. I no longer even know for certain if it *is* a bird. Maybe it's the spirit of one of the boy's departed relatives, his mother or a sister, maybe an angel come to sing him to heaven. Keep singing, then, birdie, whoever you are. We need you. I need you, while the boy lies dying in my arms.

I no longer feel the gentle rhythm of the dying boy's breathing. His body has become rigid and cold. The bird leaves its perch, flutters upward and vanishes. Perhaps it has taken the boy with him. Fly away then, my friends. Death is waiting for us all. We're just passing through this life.

We are coming to the end of this story. It is time to let it go. Ecclesiastics tells us that all our hopes, dreams and endeavors are but vanity. What more is there to say? Is it not written in first Corinthians 13? When I was a child I spoke as a child, I understood as a child, but when I became a man I put away childish things.

My life of introspection and self-doubt, my despair of not living up to my ideals and expectations, the guilt and shame regarding Linda's abortion, my failure as a writer and as a son, the sins of commission and omission as a failed Christian, my broken relationships with Carla, Linda, my mother and father, brother, all these disappointments which now seem so distant as to have happened to someone else, of what importance were they, in the end, compared to the lives of those I have shown dying around you?

So how is your life working out? Is it not meeting your hopes and expectations? We live in a broken world. It's hard being a man, but now that I am a man, I look back into the past upon the boy that I once was, and I forgive him. I'm through punishing myself. There is no shame in our not having suffered equally. We live the lives we are given, and if we are born into favorable circumstances, how does our shame help those who are not? Don't beat yourself up over it like I did. Forgive yourself, be grateful and live another day. Maybe there will be an opportunity to demonstrate generosity and kindness. Maybe your heart will be touched with love from somewhere unexpected. Maybe there is something unspeakably beautiful awaiting you. Maybe you will bring Love into the world without even knowing it.

The barefoot woman approaching me now is like a skeleton dressed in black. She carries an infant cradled in a soiled white rebozo and around her neck is an enormous wooden cross. She staggers crossing the street, but whether from the wind or weakness is unknown. Taxis and automobiles swerve to avoid her. When she reaches the sidewalk she resumes begging. Her face is like a skull with a thin layer of translucent skin wrapped tightly around it like a nylon stocking. Her eyes are covered with a milky translucent film. Her breasts sag as if withered and without milk. Her baby is so thin and lifeless that it looks as if it might be a broken doll. Everything about the infant gives the appearance of sickness. Whatever is given, it will not be enough. She meets my eyes, sees that I have no shirt or shoes, and does not beg from me. I give her everything I have, knowing that she and the baby will die anyway.

The End

Gratitude

THERE ARE MANY PEOPLE TO THANK for this project. I am grateful first of all to my wife, for her support and willingness to read multiple revisions. I want also to thank Darlene McRoberts who, perhaps unknowingly, triggered the memory that ultimately became this novel. Thanks also to her group at Sica Hall, who endured an early rough version, to the FWA group who critiqued segments of a later one, and to Sandy Hutchins Smith for her insights and enthusiasm for the novel. Finally, I want to express my appreciation for Gary Broughman for his editorial observations and first rate production. Thanks also to George Sword who read an abbreviated early draft.

All of the events and characters in this novel are fictional, with one exception, the beggar who inspired it. He was real, probably now deceased. I hope he has found peace.

About the Author

A NATIVE OF SEATTLE, MR. MACQUARRIE has lived in Mexico City, New York City, San Francisco, the mountains of New Mexico, and the Greek islands. He has worked "too many jobs to list or even remember," including employment as a merchant seaman, dishwasher, janitor, pharmacy technician, psychiatric assistant and jazz musician. In addition to *A Holy Ghost in Mexico City*, he is the author of *Hard Times in Seattle* and *The Jazz Book*.